Along the Lemon Path

Marijo Nicoletti

Copyright © 2024
All Rights Reserved

Dedication

In memory of my sweet mother, an avid reader, who encouraged me to tell the story I wanted to tell. She would often say, just start writing. Once I did begin the book, it was as if I heard her voice in my head, cheering me on.

Acknowledgment

I have often reflected on a time in my life when I lived in Italy as a young woman. It could only be described as bittersweet. While it was glorious for all the reasons that make Italy so delightful, it was marred by chaos, self-imposed, I must confess. While Along the Lemon Path is mostly a work of fiction, the year I spent in Italy was the catalyst for me to write, albeit decades later.

With much gratitude, I'm appreciative of my girlfriends who took the time to read original iterations of my manuscript. Tracey Paolone, a Licensed Professional Counselor, provided invaluable insight that assisted me in crafting the book's therapy sessions. Cena Block, an Attention Deficit Disorder (ADD) coach, helped me better understand the connection between my ADD and my comfort level with chaos which was crucial for the development of my main character.

Thank you to Jaqueline Scott who encouraged me to keep moving forward with the editing and publishing process when I all but gave up. I'm also grateful to Kim Bove for her honest feedback of what worked and what needed some tweaking. I appreciate the hard work put in by Rachel, Matthew, and the Amazon KDP team.

Finally, I'm fortunate to have a loving and supportive family. My husband, Joe, and my twin daughters, Nicolette, and Julianna have always supported my projects and new endeavors – there have been many! I'm not much of a map reader. While the story was in Italy, Joe pulled up city maps and helped guide me through avenue twists and turns to ensure accuracy. Julianna assisted me with editing early in the writing process and suggested some of the witty rhetoric.

Contents

Part I

Chapter 1
Empty Nesters
August

"I want a divorce."

Michael's devastating words roll off his tongue with such ease it's as if he stood in front of a mirror practicing his delivery for hours. I'm caught off guard by his declaration. It takes a moment for my brain to process what I'm hearing.

How in the world did we get here?

It's move-in weekend. Excited freshmen and anxious parents are hauling mini-fridges and stylish comforters into brick dorms adorned with ivy. This is a day I've been dreaming about since our twins started high school. After twenty-one campus visits from Maine to Maryland, we finally found the perfect college. It offers top-rated academic programs, a charming college town, and an idyllic quad where cherished memories will be made. The girls knew right away that this was the perfect place for them. Finally, here we are! Like any other anxious parent, I desperately hope they…we made the right decision.

Michael is always prepared. Often temperamental, he might not be the guy you call to grab a beer, but Michael is your man if you need to borrow a miter saw or require assistance with a leaky toilet. Armed with a hand drill, a dolly, a complete tool kit, and enough bungee cords for all the coeds in Myer Hall, the most sought-after freshman dorm, he gets to work unloading the girls' most treasured belongings from the bed of his super-sized pickup truck.

Dressed in khaki cargo shorts, his pockets packed with a Swiss army knife and an Allen wrench key, he pushes the dolly into the elevator, down the third-floor hallway, and into each of the girls' adjacent dorm rooms. Up and down, again and again, Michael is on a mission. He has a self-imposed time frame and is determined to meet it.

With the intensity of an Olympic athlete, Michael swiftly unloads from the dolly clearly labeled crates, overstuffed suitcases, and ample organizers, depositing them in each room with meticulous precision. His speed and efficiency make it seem as though he's in the midst of a relay race. But instead of passing a baton to a reliable teammate, he finds me prancing about in my wedges, slightly snug white jeans after a summer of overindulgence at neighborhood happy hours, and an oversized, adorable, bedazzled handbag hanging off my shoulder.

Leaning against his truck, Michael takes a well-deserved breather before hefting another load to the rooms.

"Olivia and Sienna, come here," I call out, waving for them to join me. I'm thoroughly enjoying meeting other parents, introducing myself to campus staff, and conversing with students. As I look over my shoulder, I catch Michael look at me then shake his head as he pushes himself upright. I'm undeterred by his attitude.

Looking at the quad, I reminisce about my college days, where I frolicked with friends at my small liberal arts school, known more for its party scene than its academic rigor.

"Girls, this is Fred. He handles maintenance on campus." Olivia and Sienna each shake Fred's hand, their smiles radiating warmth. Suddenly, I hear my name.

"Stephanie. A little help?" Michael scolds me in a stern tone. I turn back and notice a trickle of sweat on Michael's face.

"Coming, Michael," I reply with a cheeky chuckle, masking my momentary embarrassment. Before I walk away, I wrap up my conversation with an earnest smile.

"Fred, it's been wonderful meeting you."

I walk several steps toward the truck before I hear two sets of feet behind me. The girls must have caught their father's tone, too. They quickly retrieve pillows, blankets, and small bags from every corner of the truck's back seat, then dash up to their rooms, leaving Michael and me behind. Standing by the truck, Michael takes a long swig of water from his Yeti. His moisture-wicking t-shirt is drenched in sweat, outlining a muscular physique for a man over 50 years old. Each morning, he starts his day with a 5:00 am workout, and it shows. To cool off under the late-morning August sun, he pours water into his hands, rests the thermos on the bumper, and runs his fingers through his thinning salt-and-pepper hair. His blue eyes still sparkle despite his slightly weathered skin earned from his early years working on construction sites while putting himself through college. After a brief break, Michael heaves another load onto the dolly. We walk together up to the girls' rooms. Despite the silence, I can sense his irritation with me. Sure, I haven't helped much with loading the car back home or unpacking the truck, but building relationships is meaningful too. He'll never understand.

As Michael continues to unload the girls' belongings, I can't help but notice the excitement and nervousness in their eyes. Moving into a new dorm room can be overwhelming, especially for freshmen. I try to soak in this moment, this exciting phase that I envisioned for many years. But Michael is determined to make this process as swift as possible.

With each trip up and down the elevator, he aggressively arranges the furniture, hangs up curtains, and assembles desks. Of all the rooms in the girls' hall, the most thuds, clangs, grunts and groans come from room 642, where my husband slams tools and wood together to finalize his masterpieces. Instructions are strewn across the room—he doesn't need them. His craftiness and workmanship are evident—everything comes together perfectly.

Once we reach Olivia's room, we find the girls rummaging through their belongings. I unpack a small bin filled with toiletries off the dolly. I don't expect a gold medal, but a little acknowledgement would be nice.

"Who wears pumps to help with a move? It's just so predictable, Stephanie."

Here we go. I knew that was coming. I want to maintain peace for the sake of the girls. What does that even mean– 'just so predictable'? I attempt to defuse the situation.

"Well, to be fair, they are wedges, not pumps." I try to mask a grin, but he notices.

"Pumps or wedges, what's the difference? Either way, you've been useless all day."

That's a crushing thing to hear. I sit there, stoic, determined not to reveal my hurt feelings. The girls look at each other, and I can only imagine what they're thinking. They have an intriguing way of communicating with just a quick glance. This weekend is about them, and I won't let our bickering taint their experience. I just let it go.

"I can help you both get organized. Let's unpack your clothes and set up your toiletries. Where should we start?"

"That's okay, Mom. We've got it. Besides, there's some group social thing scheduled for our floor. I need to check the time," says Olivia.

Let's face it. Organizing isn't my forte, either. I've always struggled to maintain order, and they know it.

"Listen, there's one more load left in the trunk. I'll grab that, and how about we get out of their way?" says Michael.

"Yeah, sure. I guess it's that time."

I sit down on the edge of the bed, look down, and fold my hands on my lap. Reality is setting in. Our remaining time together is limited. Olivia pulls out her posters, paintings, and photos. She's tempering her excitement. I think she can see the bittersweet emotion on my face.

"Mom! Can you help me with this? I don't know where to hang this stuff. You're great at that." "Yeah, Mom, you're the design queen," Sienna chimes in.

It hurts that they need to uplift me after their father's attitude towards me. But I do love hearing their compliments. I do have a pretty good eye.

"If you have time, can you come to my room and help me hang my pictures, too?" asks Sienna.

"Of course, we have time. I would love to help. Let's start in Olivia's room, and then we'll work our way to your room, Sienna."

Rejuvenated, I spring up from the bed and walk over to Olivia's stash. Michael steps out as the girls, and I begin to survey the room.

"You know your father," I remark. "He's always in such a rush, but we have nowhere to be. Let's see. We'll start with the larger poster and this painting over there." I point to a blank space near the old but charming dorm room window. After I arrange a perfect layout for each respective side of their rooms, the three of us work together to stick the adhesive strips to the aged walls.

Michael eventually returns from the car with the last load. Michael takes a step back to admire his work as the last box is unpacked, and the final piece of furniture is set in place. The dorm rooms now feel like cozy sanctuaries, ready to embrace the girls and provide them with comfort and familiarity. He has played a small part in making their college experience more manageable. And I'm grateful for that side of him despite the tension he may have created throughout the process.

Our girls accompany us down to our car, briefly chatting with their roommates as we pass them on the way out.

"I would have loved to stay longer, get your bed made, and see what the finished product looks like," I say.

"They can text us pictures. I just want to hit the road after the drive here last night and the long ride ahead of me."

Like always, I'm on his schedule.

Michael and I jump into our now empty truck. I can tell he is exhausted, but I'm still excited. I offer to drive, knowing he would never conceive of such an idea. He says he can't relax when I'm behind the wheel. After a long but exhilarating weekend, we slam the car doors shut and begin our six-hour journey home, heading into the uncertainty of our life as empty nesters, leaving our twin daughters' quintessential northeastern campus in our rearview mirror.

Chapter 2
Cohabitate

During the first hour of our drive home, we toss a million thoughts back and forth—or should I say, I bounce a million thoughts off Michael, and he does a lot of head nodding. Will Olivia and Sienna make friends? Do they have everything they need? Are they prepared for the academic demands of college? I imagined parents in SUV's returning home from college move in day are engaged in similar chatter.

Michael is quiet, even more so than usual. His negative energy seems to suck the oxygen out of the two rows of our truck. Is it possible that he's still annoyed by my choice of attire? Maybe he's processing the thought of living our new lives together as empty nesters. At least that, I understand. Then, he delivers those four words abruptly, seemingly out of the blue. His disdain for me is more than frustration over my shoe selection. I suddenly grasp why he rushed to end the weekend. He couldn't wait to break the news to me.

But now, as I sit in our empty truck, surrounded by the remnants of our six-hour drive earlier that morning, Michael's words shatter the picture-perfect image I painted. The excitement and anticipation of this new chapter in our lives are replaced with a sense of dread and uncertainty.

I look at Michael, searching for any sign of hesitation or doubt in his eyes, but I see only a cold, distant stare. It's as if he has already moved on, mentally and emotionally, leaving me behind in a state of shock and confusion.

"What... what do you mean?" I manage to stammer, my voice trembling with fear and disbelief.

Michael's voice remains steady as he explains his reasons, but his words fall on deaf ears. My mind is racing, trying to make sense of it all. How did we go from planning family vacations and retirement dreams to this? Was it something I did? Something I said? Or have we gradually drifted apart, a slow erosion of the love that once bound us together?

As our situation sinks in, a wave of sadness washes over me. I think about our daughters, about the life we had built together, and the thought of tearing it all apart feels unbearable. How will they react? How will they understand that their parents, who were once inseparable, are now going their separate ways?

"What are you saying?" I ask as if he wasn't undeniably clear in his statement.

"Oh, come on, Stephanie. Stop with the act. Don't pretend like you didn't see this coming."

"Pretend? Do you think I'm pretending? Did I miss the conversation where you said, 'Stephanie, we need to talk. I'm not happy. After we drop our twins off at college, we're done?'"

But deep down, a part of me already knows the answer. The signs are hidden beneath the surface of our seemingly happy-ish marriage. Michael has been even more shut down than usual with me. Then there are the late nights at the office, the secret phone calls, and the constant complaints about me, as if I am doing nothing right. I had chosen to ignore all of this, to believe that our love was strong enough to withstand any storm.

Tears well up in my eyes.

"Did I really need to tell you? We... we haven't been happy for some time. Let's face it. We've been holding on for the kids."

"Don't gaslight me, Michael. If you aren't happy, that's your story, not mine." I point directly at him. "You damn well should've talked to me, not just dumped this on me like this."

Michael's body language is so nonchalant that it's as if he's telling me he has changed his mind about dinner. How can he be so cavalier? It has always fascinated me how he can casually detach himself from an emotional conversation.

"I've known you for over twenty years, so..."

"So what? Tell me, Michael! So, you could read my mind? Tell me what you've seen that screams I'm unhappy? Was it something I said during dinner last week or maybe during our after-work cocktail hour? And let me get this straight. When we had sex the other night, were you thinking, 'Wow, she seems so miserable?'

I pause before winding myself up as I realize this will be a long ride home.

"Or maybe you've been collecting all of this data about my discontent on one of the many little spreadsheets you keep, tracking absolutely every life detail."

"What the hell, Stephanie. Spreadsheets? What are you even talking about? Are you knocking on my spreadsheets? That's where this conversation is going? Do you want to have a conver... At least I have spreadsheets!" Michael snaps back.

I feel the tension in the truck escalating. The engine roars louder, and the trees become fleeting blurs. I think of myself careening down the highway.

"Are you leaving me because I'm not an Excel expert? Really, Michael, I'll take a class if that's what it takes to keep us together," I suggest as I tuck my hair behind my ears in a flirty attempt to diffuse the situation.

"Okay, you want to be cute, Steph," Michael begins. "I want to have a serious conversation with you for once. This isn't about spreadsheets or sex the other night."

"Now you want to talk? Okay, let's talk. Believe it or not, Michael, you're telling me you want a divorce out of the blue! I don't know how I'm supposed to respond. What's the appropriate pre-scripted response? Why don't you tell me, and I'll recite it."

"Look, Stephanie. I will always care about you." "For God's sake! How cliché could you possibly be?"

"Stephanie, stop!"

We both pause to catch our breath. Michael is the planning type. This conversation must have been brewing in his head for a while, but I'm trying to understand what the hell is happening? It's all new information to me. I don't know... maybe I have once and for all driven him away?

When we first started dating, Michael loved my carefree spirit. He said my spontaneity delighted him in contrast to his own rigidity. However, after we married, it didn't take long before my fly-by-the-seat-of-my-pants approach to life became burdensome, even irritating. But this? I saw this new chapter as an opportunity to breathe life into our marriage, prioritize ourselves, and rekindle our romance. Clearly, he sees this new chapter as 'his chapter.' I'm blindsided that he doesn't want to work things out between us after more than twenty years of marriage.

It suddenly sinks in. "Who is she?"

That has to be it. He's leaving me for another woman. No matter how challenging I might be to Michael, I'm still a partner waiting for him with a delicious hot meal at the end of a long workday and, on occasion, a somewhat steamy enough bedroom at the end of the night. Let's face it. Men don't leave unless someone else is in the dugout, ready to come up to bat.

"It isn't about that, Stephanie!"

"No? Like it wasn't about that ten years ago when you cheated on me?"

"This is nothing like ten years ago, and you know it. We were in a bad place, but we needed to hold the family together for the girls' sake. I'm at the point where I want to choose how I live my life. That sounds selfish when I say it out loud."

"Ya think? It is incredibly selfish. Let me get this straight. We agree that we owed our girls to work on our relationship for them when they were young, but you don't think you owe it to me to at least try and work things between us? ...got it!"

Suddenly overheating, I crank up the air conditioning. I'm

feeling lightheaded. My brain is spinning. Google Maps tells me we have just under four more hours to go. I don't know how to hold on without losing it for the rest of the drive.

"It's not that I don't owe you anything or that I'm trying to be selfish. Like I said, I want you to be happy too. I just don't think we are living our best lives together. I'm not blaming you, Stephanie. We are just different people."

"Well, it sounds like you're blaming me."

"No, I'm not. Not at all. It's just that I don't like how we..."

"We what, Michael?"

I wait, aghast, for him to share some groundbreaking revelation I could even remotely get behind. "I don't like how we... I don't know… cohabitate."

Beyond astounded, I become agitated.

"You don't like how we cohabitate?! Wait until I tell my friends this."

"Jesus, Stephanie. Is that all you care about? What are your friends going to think? You have always been so wrapped up in your damn friends and what they think."

"I won't apologize for having good friends, but that isn't my main concern. I care that you've made a unilateral decision to end our marriage, and all you can say is we don't cohabitate well."

"Look. What I'm saying is I want a more peaceful household. I want organization. I want consistency. I have lived our entire marriage with you creating... chaos and drama. Our home has always made me feel unsettled. You are a..."

"Well, I am so glad you aren't blaming me. Go ahead, Michael. Tell me what I am." I dramatically throw my arms in the air.

"A scatterbrain. You are, Stephanie. I hate to say it out loud, but it's true. You lose everything. How many times have you run out of gas? You start projects and don't finish them. They would never get done if I didn't remind you to take care of the most basic chores. You wore pumps or wedges or whatever the hell they are to move your daughters into college. Sometimes, it feels almost like having a third kid!"

I'm initially speechless. That's rare. I'm always good for an off-the-cuff quip. The problem is, he isn't wrong. I fell short of maintaining an organized household while raising our children. Clearly, it has worn thin on Michael. He's sick of it. He's sick of me.

"Okay, so maybe I struggled a little."

"A little?"

He genuinely chuckles and shakes his head. Michael replaces his left hand on the steering wheel with his right hand. I can feel his discomfort. The Michael I know wanted to shove this news on me and be done with the conversation. Doesn't he know me better than that?

"Really? Just a little? I don't want to be insulting, but let's face it, Stephanie."

"You think you haven't already been insulting? All you have done is insult me. The biggest insult of all is that you are just calling it quits. Why don't we get help? Maybe we can go to therapy? I don't know. Maybe I could go to therapy. Find out why..."

I pause before finishing my thoughts.

"Or, or, we can get one of those organizers. Beth has a fabulous lady who helps her out around the house. I can ask Beth for her number. Why can't we or I... Maybe I need to make some changes? I'm sure we can find a compromise?"

I hear the panic in my voice. Michael's foot lets up on the pedal. He's silent. It's as if he thought through all these rebuttals and isn't buying any of them. I'm disgusted with myself. I sound so desperate. So pathetic. I wish I was the type of woman who could say, 'Really? You're leaving me? Well, fuck you and the woman you're seeing.' Instead, I'm falling apart and making a fool out of myself.

"Stephanie, it's not that simple. This decision didn't come out of nowhere. We've been drifting apart for a while now. Come on Stephanie. I have talked to you about this for years, and nothing has changed."

"Oh, okay Mr. Perfect. And you do nothing wrong."

"I never said I was perfect. I'm just saying, you know. Nothing changes. Nothing gets better."

My chest tightens, and I feel like the truck's interior is caving around me. I'm having a panic attack. I've never had one before, but I know what they look like. I've helped Michael through them many times before. I can look at him and see if he needs more space or air. If we were with other people and I saw an attack overcoming Michael, I would make up an excuse to pull him away from a situation and talk him through his feelings. That's what you do for the person you love. Does he think this other woman will know him like that or even care? I gently put my hand over my heart to keep it from beating out of my chest. His silence is deafening, even worse, dismissive.

I take another approach, this time, more out of anger than in the spirit of repairing our marriage.

I shake my head and chuckle quietly through my gritted teeth. "Well Michael. You're taking a page from your dad's playbook, right?" That is a purposeful hit below the belt.

Michael immediately roars. "I am not my father! Don't you dare compare me to him?" The car lurches forward.

Michael thrives on control. He rarely elevates his voice. He certainly can demonstrate anger, but it manifests as an internal slow burn or a well-pointed silent treatment to demonstrate his disdain. Clenched teeth and squeezed fists are his equivalent to a screaming fit. Comparing him to his father has always been a way to go in for the kill. He can't possibly think I would allow him to walk out on me without me landing a well-deserved punch.

Michael dials back his tone with a more diminished voice. "Please... Don't compare me to my father."

Dammit. How does he do that–so quickly recomposed.

"This isn't like that. I did my job. I got to the finish line. The girls are eighteen. I didn't walk out on two little kids."

And there you have it. Our family was a job for him to endure until our girls left the house. He made it to see them off to college, far more than his dad did for him. Bar is extremely low, and he managed to clear it.

This conversation has drained me. I feel defeated. The hostile bickering in the car is replaced with uncomfortable silence. Still, I don't have the energy for any additional dialogue. Three. More. Hours.

Michael resumes the conversation but with a more compassionate approach. It feels insincere, though. He wants to push through the rest of the drive home.

"Look, Steph."

"Don't 'Steph' me!" I scream while clasping the leather door panel.

"Steph" is reserved for tender moments, playful encounters, or endearing conversations. "Steph" is not allowed when he's canceling me. I let it go once, but not anymore.

"Okay... Stephanie. You're a wonderful mother and an amazing person."

"You know, it's funny to hear you say that. You spent most of our marriage making me feel anything but wonderful or amazing."

"That isn't true. Our girls are outstanding. I always tell people you are a fantastic mom and give you props for how they turned out. But you know how I am. I like things a certain way. You and I don't mesh in that department."

"You mean as cohabitors?"

Michael's face softens, his eyes filled with regret and frustration. "I wish I never used that word. I am really sorry. This decision didn't come out of nowhere. We've been drifting apart for a while now. I feel like one day, you'll think this was the right decision for both of us."

I so badly want to scream. What gives him the right to tell me how I should or will feel? Despite all the ups and downs throughout our relationship, I never stopped loving him. Apparently, that wasn't reciprocated.

He sighs, his gaze fixed on the road ahead. "I'm sorry this is happening right now. And I didn't want to burden you with this during such an emotional time, ya know, with the girls leaving. But I don't see the point in hanging on any longer."

"Okay, can you just stop?" I snap out of frustration. "I just need to think. I need silence. You've had time to process this. I haven't. I can't talk anymore."

I'm sure he's relieved to hear I'm over the conversation.

"I get that. All I can say is I'm really, really sorry."

I don't give a shit if he's sorry. My anger grows with each passing mile. I turn my head and try to lose myself in the trees outside the truck as they pass my window. I crack the window, but I get no relief from the still, hot air. The silence in the car is suffocating, the weight of our crumbling marriage hanging heavy in the air. I struggle to find the right words, my mind racing with a mix of anger, sadness, and confusion. How did we end up here? How did we let our love slip away without even realizing it?

I want to ask Michael to pull over so I can get out and have some time alone, but that would delay the ride. I need to get home. I need to crawl in bed and pretend none of this is happening. I spend the rest of the ride home replaying our conversations from the past couple of months in my head. How long did he know this conversation was coming? I question everything about myself, how I feel in our relationship, who Michael is as a husband, and how we got to this point. What did I miss?

As we continue our journey home, the million racing thoughts that filled my mind are replaced by a single question: What comes next? The future that once seemed secure and planned now feels uncertain and daunting. Two. More. Hours.

Chapter 3
Triumph or Tragedy
October

"Hear me out," insists Ellen. "I need to show you something."

My best neighborhood friend, Ellen, stops by to check on me as she has been doing since Michael left me.

"Go get your laptop... Trust me on this."

Ellen isn't the kind of person you say no to. She runs a tight ship at home; her husband, Phillip, and four children toe the line. Reports are run for budgets, monthly calendars are posted, and everything rests in its assigned space. Sitting in a reclined position in my sparsely decorated condo, I tilt my head to the right and stare at Ellen.

"Do I have to?" I ask like a petulant teenager responding to her parent.

"Yes, you do. Go," Ellen shoos me away.

Dressed in baggy sweatpants and an ancient college sweatshirt, I let out a huge exhale as I slowly stand up from my couch and shuffle to the kitchen island, just steps away from where I had been sitting. I catch my reflection in the living room window— as if I could feel any worse, I notice a dusting of Cheetos powder brushed across my right cheek. I wipe the orange debris from my face with the sweatshirt sleeve. I rummage through a pile of unopened mail, shoving a t-shirt to the right and a two-day-old Chinese take-out container to the left. As I carelessly move a heap of miscellaneous junk that I plan on organizing at some point, I suddenly hear a clunk and immediately look down. It's the familiar sound of my car keys crashing into my ceramic tile kitchen floor.

"Oh, there they are."

To call them a set of "car" keys would be an understatement.

I lift the clustered mess of iron by the heaping bunch of expired grocery store loyalty key tags. You would think the large valet key for a car that I sold nearly a decade ago and the near dozen superfluous keychain rings would be easy to keep track of. And yet, my keys have been missing for at least two days. I consider this discovery a win.

I turn my head to look at Ellen and smirk, proud of my 'huge success,' and I half expect her to be proud of me.

Finally, after I ransack the kitchen island clutter, I find my buried laptop.

"Stephanie, when was the last time you were outside?" Ellen asks in a mildly concerned tone. She clearly noticed my discovery; however, she must have seen my 'huge success' as less of a triumph and more of a tragedy.

"What day is it?" "It's Friday."

"Uhhh, Tuesday maybe? No, Wednesday. I went to Beans and Bagels Wednesday morning."

Ellen purses her lips but decides that's a discussion for another day.

I reach down and pick up a pair of reading glasses that had fallen from the muddled mess. They're slightly crooked, a testament to the neglect that has consumed my life since Michael left. I put them on, adjusting them to sit properly on my face and make my way back to the couch where Ellen awaits.

Ellen, ever the organized and efficient friend, has already opened my laptop and is waiting for me to sit down. I plop down on my dingy couch that once lived in the partially finished basement of my beloved home. I sink into the worn-out cushions and take a deep breath.

Ellen has perched my laptop on my beautiful mid-century modern coffee table that Michael and I purchased a year ago. I love this table. Screw how it looks with this nasty couch, but there was no way I was leaving it behind for some other woman to enjoy her morning coffee.

"What is it, Ellen?" I ask, my voice tinged with a mix of curiosity and exhaustion.

She smiles, her eyes filled with a glimmer of excitement. Ellen begins banging away on the keyboard.

Despite months going by, the weight of my current situation feels heavier than ever–Ellen can tell. I trust her judgment and hope that whatever she wants to show me will bring some much-needed clarity…or, at the very least, distraction.

"I stumbled upon something yesterday that might just change your perspective, Stephanie. For reasons I couldn't begin to understand, I saw this ad on Facebook about a writer's tour through Italy for wannabe authors. These ads usually drive me nuts, but this time, I was intrigued by it."

"Maybe you googled Italian tours?" I suggest with the tone of a condescending fifteen-year-old.

"Ah, makes sense. I was looking at trips for our 25th... Sorry."

Ellen stops short, quickly recognizing it's not a great time to talk about her romantic anniversary getaway with her husband, but it is a reminder that as I sit here wallowing away in my sorrow, life is moving forward outside these four walls. As Ellen taps away on my laptop, she begins to talk about what she found.

"Anyways, I have heard of bike riding trips through Italy, Italian wine tours, or cooking tours, but I have never heard of book writing tours. Take a look. I immediately thought of you."

I raise an eyebrow, intrigued yet skeptical.

I dreamt in the past that Michael and I would retire in Italy in a small villa while writing the novel waiting to be extracted from my brain. Ellen turns the laptop towards me. The website displays lots of smiling people, piles of books, gorgeous food displays, writing journals, and amazing stock photos of the Italian countryside.

She pauses, scanning for a reaction.

"Maybe this is some sort of message," she says seriously. "This could be a sign that you're meant to do this trip."

"Or it could mean I am one of many delusional wannabe writers out there who thinks the only thing standing between them and the next Pulitzer Prize-winning novel is a book writing trip to Italy."

"Really? That's what you think? Come on, Stephanie, I know you're better than that."

Ellen knows me well, and even though I'm not immediately willing to admit it, the trip does look amazing.

Ellen leans forward, her voice filled with conviction. "Stephanie, sometimes all it takes is knowing that you're not alone. That someone out there has gone through what you're going through and has come out stronger on the other side. This might just offer you that sense of connection and hope…plus how many times have you told me about your dream to go back to Italy one day and write."

She's right. After a few drinks, the ladies would ask me to tell them more about my future novel. I would give them chunks of the story, and everyone seemed to want more. Joining a travel writing tour in Italy sounds amazing. However, at this moment, the thought of moving from this couch, packing a bag, and getting on a plane sounds overwhelming. I feel so defeated in my life that I know I'm not in the position to commit to a trip like that.

I take a moment to absorb her words. I've been feeling isolated and lost, as if no one could truly understand the pain and confusion I'm experiencing. Maybe this trip could provide the solace and guidance I desperately need.

With a nod, I reach for the laptop. "Let me take a look at this."

My fingers hover over the keyboard for a moment. Am I really entertaining this right now? To appease Ellen, I click the mouse a few times to feign interest, but my curiosity takes over.

I can't help but feel a mix of excitement and skepticism as I gaze at the website.

I feel an uncontrollable spark of anticipation and apprehension. As each page loads, I can't help but wonder if this could truly make a difference in my life. But a part of me can't help but question if it's just another way to distract myself from the pain and emptiness I feel inside.

I abruptly snap out of my trance and turn the computer back towards Ellen. I wrack my brain for any excuse to steer her away from the idea.

"It starts August 15th. I will most likely be driving the girls back to college for their second year of school. August is not a good time for a trip like that." It's obvious I'm grasping at straws.

Ellen does a slow clap. "Bravo. You really are a natural storyteller. This is perfect for you. Look how quickly you came up with that eloquent story to back out of this trip."

Ellen pauses a moment before continuing.

"Be honest. You have no idea when Olivia and Sienna's classes begin next year. Besides, your daughters have another parent who can help them move back in."

Ellen tilts her head and gives me the 'Ellen look' that I have come to know over the years.

"Let's face it, Stephanie, we all know you're not much for heavy lifting anyway."

We both chuckle. It's as if she was with my family when Michael and I moved the girls into their dorms almost two months ago. She's right, though. I'm 5'1" on a good day, and my idea of a workout is a power shopping spree with my friends followed by lunch. No matter how low I feel, Ellen is always good for the hard truth and a good laugh.

"Hell, I'll take them back to college if need be. Come to think about it, I don't even know why we are having this discussion. Sienna and Olivia are the most competent young adults I know. I'm pretty sure they could figure out how to get themselves to school on their own."

I crack a small smile thinking about my girls. I'm so proud of what capable problem solvers they've always been. Maybe it's some sort of twin thing, or maybe my own deficiencies as a mom. Either way they are exceptionally efficient and always have been. I was such a disorganized parent that it was hard enough to manage myself, let alone organize the household like other moms. They ended up figuring things out on their own. I always felt like my inadequacies inadvertently contributed to their independence. At least, that's what I always told myself to make myself feel better for falling short of June Cleaver.

One Saturday morning, when they were about nine years old, I woke up to the sound of a whirring hand drill. I rolled over and saw the empty space in our king bed where Michael slept, so I assumed he had gotten an early start on a weekend project. But when I walked into one of the girls' bedrooms, I saw them assembling a desk we had purchased months earlier but had not yet assembled. Or should I say, Michael had not yet assembled. Naturally, I deemed that to be a 'Michael job' and never even entertained the thought of pulling out the drill, spreading the wood, the nuts, and the bolts in an organized fashion all over the floor, and, with instructions in hand, putting together a desk. That is exactly what they did, not once but twice, for each of the two desks. I was amazed at the initiative they took at just nine years old. Since I was always my own worst critic, my pride in their actions also emphasized the disappointment I felt in myself for never taking on such an endeavor. But whatever the reason may be, objectively speaking, they have always been quite impressive.

Ellen's voice breaks through my thoughts, her tone filled

with genuine belief in me. "Stephanie, I know you have a story to tell. I've seen the way you light up when you talk about writing, about your dreams of retiring in Italy and penning that novel. This trip could be the push you need to finally start turning those dreams into a reality."

Like the good friend Ellen had been to me since the day I moved into the neighborhood, I know she's just looking out for me. You couldn't ask for a more fabulous round-the-clock girlfriend. A few days after Michael left me, she abandoned her groceries in the checkout line to be by my side when I called her as I was too distraught to get out of bed.

When we moved into our sought-after neighborhood fifteen years ago, establishing roots in our newly constructed colonial home just miles outside of Washington, D.C, was like a dream come true. There were tons of kids for Olivia and Sienna and fabulous moms for me. Michael reluctantly engaged with the husbands in the neighborhood from time to time for an after-work beer, but he thought they were pretentious. I don't disagree with him. Although ambitious and successful, Michael's different from a lot of the neighborhood guys. Despite his engineering degree, he's maintained his blue-collar mentality that emerged while working in construction as a means of paying his way through college. I always found that to be an attractive trait in Michael.

Like neighborhoods everywhere, gossiping was also part of our reality. I can't begin to imagine how quickly the news that Michael left me bounced from one kitchen table to another. It would have been too juicy not to discuss. Admittedly, I, too, would not have been above seeking details had it been one of the other women who had been ceremoniously dumped during a six-hour drive home. Nonetheless, I also would have been there for my friend in any way she wanted me to be available, and if I asked, the whole gaggle of ladies would be available for me.

Ellen is the only friend I have allowed into my diminutive world since our separation. She has a way of keeping me calm despite my elevated anxiety. I think her demeanor is predictable because of how she was raised. I met her family many times. Even unsociable Michael enjoyed Ellen's parents, her brother Patrick, and her sister Shannon.

One night, Ellen and her husband Phillip invited our family for a barbecue when her parents were in town. Ellen and her parents were reminiscing about a 'huge' fight her parents had when Ellen was a kid. They laughed as they recalled back and forth debate that arose regarding the most effective way to manage the household's incoming mail. As I listened intently, I couldn't help but wonder when we would get to the part where an Italian bisque lamp was thrown down the steps only to crash to a tile floor below and obliterate into a million pieces. When my parents fought, they fought. A family heirloom meeting its demise by shattering in our foyer was an unfortunate end to a valuable fixture but not an isolated incident of violence during my childhood. It's just how I grew up. Apparently, disagreements over where to stack mail were as dicey as they got in the Pryerton home.

Ellen and I sit in silence. I feel safe with her next to me. The shock still has not worn off. Talking about my girls while she attempts to help me piece my life back together feels so surreal. If someone had told me mid-summer while the girls and I rummaged through department stores for dorm room apparel that my beloved home on my tree-lined cul-de-sac would soon be occupied by another family, I would have never believed it. But here we are.

Ellen breaks the silence. She wants me to look at the website again. It's the least I could do. I can't deny it. This writing tour is right up my alley. I take a deep breath, feeling a mix of fear and excitement bubbling within me. The thought of immersing myself in the beauty of Italy, surrounded by fellow writers and guided by experienced mentors, is undeniably enticing. It's a chance to step outside of my comfort zone, challenge myself, and rediscover the passion that has been buried beneath my grief.

I hold these thoughts close to the vest for the moment. If I show an inkling of excitement, Ellen will pounce on that exuberance and push me harder. As I scroll through the website, I can't help but think what could possibly be more enchanting than spending two glorious weeks traveling through Italian cities, taking VIP museum tours, meandering through a Tuscan vineyard, and, best of all, participating in writing seminars with assistance from published authors. I could almost imagine myself sitting at a farmhouse table, with white lights above, sipping wine with other hopeful writers as I looked out on the rolling hills of a Tuscan village.

"You really think I should do it?" I ask, my voice filled with a mix of hope and uncertainty.

Ellen nods, her eyes shining with encouragement. "Absolutely, Stephanie. Life is too short to let fear hold you back. This trip could be the start of something incredible for you, a chance to reignite your love for writing and to find healing in the process."

I take another look at the website, the images of Italy calling out to me, beckoning me to take a leap of faith. Italy and me, well, we have a history. After college, I moved to Italy, fulfilling a dream to live in my ancestral land. However, at that point in my life, I wasn't emotionally prepared for such a move, and that escapade didn't end well, to say the least.

My eyes linger on the images of smiling writers, picturesque landscapes, and the promise of creative inspiration. It's as if the universe is nudging me, reminding me that it's never too late to pursue my passions and follow my dreams.

Just as I am about to concede defeat, I assure Ellen. "It's not a 'no,' but I need to work on myself before I take the plunge." Normally, I would jump on an opportunity like this without thinking things through. I need to take things slow right now.

Ellen humors me. "That sounds like a healthy approach. I'm proud of you. Use this trip as motivation to invest in yourself now so you can be ready for this tour. August is a long time from now. You have ten months to work through your stuff."

"Do you know how much stuff I have? I need more like ten years."

"Well then. Looks like you better get started," Ellen insists. "You have been talking about getting your book from your head to blank pages for years. Just picture it for a second. This is the perfect time in your life to take a trip like this."

It's true. I don't really have a life right now. The girls are thriving at college. I got a nice chunk of change after selling the house. Michael has been quite generous with the finances. I'm... in between jobs.

"You've been wallowing away in this condo, in your bed, and on this shitty couch since Michael left you. I can't imagine how hard this must be for you. I'm here to help, but it's time for you to make some moves. It's going to take effort on your part. I don't mean to be harsh, but look around. I can track what you have eaten this week just by looking at the empty food cartons. Whatever you didn't put in storage is scattered around this place in unpacked boxes. I'm not even convinced you're showering regularly."

"Okay. Okay. Let's not kick the old dog when she's down."

"Whatever you want to call it doesn't change the fact that it needs to be said. Sorry, not sorry. You're going through a divorce, you moved out of your beloved home, the girls are away at college...I get it...it sucks, but you aren't alone. You have friends and family who love you and we're all here for you. Think of this as an opportunity to focus on yourself.

Ellen's words hit me like a firm wake-up call. "You win. I give up. I don't like you very much right now, but I know you're right."

"Well lucky for me, I'm not running for mayor and looking for your vote. I just want to see you happy...like the old Stephanie I know and love."

"I will save the website link. Maybe it will motivate me. You know Ellen, it might look like I have been sitting on this 'shitty couch' for two months doing nothing, but I have been doing a lot of thinking." I double-tap my temple with my finger.

"A light went off one night after binge-watching Netflix. I need to confront the crap that has been holding me back for years– my whole life, really. If I'm going to make changes, I need to work on myself before I can move forward."

"Revelations are fabulous. Great first step. But seriously. Don't think I'm going to let you get away with talk and no action. I know this is your calling."

This is exactly what I need, but when the time is right. I don't want to write just any story; I want to write a story with a perfect ending.

Chapter 4
Let the Unraveling Begin
Late October

I step into the office for my first counseling session, feeling a great sense of trepidation. I sink into the plush leather chair in the sleek, modern waiting room, anxiously waiting to hear my name called. It's hard to fathom that I've never sought therapy for myself before despite enduring years of internal emotional turmoil. The thought of revisiting past life events, particularly the tumultuous period in my mini-marriage meltdown with Michael a decade ago, makes my stomach churn.

Although we eventually chose to stay together, we only had a handful of minimally productive sessions with a marriage counselor. The idea of delving back into that chapter of my life fills me with dread.

Ever since Ellen introduced me to the writing tour, I've allowed myself to feel a glimmer of hope thinking about my future. It may be a long and arduous journey ahead, but envisioning that trip provides me with a modicum of motivation. Why can't I be one of those radiant faces pictured on the writing tour website, basking in the Tuscan sun with a glass of wine and a laptop before me?

Cautiously optimistic and strangely exhilarated, I put on the face of someone who is ready to unpack the trauma that has burdened me for far too many years. It has hitched a free ride on my back for far too long, and it's time to shed the weight. As soon as I hear my name, I take a slow stride into Sondra's office, settling myself directly across from her and exhaling deeply.

Sondra possesses a captivating allure, drawing attention without being distractingly beautiful. Her light brown hair cascades just below her shoulders, and her green eyes stand out against her fitted purple top. A flowy skirt and high boots complete her ensemble, exuding a well-crafted blend of bohemian and chic. I've always envied women like her, effortlessly projecting an image of having it all together.

Tall and slender, she confidently owns her style, a feat that my shorter, ever-expanding frame since indulging during our separation cannot pull off. My thoughts drift to a different realm. "Who are these women who stop eating and lose weight when their husbands leave them?" I find myself spiraling into self-doubt even before therapy has begun. Not one word in therapy has yet to be spoken and I'm already visiting my old friend, 'self-doubt.' Sondra has no idea what she's in for with me.

Sondra inquires, "Hi Stephanie, it's so nice to meet you. Could you share a bit about what has brought you here today?"

"Well, my husband... after 23 years of marriage, he left me about two months ago, and I've been struggling to cope," I respond.

"That's a lot to deal with." Sondra pauses, presumably to allow me to absorb her words. I imagine she learned this technique early in her training. It's effective. It has been a lot, and I feel affirmed. Looking down, I simply nod as I fight back tears.

"Stephanie. Have you experienced feelings of wanting to cause harm to yourself?" I know she needs to ask me that, but it is still hard to hear.

"Hurting myself hasn't ever crossed my mind. I have had dark moments, but I have never had a desire to harm myself."

"Okay. Understandable." There's that pause again. "Let's talk more about your difficulty with coping. First of all, give yourself credit. You made a brave decision to come here today. Congratulations. What prompted you to take this step?" Sondra gently pushes.

Now I'm the one needing to pause and really think about why I'm here. I can't possibly say Ellen made me do it and if you knew Ellen, you would understand saying no is not an option. I come up with a response. "I want to achieve emotional well-being for myself, my daughters, and my friends."

"That's a wonderful goal. Was there something specific that led you to take these initial steps?" Sondra nudges me a little further.

"This will probably sound ridiculous." I hesitate.

"We're in a safe space, Stephanie, and your feelings are valid," Sondra reassures me, her tone comforting and caring. I already feel like I'm in the right place. I explain to her that since Michael left me, I've been consumed by fear and, at times, unable to even move. I can't imagine living a vibrant, active life like I used to.

"That can be incredibly debilitating," Sondra acknowledges.

"It feels that way. I think I found a reason to take action and make changes in my life."

"Look, there's no wrong reason to start. Tell me more about this inspiration," Sondra encourages.

"My friend told me about a writer's trip through Italy. You know. For people who…if someone wants to…well, for aspiring authors. It actually sounds perfect for me."

I chuckle in embarrassment. Aspiring author'…so lofty. But I'm reassured by a smile from across the table.

"Emotionally, I'm not in a place to embark on such an adventure. Hell, I can barely handle something as simple as grocery shopping without falling apart. It took all my strength just to come here. I thought that…maybe if I work on my mental health, I'll be in a better position to go. It's only a two-week tour, so it's not like it's that big a deal, but I can't wrap my head around going at this point. I've always had a passion for writing. Who knows, maybe it could be the start of something new for me."

Am I rambling? I'm rambling. I don't know how this process works. Sondra gives me the space to gather my thoughts. We sit face to face, a unique three-legged table adorned with a succulent and a box of tissues separating us.

"There's something else about traveling to Italy. Almost 30 years ago, after graduating from college, I moved to Italy…and it ended in disaster. I've always dreamed of having a second chance…of righting that wrong. You know, sort of like a do-over. This writer's trip wouldn't exactly be a move to Italy, but it feels like a good place to start," I confess.

Sondra chuckles softly, her eyes sparkling with amusement. "It does sound incredible, doesn't it? The idea of exploring new places, immersing yourself in the beauty of Italy, and indulging in your passion for writing. It's no wonder you feel a surge of excitement just thinking about it."

I nod eagerly, a grin starting to spread across my face. "It would be a dream come true. I can already picture myself strolling through the charming streets of Tuscany, sipping on a glass of wine, and feeling inspired to write. It's a chance for me to escape the confines of my current situation and embrace a new chapter in my life."

Sondra leans back in her chair, her eyes filled with encouragement. "Stephanie, that vision you have is powerful. It's a glimpse of the possibilities that lie ahead for you. And while the tour may not be happening right now, it represents something much more significant. It symbolizes your desire for growth, healing, and a fresh start."

Her words resonate deeply within me, and I feel a renewed sense of determination.

I straighten my posture, feeling a surge of confidence as if I had already secured my spot on the tour, booked my flight, and packed my bags. Sondra continues her voice steady and understanding. "It's important to prioritize your mental well-being before embarking on a goal like this, especially considering your past experience in Italy. But before we delve into that and your marriage, let's talk about your childhood."

And so, the unraveling begins. As the door to my memories opens, I surprise myself with how easily I divulge family secrets that have long been buried beneath the surface.

Sondra prods me gently. "You mentioned feeling a sense of guilt in your childhood home. Can you explain why?"

I feel a knot forming in my stomach, my grip on the chair tightening. "My father was incredibly abusive to my family, but somehow, I was spared from his abuse."

"Explain what makes you think you were insulated from your father's abuse?"

Sondra tilts her head slightly, a sign that she's fully engaged in listening. I explained to her the powerlessness I felt as a child, how my father's treatment towards my family was cruel, yet he showered me with love and affection. The stark contrast in his treatment pained me deeply.

"That must have been incredibly difficult for you to process as a child. Can you tell me more about your interactions with your father during that time?"

I can't help but smile as I recall those memories, and Sondra warmly smiles back at me. "He used to call me Princess, telling me that I was the princess of the world. I genuinely believed I was the actual princess of the entire world."

"Of course, I told all my friends that I was the one and only world's princess."

Sondra chuckles lightly. "I'm sure your friends set you straight." She says in a mildly teasing tone.

I nod, a laugh escaping my lips. "They sure did. I went home and asked my father why they would say that. He simply replied, 'You are MY princess of the whole world.' OH, I cried and threw a fit because I wanted to be the actual princess of the whole world."

Sondra and I share a genuine laugh. "That's incredibly sweet. Finding out you didn't actually rule the world was probably the first of many disappointments in life," she quips.

I nod in agreement. "Isn't that the truth?"

"Kidding aside, even though it was a letdown to find out you weren't an actual princess, you certainly felt your father's love and approval."

"Absolutely. That's why I've been gutted with guilt since I was a kid."

Sondra responds with empathy. "As a child, Stephanie, you craved and deserved your father's love. Children have a keen sense of injustice, even if they can't articulate it. From a young age, you understood the difference between what was fair and what wasn't in your home."

I sigh, feeling the weight of those memories. "Yes, it was incredibly confusing."

"Wasn't his mistreatment of your family abusive to all of you?" Sondra probes gently.

I hesitate before answering. "I suppose so," I finally admit, my agreement still tinged with uncertainty.

"It must have been incredibly confusing and unsettling for you. Can you tell me more about your father's inconsistent behavior?"

Sondra leans in, crossing her knee and resting her forearms on it, fully engaged in our conversation.

"My mother was such a kind and loving woman. But my father unleashed his anger and frustrations on her. He would yell, call her names, demean her. And he was particularly cruel to one of my brothers, Anthony. My mom had a soft spot for him. My brother was just a kid, innocent and undeserving of my father's wrath, but my father targeted him to hurt my mom."

I take a moment to collect my thoughts, feeling the weight of those memories resurface. Sondra reassures me, urging me to take my time.

"I remember one night vividly. He wasn't even drunk yet, which was a rarity. He and my mother were arguing about money.

He refused to give up his failing business venture and get a stable job. The bills were piling up. My father was screaming at my mother, cursing at her. He looked so enraged, like he was going to hit her."

Sondra asks, her voice tender. "Did he often physically harm your mother?"

I pause, searching my memories. "I remember a few instances of him hitting her when I was a young child, but his preferred form of abuse towards her was verbal."

"Please, continue. What happened next that night?"

"He roared like an untamed animal; it was frightening and intimidating. Sadly, not an isolated incident."

I feel a shiver run down my spine as I recall the events. "I could feel my mother's fear. After hurling every vile name at her, my father turned his anger towards Anthony."

"What happened next?"

Sondra leans in closer, her eyes focused on me. "How old were you and your brother at the time?"

"Oh gosh. I must have been seven years old at the time, so Anthony was probably nine or ten years old."

I take a deep breath, trying to steady myself.

Sondra encourages me to continue. "What happened next to Anthony?"

"He threw Anthony against the wall so forcefully that his body crumpled and sank to the floor. But what was even more devastating to Anthony, my father smashed his beloved race car set that he got for Christmas. He loved playing with that set."

"All of that anger just to get back at your mom?"

It took me years to reflect on the incident, but there was no question of what the motive was behind such anger.

"Absolutely. My father was a cruel and vindictive prick. He took pleasure in tormenting my mother, and Anthony became his favorite target to do so."

"How horrible and scary that must have been. You mentioned feeling a sense of guilt. What did your father's behavior have to do with you?"

Pausing for a moment, I gathered my thoughts before delving deeper.

"Even after all these years, the shame still lingers when I recall that night and countless others. He would berate my mother verbally and physically abuse my brother, only to turn around and treat me with love and affection. I should have stood up for them and done something to protect them. Instead, I accepted his false kindness. Even after watching what he did to Anthony that night, not twenty minutes later, he said to me, "Princess, do you want to get some ice cream?" I eagerly ran out the door and jumped in his car.

"Do you think, as a witness to the abuse, you were also traumatized?" she inquired, her voice filled with empathy.

I ponder her question before responding.

"Traumatized? Yes, I would say so but because of what I witnessed, not what I endured. I never thought I had the right to complain, though."

"You were just a child, merely seven years old. You were innocent. It was never your responsibility to shield your mother and brother. It must have been perplexing for you to process your father's kindness towards you while inflicting pain on your loved ones. And deep down, you must have feared that you could be his next target. You were a victim, just like the rest of your family, whether you were an observer or in direct line of fire."

Memories of growing up with the persistent fear of becoming his target resurfaced. "I do remember living in constant fear that one day he would turn his wrath towards me, but it never happened," I confessed.

Sondra interjects, her voice filled with understanding. "Of course, that fear was only natural. If he could harm one family member, he could harm any of you."

Sondra takes a moment to allow that thought to marinate.

"As a child, Stephanie, your instinct was to protect yourself. You assumed the adults in your life would protect you, but given your father's behavior, you couldn't trust that they would. Your home was never a safe haven; even as a young child, you understood that to be the case."

Thoughts of my daughters flood my mind, and I never wanted them to feel like they had to be family protectors as children. Michael wasn't abused like my brother but he endured years of neglect by his father. We realized how important it was for our children to never feel the weight of such responsibility. Regardless of any conflicts, our daughters were always showered with love and affection from both of us.

I return to my own childhood. "But someone had to protect them!" I declare as if it were an unspoken expectation for me as a young child to bear the burden of family protector.

"You were not that someone, especially not at that age. The terrible abuse your mother and brother endured was neither your fault nor your responsibility to fix," Sondra reassures me.

We sit in silence, allowing her words to sink in. "That was a lot to process today. Let's continue our conversation next week," she suggests, sensing my mental exhaustion.

Leaving her office, I find solace on a bench outside. I wrap myself tightly in my heavy wool sweater jacket, and shame pours over me. I neglected to share something etched in my brain with Sondra since that night nearly forty years ago. There was a moment when time stood still. As I left the house with my father, ready to indulge in ice cream, I paused at the doorway. I turned back to see my brother standing over the wreckage of his beloved car set. Our eyes locked for what felt like an eternity. His dark brown eyes conveyed a depth of pain that I did not comprehend at the time. I turned back around, ran out the door, and jumped in the car with the very man who tormented him. I have never gotten past the look in my brother's eyes.

Chapter 5
Jersey Girl
Late November

I brush off the chill of the outside air as I enter the sushi restaurant, a few minutes behind schedule, to meet Ellen. I'm relieved she chose a quiet corner towards the back, away from prying eyes. It's been three months since Michael left me, and I still haven't seen the whole clammer of ladies. I haven't had to face their judgmental gazes. A chance meeting at this point would be awkward. I'm still not ready to face the barrage of questions. I'm deeply embarrassed about the demise of my and Michael's marriage. Maybe Michael was right–I care about what my friends think.

As I approach the table, Ellen stands up and envelops me in a warm hug. Her usual smile lights up the dark, secluded corner of the restaurant. Ellen's Irish heritage shines through with her reddish blonde hair and blue eyes. Given her 'All American' girl next door looks, you would never guess she's over 50.

Michael never found her understated appearance to be particularly attractive. Women, however, universally envy her youthful glow. 'Stay out of the sun and use a good moisturizer' is her usual response when asked her secrets for maintaining youthful skin.

Our styles couldn't be more different from one another. She dons a flannel shirt, a Patagonia vest, jeans, loafers, and pearls. No matter the outfit, she always wears those pearls, a gift from her mother before she gets married. On the other hand, I look like I just stepped out of a New Jersey reality TV show with my big hair, oversized bag, chunky jewelry, and high heels. I'm definitely overdressed for a casual sushi dinner on a random Tuesday. As they say, you can take the girl out of Jersey…

At some point, Michael stopped finding my attire appealing or amusing. Initially, he thought I was the sexiest woman in the room, partly because of my stiletto heels. But like many things about me, wearing heels went from desirable to irritating.

Ellen and I quickly catch up, exchanging pleasantries and updates on our lives.

"Stephanie, you look so good. You look like you, not like that disheveled woman I last saw wallowing away on that crappy couch."

"Thank you. I'm beginning to feel more like my old self every day. I gotta admit… some days it's still a struggle to get dressed." As I take off my printed jacket and sling it on the back of my chair, I can't help but recall how much of a mess I was the last time Ellen saw me. I've made some progress since then, but putting together the pieces of my old self is still a challenge.

We order our food and start talking about Thanksgiving. I share how Michael, the girls, and I spent the day together to make it easier on them. They had much to share about their college experiences, classes, and new friends. Thanksgiving dinner conversation flowed easily. It wasn't as awkward as I had anticipated. Returning home to my condo instead of our family house was tough for them, but they handled it as well as expected.

"Selling the house is what you thought was necessary."

I respond. "At the time, I thought living in that big house, alone, with all those family memories would be tortuous. Maybe I made a hasty decision to immediately sell it. Anyways, it turns out that I'm just as unhappy in my miniscule condo."

"Well, what's done is done. The girls are resilient, and quickly adjusted. And you're doing better, right?"

Ellen rests her hand on me and looks sympathetically in my eyes, trying to detect my true state of mind.

"Yeah, yeah. I'm okay. Really. I am." I assure Ellen.

"Well, how about you, Ellen? How was your holiday?" Apologizing for not being able to visit, Ellen explains that her parents needed her help after her father's hip surgery, and then she was knocked out with bronchitis. It's been a crazy month for her, she explains to me. Listening to Ellen makes me realize that I've become so absorbed in my grief that I've failed to be a good friend. Add it to my list of failures.

"My parents, brother's family, and sister's family all came over. It was the usual. We ate too much and argued about everything. Good times had by all."

I seize the opportunity to challenge Ellen. "Oh, come on. Your family fights? I can't believe it. How could the perfect American family possibly have disagreements?"

"That's hilarious. I can't wait to tell Patrick and Shannon. Don't get me wrong, our parents were amazing, but our household was far from perfect."

"Your family always seems so close-knit. I assumed your childhood home was always harmonious." "I had a great upbringing, don't get me wrong. But we had family drama like everyone else."

The server brings us tea. We ordered miso soup and sushi to share. Ellen asks for extra wasabi for her sushi. "Well, that explains the sharp tongue," I tease. She grins but continues.

"Anyway, I have fantastic family memories, but I also remember a lot of turmoil. My mom always said she had these incredible friends in the neighborhood who supported one another."

"I guess some things never change," I reply.

I'm not sure if I feel sad or relieved to hear about Ellen's flawed family. The image of a flawless family I had in my mind shatters, but there's some comfort in knowing that not everything is as perfect as it seems.

I can tell Ellen is looking for a way to change the subject off of her.

"Look. You and Michael did the mature thing by spending dinner together." She cringes. "God, I hate complimenting that jerk." We both laugh.

We have been pretty civil throughout this whole process. Michael and I each visited our girls separately to talk with them. Olivia and Sienna processed the news differently from one another. Olivia seemed upset but didn't ask any questions or have much of a response. She's always been a lot like her father but a far superior version. Sienna is all spit and fire. I wonder where she gets that? Emotional and confrontational, she had a whole lot to say about our separation. She has been angry, mostly at Michael, but it's occasionally directed at me. At least I know where she stands.

"We're trying to be mature with one another. We've definitely hit some bumps along the way though." Before I look up from my tea, I see Ellen's wondering stare… she won't let me skate past that one.

"I don't think I told you. When Michael first ended things, he tried to convince me that it would be best for the girls if we said we mutually decided to dissolve our marriage?"

Ellen's jaw drops. "Best for the girls or best for him?"

"Exactly! He didn't want to seem like the bad guy. I refused. I told him he needed to own his decision. I told the girls I would do anything to make our marriage work. I did kinda lay it on thick." It feels good to admit that out loud.

Ellen laughs. "Now that's the warrior Stephanie I know. Hey, whatever the reason, they should know the truth. I don't blame you. He made his bed."

The food arrives, and I look down in mild embarrassment. I quickly dunk my spoon in the soup as Ellen mixes wasabi and soy sauce with chopsticks before the server walks off.

"Yeah. I will not be some bitter woman demeaning their father, but I'm also not going to allow him to rewrite history." I state firmly as I drop my spoon in my miso soup. Ellen sits back, seemingly appreciative of the fight I display in my tone.

"Honestly, the girls made a few snide remarks about their father over the weekend, and as much as I should have shut that down, I admittedly enjoyed their condemnation. I even added fuel to the fire a couple of times. On second thought, maybe I am condemned to a life of bitterness. I will add it to my list of topics for therapy." Ellen and I laugh then she lowers her voice.

"I'm actually not surprised. You know he wanted to convince you to tell the girls a revised version of events to benefit him. Michael has always been a little...manipulative like that with you, don't you think?" Ellen awkwardly asks.

"What do you mean?"

"Don't you think Michael used to make you feel..." "Feel like what?"

"I don't know - you were a burden or maybe more disruptive than productive to your household."

Ellen recalls something that happened one night when Michael made a rare appearance at a neighborhood party. He had too much to drink, which was also unlike him. He complained that the house was a mess when he got home. Since I was 'only working part-time,' he said there was no excuse for me not to keep up with the house. I cooked for the party, helped the girls with a school project, and prepared decorations for an upcoming school event, yet my contribution still fell short. He minimized me in front of everyone. At the time, I remember laughing in a weak attempt to pretend I thought he was funny, but I felt humiliated, and everyone knew it.

"You're right. I had my own insecurities, and he preyed on them to make me feel like I was inept as a wife and mother. I'm beginning to see that more clearly than ever before."

Ellen quickly reacts.

"Stephanie, you were an amazing wife and the best mom. Your house wasn't always perfect. Whose house is?"

"Uhhh, yours??" I quickly respond.

"Oh, come on. Hardly. Maybe you struggled with your home

more than some, but that didn't define you as a wife and mother."

"Well, that's diplomatic. Do you know how often I found my girls on top of a huge heap of clean clothes in the morning, looking for matching socks? The funny thing is, they would make a game out of it. The first to find a matching pair would declare themselves the winner."

I smile as I reflect on one or the other, sitting on a heaping pile of clean clothes, holding matching socks in the air like a victor. It was part of their morning routine. I knew it was chaotic at the time but thinking about it now warms my heart.

"It always felt like our household disorganization or my disorganization, was our family's dirty little secret. What kind of mother can't even manage laundry for the family?"

"Seriously, Stephanie? Busy moms everywhere. So, Michael didn't walk into a house in tip-top shape, roast on the table, you in nothing but an apron."

I chuckle, but Michael never truly respected or appreciated all I did for our family. He made me feel inadequate. How didn't I see it then, or did I bury my head in the sand? As painful as it is to acknowledge the truth, it's liberating now to begin seeing through his manipulation.

"Michael didn't give you the respect you earned for everything you did for the family. You were as committed to your family as we were, even if you felt 'less than' because of your husband."

I think I accepted his snide comments because his behavior was minimal compared to what I witnessed as a kid. Michael never called me foul names or wished death upon my family like my father did to my mother. So, from my perspective, that made Michael the husband of the year. My whole image of what is "normal" is distorted.

I slurp a spoonful of soup as we sit silently, allowing our conversation to marinate. She finally breaks the silence, and in true form, Ellen cracks a joke to lighten the atmosphere. We wrap up our dinner, give each other a warm hug then walk back into the chill of the night. I smile as I wrap my animal-printed jacket tighter to guard against the cold. Those two hours with my dear friend, eating sushi and catching up about Thanksgiving, were the most normal I have felt since Michael and I pulled away from our girls' college campus. Progress?

Chapter 6
Holiday Tradition
December

After two months of therapy, a routine has emerged during my sessions with Sondra. Amidst the upheaval of my life, the predictability of therapy oddly comforts me.

However, the impending holiday season brings discomfort. Lights twinkle, and Christmas melodies echo everywhere, yet I struggle to embrace the festive spirit.

"How are you feeling?" Sondra's perceptive inquiry slices through my thoughts. "You seem a little tense today."

"I feel unsettled."

"What's going on?"

"Well, Christmas break is approaching. I'm anxious about the girls coming home. I can't wait for them to be here, but…"

"You're apprehensive." Sondra nods empathetically.

I reach for a tissue, a familiar ritual, but today, unexpected tears blur my vision. Despite navigating through intense sessions – guilt, childhood memories, discussions about low self-esteem, and my husband's abrupt departure – the thought of disappointing my daughters during the holidays makes me weep.

"I'm sorry."

"Don't apologize. Take your time," reassures Sondra.

I believed I made so much progress during our sessions until those dreaded fucking Christmas cards started to flood my mailbox. Each family beamed in front of a fireplace adorned in matching pajamas. I grimace at their perfect joy, resenting my own lack thereof. Am I a terrible person? Do I wish misery upon others just because my condo lacks holiday cheer? Do I want my friends and family to suffer because it's less than two weeks from Christmas, and there are no dangling stockings or elaborate holiday decorations in my crappy little condo? Hell, even dogs in reindeer sweaters irritate me. The girls and I begged, but Michael vetoed the idea of having a pet, claiming he'd end up caring for it. Did I have a voice in our home at all? How did I allow that?

"What's going on?" Sondra breaks my spiraling train of thought.

"I've always loved Christmas—the cooking, baking, decorating. It's going to be so different for my girls this year."

"Will the girls stay with you the whole time?"

"My condo will be their base, but they'll also spend time with their father."

"Year one after a break-up is full of firsts. It's understandable to feel trepidation. What specifically concerns you about their visit?"

"I don't want to disappoint Olivia and Sienna. Christmas has always been special for us, and this year feels like it'll fall flat."

"Stephanie, the holidays will look a lot different this year. But, even though your situation has changed, you can make their visit special in a different way. Have you thought about maintaining old traditions while incorporating new ones?"

I tell Sondra about the turmoil I've been in, fixating on what I've lost. This is probably no shock to her—we've gotten to know each other quite a bit over the past six or so sessions. Well, I guess she's gotten to know a lot about me…

I dwell on the grand Christmas trees we used to adorn our home with, trees that now couldn't fit through my condo's door. We hosted extravagant parties before Christmas, although Michael always grumbled about them. To Michael, the only upside was the pre-party cleaning, which in his world meant shoving clutter under beds, into closets, and deep into the recesses of our basement. Despite the chaos, my home exuded festive charm. This year, my daughters will return from school to a drab and sterile space. I confide in Sondra, fearing that once they arrive, they'll yearn to escape to college.

"Let's face it. No matter where you live, your girls are gaining independence and will probably home, yearning to get back to school. If they do, don't take it as an immediate repudiation of your condo." Sondra assures me.

"True, true. They have made lots of friends. You might be right about that," I acknowledge, finding solace in her perspective.

Dabbing a few remaining tears, I crumple the used tissue in my hand and rest it on my lap. I take a deep breath, anticipating Sondra's direction for our conversation.

"It sounds like you made the holidays beautiful for your family. Your daughters grew up with a house full of decorations, excitement, and good food during Christmas. Tell me about some of your holiday traditions," Sondra's smile signals a shift to a more cheerful discussion.

"As you know, I'm Italian, well, Italian-American. Either way, it's all about the food," I chuckle.

"You can't go wrong with Italian cuisine. What foods do you prepare?" She inquires, interested in our culinary customs.

"Baking together is one of our traditions. In all honesty, I'm a terrible baker. Now, I can cook." I say with emphasis. "There's freedom with cooking. It's done by feel and by taste. I rarely use a recipe or measure ingredients." I pause." Baking, however, requires precision, which never went well with my personality. You must know that about me by now." We chuckle, and Sondra nods in understanding.

I delve into the memories of baking Italian cookies with my grandmother and mother when I was young. Their tales of family and Italy became intertwined with the tradition of baking holiday cookies. I carried that tradition on through the generations with my girls.

"Baking is a wonderful tradition to pass on from one generation to the next. I assume you have a kitchen in your condo," Sondra remarks.

I laugh softly. "Yes, I do indeed."

Sondra guides me back to cherished traditions, especially baking Italian cookies. Despite my apprehension about my condo's limitations, she encourages me to focus on creating a comforting experience for my daughters. She nudges me to see my control over this holiday season separate from past narratives.

"When we talk about maintaining old traditions, you can sustain this to convey a sense of normalcy for all three of you when your daughters get home. At this age, whether they tell you or not, they will find comfort in baking together like you've always done. Do your girls enjoy baking?"

"They love it, and in fact, they are way better bakers than me. Olivia especially. She has mastered my grandmother's biscotti recipe. Making the dough is an exact science–I guess she inherited Michael's engineering brain. Every spec of ingredient and process is followed exactly, but she adds some unique twist. I'm not kidding…they are bakery quality."

"Wow. They do sound amazing," Sondra's big smile feels inviting. I continue. "Sienna loves making Italian Iced Cookies, a butter and sugar cookie combo with icing and sprinkles. My mom called them an 'Italian classic.' We make all sorts of cookies and give them away to the neighbors. Every year, we shop together for toys and toiletries, pack tins full of cookies, and take care packages to a local women's shelter."

"You're making my mouth water talking about the cookies and what a lovely thing to do with your girls over the holidays. I'm sure they would enjoy baking and donating gifts like you have done every year."

Sondra fosters a warmth that feels more like a casual chat than a therapy session. She avoids note-taking, making our discussions feel natural without any added pressure.

"Yeah. Sienna has already asked me when we would be baking and shopping for gifts to donate. I lied and pretended I had everything planned, but I can't even motivate myself to buy flour."

"What is it about shopping for ingredients that's so hard?"

I recount to Sondra how I used to relish strolling through the aisles, discovering new flavors, or selecting the perfect ingredients for my culinary creations. But last week, amid the baking aisle, I repeatedly picked up and put down flour, sugar, and baking powder. I couldn't shake the image of my girls and me in our spacious, gourmet kitchen, joyfully rolling dough trays of treats coming in and out of the double ovens. The thought struck me: "What was I thinking, selling that house?" I clench my fists. "I can't imagine a similar experience in my current kitchen."

"At that point in your life, selling the home felt necessary. Try focusing on the goals– maintaining traditions and giving back to others. Work on letting go of the physical space. How does that sit with you?"

I exhale deeply, shaking my head. "I will try. I promise to work on it." "What other food traditions are important to your family?"

"Have you heard of the Festa dei sette pesci, Feast of the Seven Fishes?" Sondra shakes her head. "No, what's that?"

"Italian-Americans celebrate Christmas Eve by serving seven fish dishes."

I throw my hands in the air. "Don't ask why. I don't even remember the reason, but it's tradition, and everyone loves it."

Sondra probes further. "Did you grow up with this tradition too?"

"Yes. My father was an amazing cook. He handled most of the Christmas Eve meal preparation. He fried calamari, baked flounder, and made Italian bacalao, a cod dish. But the family favorite was always a pasta dish, pasta vongole–clams or mussels with spaghetti or linguine in a white wine sauce."

"Really, as long as the dish included something from the sea, it made it onto the menu. Am I catching on to how it works?" Sondra suggests.

"Exactly!" I become more animated as I continue.

"He also made these smelts which were dipped in flour and fried. They are these disgusting little fish with beady eyes that remind me of bait…just nasty. I don't make them."

"I have to agree with you, but other than - smelts? - It all sounds amazing."

For a moment, it feels like I'm talking with a friend, not my therapist. Reminiscing about my annual Christmas Eve dinner with Sondra feels surprisingly nourishing rather than depressing. Since she doesn't take notes during our sessions, we are just two ladies chit-chatting. One time, I asked her why she didn't take notes. She said she learned years ago that note-taking could be intimidating. With every pen stroke, she noticed some clients staring at the pad and becoming more focused on her writing than our discussion. That would have been me, especially with all my insecurities.

"How did your father learn how to cook so well?"

"My grandfather owned restaurants. He grew up learning to cook from Italian chefs. He used to say he started working when he was nine years old. I don't know if that was one of his classic exaggerations or not, but he more than knew his way around the kitchen."

"So many wonderful Christmas memories." Sondra pauses before delving in deeper.

"What comes to mind when you think about the holidays as a child?"

I swiftly return to reality. Sondra isn't my girlfriend. Besides the fact that she's married with a fourteen-year-old son and she runs, I know nothing about her. I don't even know where she's from. It's strange, isn't it? To share all this information with a person and not know the tiniest details of the other's life? She knows many of my deepest thoughts; the good, the bad, and the embarrassing. I have grown to appreciate and cherish my sessions with Sondra. I feel this burning desire to ask her about her life, but I refrain. This is where I come to dig up bones buried for decades, not to chat over coffee. She steers our conversation to childhood memories, where the volatility of my father shaped holiday experiences.

"At times, it was magical. Other times, it spiraled into chaos, ya know, depending on his mood, how much he drank or if we were spending the holidays with relatives. One year, we were so excited for my aunt's annual New Year's Eve party. There was always so much food, music, all my cousins were there. It was always such a big deal. I remember I picked out one of my new outfits I just got for Christmas. Then, seemingly out of nowhere, a dark cloud came over my father. He decided we were staying home, and that was that. My mother did her best to scrounge up a meal and play games but we were devastated. Anthony and I stood on the front steps and banged pots together at midnight. I guess we were trying to make the best of it but it was so disheartening. It was always the same though. If we had plans with family, would my dad get pissed off and change his mind. Christmas Eve–would he cancel our plans at the eleventh hour? The fear of let down and disappointment made it difficult to feel settled around the holidays."

"You're likening the holiday season to the general atmosphere of your childhood home—volatile and unpredictable. Your father controlled the narrative."

"It was crazy! My dad would harbor anger towards one family member or another. At the time, we never knew what exactly triggered him. Anything could happen. There could be screaming or shouting or he would even throw out food after it was prepared. I can't fathom how heart-wrenching it must have been for my own mother. Other years were completely different though. There would be lots of food, family, games - some years were great! You just didn't know what you were going to get year to year."

"How upsetting for all of you. Could you be aiming for an ideal Christmas for your daughters because your childhood holidays were so fraught with stress? Maybe you yearn for the consistency for your children you didn't have back then."

"Maybe." I sit quietly for a few moments, remembering something that happened several years ago. "About two years after moving into our new home, Michael mentioned keeping our spending in check due to the expenses we'd incurred with the house that year. It triggered such an immature, almost childlike response from me. I cried and cried. He wasn't suggesting canceling Christmas or anything drastic, just asking for mindfulness in our spending. Initially, Michael was understandably upset by my reaction. He used harsh words—selfish, immature, ungrateful—I heard it all. All I could manage to express was that Christmas had to be perfect for our girls. Eventually, I composed myself, embarrassed by my outburst, and offered an apology. It was no easy feat for either of us to apologize. Surprisingly, he responded with tenderness, understanding the weight of the moment. I distinctly recall him embracing me and conveying his understanding."

My eyes well up with tears again. I reach for the same crumpled tissues to dab my eyes, vividly reliving that profound moment between us.

"Sounds like Michael was supportive once he realized this was something deep-seeded."

"Absolutely. Looking back on the situation, he was uncharacteristically empathetic.

Michael has his own issues with holiday and birthday memories. I probably didn't give him enough credit at the time for how he handled the situation."

"How did that Christmas end up that year?" I smile. "It was perfect."

"Let's revisit something you mentioned. You described your reaction to Michael's request as 'childlike.' As a child, the holiday outcome was beyond your control—your family's experience was dictated by your father. As an adult, raising your children and creating a special holiday for your girls was within your grasp. It was something you could control. When Michael asked you to tighten the belt, you reacted immaturely. It sounds like your reaction mirrored that lack of control from your childhood. It was like regressing to that child who lacked agency. Your resistance to Michael's request was an attempt to seize control, something you didn't have growing up. While his urge to demonstrate financial caution was reasonable, what you heard echoed the narrative of control your father always wielded."

"Wow. I'm blown away. That. That. That makes a lot of sense. It's sad when you think about it, isn't it?"

"What strikes you as sad about it?"

"As an adult, a mother, and a wife, having a meltdown and throwing a tantrum over echoes of my father's behavior from my childhood feels misplaced."

"And what were you fighting for when throwing that tantrum?"

"My girls," I say firmly. "I wanted them to always have the best Christmas imaginable. I never wanted them to experience what I went through as a child."

"Well then, that sounds like a protective, devoted mother looking out for her children. You wanted only the best for them. Not that sad at all if you think of it that way, is it?"

I shake my head in agreement as Sondra allows a moment before continuing.

"Fast-forward to today. You still want to share a wonderful holiday season with your girls, right?"

"You absolutely can. Decorate together, bake cookies, and donate toys as you do every year. But take a moment to sit down and develop new traditions together.

Recognize that you have control over the holidays with your daughters now. You aren't at the mercy of your father's influence or Michael's concerns. And the holidays were never about the beautiful home that you had them in. It'll be different, but there's no reason it can't be fabulous."

I giggle. Oh, she knows I love that word.

I leave my session with Sondra with newfound clarity.

Chapter 7
Homecoming
December

I look out the window and see Olivia and Sienna step out of their cab. The crisp evening winter air embraces them as they stand outside my building. I nearly float down the steps to greet them suddenly, not feeling so embarrassed by the condo. The street is adorned with twinkling lights, the lobby glittered with decorations and smells of pine.

Festive music bellows in the hallways. As they approach the door, I can tell a familiar warmth envelops them—the essence of home, albeit in a different setting.

I shriek with excitement as I clamor to let them into the building. "You're here!" I exclaim, pulling them both into a tight embrace. The three of us carry too many bags through the halls to my front door–I should say they have, but I drag. Something I never helped with in the past. That was a Michael job, but there is something so effortless about my jumping in... My girls laugh as I stumble over bag straps and whack into walls. Still ineffective, but happy to help.

My hands shake with excitement as I fumble my keys into the lock. I slowly open the door and we're all met with the smell of nearly a dozen Christmas candles of varied scents.

"Wow, look at this," Sienna says, a smile tugging at the corners of her lips. "Mom's really gone all out with the Christmas decorations."

My condo's windows glow with the soft hue of Christmas lights, and a wreath adorns all the doors. It's a quaint yet cheerful welcome. I could see the excitement bubble within them as they exchange glances, eager to explore.

"Let's see what you've done with the place since Thanksgiving," Olivia suggests, rushing for their new bedroom door.

"It looks amazing, Mom," Sienna says, enjoying the festive ambiance.

I beam with pride. "I wanted it to feel like home, especially for the holidays." Olivia nodded, glancing around. "You've definitely nailed it."

We share a moment, surrounded by the glow of the season and the comfort of being together.

"I've missed you both," I say, my voice tinged with emotion.

"We've missed you too, Mom," Olivia replies, a softness in her tone. Sienna, not being the soft, cuddly type, agrees. I can feel the cringe coming off her, but she plays it off well. It warms my heart that they haven't changed a bit.

A crackling fireplace on the TV replaces the presence of our warm booming fireplace. Brisk, snowy air flows through the windows of my sleek, modern condo, lending a cozy feel to the space. Sienna settles onto the sofa, Olivia and I flanking her, each armed with a cup of hot cocoa and a determination to infuse cheer into our new reality. I'll say it's coming a lot easier than expected. My condo has never felt like such a home. I'm now seeing it in a whole new light.

"Okay, Mom," Olivia says, a spark of excitement in her eyes, "let's brainstorm new traditions." I was too excited to tell the girls about my newfound clarity with Sondra. Sienna nods eagerly. "Definitely! Something that makes this place feel like home."

They toss ideas, from a themed dinner night to a weekend getaway, each suggestion accompanied by laughter and shared memories.

"It is kinda weird not having so many people around," Sienna admits a tinge of wistfulness in her voice. Our house used to be bustling with friends and family during the holidays.

Olivia quickly glances at Sienna as if to say, 'Way to ruin

the mood.' Then, a silent look shot back the other way. Watching these two communicate in utter silence. An overall understanding passes between them.

Olivia pipes up. "What if we throw a neighborhood party? It could help you reconnect with friends, Mom. You've mentioned that you miss the ladies." Oh, now I see. This had to be planned. It's as if Ellen called them and nudged them to say that.

Sienna nods enthusiastically. "Yeah! We could organize games and cook seven fish, even if the party is after Christmas Eve."

A glimmer of sadness runs through me. What they want most is what they had before. Then, it dawns on me, and I feel an immense sense of satisfaction. What they want is what they used to have. Had. They cherish the perfect holidays, which I fretted over and provided to them all those years.

My eyes brighten at the prospect. "That's a fantastic idea! It has been a while since I've caught up with everyone."

Together, we outline plans for this holiday event. My condo is buzzing with newfound energy and excitement. As they draft invitations and discuss potential activities, I am grateful for my daughters' insight. They recognize my need for connection amidst the changes post-divorce.

Even with college commitments and hectic schedules, their dedication to my well-being shines through with a perfectly crafted plan to get me back to my old self.

In my condo, amidst the clatter of planning and laughter, I understand that family traditions are not solely about upholding the past but about adapting to change and nurturing relationships. And in that shared decision to create a new tradition, we are forging a path to a deeper, more resilient bond.

Chapter 8
Trauma
End of December

I return to therapy a few days after Christmas with a tin brimming with cookies.

"Oh my gosh. How thoughtful of you. I can't wait to dig into them. Looks like you did some baking over the holidays." Sondra exclaims.

"Just like old times," I reply, grinning. "We shared them with friends and donated some to the women's shelter."

"I'm sure that made you feel good," Sondra observes.

"Humbled but good. It's been a tough four months since Michael left, but I'm not in danger. I'm financially secure. My girls are healthy and safe. Yeah, 'humbling' feels like the right word."

"Why do you feel so humbled?" Sondra inquires.

"The last time I was here, I was drowning in sorrow because I no longer lived in my big house with those massive Christmas trees. I erratically chose to sell the home when we separated. At the shelter, I saw those women trying to keep themselves safe and protect their children. I felt... shame. Like, who am I to complain?"

"Everything is relative. You have every right to grieve the loss of a twenty-year marriage without guilt. You can empathize with others while taking care of yourself. No apologies. How does that sit with you?"

"It makes sense. I deserve my own peace of mind without comparing myself to others. I understand that" I affirm, convincing myself of my entitlement to my sorrow.

Sondra continues, "How are things with you and your girls?"

"Well, I took your advice. Besides baking, we're planning a fabulous first annual party in January. Maybe this will be our new tradition."

"I'm glad it went well. How did having your girls split their time between you and Michael feel?"

"It wasn't strange having them visit their father. It felt odd without Michael at our side, especially during the seven-fish Christmas Eve feast he adored. The tradition held value for him," I smile, thinking about how excited he would get about Christmas Eve.

"My feelings for him are so complicated. I've been grappling with such fury – working on managing it. Yet, there was a genuine sadness that he wasn't there with us. He's already with another woman, for God's sake! I know he doesn't deserve my warm sentiments, but I can't control my feelings."

"Breakups, especially after long relationships, stir up complex emotions. Let's face it, most people aren't all right or all wrong. All good or all bad," she remarks.

"You mean I'm not perfect? I don't believe it," I joke, though knowing therapy has forced me to become introspective and painfully honest with myself. Michael should've communicated his unhappiness, but I realize we both share responsibility for the unhealthy aspects of our relationship. Like she said, nothing is black and white.

"Together, you raised two amazing young women, and it's clear there was love between you two. It's okay to feel conflicted," she reassures.

"You mentioned that Michael had it rough growing up too. In what way was it rough?" I take a deep breath.

I open up to Sondra about Michael's upbringing. His father abandoned him and his mom when he was just eleven years old, for a woman who had a lot of money, leaving Michael and his mother to struggle financially. While his father lived luxuriously, Michael grew up fast, shouldering the responsibility of bills, from the time he started working at fourteen. Despite my complaints about

Michael to Sondra, I always admired how he cared for his mom. As dysfunctional as my family was growing up, he felt like his situation was worse, constantly fighting to stay above water. I think that's why the holidays were so significant to him.

As Sondra leans in, listening intently, she remarks, "You both faced childhood challenges no kid should endure. Do you think these experiences impacted your relationship dynamics?"

"Absolutely," I respond. "Michael took on so much responsibility as a child that our roles were distorted. It was like he took on a parental role with me, too. When he left me, he said I was like a third child sometimes."

"Your relationship was defined by an imbalance of power," she says. "Given the violence in your childhood home, it's not surprising that your emotional development was impacted. You both struggled to navigate your marriage without learning healthy tools growing up."

Sondra's insight into the dynamics of our relationship hit hard. It's true—we were both stumbling through our marriage without the necessary healthy tools. The weight of our childhood experiences had shaped our relationship in ways I hadn't fully grasped until that moment.

She shifts gears in our conversation. "How did you and Michael first meet?" she asked.

"Well, when we were both around twenty-five years old, we went to the same cafe every morning on our way to work. Looking back, we were so young," I reflect. "I was an inside salesperson for a downtown D.C. learning center, and Michael was working his way through college. I think it was his last semester. Would you believe he still works for that same company today?" I ask rhetorically.

"After graduating with an engineering degree, he earned promotions, and the company even paid for his grad school. He's made quite a career for himself. I'll give him that. You know it's funny. He's so loyal to that company. He has stuck with his company despite other job offers for more money." "What do you find to be funny about that?" Asks Sondra.

"Because the nerve of him," I exclaim, my voice rising. "He'd never leave his company because they supported him through school, showed commitment, and treated him well." I calm myself.

"What about me? Haven't I always been by his side? I didn't deserve his loyalty? He gives more respect to that stupid company than he shows me."

I could feel my frustration building, almost sure that Sondra could sense my irritation.

"You mentioned Michael valued consistency and predictability. Maybe his company represents that to him," she suggests.

"Yeah, maybe," I concede with a sigh. "He's made it clear I lack in that department. And to rub salt in the wound, his boss is a real pain in the ass. Oh, but try telling Michael that. He thinks the guy could do no wrong."

I take a moment to snap out of that spiral.

"Let's see. Sorry. I lost my train of thought. Where was I?"

"That's okay. Take your time. You were talking about how you two met," Sondra prompts me.

"Right. As I said, we both frequented the same coffee spot every morning. We noticed each other for weeks. We'd shared glances before but never really spoke a word to one another. Once I got to my office with my coffee, my work friends would tease me and ask if I talked to the 'early morning café man.' Then, one morning, he took a chance and arrived earlier than usual and ordered me my usual coffee with cream and a biscotti—he'd obviously overheard my order before."

As I recount the memory, my internal temperature decreases, allowing me to relax slightly in my chair.

"When I walked into the café that morning, he said to me, 'No pressure, would you like to have breakfast with me?' How could anyone resist such a romantic gesture? I didn't know if I was more excited about meeting him or bragging that I'd finally met the elusive 'morning café man.'"

A laugh escapes me, and Sondra returns a warm smile.

"What attracted you two to each other?" Sondra inquires gently.

"It started like many young couples do. He was charmingly cute. Michael later told me he couldn't help but notice my boobs and admired my hair. Sounds silly, but big hair was a thing for Jersey girls in the '80s," I chuckle softly, reminiscing.

I momentarily think back to how happy we were in the early days–a bittersweet feeling.

"I was attracted to his physique. I imagined his strong arms around me, keeping me safe and secure."

"It's obvious that you and Michael developed a strong connection."

"At first, it seemed that way," I muse. "I don't know. Not just the beginning, but many of our years together seemed good... Maybe it was always a struggle, and I was blind to it. It's all still so confusing to me."

"Stephanie, deciphering your own becomes a puzzle when you've never seen a healthy relationship. Making matters more challenging, Michael didn't openly communicate how he was feeling when he left you. Maybe he didn't know how to talk with you, but you aren't a mind reader," Sondra noted. "Continue. What happened next?"

"So, we got serious pretty quickly. Sadly, our connection was built on discussing our family chaos. We identified with one another in that way. We found solace in our shared dysfunction."

Sondra explains. "That makes sense. As young adults, you

were both working through childhood trauma. It was like you were each other's therapist."

"Well, if that's the case, we need to refund each other for our services."

Chapter 9
Holiday Cheer
Beginning of January

As the cool winter breeze drifts through the neighborhood, a newfound sense of purpose permeates the walls of my condo. My place has a buzz about it. Olivia and Sienna, with their unwavering optimism, bring an energy missing from what I now call home.

Together, we dive into prepping for the party. The living room becomes the creative hub, piling onto my already-decorated condo with even more glitz and glam. Memories surface as decorations from boxes that I was hesitant to unpack alone—each piece a nostalgic whisper of celebrations past. However, with the girls by my side, the emotions are more pleasant than daunting to confront. With twinkling lights, the aroma of freshly baked cookies, and decorations from Christmases past, the condo truly starts to emulate my once grand, warm, and joyful home.

Invitations adorned with glistening snowflakes, simply stating "Come Join Us!" found their way to neighbors, old and new. Secretly, I hope to rekindle connections that drifted apart since the whole divorce drama. I think I'm ready to rejuvenate those relationships I let slip away. I considered adding in some new neighbors would mask my efforts.

On the day of the party, an early doorbell signals Ellen's arrival. No sooner does the quick chime end Ellen comes flying into my living room with open arms squealing to my girls to give her a hug. Just like old times. I remember Michael made a snide comment a few years back about how Ellen just waltzed into our home at any moment like she owned the place. After that, the doorbell served as a warning more than anything. A battle Michael never chose to take on.

Olivia and Sienna giggle in response to Ellen's warmth. It feels like a familiar melody playing in a forgotten corner of my mind—Ellen's effortless warmth is unmatched. As she prods around, taking in the festive decorations, Ellen's vibrant energy infuses a sense of joy into the room that no decoration could achieve.

"Stephanie, this place is unbelievable! Girls, remember what a mess this place was right after she moved in."

"Jesus, Ellen. You're gonna ruin my perfectly crafted facade. Don't listen to her girls."

"She's right, mom," Olivia agrees. "I can't believe how much you have done to the place since Thanksgiving."

"How can I help, Steph?"

We spend the next few hours putting on the finishing touches.

Then the doorbell chimes repeatedly, signaling our old neighbors' arrival– anticipation and nerves swirl within me. Laughter and familiar faces fill the rooms, wrapping us in this cozy blanket of familiarity. In the soft glow of lights and flickering candles, conversations flowed effortlessly, stitching together fragments of joint memories and tales waiting to be shared.

Melissa grabs my arm and pulls me aside. "Stephanie, your new place is simply charming," she exclaims, enveloping me in a warm hug.

All the girls gather around.

"Thank you, Melissa! It's been quite the adjustment, but I'm glad to have everyone here," I reply, feeling a surge of pride wash over me.

"By the way, separation serves you well. You look great!" Sarah jumps right over the elephant in the middle of the room in the best possible way. You can never go wrong, kicking things off with a compliment. Just like that, the conversation fills the room like old times.

"Thanks! I lost some weight I packed on immediately after Michael left me. Some people get depressed and can't eat. Me, on the other hand… I was quickly on a first name basis with all the town deliverers. Ellen can tell you all about it."

"Hey, you do look great, and if you found comfort in extra lo mein when your life was falling apart, who am I to judge?" Ellen teases me as she downs another swig of her light beer. The ladies nervously wait for my reaction. I laugh loudly. I love it! Tease me. Taunt me. Just don't walk on eggshells around me. Ellen gets me.

With her serene demeanor, Janet adds, "This place has such positive energy. You must get a brilliant morning sun from those large windows." Janet pontificates, pointing to the row of windows of the main living space.

"That's right, I've been meaning to join your classes, Janet. I could use some zen in my life," I chuckle, feeling a flicker of excitement at the prospect.

"I've been brewing up some fun activities for the new year. Do you know about goat yoga?" Janet says.

"Goat yoga?" I echo.

"Yes! Picture this: yoga poses - wait for it - adorable little goats joining in. It's been proven that goats contribute to mental and physical wellness. It's gonna be a blast!" Janet's enthusiasm is infectious.

"Hey, I'm up for trying anything that will improve my mental and physical well-being. Count me in! Anyone else?" All the girls commit in solidarity.

"Fantastic! I'll send you all the details. It's a perfect way to unwind after the holidays." Janet says, her smile widening.

Sarah says with a smirk. "We all know Stephanie is gonna put us to shame."

Lisa recalls. "Oh my God, Sarah. You're right. It's coming back to me. Remember Stephanie doing those flying splits? Stephanie, you've always been flexible." We all laugh, thinking about me in my family room, lifting my leg high over my head and crashing down on my hardwood floor into a split.

"Trust me. No one wants to see me attempt that now unless you are prepared to scrape me off the ground." We all roar.

The ladies and I talk about our children, their husbands, jobs, and the holidays for hours, non-stop. I share separation updates and tell them about my therapy sessions. After avoiding them for months, I'm disappointed to have sold them so short. I should have known they would have been nothing but supportive. Curious but supportive. I missed them and it feels amazing to reconnect.

Meanwhile, Olivia and Sienna are yapping away with the neighborhood kids, swapping tales and giggles like they did for years. Their chatter and laughter reverberate through the room, intertwining seamlessly with the adult conversations.

It warms my heart to remember how the neighborhood kids felt in my home. Shoes, jackets, and snacks scattered around didn't bother me. When I say 'snacks,' it wasn't just chips and soda; they loved the pasta dishes and huge salads I'd whip up for after-school treats. Michael wasn't thrilled returning home from work to a household of twelve-year-olds running amuck. The house echoed with loud music, balls bouncing off walls, and shrieking pre-teens. For me, having a full home was a parenting victory. Not all might think so.

Like I did back then, amidst the joyous chaos of our party, I find solace—not just in the rekindling of friendships, but in the realization that this home, now adorned with the laughter and warmth of cherished company, is a canvas waiting to be painted with new memories and new traditions.

Chapter 10
Early March
Vicious Cycle

After my third yoga class, Janet offered me a job managing her studio's social media accounts, knowing I was often hailed as the group's 'queen of social media.' Janet believes leveraging her social platforms is a perfect fit for me. In our first monthly budget meeting, she showers me with compliments.

"You're a genius. Truly. Since you started, business has surged 12% in just two months."

Initially, it was about creating Facebook, Instagram, and Twitter content. However, my enthusiasm led me to propose a blog to attract new clients. Each week, I craft articles on health, wellness, or topics to stir up interest in yoga.

"I never considered this as an additional income stream. Creating a blog was one thing, but now we have two clients advertising on our site. We're earning without spending on marketing!" Janet's excitement is palpable, and it's flattering to hear her enthusiastic response.

During my marriage, I'd often plunge wholeheartedly into new ideas with intense fervor to turn around and passionately dive into the next great idea. To put it short–I struggled with follow-through. I was a serial business starter, inventor, and creator. Our basement became a graveyard of failed endeavors—imaginative wine bottle holders and trendy accessories destined for success piled up in a dark room in neat boxes Michael organized. If you dared to tour the room, you would have found multiple 'Shark Tank' worthy products waiting to be discovered. I had ideas but lacked the structured plans to see them through. It became a cycle: start, lose interest, and move on. Sometimes, the wind just blew me in a different direction.

Over time, I recognized the pattern but felt powerless to

control it. Instead, I bought into the narrative that I burdened my family while Michael was the savior with every business collapse. It was a pattern that repeated itself many times. I realized recently that what needed saving most was my self-esteem, and Michael hindered rather than boosted my self-perception.

Life seems to be falling into place in a way I could not have imagined seven months prior during that infamous car ride home. The girls are thriving in their second semester, and I've settled into a steady routine. I've dedicated myself to workouts, a healthy diet, and making meaningful progress in my sessions with Sondra. Janet has graciously given me space to contribute to the business strategy. I've tailored a marketing campaign to target women over fifty, recognizing they have both disposable income and available time. My confidence is growing in part because of the studio's successes. Janet's praise, though I deflect it, serves as a much-needed boost to my confidence.

I'm also consciously working on recognizing my behavioral patterns and limitations.

Daily meditation serves as a gentle reminder that balance is essential—slow and steady progress is the key, especially with attention deficit disorder. I feel like I'm finally moving forward positively.

In the past, when my creativity surged, it felt like an exhilarating adrenaline rush that propelled me through my newest endeavor. I wanted so badly for this thing, whatever it was, to 'takeoff' so everyone around me would be blown away at my great success.

Predictably, I became obsessed and then overwhelmed with too many batons twirling at once. Ultimately, they all came crashing down. Once my disorganization was in overdrive, I started to unravel. My disorganization spiraled and affected my home life. My thoughts became muddled, the house fell into disarray, the weight piled on, and I felt utterly out of control. It was a vicious cycle. My behavior starkly contrasted with Michael's structure and consistent approach to life. He easily became frustrated with me and even lashed out at me, and his occasional outbursts only reinforced and amplified my self-loathing. Certainly, while my struggles with self-esteem weren't solely his fault, therapy has helped me see how he inadvertently reinforced the negative thoughts in my head. Better late than never.

Chapter 11
Chaos
Late March

I walk into Sondra's office for our regularly scheduled appointment.

"It's good to see you, Stephanie. You look well." Sondra beams with pride. I cheerfully reply, "Thank you. Dare, I say, I feel good."

"I detect some hesitation in that admission. What's on your mind?" "Things are going really well, actually."

"Glad to hear that. What's going well for you?"

I reach outside my comfort zone to admit, "Well, for one, the yoga studio. It's growing, and Janet often credits me for the studio's successes. I feel like maybe, you know, she's right. My input. I'm making a difference?"

"That's fantastic. Stephanie, I'm sure you are contributing to its success. It's okay to admit it." Sondra responds enthusiastically.

I look down and smile.

"Tell me what else is going well," asks Sondra.

"I don't know how to explain it. It's not any one thing but rather how I feel. I feel much calmer. My thoughts are settled and not going off in a million directions. I don't feel as scattered if that makes sense?" It's a challenge for me to concede that my life is coming together positively. I collect my thoughts and then continue. "It's hard to explain."

"You are wondering when the other shoe will drop."

"Yes, exactly. I didn't know you are a mind reader too." We both chuckle.

"You've talked about experiencing ebbs and flows throughout your life. You have grown to expect this is just another swing in that flow. Does anything feel different this time?"

I take a moment to think about her question.

"I think I do, you know, feel different than in the past. I am more mindful this time and more in control of my actions and thoughts."

Sondra explains. "You're becoming more cognizant. Since you're in a more mindful space and doing the hard work to put yourself on a better path, your thought process will continue to improve over time. Because you are sharpening your ability to recognize when you're falling into old patterns, you are developing tools to avoid slipping into old habits. This will continue to become more natural over time. Just ensure you credit yourself for successes so you identify the wins and not question them. When you leave here today, I challenge you to embrace and not fear success."

I nod my head as I allow my 'homework assignment' to sink in. "How are you feeling on the Adderall?"

Sondra referred me to a psychiatrist who diagnosed me with ADD and prescribed a low dose of medication to me.

"I think it helps a lot. I feel more focused on the medication. I'm more productive. I also wonder how it could have changed my life had I taken medication as a child."

"Medication may have helped you with your ADD as a child. However, there were significant challenges in your home that needed addressing. Medicine, alone, wouldn't have prevented growing up in a toxic environment." Sondra looks at me as if she is looking for a sign that I'm tracking with her. I nod in agreement.

"Did your parents or a doctor ever talk with you about ADD when you were a child?"

I let out a *Huh*, "No one was in tune with my ADD. I was a pretty easy kid. I did well enough in school and didn't really cause much of a fuss. The signs should have been obvious to my parents, though. I was also horribly disorganized. My room was always messy, and all my books or whatever we carried back then were disheveled. I always struggled to hold things together, ya know. I think we had so much going on that my messy binders were not on anyone's radar."

Sondra understands. "For sure. If you were not a disruptor, your ADD probably went unseen and in fairness to your parents, especially back then."

Sondra changes direction. "Speaking of emotional challenges, during our earlier session, you mentioned that your mom suffered from depression. I would like to circle back to that."

"I don't know if my mom was clinically depressed. It didn't seem like that when she finally left my father later in life. But dealing with his shit for so long eventually broke her. I remember this one horrible day when I was probably about 10 years old. My mom was lying on the couch during the day in a tattered old robe. I don't know why her robe stood out, but she looked awful. She was distraught, absolutely despondent, and turning to me for answers. She asked me what she should do. I obviously didn't have answers to give. As a 10-year-old, what did I know? All I wanted to do was go outside and play with my friends. In retrospect, she must have been in such a state of despair to turn to me for help."

"Do you feel you should have done more for your mom?"

"I do. She was my mother, and I walked out on her in a dark moment to be with my friends. She was literally pleading for help."

Sondra asks me. "Do you see a pattern? You, as a child, felt responsible for the mental well-being of your mother. As we talked before, it was not your responsibility to take care of everyone or anyone for that matter. It must have been so traumatic for you to see your mother in such a bad mental state with no ability to help her. I know she didn't mean any harm to you, but that was a lot of pressure to put on a 10-year-old."

I adored my mother and hate to think I'm portraying her unfavorably. I'm also committed to improving my mental health, so I know I need to be transparent. Yet, I feel compelled to defend her honor.

"My mother was wonderful, and I know she would agree with you. I'm sure she regretted imposing her issues on me. I wanted her to be present for me as a parent, but she was so incapacitated. I think about that Italian Bisque lamp crashing down the steps." I recall, deep in my thoughts.

"You have mentioned that lamp a time or two before. Tell me the significance of it."

"It was my mom who threw it," I reveal. It was previously assumed that my father threw the lamp down the steps. After all, he was the violent parent, not my mother.

Sondra asks. "You have shared many stories of violence and dysfunction since we started meeting. What about your mother throwing the lamp makes it so significant?"

"I witnessed my mom's depression. I've seen her so distraught that, at times, she couldn't get off the couch, but as a person, she was a calm and docile person, unlike my father. The fact that my mom had emotionally deteriorated to the point that she would throw the lamp from the top of the steps to the floor below was scary."

Sondra explains. "As a child, you were looking for stability from someone and asking yourself where is my safe place. That act by your mother made you question if she was that person. Unpredictability in a household impacts development and maturity. In your case, it seems like you compensated the best you could. All along, however, this chaotic atmosphere had an impact on how you viewed yourself, your self-worth, and your personal security."

After Sondra allows time for me to process, she continues. "We tend to return to something comfortable; in your case, chaos was like comfort food to you. When your life decisions lead to destructive patterns, it's familiar ground. It makes sense to you. However, now that you see yourself going in the right direction, making positive strides, and staying organized in your thoughts and behaviors, you feel hesitant because you are waiting for it all to fall apart. There is no road map for your new and improved behaviors since you never grew accustomed to this path. Whether you know it or not, you ask yourself, when will I revert to the old me, where life is familiar, warm, and cozy...and unhealthy."

I cringe when I think about my choices: reckless spending, risky behavior, faulty decision-making, and, of course, my epic failure in Italy.

"One more thing. I would like to revisit your feeling of survivor's guilt. Suppose anything can sneak up on you and dismantle your progress. Are you falling into the trap of thinking you don't deserve success and happiness? If you see yourself slipping into old patterns, I would like you to journal your thoughts and feelings. Try and identify the impetus causing you to take a step back. How does that sound?"

"Wow. It's a lot. So much happens in our brains subconsciously. Yeah, sure. I will try to be more aware of my behavior and journal my thoughts."

After this session, I feel particularly exhausted but am motivated to accept Sondra's challenge. I also can't help but feel guilty for how I portrayed my mom. And there is that guilt again. Old habits die hard. That journal is going to see lots of action.

Chapter 12
Midday Salad
Early April

Deep in thought while enjoying my morning coffee, I'm startled by the sound of my ringtone. I look down to check the number. My stomach drops. I take a deep breath.

"Hello, Michael."

Eight months have passed since our separation. A simple 'hello' causes me to tremble. Since the girls returned to school for their 2nd semester, other than a few text messages, there hasn't been any communication between us. Overall, it's been surprisingly easy to unravel our 23-year marriage. A legal separation agreement was drawn up shortly after he left me. We quickly sold the house, paid off our debts and divided assets. I didn't have the strength for an exhaustive property search, so I hastily signed a year lease for the first nice enough condo I found.

Given the age of our girls, there are no custody battles to be had. Always the planner, Michael began saving for the girls' college education and even a wedding fund when they were born.

What else do we have to talk about? When he asks me to go out for lunch, I imagine how that encounter will go. I will nervously ramble on about nothing then we will discuss hammering a final nail in the coffin of our defunct relationship. For eight months, I have known this day would eventually come, yet it feels like this phone call crept up on me out of nowhere.

It's a beautiful spring day. I park my car on Main St., then walk 2 blocks to meet him at a charming café not far from the yoga studio. I'm wearing a new outfit: jeans and a red wrap shirt, tied tight around my waist to accentuate my more fit figure. It's casual enough that it looks like I could have pulled it from the back of my closet. I don't want him to think I care that much about seeing him. Michael, already waiting for me, stands up and pulls out my chair at our quaint window seat. I don't know what to do. Do I hug him or even kiss him on the cheek? I just sit down and let out a huge exhale that I hope he doesn't hear.

"Stephanie. You look great."

Michael stares intensely at me. I grumble an uncommitted thank you, then look to my left, catching a glimpse outside the window of smiling people, young and old, passing by enjoying spring's first bloom, seemingly without a care in the world. By comparison, sitting down to lunch at a small marble-top table with the man I had eaten with daily for well over 20 years, it feels like I'm pursuing a Herculean endeavor. Throwing up all over the table is not entirely out of the realm of possibilities at this point.

"You seem so...calm," Michael observes as he continues to stare at me.

What an odd thing to say. Besides, if only he knew, he is well within the line of fire of whatever is gurgling in my stomach. Thankfully, he can't tell that I am barely holding it together. I have no intention of conceding that to him either. Instead, I sit tall, tuck my hair behind my ear and fake it.

"Thank you. I actually feel really good." I smile big.

Michael doesn't look like himself. He had always maintained a fit physique, given his daily workouts and controlled diet. He looks like he gained a few pounds, and he's in need of a haircut. His clothes even look uncharacteristically unkempt for him.

We engage in small talk about our girls, the menu, the weather and whatever we could think about to keep a superficial conversation flowing.

"I hear you have been working for Janet. Did she tell you I ran into her? She said you are doing great things for the studio."

"Oh, I think she mentioned it."

And there's another lie. Janet came running into the studio that day and asked me, 'Guess who' I just spent the last 15 minutes talking to at the bank. I made her recite every single word of their conversation. Michael looks disappointed when I imply that my conversation with Janet was no more than a blip on the screen.

I begin to perk up as I describe what I have been doing at the studio. I tell him about the blog, my social media posts and our month-over-month increase in revenue. When I finish delivering my 'state of the union' about the studio, there is suddenly an awkward silence. Well, it feels awkward to me, but probably not to Michael. Sitting in silence was never uncomfortable to him, and in fact, he would often prefer it.

My heart pounds out of my chest as I wait for him to initiate the divorce conversation. Why did I even agree to have lunch with him? I should have said send the papers to my lawyer and leave it at that. My nervous energy finally gets the best of me, and I drive the affable conversation off the tracks. Staring at my bowl full of a variety of greens, grains, and goat cheese, topped with medium rare salmon, I plunge my fork into my salad. Skewered with arugula, draped in a creamy parmesan lemon dressing, I wave my fork to the left and then to the right to punctuate each name's pronunciation when I ask.

"How's Marissa or Mellissa?"

Michael's body stiffens. "It's Missy. Just Missy."

I re-ask the question. "Oh, okay. How is Missy just Missy?"

After a brief moment, he responds. "We broke up."

"Oh, I am so sorry to hear that."

My goal isn't to say that with a flicker of snark, but at that moment, my tone isn't under the control of my tongue. Michael tilts his head to the side as if to acknowledge he is on to me. He and Missy started dating two months after he left me. At least, that is what he told our girls. I never had proof he cheated on me, but my gut tells me he was dating her while we were still together. Michael takes a deep breath and then continues.

"Stephanie, I made the biggest mistake of my life." I sarcastically respond. "Oh no. What did you do now?"

Based on how I respond, it's clear that my tone is still under the control of an outside force. I can't help myself. I played nice for the first 30 minutes, but I clearly have deep-seated resentment for the way he ended our relationship despite months of therapy.

"I'm referring to our separation. I am so sorry for what I did to you. I regret leaving you. I think I was really scared when the girls went away to school. Our entire focus was always on them. Their activities. Their school. Many of our friends were friends we made because of them. When they left for college, rather than focusing on us, I quit. I just gave up. I'm so sorry I did that to us, that I did that to you. I want to fight for our relationship. I want us to get back together. I want us to be a family again."

What! Is! He! Saying! Should I cry? Should I scream? Maybe I should toss my salad to the floor and storm out of the restaurant. Or do I just fall into his arms and never let go? I set the fork on the edge of my oversized, oblong-shaped bowl and attempt to take in what I am hearing.

"I don't even know what to say, nor can I even believe what I am hearing. I fully expected that you called me to talk about a divorce."

"What? Noooo," he replies as he puts his colossal cheeseburger down. "What would make you think that?"

"Are you kidding me, Michael? Why wouldn't I think that's why you wanted to see me? It's not like you have checked in on me to see how I'm coping after you dumped me. Other than a few empty apologies early on, you never reached out to say, 'Stephanie, I'm sure this is tough. How are you?' Instead, after eight months, you call me, snap your fingers and want to get back together?"

"Obviously, Stephanie, it's your choice. I realize I can't snap my fingers to get what I want."

"Are you sure you don't think that?"

I sit back on my chair and cross my arms across my chest.

"You're right. I'm a horrible communicator. I'm committed to doing better. I promise. I wanted to call, but I didn't know what to say or if it would make things worse for you."

A rare admission, Michael acknowledging his communication needs improvement surprises me. "Well, you hurt me. You hurt me badly." The busboy returns and refills our water glasses. It gives us a chance to collect ourselves. I feel my insides burning. The young man leaves our table, and I continue the conversation.

"So, is this how it works? You have an affair every 10 or so years, and then you come running back to me when you tire of your new relationship, or more likely, they tire of you? Am I to understand that is how you operate? Should I put a reminder on my calendar for when we are 61, and we will go for round three of this, Michael?"

Because my voice elevates, I become hyper-aware of our surroundings. Luckily, we are in between lunch and dinner. The café isn't as busy as when I first walked in. No one is sitting next to us, although given my flailing arms, we must be a sideshow for pedestrians passing by the window.

"This is nothing like what happened 10 years ago. First, I didn't even sleep with Missy before I left you. Secondly, we were in a bad place 10 years ago. I took the first step, but you know neither of us were happy. This time, I left out of fear. I was scared."

Michael and I hit a rough patch previously in our marriage. Rather than working things out with me, he responded by engaging in a 3-month relationship with a woman he met one night at a work event. After discovering his affair, I had revenge sex with a handsome enough, slightly younger man I met at work. At the time, I truly felt justified in sleeping with him since I didn't start the infidelity. Our marriage was in a state of crisis. Despite our marriage's state of affairs, we decided to work things out, probably more for the girls than for each other. We went to not nearly enough sessions of couple's therapy. Over time, we pieced our marriage back together.

Albeit not perfect, things were good enough between us. At least that's what I thought. I was caught off guard when Michael left me in August, and now I'm blind-sided by him wanting to repair our marriage. My radar is clearly way off. My voice raises as I respond.

"Let me explain something to you, Michael. Focusing on our children, their school and their activities is called parenting. It's what parents do. And another thing. You chose to run into the arms of another woman 10 years ago before deciding to work on rebuilding our relationship. You did the same thing again eight months ago whether you slept with 'Missiyyyy' before or after you left me."

I stop to take a breath, then continue. "You know the worst part about this is? I am moving on. I am making my own way in life without you, and here you are, out of the blue, wanting to get back together. In fact, I have been doing quite well without you in my life, so fuck you for your timing."

Silence. We wait. Who will speak next? God, that felt good. I'm not sure where we go from here but no matter what I decide, I stood up to him. Even if I do break down and take him back, I feel a tinge of control. I take my voice down a notch and continue the conversation.

"Michael, do you know how many times in the first few months after you left I dreamed about you coming back to me? Even though I had said 10 years ago I would never again take you back if you left me, I would have crawled back to you if you asked. I hate that I was that week, but it's the truth."

Michael, seemingly stunned, finally responds. I think he really thought I would bat my eyes, thank him and run into his arms.

"Stephanie, I know this is a lot for me to throw at you over lunch. You can't imagine how sorry I am and so angry with myself for the way I treated you during our car ride home. You certainly didn't deserve that."

"Damn right, I didn't deserve it. You were awful to me that day. You dumped me mid-drive like I was something that needed to be discarded before we reached our cul-de-sac. Besides, I thought you couldn't 'cohabitate' with me. Remember that fun word?" I am sure he had hoped he would never again hear that word. "Oh, and suddenly, you think you can live with me and all my chaos. Eight months ago, you said you couldn't."

"I apologize from the bottom of my heart that I said those terrible things to you. They were just excuses. The truth is, I miss everything about you. Well, you know, most everything." He nervously crumbles his napkin and then stuffs it under his plate. My mouth slightly opened, and I tilt my head to convey, are you really going to say 'most everything?' How about you miss every inch of me?

"Look. I never stopped loving you. I can't explain why I left other than I had no vision of us as a couple, just the two of us, without our girls. Now, I can't imagine my life without you. Please give us a chance. We can take it slow."

I'm confused and unsure as to what I want. We are locked in a conversation about something I couldn't even fathom an hour earlier in the day. "I'm leaving. I just can't anymore with this conversation."

I remove my napkin from my lap and throw it down on the table. I stand up, remove my handbag from the back of my chair and whip it over my shoulder.

"You are right about one thing. This is all too much to handle over a midday salad."

I begin to walk out but suddenly stop dead in my tracks and I even surprise myself when I turn back and firmly speak to Michael.

"I make no promises about our future together, but I will give our relationship a try on a very short leash. We will start slowly and see where things take us. Our girls will not know about this. It will stay between us before we involve them in our nuttiness. I certainly don't want them to have to go through another breakup if things don't work out."

Our eyes connect, but no other word is spoken. I imagine Michael must be stunned at how I have taken control of this encounter. I flip my bag back over my shoulder, turn back around and walk towards the door. The clapping of my heels on the Mediterranean tile floor is the only sound heard throughout the bistro. I immediately question my decision, yet I know I would never forgive myself if I didn't at least give us another chance.

Chapter 13
Job Hopping
Late April

Janet scheduled a planning meeting with me at the studio to review sales and strategize upcoming marketing campaigns.

"Janet, this is going to be a great space for the juice bar. There will even be plenty of room for a few seats too." I point to the far end of the studio, currently wide open ready for renovation. "An exterior door to generate walk-in business is a huge game changer."

Janet brandishes a big smile. "It's going to be great, right? The landlord, fingers crossed, will approve the renovation proposal this week. Randy is working out the financing. The market analysis was positive, so with your social media magic, it's going to be a huge success."

I brush off her compliment, but the truth is, I relish in her vote of confidence. I've had a few career highlights and a fair share of professional failures. Thriving at the yoga studio is significant to me. In addition to being my boss, Janet is also my longtime friend. She knows that after years of feeling minimized, her encouragement is cherished. We wrap up our meeting but Janet has one more topic to initiate. She pulls down a yoga mat from the wall and throws it on the floor. I follow her lead. We each stretch as we talk.

"Stephanie, I can't help to notice how well you are doing in class." I'm flattered that she notices. I offer an exaggerated response. "Thanks, but let's hope so. I take like 100 yoga classes a week."

Janet chuckles. "Listen. I was thinking. How would you like to get certified to teach classes?"

I didn't see that coming. If you were to conjure an image of what a yoga instructor looks like, it would be Janet. Her exquisite, tall, and lean body captures the attention of men and women when she walks into a room. She maintains her beauty and her figure with high-end facial products, healthy eating, regular exercise and an occasional nip and tuck here and there.

I chuckle, then ask, "Janet, what about me, screams yoga instructor?" I have lost weight over the previous few months, and my yoga skills are improving. But I've never thought of myself as a fitness instructor type. Short and, let's say, curvy, I don't have the body type that one imagines when you say yoga instructor, but maybe my view is outdated.

"We have been focused on expanding our women over 50 and 60 markets, and the ladies adore you. More importantly, they trust you. When you conduct studio tours, I see how engaged you are with them and how they respond to you. We have been talking about adding additional morning classes when our older clientele is available, and I think you would be a great fit for them."

The thought of earning a little extra money doesn't hurt my feelings. Maybe this is the part of my life story where I reimagine myself in a different way than I had always seen myself. Sure, I don't have Janet's long and lean body that contorts into all sorts of positions, but I'm pushing my limits. Much of my life has been focused on what I can't do. What if I think about what I can accomplish?

"Interesting proposal. I will definitely think about it. Admittedly, it sounds kinda exciting. It's way outside of my comfort zone but a little discomfort never hurt anyone." I say as I take one additional, long stretch.

Janet smiles, reaches across her mat and gives me a high five. "I'll take that as a yes." She quickly redirects the conversation. "Sooo. How are things going with Michael?"

"We are taking things slowly, but you know, we're getting along, I guess." Janet quips. "Ahhh., taking things slow means you aren't sleeping with him?"

"Well, not that slowly. When Michael and I had our first 'official date' after our lunch debacle, we talked about waiting before sleeping together. I couldn't think of a good reason to wait. After all, he is still my husband. I guess I'm easy because I put out the first night we got together."

Janet laughs and then presses on. "How's the sex?" We both stand up, then walk to the wall, wipe down the mats and return them to the wall hooks.

"It's like putting on an old pair of jeans. They feel familiar and comfortable, and I know exactly what goes well with them. We have only been out a few times." I pause and then provide a more thoughtful response. "I guess I'm enjoying the intimacy more than the sex, you know? It's been nice waking up to him, but it also feels good having my own place when we aren't together."

"I could understand that." Janet hesitates and then asks. "Do you see yourself staying with him?" None of my friends have directly told me that rekindling my relationship with Michael is a bad idea, but I sense their skepticism about him. They remember Michael as that guy who hurled condescending comments at me and then carelessly left me. It's as if they are taking a wait and see approach before accepting Michael has changed.

"I don't know what we are doing today, let alone next month or next year. I have my reservations. I still don't know if this is good for me or not."

"At least you are open as to whether it's the right thing or not. You know what I'm saying?" Asks Janet.

"I get it. I mean, he wants to go all in, but I told him we need to do this on my timeline. It's ironic, ya know. He was pushing me to go all in after I practically begged him not to leave in the first place."

"Well, you're evolving. It's different now for you."

"Exactly. I'm making so much progress with Sondra. The last thing I want to do is regress by returning to old habits. I was devastated when he left me. I would have continued with our dysfunction forever. One thing I know for sure is that I won't put up with the same old relationship. If I see a hint of our old dynamics, I'm out, you know." I'm not sure if I'm trying to convince Jeanet or me.

Janet offers enthusiastically. "Yes. That's right. You didn't ask him to come back. He asked you to get back together. Tell him what you want and be firm. You're in the driver's seat."

Janet is right. If we are going to stay together, it needs to be on my terms. The man I loved for over two decades, the father of my children, is begging me to revive our relationship, and my heart says yes, but my gut is telling me not so fast.

Chapter 14
Stronger
Late April

"How have you and Michael been doing?" Asks Sondra.

"Um. Pleasant. Comfortable. Nothing all that deep, really. I guess we're trucking along well enough."

"I see. Is that enough for you?"

I consider her question deeply. "I don't know. Probably not. I enjoy his company. Sort of."

"Is it his company or just having company? I remember before Michael returned, you mentioned feeling lonely at times."

"I don't know. Probably a little of both. Even if our marriage wasn't always pleasant, there was security in having someone come home to me. It's comforting having someone around on the nights we spend together."

I've never felt judged by Sondra until this moment. I'm sure it's in my head, but it feels like she disapproves of my relationship with Michael. Maybe she should judge me for getting back together with him after all the work she and I have done together. Since resuming our relationship, I explain to Sondra it's not like Michael and I have fixed anything. If I'm being completely honest with myself, I haven't wanted to rock the boat, so I purposely avoid conversations that I know are significant but potentially controversial.

Sondra asks, "What conversations should you be initiating with Michael?"

"Lots of stuff. For starters, we haven't dealt with the fact that he gave up on us, on me, not once but twice during our marriage. I probably should address how he used to minimize me. He's been fine since getting back together but in the past, he contributed to me feeling insecure. I want him to acknowledge that behavior so it's not repeated."

"Sounds like it's important to you that he takes responsibility for how he's made you feel throughout your relationship."

"It's important to me that he digs deep." I nervously concede, "I mean, I'm open, ya know, if I need to be aware of…adjustments I need to make."

"Makes sense. It's a give-and-take. What requirements do you have for Michael?"

"Well, for starters, I'm working with you to figure out my issues. He needs to do the same hard work on himself. We also need couple's therapy. Do I have a right to require him to make the same investment in himself that I'm making?"

"The short answer is yes. You each have the right to set any boundaries you want. Are you willing to hold his feet to the fire?"

"If I learned anything since starting therapy, childhood trauma doesn't age well. It's not easy dredging up painful memories, but I know I'm better off because of our sessions, and I think therapy would help him to be a better partner. Yes. I think I'm willing to hold him to it."

"You answered your own question," Sondra confirms.

"I have, haven't I. Michael isn't a big fan of therapy. I'm not sure how he will respond to the request or should I say requirement."

Sondra pauses. She reads me well. My brain is churning. She sits back, crosses her right leg over her left, and takes the conversation elsewhere.

"You started to tell me that Michael is more like your father than you thought when you met him. How so?"

I explain to Sondra that I would have never dated Michael if I thought he was anything like my father. Initially, they didn't seem similar to one another. He certainly was never vulgar or anywhere near as abusive as my father was, but in the months since our separation, I see some similarities. Michael and my father projected they were tough, strong men but hidden behind that facade are weaknesses and insecurities.

As it turns out, my mom was stronger than my father. She had to be to make it 40 years with him. As she got older, she gained strength and lived out her later years very much on her own terms. Maybe in our family, the women gain momentum with age.

Sondra suggests. "With the proper physical and emotional

self-care, you certainly are positioning yourself to grow stronger and more independent with age….like your mom."

Sondra re-adjusts her legs again. I know this adjustment signals another transition in conversation. "Speaking of your father, you mentioned you understood better when you were older why your father had anger towards his family. What did you mean by that?"

I take a deep breath and share details about my dad's family history. My father's family was and is wonderful but he was always mad at one family member or another. I think his family was a painful reminder of his volatile childhood. He must have sabotaged his relationship with them to protect himself from memories. My dad told us all the time how horribly abusive his father was to him, his mother and siblings.

"Unfortunately, abused children very often grow up to be abusers themselves. What else happened to your father?" Sondra asks, sensing there's more to the story.

When our father died, Anthony and I divided and conquered to arrange a memorial service for him. We didn't plan anything elaborate. A Catholic mass followed by a luncheon was scheduled for family and a few friends. My father had remarried a lovely woman a few years after he and my mother divorced, but she deferred to us to plan the day. Given his flair for finding good women, she tirelessly cared for him until his death. By the time my father passed away, Eva was physically and emotionally exhausted by my father.

Initially, Eva was enticed by his charismatic personality, but year by year, my father zapped her energy. One can only suppress their true colors for so long. His authentic self eventually emerged. Eva was increasingly isolated from her friends and family. It was clear to her that living with him meant navigating through the ups of his dynamic personality and the downs of his dark side.

It was always sad to me that someone so gifted and intelligent was unable to retain relationships. He was not only a talented cook, but he was also an amazing singer, a talented artist and a captivating orator. Despite not having a formal education, he was truly brilliant. My father held multiple patents and spoke eloquently on a multitude of topics. Unfortunately, despite his alluring qualities, I remember him as an imposing figure who terrorized my family. The most substantial legacy left to us was his mistreatment of those closest to him.

I had an on-and-off relationship with my father after he and my mother divorced. Despite attempts to retain a connection, every time I reached out to him, all he could do was project hateful, vulgar rhetoric at me about my mother. "We will try again next week, Dad," I told him each time we spoke, and he continued to repeat the same rhetoric until I stopped calling him altogether. Weeks turned to months, months to years. Eventually, his rage subsided and while we never again were close, we resumed a relationship.

Sondra says, "Based on what you told me about your father, it sounds like, by the time he passed away, you and your brothers had come to terms with your childhood."

"We each made peace with our past in our own way."

"From what you explained, your father continued fighting his internal demons throughout his whole life."

"Yeah, I would say the demons won. When he died, my brother and I learned that he suffered even more profoundly than we had previously known."

"It must have been terrible to find that out after his death. What did you learn about his past?"

I share with Sondra that after the luncheon, Anthony and I said our goodbyes to friends and family who came to pay their respects. As we were all leaving, our cousin Eddie handed my brother a letter like you would hand a groom a card stuffed with cash on his wedding day. Eddie told us that my father had written him the letter a year prior, and now that our dad had passed away, he wanted to share it with us. Eddie always had a soft spot for my dad but also understood why we had animosity towards him. If I had to guess, he wanted us to read my dad's letter so we could better empathize and maybe even forgive my father's abusive behavior towards our family. When Anthony and I got back to his house, my brother read the letter out loud.

My father wrote to Eddie that he admired how open Eddie had been about the sexual abuse he endured as a child. Because of Eddie's openness about the abuse he endured, I assume my father felt comfortable writing to Eddie about his own childhood pain. My father wrote that he had been sexually abused between the ages of 11 and 13. As if that wasn't already shocking enough, he detailed the violent sexual abuse he suffered for two years at the hands of his father's bodyguard.

Listening to my brother read the letter, I didn't know what to process first; My grandfather had a bodyguard, or my father had been brutally raped for two years. I had heard grumblings of my grandfather's mafia connections throughout my childhood, but I didn't realize until that day just how extensive my grandfather's mafia ties were, hence the bodyguard. Although that was shocking to hear, even more disturbing, my father lived through such horrific abuse as a child and buried his secret deep in his soul.

"That was a lot for you to process on the day of your father's memorial service. Did it make you feel any differently about him? Maybe more empathetic or more forgiving of him for how he treated your family like your cousin Eddie hoped?"

I had given this thought in the years since my brother, and I read that letter. "I mean, yeah, sure, it makes a difference knowing the horrors he experienced. I have compassion for what a tortured soul my father must have been. Not only was he violently raped, but he also didn't feel safe to go to his own abusive father about his rapist. It explains so much about his behavior and how he treated others. My father was so untrusting of others and often thought the worst of people. I get it! His father and this rapist let him down! We used to be so frustrated when my father didn't allow us to see the family, but in retrospect, seeing them must have been a horrible reminder of the violence he endured. Sadly, I understood him better after his death."

I pause, and Sondra quietly waits for me to continue. "I feel conflicted, ya know? He was still abusive to my family, and it's unacceptable. Just like his life was impacted by his father and that other evil man, our lives were impacted by him. I'm not sure if that sounds insensitive, but I can't completely give him a pass because of what he endured, even if it was horrific. Like you have been telling me all along, it was my father's responsibility to be emotionally healthy for his family."

Sondra is calm in her response. "You are correct. Every child deserves to be supported by loving parents. Your father failed to do that. As an adult, you now know what contributed to his behavior towards your family, and it isn't easy to know what to do with that information. Should he have gotten help before becoming a husband and parent? Absolutely. Was it common for men to seek therapy 50 or 60 years ago? No way, especially if it meant talking about sexual abuse. He very predictably buried what happened to him. That pain festered, and then he emotionally and physically became an abuser. It certainly doesn't give him a pass. It does, however, provide some clarity."

It's not surprising that my father never went to therapy for all the reasons Sondra mentions. However, I also can't help but wonder how life would have been different if he had. Even though learning about the abuse he endured helps to put the puzzle pieces together, it doesn't change the fact that, as a man, he was exceptional in so many ways but not in the way that mattered most.

Chapter 15
Never Better
Early May

"Stephanie, your condo looks great! Where is all your stuff?" Michael yells at me from the family room, probably louder than he needs to. The kitchen is just a few steps away from where he is sitting on my new, apartment-sized, white linen sectional. I had always wanted a white couch, but Michael overruled me. He didn't think we could keep it clean. How did I allow him to get away with that? It felt so good to replace the old, shabby couch I moved from my basement to the condo. It used to be more of a jungle gym for the kids and their friends than a place to recline. Once in the condo, many days turned into nights, lying listlessly on it, completely despondent over the loss of my marriage. It was cathartic to replace it with a beautiful new addition to the room. The cherry on top is – the freedom to purchase what I want without consulting anyone.

It's the first time that he has seen my condo since Thanksgiving. I still had boxes to unpack and pictures to hang when he had dinner with the girls and me. So much has changed since then. Not only am I experiencing a personal overhaul, but so has my quaint, rented condo.

He's right. The condo does look fabulous. How I hated it the first few months after moving in. It was such a departure from my roomy, three car garage brick colonial situated on a ½ acre. And what do you know? Size really doesn't matter. Nine months later, the place I now call home is everything I need. No longer do I view it as a symbol of my failed marriage but rather as a haven for my rebirth. Small with modern finishings, it's fresh, bright, and best of all, it's mine and mine alone.

"I decided to go with a minimalist approach to decorating. It's easier for me to keep things organized. I don't need to tell you. Maintaining order…well, you know."

Michael awkwardly grins and quickly looks away. He probably realizes that's a conversation that could quickly derail. Part of getting my life together includes managing my ADD. Decluttering is key to staying organized both mentally and physically. Just a few plants, a couple of candles, a few of my favorite pictures of the girls, and a throw blanket create an inviting vibe. With a little help from my friends, I'm proud of my warm and cozy place, which is best suited for one.

I provide additional details. "I have a storage unit, and I sold a lot of my…our things that neither of us wanted. I held on to that stuff for a while. You know, after the separation and all. At first, I had a hard time letting go. It felt like holding onto tables, chairs, or paintings was holding our family together. At least that is what Sondra helped me realize."

Michael's whole demeanor changes. He drops his shoulders. "Stephanie, I'm sorry. I put you in such emotional turmoil."

I assure Michael. "I don't want you to feel bad. I am sharing just to let you know that I worked through this stuff, and honestly, it feels good to be transparent." I flash him a reassuring smile. What he doesn't realize is that I'm dropping seeds for a future, deeper conversation. After pulling two wine glasses from the glass holder mounted under a kitchen cabinet, I place them on the counter next to the bottle of red I bought earlier in the day. Dating my husband is bizarre. On the one hand, I'm processing the demise of our marriage each week in therapy while simultaneously working on rebuilding our relationship together. I'm a living, breathing oxymoron.

We had been spending our date nights at his house, but tonight, we ate at a new French bistro in my neighborhood, so it made sense to come back to my place. I told myself that I would talk with Michael tonight about my requirements for reconciling a long-term relationship. I'm anxious.

His reaction to the conversation will be crucial to a future together or to the final demise of a life together. As I open the bottle of wine, Michael strolls into the kitchen.

"You have a juice bullet. How do you like it?" He extends his hand and double-taps the juice bullet squeezed into a corner of my countertop next to the refrigerator. He, too, seems to have nervous energy tonight.

"I'm trying out different concoctions. Janet is expanding the business by opening a juice bar, so I've been experimenting with different shakes. So far, I've tried a spinach and kale shake with apple. Let's see, some berry mixtures...lots of different blends. Of course, the juice bar will have a commercial blender, but we are trying out menu ideas. Do you have a juicer?"

Michael confesses as he grabs his stomach. "No, but I probably should. I don't know if you noticed, but I put on a few pounds." Michael put on more than a few pounds. It would be impossible not to notice. He has always been within five pounds of what he weighed when we first met, so it is odd to see him this heavy. It is far for me to judge or even acknowledge someone's weight gain. God knows I have had my own struggles over the years.

I suggest. "Start juicing and maybe consider some yoga classes. You will lose weight, I mean if that's what you want to do." I pause, not sure if I'm pushing too forcefully. "The classes are great for mind and body. I know you probably think you aren't a yoga kind of guy, but you might be surprised."

"You're right about that. I really don't see myself taking a yoga class. I'm more of a pump-iron kind of guy, but who knows. Maybe I should give it a try. I know I need to do something."

We sit down at my glass dinette table for 2, just adjacent to the kitchen cabinets.

"Speaking of yoga classes, I'm in the process of getting certified to be an instructor. Can you imagine? Me, a yoga instructor?"

"Wow, you are becoming an instructor now. That is a little surprising, to be honest. I... I… I never really thought of you as the yoga instructor type. Janet, for sure, but you?"

As they say, be careful what you ask. Albeit rhetorical, I did, in fact, ask him if he could imagine me as an instructor. I don't respond.

"This yoga thing has really become a huge part of your life."

How condescending. This yoga thing is my job, and I take a lot of pride in it. I decide that I can't let that comment pass, too.

"It really is a happy place for me. Besides, it is my actual job, not just a thing." "Oh, yeah, yeah, of course." Michael quickly responds.

I take a sip of wine and a deep breath. "I'm doing a lotta different stuff for the studio. The job has been really gratifying to me. I feel…accomplished with the studio. I haven't felt that in a long time. Oh, and when my day is over, I have also knocked out a workout, so you can't beat it."

"Well, I am glad you are happy."

I can't get a read from Michael. Was that sincere? He says he's happy for me, but I sense that he doesn't respect what I do. I realize that tonight must be the night for us to talk about relationship expectations. Just as I am about to initiate "the talk," he picks up a bundle of fabric sitting on the edge of the circular table.

"What do you have going on here?" Michael asks as he picks up my newest creation and opens it up.

I smile big. "Oh, that's a prototype. I have this idea for an apron that doubles as a tool holder. You always took care of hanging pictures and small home repairs, and I don't know - drilling holes. Now that I live alone, I've started doing home projects. I came up with an idea for a cute apron-tool holster combo to hold anything from a spatula in the kitchen to a screwdriver in the family room." I smile as I feign delivering a marketing pitch. I then mentioned that I'm writing an article for our healthy living blog about women living on their own for the first time and mastering home repairs.

Michael blurts out, "Jesus, Stephanie. I thought you were in therapy."

"Excuse me. What the hell are you saying, Michael?"

He charges forward. "You are inventing an apron for tools, writing a blog, trying out juices, becoming a yoga instructor. What were you telling me over dinner? You are taking a writing trip through Italy so you can write a novel? You haven't changed a bit. I thought therapy would...you know."

I push back. "No, I don't know. Why don't you tell me?"

"Settle you down. It sounds like you are still all over the place." I'm beyond pissed off and in complete disbelief.

"Settle me down. Do you think I need to be settled down?

What year is it again? 1952?" Michael quickly attempts to backtrack.

"Look, I don't mean it like that."

"Just how the fuck did you mean it? First of all, I don't need to be settled down. Secondly, I go to therapy to process my childhood, figure out why I have made the life choices I have made, and empower me not to take shit from men anymore."

I pause to allow that to sink in. I then unleash a rant on him. "I'm not in therapy to stop being me. You never appreciated me for who I was…as a person. Therapy is one of the best things I have ever done. I'm not trying to change who I am, but rather, I want to find peace, be happy, and live a mentally and physically healthy life. It has been and will continue to be wonderful for me. You know what, Michael, maybe you should try it sometime. I'm at least working on myself. You are the one still trapped inside your head and blurting out your little insults at me. You can't even decide one year to the next if you want to still be married to me. And I'm all over the place? What about you? I'm not trying to be rude, but honestly, Michael, you look terrible, even unkempt. Speaking from the perspective of wanting my children to have the happiest and mentally healthiest parents possible, I really think you should get help. It was long overdue for me, and I think it is long overdue for you."

We sit in silence before Michael responds.

"I am sorry for what I said. Really, that was out of line. I should never have implied there is something wrong with you. And for the record, I never not appreciated who you are or your interests."

"Be honest, Michael. You never supported my projects."

"Your projects? I just wanted you to hold down a stable job. Was that too much to ask? Your so-called projects ended up costing me money."

"Oh, please. Yeah, sure, maybe I would become overly zealous about a business endeavor, but you acted like I financially ruined us. Let's face it, Michael. There was always something wrong with me. If it wasn't one of my projects, I didn't keep the house clean enough, or I didn't have a job that worked for the family. You didn't care for my social life. I didn't have enough structure with the girls. I never had the appropriate outfit on. I was too outspoken about politics. There was always something about me that didn't meet your standards." I mumble out loud, quietly, more to myself than to Michael. "It's never going to change, is it?"

"That's not true. Stephanie. I sometimes don't say things the right way. But that doesn't mean I don't love you. There's nothing wrong with you, Stephanie."

"You know what, Michael? After months of therapy, I finally know that. There is absolutely nothing wrong with me. I'm just not convinced you know that."

"Of course, I know that."

"Why then did you leave me? You cheated on me 10 years ago. You left me eight months ago. Both times, you never even talked with me about how you were feeling. You just announced you were leaving, and within six weeks, my house was sold, I moved to this place, and my girls started college. My entire world turned upside down."

Michael's voice elevates. "Stephanie. I am sorry. I didn't handle that the right way, but we talked about it."

"Yeah, sure, during a car ride, then as soon as we got home, you left. What was it that you said? You had no vision for us without the kids. That's just bullshit, and you know it."

I release all my frustrations on him. We sit quietly to allow the temperature to drop. I knew I wanted to talk with Michael, but this wasn't at all what I had in mind. It feels good to let it out.

"Do you know what I just realized? I have no vision for us in this relationship. I just don't see it. I can't slip back into our old patterns. It's not who I am anymore. I spent so many years doubting myself."

"Oh, and that's all my fault."

"No. It's not. However, our relationship contributed to my insecurities rather than empowered me, which is what a relationship should do for each other. I now know how toxic it was, and my gut tells me that it won't change if we stay together. I'm making healthy changes in my life. I'm not saying I have all of life figured out, Michael, but I'm much better off than I was eight months ago when you left me. I will always love you and want the best for you. But I can't do this with you. I won't do this anymore."

I pause, then I suddenly have such clarity when I look directly into Michael's eyes and say, "I think it is time for you to go."

Michael seems stunned. He stares down at the table a moment longer, then stands up and walks out the door without looking back. I call Ellen, and as soon as she answers, I quietly tell her.

"It's over. Michael is gone...For good."

"I'm so sorry, sweety. I can come right over with two spoons. Chocolate chip or rocky road?" I think about it for a few seconds, then state it emphatically. "Neither. I think I'm good."

I have never felt so in control of my life and sure of myself. If someone told me eight months ago that I would be ending my relationship with Michael, I would assume I landed in an alternate universe. Making this decisive decision makes me believe I'm on my way to becoming the best version of myself that I have ever been.

Chapter 16
I'm Ready
June

I love the hustle and bustle of my condo with the girls home for the summer. Even if it means tripping over shoes left in the middle of the floor or competing for the one full bathroom, my home feels alive. I hardly recognize the woman who picked out comforters and bath towels with them this time last year in preparation for their first year of college. Working on my personal growth is still a work in process, but my girls returned home for the summer to a mentally stronger and physically more fit mother.

The yoga studio is absolutely exploding. We worried about a summer drop-off, but on the contrary, classes are packed. I love teaching morning sessions, and nothing makes me prouder than standing in front of my class and seeing my daughters in a downward-facing dog. The juice bar construction is moving forward, and the blog is active. Janet never misses an opportunity to remind me how instrumental I have been to the success of the business. I can't wait for my trip to Italy. I made my final payment to the tour company last week, and I squeeze in a few hours each week to work on the pre-tour writing samples. The guy running the program, Gianni Ciabattini, requested we submit summaries of the book we intend on writing and a 500-word autobiographical essay. I get him wanting the book summary, but who knows why he wants to know about us. Whatever the reason, after months of therapy, I knocked that out easily. I probably overshared, but once I started writing my personal story, it poured out of me like water flowing from a mountain.

Work and writing are keeping me busy, and on Friday nights, I often visit the ladies in my old neighborhood for happy hour. Life feels active, alive, and, best of all, healthy. I know more work needs to be done, but I'm moving in the right direction.

Chapter 17
Connected
July

Sitting across from Sondra for the first time in several weeks, I proudly display my JT Yoga wear.

"Stephanie, you look fantastic."

I sit a little taller and smile big. After a pause, she asks. "Are you and the girls still doing well together?"

"Yeah, I think it's going well," I respond cheerfully. "I love having them home. We have our moments, believe me, but overall, we've fallen into a routine that works for us."

Sondra responds. "Glad to hear it. The last time you were here, you were starting to get excited about your trip to Italy. How are you feeling as the date gets closer?"

"Mixed feelings. It's a combination of excitement, intrigue, and fear all rolled up in one." Sondra assures me. "That's understandable. It's a big trip! What excites you most about the trip?"

"The tour leader required us to write a book summary. It's dreadfully obvious how much expert writing assistance I need. Beyond the writing assistance, I can't wait for the museums, the sites, and the amazing Italian food. Oh, I really want a good cappuccino."

"That all sounds wonderful." Sondra smiles, takes a beat, then continues.

"You've mentioned before that this trip will be a 2nd chance at an Italian experience, given how things ended the last time you were there. What happened the last time you were there?"

Sondra listens intently as I describe my early days in Italy when I moved over two decades ago. It was a dream to move to Italy and completely immerse myself in the culture. I was hired as a summer nanny for a wealthy family to care for their 5-year-old son. We split our time between their magnificent villa perched in the hills, overlooking Florence, and their stunning seaside home. At first, it felt like I was living the dream I imagined. They had a cook whom I adored. I helped her prepare meals. We used fresh herbs from their garden delicious tomatoes, and I recall cooking the most delicious fava beans that I have ever eaten.

"That sounds like an amazing experience for a young woman. Did you learn to speak Italian?"

"I wasn't fluent by the end of the summer, but I could get around. Believe it or not, I learned a lot from the 5-year-old."

"Yeah, I get that. He probably just talked and talked and assumed everyone around him needed to understand him." Sondra suggests as she smiles, perhaps reminiscing about her own son as a small child.

"What a memorable life experience for you. Based on what you have told me, this story takes a turn, though. What happened?"

I tell Sondra that it was initially magical. The summer job came to an end, and I began to travel on my own. I made my way to Rome and immediately met a young woman, coincidentally, also from New Jersey. I dig deep to recall her name, then exclaim. "Lisa! That was it. She and I really hit it off."

I smile, thinking about this person I hadn't thought about in years. She had a huge personality and was up for anything. We toured the city, ate everything, and joked with one another like we had known each other forever.

"We took a break from touring and sat on a slab of marble under an archway at some historic building not far from the Colosseum. Two guys walked by us, and one of them said something in Italian like - you could catch a cold sitting there since it's drafty between the archways."

"Ouch, cringy pick-up line." Sondra teases.

"I know, right! By this point, I apparently thought I was more fluent than I was. I thought he was telling us to move because we were in the way. I responded in Italian and said something with a little New Jersey snark like who are you to tell us to move? The guy repeated himself but spoke slowly and used gestures. I finally got the gist of what he was saying."

"That really does sound like the start of a romantic comedy," Sondra says while laughing. "Yeah, well, it ended more like a horror film than one of those cute romantic comedies."

I chuckle, and Sondra smiles back. "I fell for the guy. He was cute. Funny. We communicated the best we could. My new girlfriend didn't speak Italian, so I was the official interpreter for the four of us. The boys took us to their favorite city spots, and we had a great time."

"What interested you about this guy you met in Rome, other than he was cute?" "Well, I was 21, so the fact that he was cute seemed like a pretty good start."

"Yes, yes. Fair enough."

"I don't know. It was exciting. Speaking only in Italian fooled me into thinking I was acting out some romantic Italian story."

"I can see that. What happened next?"

I told Sondra the story of Sami. "Lisa returned to the States, and Sami and I...his name is Samir, but he went by Sami... Anyways, he and I went to Milan together for a few days, then we returned to Rome."

"Ok. You're back in Rome. Was it time for you to return to the States?" Asks Sondra.

"Yes. I should have boarded a plane and gone home. Instead, I canceled my ticket, broke up with Glenn and moved in with Sami, someone I literally met on the streets of Rome two weeks earlier."

Sondra asks. "What did your parents say about you staying

in Italy?"

"They were pissed and scared. I moved in with a guy I barely knew, 6,000 miles from home. I had very little money and absolutely no plan in place. It was an erratic decision. I know I would be devastated if one of my daughters moved in with some guy she just met."

"Stephanie, we have talked a lot about your upbringing. Do you think the unpredictability of your earlier years impacted your decision-making when you were in Italy? You had developed a level of comfort with chaos. Is it surprising that your first grown-up decision after college was, like you said, erratic?"

I agree. "Not surprising at all. I mean, I get it now. I didn't connect the dots prior to therapy, but now, it all makes sense."

"People follow patterns unless there is some sort of disruptor, like therapy. It sounds like a shameless plug for therapy, I know," Sondra quips.

I smile at Sondra. I know she's right.

Sondra continues. "I'm confident that if one day you follow through with a 2nd move to Italy, you will approach it differently. Not only are you older and more mature, but you have also developed a sense of self. You're more organized in your thought process. Tell me about your relationship with Sami."

Many months of therapy have passed, and I have talked with Sondra about my troublesome childhood, my relationship with Michael, motherhood, and career mishaps, but I never discussed with her the details of something as monumental as a marriage to a man I met when I was 21 years old. As significant as the relationship was to me at the time, it now feels like ancient history. More recently, memories of my time in Italy have flooded back to me, most likely because of my upcoming writing tour. Prior to this summer, I rarely thought about my time living with Sami in Italy.

I rehash bits and pieces of my life with Sami. We lived in an old, shared apartment in what I would say was a modest Roman neighborhood, many bus stops from the city center. I have a vivid memory of us one night in our small kitchen making a creamy rice pudding together like his mother made for him when he was a child. We poured lots of thick milk - not like the milk we have here - into a large pot of simmering rice, tasting it along the way. We had those moments, you know. Cooking…talking about our families, friends and experiences.

"Nothing is black and white. You obviously were drawn to him." I nod in agreement.

It was the late 1980's. Sami was from what was, at the time, the Macedonian region of Yugoslavia. He had emigrated to Italy a few years earlier instead of submitting to compulsory military service. The ruling government was oppressive towards his people, Macedonian Albanian Muslims. He left his family and moved to Italy rather than serve in the military for the oppressive government. I remember feeling mesmerized by his stories about his homeland, the politics, his family….it was all so interesting to me. We were two lost souls searching for something in a foreign country. There was something sadly romantic about that connection.

After listening intently, Sondra responds. "Stephanie, that's heavy stuff. It's almost poetic. If there was a happy ending, I would call it a lovely genesis to a relationship."

"There were sweet spots, for sure." I submit. "What went wrong?" She asks.

"You don't have to be Freud to recognize the similarities between Sami and my father. Sami was smart, dynamic, and compelling, just like my father. Unfortunately, he was also jealous, possessive, and abusive...also like my father. I made excuses for him because of cultural differences. I told myself he just needed time for us to better understand one another."

Sondra says. "Unfortunately, abusers tend to be master manipulators, and the one who is abused finds ways to cover up or, like you said, make excuses for them. What did you do?"

"Well, I did what every person does when they are in an abusive relationship thousands of miles from home - I married him. In Italy."

"Oh wow. That's a big deal. Did you realize at the time that it wasn't the best choice?"

"Honestly, who knows what the hell I was thinking. I just didn't think much of it. He said let's get married. It will make it easier for him to move to the States. I said, "Why not.""

"Sounds like you created a narrative in your head and justified your decision." Sondra pauses for me to think through her statement. "What did your parents say at the time?" Sondra asks.

I look down, embarrassed to answer. "I was scared they would have killed me. Not literally, ya know, but obviously they wouldn't have approved."

"You didn't tell them," Sondra says, her voice lowered.

"No, not initially." I shared with Sondra that after three months of living with Sami in Rome, I returned to my parent's home in New Jersey. Once Sami's visa was approved, he moved in with me and my parents. Our relationship got progressively worse in New Jersey. As much as I tried to hide his abusive behavior from my mom, she read right through him. She couldn't stand him.

Sondra asks. "You left an adoring man and ended up in a dysfunctional relationship with someone who mistreated you. Did something about your relationship with Glen scare you?"

"I didn't feel like I was good enough for Glen. He was mature. Stable. Put together. His family was amazing. I felt inadequate compared to him. On some level, I realized I was a mess. In many ways, I had more in common with Sami despite our differences. Sami was familiar to me in all the worst ways. I guess Sami was as damaged as me, and we connected on that dysfunction."

"Interesting. You and Michael connected for similar reasons. You were drawn to men who you perceived as damaged, one way or another, like you."

I joke. "Well, I guess you can say I have a type."

Sondra smiles. "Had a type." She emphasizes. "How did your relationship end?"

"Our relationship continued to spiral further out of control, and I guess I finally had enough. I left him. He stalked me and threatened me. I even had to get a restraining order against him. Far from a romantic comedy, right?" I ask rhetorically.

"I have no regrets, though. That life path led me to meet Michael, who gave me my biggest life gift, my girls. That means everything to me. Oh, also, when I met Sami, he saved me from unwittingly acting in a snuff film. That's a whole other story."

Sondra nervously half chuckles. It's as if she decided she wasn't going to open that envelope.

"Now that I know what happened the last time you lived in Italy, I can understand why you want a redo."

"I never got to enjoy the full experience I set out to find."

Sondra assures me. "The old Stephanie gravitated towards chaos. The new Stephanie is ready for her next Italian experience on her own terms."

"You know, I think I am."

Chapter 18
Monumental Moment

August

"I just buzzed your father in the building. Let's start getting your bags out of your room so we can quickly pack up the U-Haul."

Today is move-out day. The summer has flown by. Spending time together was amazing, and I think we're all ready to move forward. There's a knock at the door. I take a deep breath, turn the handle, and open the door. I haven't seen Michael since our blow-up the last time we were here together. I put a big smile on my face, and awkwardly, we hug one another. I immediately notice that he looks much better than when I had seen him last. He looks more like the Michael I used to know. Maybe he took my advice.

"Thanks, Michael, for taking the girls. I have so much to do before I leave on Wednesday for Italy."

He responds. "It's no problem. I'm looking forward to spending time with them."

"I figured you would. I'm also glad you will be there to see where they are living. Who knows the condition of these homes they are renting? They could have picked something based on proximity to cute boys, not meeting a safety checklist."

Michael laughs. "I know. I know. That's another reason I want to drive them. I have all my tools with me."

I have no doubt that Michael is more than prepared to tackle any home repair he may encounter. They each rent homes off campus with their respective friends. I'm sure there will be plenty of projects to keep him busy over the next couple of days. It's nice to engage in a normal parental conversation with him. Michael and I will never again reunite as a couple. We both know that. I do hope, however, that over time, we will have an amicable relationship with one another. Who knows? Maybe we will even share dinners or holidays together with the girls.

Olivia and Sienna come running out of their room with the excitement of 10-year-olds going to Disney World. They each call out a 'hi, dad' as they blow by him. For a split second, I see them as young, playful girls running to our family car for a road trip rather than smart, beautiful young women about to embark on their second year of college. I silently wonder, where has the time gone?

Dressed in yoga pants, a t-shirt, and sneakers, I jump in to help Michael load the U-Haul, which is already packed with furniture. All four of us work together quickly to pack our girls' remaining belongings. I give each of my daughters a big hug. They jump in the car and immediately blast their road trip playlist. We have already picked a weekend for me to visit after I return from Italy, so saying goodbye isn't too painful for me. Michael turns to me, smiles, then throws his arms open. "This…This Stephanie, is how you dress to pack a car."

Who could forget his anger last year when I wore an outfit better suited for a happy hour than moving crates into a dorm.

"Michael, do you really want to go there?" "Nope. Probably not. I'll stop talking."

"That's a good idea." We both laugh.

Standing outside of the U-Haul in silence, we don't need words to recognize that this moment is monumental. It was exactly one year since we drove our girls to school together, and the process of dissolving our marriage was initiated.

He speaks first. "What a year it has been." "It certainly has been a year." I concur.

Michael looks like he has more to say. He opens his mouth to speak, but nothing comes out. What more can be said that hasn't already been spoken.

"Michael, it's okay. I'm good. You're good, and most

importantly, our girls are amazing." Knowing him like I do, he's probably relieved that I saved him from having to figure out something profound to say to match the moment.

"Well, Stephanie, I hope you enjoy Italy. I. Umm. I'm really proud of you. I know you have a great story buried in that brain of yours waiting to be exhumed. It's going to be fantastic."

It's nice that he acknowledges my trip and my writing in a supportive way. Nice. That's all it is. I very much appreciate his kind words, but they are not crucial to my mental well-being. I don't need or crave his affirmation for me to feel validated. It feels good for me to recognize the difference.

"Do I ever have a great story buried in my head? You should be very, very nervous. I'm going to tell all our secrets for the world to read."

"Oh, you are...are you? That would be an interesting read, wouldn't it?"

We both continue to laugh as we give each other a hug, but this time, it is a warm embrace. It's the kind of hug you would give an old friend. I'm hopeful we turned a page with one another. Maybe this is the start of us finding our new normal with one another.

"Goodbye, Michael." He smiles big at me.

"Goodbye, Stephanie."

I walk away, feeling a sense of peace. I turn back and see Michael still standing in the same spot, outside of the U-Haul, staring at me. Like he said, what a difference a year has made. As I reach my front door, I feel my phone vibrate. I slide it out of my yoga pants pocket.

"Hi, Ellen."

She apologized for not being able to talk when I called her earlier.

"I couldn't leave without talking to you. I can't thank you

enough for everything. This trip would never have happened without you. You got me through so much shit. You found the tour, you encouraged me to sign up for it, and you helped me get back on my feet. You're an amazing friend."

Ellen replies. "I just pointed you in the right direction, but you did all the hard work. When you are a famous author on your worldwide book tour, you better not forget about me."

"Well, I make no promises about that, but I will bring you home the most fabulous bottle of wine from Italy."

Ellen responds. "You gotta deal. You know I'm a sucker for a good bottle of red."

Part II

Chapter 19
I'm Back

Day 1 - Rome

Two flights and twelve hours later, I finally land in Rome. Despite the lack of sleep, an adrenaline rush is fueling my elevated energy level. Crashing and burning are most likely in my future, but for now, I'm consumed with the sounds, the sights, and the smells that surround me on every corner of the city. After dropping my bags at the quaint, center city hotel reserved for our group, I walk into a café, allured in by the aroma of roasting beans drifting onto the sidewalk.

Elderly men standing at the bar throwback espresso, raucously laughing and talking, or should I say screaming, with one another. A television hangs over the expansive bar, blaring a soccer game. There is no doubt. I'm back in Rome.

After quickly inhaling a panini and a cappuccino, I walk back to the hotel for our scheduled orientation set up in the elegant hotel ballroom. Three tables, organized in a horseshoe layout, are arranged in the middle of the room. Nine chairs are neatly aligned against the tables. With the apprehension of a first-year college student, I sit down next to a woman with long curly hair, nervously fussing with a pen.

"*Benvenuti* in Italia and thank you for joining our inaugural book writing tour. Yes, you heard that right. I said inaugural. We are testing this trip out on all of you over the next couple of weeks to see if it works or not." We nervously laugh, not knowing if he's serious or not.

"Kidding, kidding." He assures us. Voice lowered, and arms crossed, he resumes. "This really is our first ever tour, but I promise, every day has been thoroughly thought out to ensure the best experience possible. If you haven't already guessed, I'm Gianni

Ciabattini, and I will lead our workshop over the next two weeks. Left to my own devices, this class would have never launched. All my gratitude goes to Ella and Ana, who worked tirelessly to pull all the pieces together."

Gianni places his hands in prayer position, rests them under his chin, and slightly bows his head towards the young woman. Standing next to a table pushed up against a wall, notebooks and supplies are neatly arranged. The lovely, stylishly dressed young women smile big and wave at us.

"On behalf of the three of us, we would like to extend a heartfelt welcome to all of you."

After a brief pause, Gianni moves to the center of the horseshoe and looks to his left and to his right as he continues. "I need to start out by congratulating all of you for joining this tour."

Gianni says. "Many people think it would be inspirational to travel to Italy and write but most people only think about this kind of adventure but don't follow through. You have all taken a leap of faith. One way to get the juices flowing when writing is to remove yourself from your bubble - ya know - get out of your comfort zone and enter a space that might be exciting but also potentially uncomfortable. Give yourself a big applause for taking a risk by joining the tour."

We awkwardly clap for ourselves while looking at one another. Ironically, Ellen said something very similar to that before I left. It makes me smile just thinking about my dear friend.

"Be prepared to soak in the beauty, the culture and the food Italy has to offer. The inspiration in my country is endless." He oozes with pride as he speaks about Italy.

"We will write most every day in hotel rooms like this, a Tuscan villa, outdoor spaces —anywhere that motivates us... Published authors will join us some days to offer their expertise to us.'

I conjured a totally different image of Gianni in my head

before today. I pictured a nerdy, not exceptionally attractive man better suited for writing than communicating. Am I the only one who notices his appeal? Gianni Ciabattini exuberantly tells us about the days ahead of us but it's his sex appeal and dynamic personality that has me clinging to every descriptive word. What is it with me and men in this country?

Ella and Ana, in a well-orchestrated manner, walk over to the tables to hand each of us packets and notebooks. Although they will handle the trip logistics, as Gianni explains, make no mistake, this is the Gianni spectacle, and he is the star of the show.

Gianni shares with us details about both his family and his career. His voice inflection, his word choice and his descriptive language are alluring, leaving no doubt as to why he has carved out a successful career as an author, a political speechwriter and a businessman, he explains, while not mincing any words. Standing about 6'0 tall, Gianni has an unrelenting mane of silver hair that makes him look like a photoshopped picture of a 'mature' model.' I'm focused on how he seamlessly runs his hands through his gorgeous hair while gliding through the hotel ballroom with the finesse of a groom dancing with his new bride. His hazel green, expressive eyes draw me in as he reveals details of his exceptional life. Instinctively, I glance at his left hand, looking for a wedding ring. I don't see one, but maybe Italians don't wear rings. Stephanie, what are you doing? You're here to write a novel, not to assess the marital status of your instructor.

Now that my attention span has run off the tracks, my thoughts take me down another rabbit hole. Why am I even on this tour? What would ever make me think I could be an author? Gianni has traveled the world, hobnobbing with the rich and politically connected. My life experiences feel so diminished as I listen to his life story. I momentarily fade from his presentation and recall the great work I have done over the past year with Sondra. I channel her voice. 'Don't psych yourself out, Stephanie. You belong here.' I resume a sense of calm. Focus on positive energy rather than self-doubt will guide me over the next two weeks.

After my temporary mental drift, I rejoin the Gianni extravaganza as he outlines the plot behind his most popular political thriller, published just over five years ago. Gianni has written eight best-selling novels. Many of his works of fiction derive from reality, based on what he observed in politics and in business. Pursuing a political and business career is in his blood.

Translated into multiple languages, Gianni's novels are not only well known throughout Italy but also beyond its borders. He tells us that Infused in the plot lines are narratives that closely resemble real-life corruption entrenched in their government. Gianni isn't without controversy, as he proudly professes. While political leaders are angered by his books, the public revere his thrillers, even to this day. They interpret his novels as 'outing' the corruption embedded between the marble pillars of the Italian Parliament buildings.

He transitions to talking about his father, who had had a successful career in finance and even had been an elected Roman government ministry official in the late 1990s. It's obvious Gianni achieved so much because of his talents, but his father also had the ability to open doors for him…different country, same shit.

Our group of nine listens intently as Gianni shares with us how his father, Alessandro, and his American mother, Lilly, met during the 1950s in England. Alessandro studied economics at Oxford while his future bride, Lilly, lived with her mother and banker father in London. England was still in the midst of its rebirth after World War II, and her father was an executive at a bank financing many of the post-war development projects. Gianni speaks fondly about growing up in Rome and summers spent in the Hamptons with his American family. That explains why he barely has a hint of an accent. It would be easy to conclude that Gianni has lived an idyllic life but if I have learned anything, things aren't always what they seem on the surface. Chances are good that skeletons are buried in the Ciabattini backyard like any other family.

Gianni projects an air of confidence, or is it arrogance? I

don't know which, but we all seem to be hooked because of his intelligence, his sense of humor and his engaging personality.

"What are ya' currently writin'?" asks Dan in a thick British, perhaps Manchester accent. Dan seems unphased when we all turn to look at him, one of only two men in the group.

Gianni raises a clenched fist to his mouth and clears his throat. "I'm focused on other projects right now, so I don't have anything in the works." He takes a few steps toward the front of the room picks up a glass of water, resting on a podium, and takes a sip. "Where was I?"

That was an odd interaction. Gianni, author and orator extraordinaire, cool and collective, seems thrown off his game by a question that he had to have anticipated. He awkwardly transitions the discussion from his writing to talk about his community outreach. It's impressive to hear how he has leveraged his popularity in positive ways but still, that was weird.

Gianni founded an art center in Rome for children and adults who don't have the means to pay for such programs. Painters, poets, sculptors, and authors gather in the center to express themselves through their chosen platforms. Not only does he personally fund the program, but he also raises money by hitting up his wealthy friends to help finance the center. "Art is crucial for mental health and well-being." He declares.

I didn't expect him to share so much about his personal story. Maybe it's intentional to adjust our mindset towards telling our stories. After learning more about his writing inspirations, Gianni tells us more about his instructional style. He explains that the program is designed to arouse our senses so we become more prolific as writers. As we travel throughout Italy, he tells us that we will spend two weeks agitating our taste buds, stimulating our sense of touch, overwhelming our vision, waking up our sense of hearing and introducing new smells to our olfactory.

Gianni wants us to sleep well before we devour Italy, but

before he wraps up the first day, he instructs us to stand up, walk around and introduce ourselves to one another. He tells us to practice using adjectives to describe ourselves as we meet one another.

"No writing today. Just get your mind thinking in descriptive terms."

Gianni encourages us to find partners for a group activity planned for the following morning. Four of us, all women appearing to be in our 50's, gravitate to one another.

Our first day comes to an end. After a brisk walk around the block, I call it a night. Gianni spoke about the journey that lies ahead of us, but I can't help but reflect on the path that led me to this lovely Roman hotel just 2 blocks from Trevi Fountain. Before drifting off to sleep, the last thought that crosses my mind is a sense of pride that I pushed through the most tumultuous time in my life to be here.

Chapter 20
Getting Acquainted
Day 2 – Rome

Before going our separate ways after orientation, the three ladies and I decided to have an early morning breakfast together. Who knows what Gianni has in store for us; developing a rapport with one another can't hurt. One of the gals, Lauren, sashays through the restaurant, offering the most exaggerated warm greeting as she sits down with us.

"Good morning, ladies. How is everyone doing? Was I the only one who struggled this morning? I must have a touch of jet lag. How is everyone doing?"

Multiple questions are layered before we can respond to the first one. I thought I was upbeat and outgoing, but Lauren is a professional on another level. I sense she might not be everyone's cup of espresso at this hour in the morning, but she presses forward.

"I'm so sorry. Did I interrupt your conversation?"

And we have another question to process. Maura, Francesca, and I all politely smile as I quickly update Lauren.

"Maura will not be participating in all of the planned tours today because she is visiting with her family who lives here, in Rome."

"You have family in Rome! That is so exciting!"

Lauren smiles huge again. I can't tell if she is the sweetest person on earth or just over the top for no good reason. One thing is clear. Lauren is as demonstrative as Maura is reserved.

"Yes. Yes. I do," Maura quietly responds with a forced smile as she fidgets with the napkin on her lap.

Lauren asks. "Are you close with your family? Oh, I am

sorry. Since I was late, I hope you all didn't already talk about this."

Maura stutters as she explains. "Um, not. No. Not especially close. It's, I would say, it's a little complicated. Just before World War II, when my mother was just seven years old, she left Italy with her brother, and her parents, well my grandparents."

Maura pauses, looks down, picks up her coffee and when she sits it back down, she knocks her fork on the ground. When she bends over to pick it up, she bangs her head on the table on the way back up. I'm beginning to wonder if this pre-meeting breakfast was a good idea. We all ask if she is okay. Her face is candy apple red. She seems to be more embarrassed than injured.

"Oh boy. Did I upset the ecosystem, or what? Here, you three were probably calmly enjoying your coffee before I tumbled in here late," says Lauren. Dressed in a sleeveless, lightweight jean wrap dress that is slightly oversized for her small frame, her complementary jewelry and flat shoes pull together Lauren's elegant look.

Maura responds. "No, no. You're good. That won't be the last head bop you will see from me on this trip."

I can tell that I will enjoy Maura's self-deprecating humor. She resumes her story.

"Where was I. Oh yes. Our family separated during World War 2. I am…we are Italian Jews. The fascist leader at the time, Mussolini, put in place antisemitic legislation called 'Racial Laws' in Italy in 1938, so it was tough on Jews. My grandparents made the decision to leave Italy. Much of my mother's family stayed in Italy. The family who stayed here in Rome assumed the non-Jewish Italians would protect them, so they didn't feel like they needed to leave. My grandmother's sisters, my great-aunts, and many of my second cousins live in Rome. That's the family I'm visiting."

Francesca exclaims. "That's incredible! Spending time with them is worth missing some of the planned tours. We will let you know if you miss anything."

"Thank you. I appreciate that," responds Maura. "I'm really excited to meet them in person but I'm hoping to also gain research for the book I am writing. I would like to learn more about their experiences before, during and after the war."

"So, your family survived the holocaust?" I ask.

"Most of our family *did* survive. Some were killed, but fortunately, most made it through the war. It was horri…" Maura stops mid-word. "Sorry. This is heavy stuff for an 8 am 'get to know ya' breakfast." We smile at Maura. Lauren lowers her tone to match the gravity of the conversation. "Don't be silly. What a fascinating family history. I know I would love to hear all about it."

Lauren reaches out and warmly touches Maura's arm. Francesca and I quickly agree with her. We are all here to write so I assume this will be one of many discussions about our books in progress. Lauren looks around as if she is about to share something secretive.

"Um. I know this must sound so dumb, but I didn't know there were Italian Jews. I have only known Italians to be Catholic. I can hear how ridiculous that sounds, hearing myself say that out loud." Lauren releases a quiet chuckle that women tend to do when they are embarrassed.

Maura reassures Lauren. "No, that doesn't sound dumb at all. I confuse people all the time when they realize I'm Italian and Jewish. Like you said, people assume I'm Catholic."

I rescue Lauren. "The things we will learn over the next 2 weeks are endless! Maura, we can't wait to hear about your family."

Francesca and Lauren agree with me as we finish our coffee and cornetto, then join the others in the hotel lobby. These ladies might be okay.

~

Gianni exuberantly greets us for the start of Day 2. "Buongiorno a Tutti. I hope you got a good night's sleep and you're all ready for a Roman adventure. We will board the bus in a few minutes and make our way to Vatican City for a private tour. You're lucky." Gianni smiles big and stands tall. Dressed in what looks to be designer jeans, a V-neck black t-shirt, and loafers, he personifies the essence of casual Italian sophisticated style. "I have a surprise for you at the Vatican. My connections throughout Italy are endless." Gianni spans his hands wide as he brags about his VIP status. I can't tell if he is trying to be witty and grandiose or if he's truly bragging about his lofty associates. Maybe somewhere in between? Strangely enough, whatever it is, I find it to be endearing.

Pointing to his eyes and then his ears, Gianni reminds us. "Remember, as we tour, think about which emotions are sparked by what you see and what you hear." He then extends his arms then pulls them inward to rest his hand on his chest. "Even more importantly, also think about how you feel and the types of adjectives you could use to describe those sentiments."

Skilled as an orator, he uses hand gestures and proper pauses to create the perfect amount of drama. It's as if he could deliver an entire soliloquy just with his hands and body.

"Transcribe your thoughts in the journal Ana and Ella gave you yesterday, or use your phone, a tablet or whatever works best for you to capture your thoughts. *Capite Tutti?*"

As our bus drives away from the hotel, crosses the Vittorio Emanuele II bridge and travels over the River Tiber on the edge of the Vatican City, I reflect on how I got here today. When Ellen recommended this tour to me 10 months earlier, I was so despondent that I could barely leave my condo. As I look out the window at the stunning villas nestled into the hills, I allow myself a momentary acknowledgment. 'You did good, Stephanie.' I feel more in control of my mental health and well-being than I can ever remember feeling. Metaphorically and physically, I'm sitting thousands of miles from where I sat on that beat-up old couch the first two months after Michael left me. No matter what happens over the next two weeks, I'm here. That might not be a victory for my eight writing colleagues, but for me, it's an astounding accomplishment. Having said that, managing life is like excelling in any skill. A pianist who masters the *Moonlight Sonata* continues to practice daily. I will take the victory lap; the work to become an even healthier me continues.

The city is as beautiful as I remember it. I look forward to viewing it through a different lens than when I explored it two decades ago. Our bus driver parks outside of the 'pedestrian only' city center. We exit the bus and begin our trek down Via della Conciliazione along with crowds of other tourists who also spill into the Piazza San Pietro. As we stand in the piazza, our eyes are drawn to the imposing presence of St. Peter's Basilica. The top of the basilica is capped with the tallest dome in the world, Gianni explained during the bus ride.

And our 'surprise' awaits us. Signora Nina Belatini will guide our tour for the day by introducing us to the magic of the Vatican City, the Sistine Chapel and St. Peter's Basilica. Nina, as she asked us to call her, isn't a Vatican tour guide. She's introduced to us by Gianni, a highly esteemed art history professor at the prestigious Sapienza Università Di Roma. Our tour group is the beneficiary of Gianni's leveraged relationships, and he takes every opportunity to remind us. I recall reading about VIP tours on the book tour website. I surmise that means university professors, not contracted tour guides, leading tours - box checked off the list.

Mature, sophisticated, and dressed stylishly, Signora Belatini typifies Italian elegance. She storms through the marble-paved hallways in her stiletto heels with the grace of a tightrope walker as our group practically jogs to keep up with her. Although I should be enthralled by Raphael's *'The Annunciation,'* my eyes are locked on her fabulous, high-waisted, summer-weight palazzo trousers, perfectly tailored to accentuate her figure. Her tan silk blouse, neatly tucked into her pants, is accented with a thin, leopard pattern belt that cinches her waist. I'm mesmerized by her designer sunglasses, perfectly mounted on top of her head, seamlessly intertwined with her hairstyle.

Maybe I'm in storytelling mode, but I sense sexual tension between Nina and Gianni. I'll keep an eye on their interactions throughout the day. Re-focus Stephanie. Pay attention to the astonishing artwork rather than the latest Italian fashion of mature women aging gracefully and real or imagined chemistry between possible old lovers. To think, I wasn't going to pack my Adderall on the trip because it isn't like 'I had a million things to do.' Thankfully, at the last minute, I tossed the bottle into my bag, 'just in case.' Note to self. Pop one of those bad boys in my mouth first thing tomorrow morning.

As we make our way into the Sistine Chapel, our group engages one another in small talk about our first impressions. I have no idea if Gianni's approach to instructing us is conventional or unorthodox; in theory, stimulating our senses to inspire creative writing sounds logical to me!

Gianna has my buy-in on multiple levels. Handsome … creative … intelligent. I'm intrigued.

"The Sistine Chapel was in the Apostolic Palace, which was the official residence of the pope." Nina guides us through a 600-year history from the time the palace was erected. Not only does she describe how popes were selected through the centuries, but also the significance behind the amazing artwork.

"The life and important events of Christ are depicted in stunning frescos by Renaissance artists such as Perugino, Botticelli, Rosselli and others."

Nina speaks English perfectly grammatically, but unlike Gianni, she has a profound Italian accent: vowels are dramatically emphasized.

"The glory of the Sistine Chapel, or…or…should I say, the 'Grand Finale', is the ceiling." Nina leans into her speech as Italians do by swinging her arms upward as she theatrically enunciates 'Grand Finale.'

"When we think about the most prolific artists of the 16th century, certainly Michelangelo must be on that list if not the top of every list. He was a Renaissance sculptor, painter, architect, and even a poet who influenced Western art. Michelangelo was the genius behind the Sistine Chapel. Pope Julius II commissioned him between 1508 - 1512 to paint over the original ceiling which was blue with stars. In my opinion, if you want to see the most beautiful art anywhere in the world, look up and gaze at the display above. I will remain silent for a few minutes so you may silently soak in the opulence offered through the masterpiece of the Sistine Chapel's ceiling."

We all dutifully abide by Nina's instructions. The nine of us crank our heads back, allowing our eyes to absorb the vibrant colors, intricate details and fantastic story told through Michelangelo's work. It's obvious that Nina is a huge Michelangelo *fan girl*. Can you blame her? How can you deny the genius behind his breathtaking artwork? When I lived in Italy before, I visited the Sistine Chapel many times. I remember that I enjoyed it well enough, but I didn't truly appreciate, on a deeper level, the true beauty tucked away between the walls of the historical treasures Rome offers.

When I lived in Italy all those years ago, Sami and I jumped on a bus from where we lived in the Boccea section of Rome. Twenty minutes later, we were in the center of the city. Travel was nowhere near as congested as it is today. We visited the Sistine Chapel and other sites whenever we wanted. I didn't value the gift at the time. How could I? Negotiating a tumultuous relationship eclipsed appreciating the city's treasures. After what feels like several minutes, Nina resumes her narrative as we return our heads to the proper position.

"It's important to understand *everything* Michelangelo was communicating with his artwork." Nina passionately explains how Michelangelo's brilliant works of art intersect with the Catholic church. Along with my cohorts, I listen keenly as we all seek inspiration from men who died almost 500 years ago.

Chapter 21
Dalliance

A true art aficionado could spend days scouring every aspect of the Vatican City, but Gianni's goal - paint broad strokes through multiple Italian settings to tantalize *all* our senses. After a productive morning, Nina leads us back to the Piazza San Pietro, where Gianni waits for our return.

Hands extended outward from his waist, palms up, Gianni asks. "Who's hungry?"

Every hand in our group shoots up. I still don't know if Caravaggio's 'The Entombment of Christ' inspired me to write, but it certainly has inspired me to eat! Since Francesca is a chef in her hometown of Brooklyn, we defer to her for a recommendation. The four of us walk just outside of the pedestrian perimeter to grab a taxi while the others in the group remain in Vatican City.

On our way to lunch, we chat about the Sistine Chapel's beautiful artwork. Lauren passionately compares the realism of the Renaissance works we just observed with the naturalism of Byzantine works of art, revealing an additional dimension to her personality. An appealing city vibe ripples down the *via* as we pull up to our destination. The inviting restaurant is situated on a bustling street lined with businesses, eateries, and shops.

Just after we are seated, I ask, "So, you are a chef. How exciting. What's your specialty?" I pluck low-hanging fruit to instigate conversation.

"Mostly Italian, but I have been venturing out and exploring other cuisines. I've been into interesting fusions these days. Yeah, it is exciting, but dear lord, is it ever exhausting. I was thinking during my flight here about the wear and tear on my body and, quite frankly, on my family after all these years."

"I can't imagine," I respond. "I owned a café and catering

company at one point with my mother for just over 2 years and between the kids, the early mornings and late nights, I couldn't do it anymore. Kudos to you for keeping it going for so many years."

Francesca continues. "Yep. That's my world. I honestly don't even know how I have stuck it out all these years."

"No exit plan as of yet, I take it?" asks Lauren. That's an interesting question. I hear Francesca say she's exhausted, but an off-ramp? Francesca didn't say anything to suggest she wanted out of the business.

"Nope. I've thought about it every which way then panic sets in. I don't know what else I would do. I end up right back where I started."

Francesca unravels her silverware and rests it on her lap. She exhales and shakes her head. Lauren *did* properly read the tea leaves.

"Yeah, that's tough. It's a vicious cycle. How did you get into cooking?" Maura asks.

"I began cooking with my maternal Italian grandmother. She was from Calabria, which is the tip of the boot if you don't know where that is."

I smile and respond. "I'm part Calabrese too. Maybe we are cousins."

"Okay. Okay. Maybe." Francesca chuckles. "I'm writing a cookbook that combines recipes with multicultural, family short stories. I got the recipes under control, but I need lots of help writing the stories!" Francesca laughs. "That's why I am here. Well, that and the wine."

I commiserate with her. "Wow. That sounds amazing. I know what you mean. I'm writing a murder mystery, and I have the story swirling around in my head, but getting it from my brain to my computer is agonizing. Oh, and I am with you. Good Italian wine doesn't hurt, does it."

Francesca's mom's family is Italian but nothing about her

father. I'm curious, but I'll wait to see if more of that story unfolds. The server approaches with a basket of bread. Francesca and Maura both speak with him fluently in Italian.

"You two are *really* fluent, aren't you? I used to speak Italian well enough to get by but these days, I'm rusty, at best," says Lauren as she takes a slice of the warm bread and passes the basket to me.

I add exuberantly. "Me too! I spoke Italian pretty well years ago, too, but not so much anymore. Like I told my…" I hesitate before continuing. "Like I said to my therapist, I spoke fairly well when I lived in Italy after college, but now, I would say I speak enough to be dangerous."

Too soon? I don't know how this whole therapy thing works when meeting new people. I'm not embarrassed about seeing a therapist, but am I oversharing with my new acquaintances by letting them know I'm a work in progress? I can't take it back now, and they don't even flinch.

"Lauren, it sounds like you have extensive art history knowledge. Did you study art, or are you an artist?" asks Maura.

"A little of each. I enjoy painting and drawing, but my major in college was art history. I spent a semester studying in Florence." Lauren pauses. She looks pensive.

"I haven't been back to Italy since then. I can't wait until we get to Florence….So many memories. I hope it's everything I remember it to be."

Lauren appears to be taken back to another time. The server returns to take our order. Gianni said we can't leave Rome without eating Pasta Carbonara. Francesca explains. "When it is made properly, it has a nice creamy sauce." Francesca slides her fingers against one another as she describes the consistency. "People think Carbonara sauce is made with cream, but it's a mixture of egg and cheese that makes it creamy. The cured meat adds a spicy, savory taste. Do we want to share the Carbonaro and the Cacio e Pepe?"

"Sounds good to me." I agree.

"Should I pick a bottle of wine? Are we all drinkers?"

"You will never hear me turning down wine," I assure Francesca.

"I would love some wine. I might need the entire bottle to prepare me for my family visit." Maura jokes.

"I wish I could drink, but I shouldn't. I might have a small splash to taste it, but that's about it." Lauren says.

Medication? Liver disease? Issues with alcohol? I'm curious…not polite to ask. She leaves it at that so of course we do as well.

Carbonaro was one of my father's specialties. Besides his classic spaghetti and gravy - tomato sauce, made with a variety of Italian meats, it was one of my favorites. I'm not familiar with Cacio e Pepe, but Gianni told us this simple four ingredient recipe of butter, cheese and pepper is also a must-try typical Roman dish. As we wait for our wine, pasta dishes and 'insalata' to arrive, I take a risk with an attempt at humor with three women I barely know. Let's see where it goes.

"Okay, ladies. Maybe the creative juices have been activated with all of this talk about agitating our senses, but did anyone else detect a hint of sexual tension between Nina and Gianni?" Initial silence was then saved by laughter. I double down.

"With all of our guest tour guides and authors he has scheduled, there is no telling what saucy romance novel we might write by the end of the two weeks."

Francesca agrees. "I see what you're seeing. He gives off a flirty vibe, for sure." "I wasn't going to say anything, but I was thinking the same thing," says Maura.

"He's kind of flirty, in a non-threatening way, don't you think?" I suggest as if I'm defending his honor. In any case, they seem down for dishing. Mission accomplished! Who doesn't like to speculate about a potential dalliance? Protective barriers begin to retreat, and the conversation opens up even further. We find common ground by talking about family, work, and the books we are writing.

I notice one odd exception. Lauren smiles when she talks about her wonderful husband, Robert, and her fabulous children, her 23-year-old daughter, Claire and 21-year-old son, Christopher.

Details about what brought her thousands of miles from home are strangely limited when asked directly about her book in progress. She looked off to one side, tucked her hair behind her ear, and then said something about considering a couple directions. It was obvious she didn't want to discuss it and the three of us received the message.

Lauren is classically beautiful with high cheekbones, aqua blue eyes and gorgeous, shiny, silver neck-length hair that very few women could pull off. She's the kind of woman who probably has always garnished attention when walking into a room. Both outfits she has worn so far look like well-tailored designer-level clothing. However, they both appear to be slightly oversized for her slight figure. Her loving demeanor makes her even more attractive, yet I sense a hint of sadness in her eyes. I can't quite put my finger on it. While I always enjoy a robust story, as kind-hearted as Lauren is, I hope my spidey senses got this hunch wrong.

"So, Maura, you are looking forward to seeing your family, yet you need a bottle of wine to prepare for it?" Francesca says in jest.

"Well…it's complicated," she replies with a chuckle. "I'm excited to meet them in person, but our families on opposite sides of the ocean have a history between us. I'm sure they will be loving towards me, but I'm a little nervous. Oh, speaking of a loving family, I probably don't want to eat too much. Italian families…There's no such thing as turning down food."

"I completely understand that. It took years for my hus…or soon-to-be ex-husband, I should say, to get used to that when visiting my family. "It still feels weird referring to Michael as my 'ex.' As much as I have adjusted to life without Michael, referring to him in the past still feels odd to me.

"You said they will be helpful with your book?" I ask. I'm curious about Maura's manuscript in progress. The topic of Italian Jews surviving the Holocaust is particularly interesting to me. I had always heard that Italians were protective of Jews in Italy who were under threat from Hitler and Mussolini.

Maura stammers as she responds to my questions. "Yeah, for sure. I'm writing about my family's escape from Italy and what it was like for my family, who remained in Italy throughout the war. There was tension between the two sides because my family, who remained in Italy throughout the war, felt a sense of abandonment when my grandparents escaped to America with my mother and uncle."

I add that there were no good options for any of them, then suggest, "What an undertaking. It sounds like you are doing such important work. Survivors are dying out, so capturing the history is a great contribution. Will you expand research beyond your family?"

"Yes! I've already spent a ton of time doing all sorts of research on this topic. Ask my husband. He'll tell you all about it."

Francesca asks. "How far back in history do you go?"

"That's a good question. I went back and forth about how much to include. I decided to begin with how Jews ended up in Italy, then how Italian Jews lived in Italy prior to the Holocaust. It's been a family affair. My eldest son, Samuel, is getting his Master's in history, so he helps out with the research. One of my cousins is working with a historian at the Jewish Museum of Rome for artifacts and historical data.

Maura seems like the perfect person to reveal her historic story. She's a pediatrician, so I assume she must be smart! I love Maura's awkward mannerisms. Her quirkiness is endearing, but I would love to give her a makeover. How have I managed to transition, in my head, from the horrors prompted by World War II's fascist leaders to Maura's untapped makeover potential? Maura's beautiful in an understated way.

It appears that she has no interest in flattering her long and lean figure. If I had her body, I would not hide it under such loose clothing. Her thick, curly, shoulder-length hair is fabulous but needs a little TLC. Just the right lip liner and a heavy gloss would be gorgeous on her plump, perfectly shaped lips. Mascara would be a game changer on her big, brown eyes. If she were one of my friends from back home, Maura wouldn't know what hit her. I would have her all gussied up somewhere between the Roman Coliseum and Florence's Statue of David. In addition to writing a best-selling novel in two weeks, I added to my 'to-do' list to convince Maura to allow me to give her a makeover.

Our piping hot Cacio e pepe arrives, beautifully displayed in a two-inch-high twirled tower. The Carbonaro follows. As we begin twirling our pasta, Maura captivates our attention as she further describes the plight of Jews in Italy during the Holocaust. It's interesting to learn from her that there has been a Jewish presence in Rome for over 2,000 years. Throughout history, some Jews were transported as slaves to Rome to build many parts of the city, and others were exiled from other countries because of their faith. Many Jews even migrated to Rome in search of economic opportunities. Regardless of why they arrived, Jews retained a vibrant culture in Rome and throughout Italy. She told us how there were times throughout history when the Jews lived acrimoniously with Catholics and other times when they were persecuted.

Maura continues. "In 1555, Pope Paul IV forced all Jews to live in a Jewish Ghetto.' There was even a huge gate to the ghetto that was locked at night. They had all sorts of other rules, too."

I interject. "I remember when I lived here 30 years ago, I visited the Jewish Ghetto."

"That's awesome." She responds. "Today, it's a beautiful

neighborhood called Quartiere Ebraico, Hebrew Quarter. Oh, and a fun fact...It is the oldest Jewish community in all of Europe."

The three of us are surprised to hear that. I suggest. "I would have guessed a city in Germany or Poland would have the oldest Jewish community in Europe. That is really interesting."

"Maura, your book is going to be amazing. I can't wait to hear more," says Francesca as we pay our check and get ready to leave. Maura looks down, uncomfortable, yet she reveals her pride through her soft smile.

Those cheekbones...I've got the perfect contour...

Chapter 22
A Promise Made at Trevi Fountain

"Is anyone else exhausted? It's only our second day, and I feel so fatigued." Lauren looks at us as if she wants our buy-in. I quickly rescue her.

"Absolutely. You need a whole fitness program to prepare for travel."

The four of us planned to meet for an early evening city stroll. Not far from our hotel, we meander through the stunning Villa Borghese, the lovely expansive gardens plopped in the middle of Rome. From the green space of the gardens, our newly minted friend group makes our way to the Piazza di Spagna. Young lovers adorn the steps in true Italian form. Their public display of affection is on stage for all to see. This brings back memories of me and Sami. Our volatile relationship was complicated. While I mostly remember him as abusive, there were affectionate moments, including romantic nights spent together on these very steps.

The four of us commandeer a slice of real estate, squeezed between a young family of three on one side and teenage girls on the other, laughing as they pose for selfies on the other. We chat while participating in Olympic skill level people watching.

I observe. "Do you know what I find to be so interesting? Italy is such a conservative country in many ways, yet you see PDAs everywhere. Just look around. Does anyone else want to yell, 'Get a room?' I need to put that in Google translation."

I pull out my phone and feign, tapping away. The ladies laugh. I often strive to provoke laughter from others. Growing up, laughing was a way of escaping the reality of our toxic home. Sondra and I discovered, together, that I've become accustomed to masking insecurities and pain with humor. While I still enjoy making people laugh, I'm also more self-aware when I attempt to be funny.

Maura responds. "It's funny you should say that. We talked about how Italians grope each other in public at my aunt's house. My cousin said that young people in Italy often live at home until they get married. It's not even uncommon for them to have curfews as adults, so without a lot of privacy at home, they come here and show their love all over the Spanish Steps."

Maura extends her long arms to provide a visual of the expansiveness of the steps.

"Curfews! I struggled to get my 19-year-old twins during the summer to abide by any rules. You know, they are adults now that they spent a year in college." They nod in agreement.

We then make our way to the majestic Fountain of Trevi. Large crowds swarm the fountain to enjoy the tradition of tossing coins into the fountain. The four of us stand several steps back, waiting for space to open on the concrete and rod iron barrier.

"It says here that Trevi comes from the Latin word 'Trevium,' which means the intersection of three streets." I read the plaque out loud as if I made an obscure discovery.

"Everyone take out your coins," Lauren, now more energized, firmly instructs us. "Does anyone know what the purpose of throwing coins into the fountain is?" Francesca asks as I dig into my oversized patterned tote bag to find a single euro.

"I can think of a million reasons we throw coins into the fountain," I suggest as I cup several coins found at the bottom of my bag and hold them up to reinforce my point.

Maura says. "You're right about that. The city makes a lot of money from this fountain. Although…I googled and found out other cool reasons for throwing coins."

"You're full of all sorts of trivia… OKAY. Let's hear them," I respond.

Maura proudly announces. "Throw one coin as a promise you will return to Italy. Throw two coins, and you will fall in love with an Italian, and if you throw three coins, you will marry your Italian love."

I ponder. "OK, are you really gonna make me consider all these options?"

Francesca asks. "Do you have any interest in falling in love again? Gianni seems to have caught your eye."

I pretend I have no idea what she's referring to.

"What? Don't you think we noticed you hanging on his every word this afternoon? Right, Lauren?"

"Yeah, I thought I detected a small crush, too." Lauren pinches her pointed thumb together for effect. "I think it's adorable, but I have been called a hopeless romantic a time or two. I also think you only live once. Leave no stone unturned."

Lauren's explanation is dramatic for a potential crush of someone I met a day ago. Maybe she's just leaning into the banter.

"OK, what did I miss? I was gone for the afternoon and Stephanie is in love with Gianni? Did I get that right? If I knew things would heat up like that, I would have rescheduled my family visit for another time."

I laugh. "Apparently, Maura, I'm madly in love with someone I met yesterday. Sure, I find him to be attractive. Who doesn't? Right? I can't be the only one." I look at three blank faces.

"Before we get all crazy, I'm a little leery about falling in love in Italy. It's a long story good for another night over a bottle of wine." I drop a life teaser for them to chew on.

"OKAY. OKAY. Well played. You changed the subject with a properly placed conundrum. Sign of a true writer," Maura observes.

"How about we table Stephanie's potential deep affection for our fearless tour leader and start with one coin to inspire a future return to Trevi Fountain?" suggests Francesca.

"Let's throw the coins together. Hold on a sec." A young couple groping one another walks by as we prepare to throw our coins into the fountain. I interrupt them and hand over my iPhone. *"Faccio una foto per favore."*

I feel so proud of myself for my 'extensive' dialogue as if I just recited the Gettysburg Address in Italian. The handsome young man cheerfully plays along. *"Uno, due, tre e lasciate."*

Standing with our back to the fountain, on his command, we simultaneously release our coins over our heads into the fountain.

"There. It's been settled. We will be back here together again, and we have a picture to remind us," I suggest facetiously.

"You don't know how much I would love for that to be true," Lauren responds as she digs into her change purse. She then lays out four coins on the concrete ledge surrounding the fountain.

"Here. Everyone take a coin." Maura, Francesca, and I look at one another as we follow Lauren's instructions. We each pick up one of Lauren's coins from the ledge.

"Our coins are our promise to return to Trevi Fountain. Save them, and one day, we will return to Trevi and toss them into the fountain."

We quietly put our coins in our handbags. As we silently walk away, I wonder what deeper meaning hides behind the Trevi Fountain promise. Our playful dialogue suddenly turned serious and for the life of me, I don't understand why.

~

None of us are up for another full meal, but there is no such thing as un giro in Rome on a warm summer night without gelato. Not far from the fountain, we walk into a gelateria on Via Dei Crociferi to enjoy what I consider to be the 8th wonder of the world.

Sitting at an outside table, we begin to scoff down a mirage of flavors.

"How was the Colosseum?" asks Maura.

Francesca looks at me and smiles. "We had a wonderful tour with another 'good friend' of Gianni's."

We chuckle like school girls when Francesca air quotes 'good friend.' I can't wait to tell Ellen that my new girlfriends have followed me into the gutter with my unfounded assumptions about Gianni and potential ex-lovers. I dig in for another spoonful of nocciola blended with stracciatella and smile as I imagine Ellen's response. 'Why am I not surprised, Stephanie? Why am I NOT surprised?'

"Kidding aside," Francesca tells Maura, "it was a fabulous tour. Lucia was as amazing as Nina. Gianni challenged us to imagine what it would have been like for the gladiators competing against wild animals in a packed arena."

"Oh, I got you something." Lauren bends over and pulls out a book she purchased for Maura at the Colosseum. "I got the Italian version. You said you want to improve your Italian reading skills. Have fun reading about gladiators and the construction of the Colosseum."

"Oh, Lauren, how thoughtful how much do I..." Lauren brushes her hand as if to say don't even think of it before Maura can finish her question. Lauren is such a kind and thoughtful person, yet there is something in her eyes that speak to me.

"Imagine what it would feel like? I guess it would feel like I was about to get my body torn apart." Maura says.

"We want to hear about your family visit," Says Francesca.

Maura lights up as she gushes about her first in-person meeting with her Roman family. She pulls out her phone and faces it, proudly scrolling through pictures of them as she begins to talk.

"They told me all about how Jews lived in Italy before the

holocaust. Accomplished in academia, business, in professional careers - many were doctors, lawyers, master tradesmen, and military servicemen. They were fully integrated into society. That's what made the betrayal particularly significant."

"Were there a lot of Italian Jews living in Rome at the time?" I ask.

"About 12,000 Jews living in Rome and over 40,000 Jews in the country. They were a minority population."

"But they made a huge impact," I offer.

"Yeah. For sure. That seemed to mean a lot to Aunt Maria. She mentioned it a few times."

Maura smiles as she continues. "Do you know what was so weird? My great-aunts reminded me so much of my mother and grandmother. They are all so stoic, emotionless in some ways but also so loving. They felt familiar to me."

"Funny how those family genes work," Francesca says. "In your family's case, they share genes, but they also had shared experiences, fighting for survival, whether it was escaping Italy or making it through the war."

Laura asks. "Did your mom and grandmother talk much about their experiences?"

"No, not really. I guess they preferred burying that stuff instead of dealing with it."

Francesca says. "They must have all had PTSD. It would have been horrific to return to that moment in time. I have read stories about current-day survivors of genocide or torture getting therapy. My guess is that didn't happen back then."

Maura responds. "Yeah, totally. They just brushed themselves off and carried on, but truly, they would have benefitted from therapy. Generations going forward would also have benefited too…trust me." Maura extends her pointer fingers and then directs back towards herself.

Listening to Francesca and Maura reminds me of a conversation with Sondra about how unrealistic it was for my dad to get therapy after the abuse he suffered. So much pain left to fester. I dig my spoon back into the cup to scoop out the few remaining bites of my melting nutty flavored gelato and slip it into my mouth.

"What did your aunts and cousins tell you about what happened with your family?"

"Let's see. You guys are going to run from me tomorrow. I got our cheery, upbeat morning coffee rolling by telling you all about the 1938 Racial Laws, and now we get to talk about the horrors my family experienced."

We all laugh, then assure her we are hooked and want to hear more. Maura tells us that the racial laws were a turning point in Italy. Jews were forced out of their jobs, and kids weren't even allowed back to school, literally overnight. Her grandparents immediately created a plan to escape Italy. It took them a couple of months to iron out a safe path to leave but they were sure leaving was their only way to survive. Maura's Aunt Marie said that her grandmother begged the whole family to leave with them, but everyone else was determined to remain in Italy.

Maura continues. "Ultimately, my grandparents, mother and uncle made their way to Trieste from Rome to take a ship to New York. There is this little-known story about a small number of Jews who migrated by ship to the United States right after those 1938 racial laws. They were on one of those ships that got out of Italy and made its way to America before it was too late to leave."

I feel my chair pushed from behind. I look up and see a beautiful young mother smile down at me. *"Scuzi,"* she says to me as she brushes my chair, gripping her young son's hand, as they make their way inside to delight in a cup of creamy gelato.

"Reaching Trieste," Maura continues, "from Rome while Jews were restricted to travel was tricky. This guy helped them out. My grandfather was a doctor. Well, years earlier, my grandfather took care of this man's daughter, and he felt indebted to my grandfather."

Maura takes a bite of her gelato and then rests the spoon on the cup. "Details are sketchy, but this guy drove my family to a farm near Florence. They hid out for a few days with some family, then drove to the next secure destination, then the following safe place until they made their way to the Port of Trieste."

Francesca says. "Can you imagine how agonizing that must have been for your grandmother? She en trusted her children's lives into the hands of strangers."

"Yeah, any of them could have been a Mussolini sympathizer. Fortunately, they reached Trieste and boarded the *Avventuriera* with two small suitcases and hardly any money. Years ago, I remember my grandmother telling me that she never imagined feeling so lucky with so little. She was convinced they escaped death."

Maura leans over, placing her elbows on the rod iron table, crosses her hands and tells us more about her family.

"During our conversation today, my 2nd cousins Rachael, Ana and I discovered something we had in common. We talked about living under a cloud of gloom as children on both sides of the ocean. My brother and I weren't allowed to have bad days. I'm exaggerating, of course, but if we didn't like dinner, or we had too much homework or didn't have friends to play with, the response was something like, 'Oh, you think you have it so bad. I barely escaped with my life when I was seven years old.' We learned to push those feelings down. My cousins felt the same way with their parents. Over the years, we bottled up our feelings," Maura teases. "I come by nervous energy naturally."

I add. "Believe me, I have my masters in family dysfunction, so I can relate." Lauren concurs. "Don't we all? Don't even get me started about my mother."

Interesting. That is unexpected. I sense a deeper story behind

Lauren's seemingly ideal life but I didn't expect her to say that. I love how people never fail to surprise me. Gelato cups stuffed with napkins and spoons rest in the center of the rod iron table. None of us are making a move to leave. The conversation is engaging, and the gentle summer breeze is refreshing. The crowd begins to dissipate around us. Maura sits pensive and then continues.

"My aunts told me that life became even more brutal for my family here in Rome. Jews throughout Europe were starting to be rounded up, sent to concentration camps, and killed. My aunts said during this time, they were hanging on...managing...daily life was awful, but they were in survival mode. They took care of one another in the Jewish community, and many non-Jews took risks to help them."

I ask Maura a question I had been thinking about since she began telling us her family's story. "I always heard that Italians were protective of their Jewish community more than in other countries. Did you uncover that in your research?"

"To an extent. Yes. Many Italians quietly resisted fascism and weren't in favor of the Racial Laws. There were government officials, Vatican officials, and, you know, average Italians who helped Jews before a raid or did what they could. Having said that, my aunt said something that translates to 'where was the outrage' in reference to the Racial Laws. She believes that Italians still could have done more and the monarchy also had blood on their hands. King Victor Emmanuel III supported fascism and supported Mussolini. I think it's an important aspect of the story, but I am not sure how much to include in the book. Hopefully, Gianni will have good insight about that too. Overall, Stephanie, I think Italians were more supportive of their Jewish communities than many other countries but could have done more."

Francesca asks. "How did your family who remained in Italy survive?"

"Well, they didn't all survive but most of my family did make it out. Someone in the family was a scientist. I remember my grandparents used to say he was a brilliant man...a little strange but brilliant. Before the war, he had some big government job. His friends alerted him when it was time for the family to go hide and even connected my family with safe houses. Everyone remained hidden until the war ended about a year later. There were some Italians who were paid to shelter Jews, but most weren't. They were courageous heroes who risked their own lives to shelter Jewish families. During our conversation today, Aunt Rosa pointed her arthritic finger toward my computer as I was taking notes and directed me to type that. She thought it was critical to make it clear that despite the failures of many Italians, there were many ordinary people who stepped up by risking their own lives to save others."

I notice some of the employees begin to pull the tables inside. Maura notices, too.

"One last story from today - I think these guys want to go home. This was so terrifying. My Aunt Rosa, Aunt Maria, and their mother, who was my grandmother's sister, hid in an elderly couple's rural farmhouse outside of Rome. My aunt said they probably had it better than many Jews since the home was so isolated. They had some freedom to move around the house, and they even played outside occasionally. You couldn't do that in the city. Food was limited, but they said there was enough to get by. Every night, they crawled into a small pocket in the attic and remained quiet all night. My Aunt Maria said her mother would find ways to make games out of quiet time."

Francesca, Lauren, and I lean in, compelled by Maura's story.

"One night, while they were tucked in their tiny little space when, German soldiers pounded on the door and demanded to enter the home. It wasn't uncommon for Germans to raid homes during the night in rural areas. Aunt Rosa recalled hearing the *clunk...clunk...clunk...clunk* of their heavy boots. She said they were trembling with fear."

"Oh my gosh, how old were they?"

"They are similar in age to my mother, so about seven and five years old. My Aunt Rosa said she could feel her heart pounding out of her chest. Even though she was so young and did not understand what was going on, she understood if they were caught, something really bad would happen to them. The soldiers pounced around the house, looking for signs that more people were living there, but they didn't find any evidence. The homeowners and my great aunt always made sure there weren't extra clothes, dishes or anything around the house that would look like more people lived there. The couple hiding them, my two aunts and my great aunt, used only two plates during meals in case German soldiers unexpectedly showed up and my family had to quickly hide. They wouldn't have to worry about extra plates. The soldiers eventually left that night, but to this day, Aunt Rosa asks people to remove their shoes when they come into her house. The sound of shoes clapping on the floor still scares her."

"What a horrible memory for them. It's still traumatic, all these years later," says Francesca.

"Oh, it is," confirms Maura. "They said they were always terrified after that night until Italy was finally liberated; the war was over, and Jews emerged from their secluded locations. They waited to see who emerged and who was lost. Several distant family relatives were killed, but my immediate family survived, except for my grandmother's brother, Arturo."

"What an incredible story. It's devastating yet inspiring," says Lauren.

Maura responds. "Yeah, my book won't be the 'must-read summer novel' stuffed in every beach bag. It is definitely a very specific niche, that's for sure. I look at it as a tribute to my family and my Jewish Italian heritage."

Lauren reminds us. "You are doing important work. Before yesterday morning, I didn't even know there were Italian Jews. I have learned so much in a day and a half."

"I hope so! I know one thing; it's been cathartic for my mother and my aunts to tell their stories." Francesca says. "When they were younger, they didn't talk about their experiences, probably to protect their own mental health. Now that they are older, they know how important it is to keep the story alive."

I look to the left and to the right and think, if these Roman streets could talk, they would tell countless stories of resilience. Quietly, we stand up, throw away our gelato cups and begin our short walk back to the hotel. Listening to Maura's gripping story is a compelling reminder. Albeit most often not as traumatizing as what Maura's family endured, pushing through adversity and the process of reinventing oneself throughout life is a never-ending journey.

Chapter 23
Roman Gladiator

"*Buon giorno studenti.* We spent a glorious day yesterday touring Rome, and I know many of you had a fantastic night taking in additional sites." We are back in the ballroom, sitting in the horseshoe layout, where we met on day one. Gianni's melodious voice bounces off each wall. Gliding from one point to another, all eyes follow him as if we are watching a tennis match.

"During today's writing clinic, I invite you to include techniques we discussed during yesterday's tours. Challenge yourself to recall how you felt, what you saw, what you heard and even what you tasted for those of you who enjoyed the wonderful flavors that Rome has to offer. A *mezzogiorno*, we will jump on a bus and head out to Napoli. As you can see, we have a guest. Tommaso Rossini will help with our breakout writing session. Signor Rossini is a published author best known for his suspense and thriller novels. He's highly acclaimed with an unmatched ability to create crystal clear visuals for readers, painting such vivid images that it is as if you are watching a movie instead of reading a novel. His writing is just remarkable."

Gianni dramatically extends his arm towards Tommaso as if he is welcoming Miss America to the stage. Our group awkwardly applauds while we turn our attention to Tommaso. He gently nods his head. One foot crossed over another, arms folded over his body, Tommaso is leaning against a table as if it's there for the sole purpose of holding him up. His level of excitement doesn't mirror Gianni's robust introduction.

Gianni's a born showman who seems to thrive on attention; by contrast, Tommaso looks lackluster, as if he's sitting in the doctor's office, waiting for his name to be called. He offers a few unmemorable words, completely underwhelming relative to the praise bestowed by Gianni. After Tommaso's limp acknowledgment, Gianni resumes command of the helm of the ship.

"*Allora*. Look around the room."

Our eyes shift to three of the room corners, observing easels with poster boards on each easel.

"As I call your group, move with your fellow authors to the poster located in each corner of our room."

Gianni points to each of the three posters using flight attendant signals as he directs us.

"Group 1, head over to the 'Conflicts' poster. Let's have group 2...go to the 'Character Traits.' Where is my 3rd group? You will start out with 'Settings and themes' in the back of the room."

Ella and Ana created artistic posters and neatly displayed markers representing every hue of the color wheel. Gianni describes our activity. We should work with our groups and identify words representing conflicts, characters and settings. Once completed, he tells us, we will spend 60 minutes working independently on our novels.

"Does anyone have questions?" Diane eagerly raises her hand to a firm position. "And what exactly does this have to do with writing our books?"

I mumble to myself louder than I thought. "She's one of those."

Maura looks at me and smiles.

"Oh, sorry. Did I say that out loud?" Maura leans in and shields her mouth.

"I think we're all thinking the same thing." I smile back at her.

Gianni claps his hands together in front of his body and professes.

"Thank you, Diane, for asking. I could understand why you

would wonder what an arts and crafts activity has to do with writing a book." Gianna explains in his most convincing voice.

"I request that you recall our initial orientation when I asked you to trust the process even if it seems like it does NOT make much sense. Well, this is one of those times. You are fine-tuned athletes preparing for the World Cup. This is your warm-up training. Diane, in due time, it will all make sense. Let's get started."

Francesca immediately picks up a marker and leads the four of us like a coach, rallying her team to victory. Gianni said nothing about this being a competition, but try telling Francesca that! She displays an enviable ability to lead, to organize and to inspire. I guess you can't just shut down that competitive spirit after years of running restaurants. God, I wish I were more like her. How quickly things change in my head. One day, I'm gazing out a bus window feeling like a Roman *conquistador*, and the next day, I am riddled with self-doubt, comparing what I observe as Francesca's excellence to my own mediocrity. It's a curse that has plagued me my whole life.

Sondra prepared me for these pitfalls. Over time, my conqueror moments would win out. I assure myself that I will get there. Our group activity ends and each of us works independently on our novels. My Adderall has kicked in, and I feel like I'm in a zone. Just over my left ear, I hear a voice.

"Stephanie, how is it coming along?"

My heart races as Gianni pulls up a chair next to me.

"Oh, you know. Writing. Rewriting. Deleting. I don't think…I'm not sure how…"

I'm so out of sorts that I literally stop talking mid-sentence.

"Stephanie, if you would allow me to intervene. Let's take a positive approach. Our goal is to improve our writing skills, enhance our techniques and leave here after two weeks with a solid structure for your book. Take a deep breath." Inhale, exhale, I listen to his direction. With your permission, may I?" Gianni reaches out for my laptop. He facilitates high-octane presentations to the group yet one on one, Gianni is surprisingly reserved, gentle even. He stares into my eyes so deeply that I feel exposed. As he reads my narrative, I squirm in my chair like a 4th grader waiting for her teacher to review her work. "This is a creative, well-developed narrative, Stephanie."

I melt just hearing him say, Stephanie. I hope he doesn't notice my reaction. I don't remember ever having such an immediate attraction to someone, at least not in many years.

"Based on the pre-work sample writing submitted before the trip and this narrative, I'm impressed with your storytelling skills. Your ability to develop a plot is strong. You know how to capture the reader. However, let's work together to figure out over the next few days what is holding you back from digging deeper and becoming more vulnerable. We want to peel away another layer of the onion. Do you understand what I mean?"

I nod my head, barely knowing what I am agreeing to. What I *do* know, however, is that onions are a central theme in my life. They keep popping up. Whether I am in Virginia sitting in Sondra's office talking about peeling layers of my life like an onion or in Rome, writing a narrative, it would appear I have onions with excess layers. If there were to be a metaphor for my life, words like white, red and Vidalia would be part of the equation.

"Stephanie, indulge me, please, if you will. Close your eyes, listen to my voice, and follow my instructions in your head."

I dutifully follow along. "Before you take a dip into the sea, I want you to kick off your sandals." Gianni pauses with each direction. "Remove your hat. Slip out of your bathing suit cover-up. Throw your sunglasses on the towel." I quietly wait for his next instruction but instead, he asks me a question. "How do you feel?"

His voice is calming. I could almost feel the warmth of his breath. No wonder Francesca 'accused' me of hanging on his every word. It's more like clutching onto his every word.

"I feel...naked," I respond as I open my eyes. Where did that come from?

He pauses before confirming. "Yes, Stephanie. Naked. That is exactly how I want you." Gianni pauses and then finishes his sentence, "To feel when you write."

Gianni slowly stands up in silence and then drifts away to help Penny without speaking another word. I utter out loud to myself. *"What the hell just happened?*

Chapter 24
Jolted

Day 3 - Naples

After a three-hour bus ride, Gianni pops up from his first-row seat.

"*Benvenuti* a Napoli. In a few minutes, we will pull up to our stunning hotel. Be prepared for a spectacular view of the Island of Capri and Mt. Vesuvius. Look for the panoramic explosion in every direction. You just might start writing before you exit the bus." He seems to be amused with himself.

We have already become accustomed to Gianni's flair for the dramatic, but as we enter the hotel property, it's clear that he isn't exaggerating...this time. The view is truly remarkable.

Descending from the bus, I feel an electric bolt penetrate my body as Gianni accidentally brushes my arm in passing… something so benign yet so combustible. I'm quietly embarrassed by how I feel. Even worse, I'm concerned my private thoughts are obvious to others.

Lauren approaches me. "Are you Okay? You look a little...flushed."

"Yes. Oh, I am fine. You know it's just a little…ahh, you know." I suddenly can't find words. "Hot? Were you going to say hot?"

"Yes…yes, yes. That's exactly right. I was going to say hot." I'm barely coherent as I attempt to explain to Lauren the complex concept of feeling overheated. The problem is, I know exactly what is ailing me, and it isn't the elevated early evening temperature in Naples but the steamy sensation generated by Gianni. Teasing the ladies about my attraction to him was entertaining, but truly admitting that I'm smitten with the sexy writing instructor feels humiliating, not to mention cliché. I know I've been out of the game for a long time, but I'm not completely naïve. Surely, he's been down this via before with adoring fans. As our group trickles into the hotel lobby, Gianni's voice carries throughout the open space.

"Don't forget. Meet right here in the lobby at 7:00 pm. We have an unforgettable night planned." "I need some of his energy," Francesca comments as we disperse to our respective hotel rooms.

~

At precisely 7:00, our slightly rejuvenated tour group gathers in the lobby. After a 10-minute bus ride from our seafront hotel, we end up at the Castel Nuovo. Our newest personal tour guide, Giuseppe Lorenzo, greets us with a warm welcome to the historic, medieval fortress constructed between 1279 and 1284. At least that is what it says in the brochure Ella gave us.

Standing side by side, Giuseppe appears slight in comparison to Gianni with his grandiose presence both in his build and his personality. Gianni brags about Signor Lorenzo while gently resting his hand on Giuseppe's shoulder.

"He's a legend in Napoli. Not only is he a brilliant historian but Signor Lorenzo is a descendent of the House of Caracciolo, a prominent aristocratic family from the Kingdom of Naples. What I love most about Giuseppe Lorenzo is that he has provided generous financial contributions throughout Naples, following in the footsteps of his philanthropic family." Gianni seems to value giving back. He's boasting about Giuseppe's family philanthropy and he was so obviously proud when talking about his arts center.

I whisper to Francesca, standing to my right. "Should we trust him? Do you remember what Maura told us about King Victor Emmanuel III and his support for fascism? I'm now skeptical of the Royals. What do you think?" Francesca flashes a smile at me.

"Stephanie, you crack me up. You might be right about the whole family thing, but I don't know… I think he has kind eyes, though. Don't ya think." Francesca might be right. There is something endearing about him. During the tour, the four of us talk about the stunning descending sun. Directed at the castle, flood lights add an additional allure to the already mystifying setting. The only other time I had been in Naples, Sami and I secured our marriage license through the U.S. consulate which was required to marry in Rome. We certainly weren't enjoying sunset excursions at a castle that day but rather shuffling through bureaucracy to enter an ill-conceived marriage.

Standing on the front grounds, I announce to the group. "Does anyone else suddenly want to play chess?"

"As the young lady mentioned, the five round towers, which of course look like the rook on a chess board, were built both as a defensive wall and it is a beautiful architectural accomplishment. As we can see, the towers along with the triumph arch are celebrated as a Neapolitan Renaissance masterpiece."

I didn't hear another word after Giuseppe said, 'Young lady.' I take that as my own triumph. Over the next hour and a half, we explore the history and charm of Castel Nuovo.

"Locally, you will hear the castle referred to as Maschio Angioino, the original builders. Many travelers to Naples are surprised to hear that Castel Nuovo continued to seat kings of Naples until the early 19th century. Let's look at the exceptional artwork housed in the Castel Nuovo."

I quietly wonder how long it will take for Gianni to remind us to soak in Giotto's frescoes and the multi-century Neapolitan paintings from the 1600s through the more contemporary 1900s paintings. As if he read my mind, Gianni speaks up to tell us to look deep into the contrasting colors, the lines, and the stories behind the paintings. I laugh to myself, thinking how well I know him already. What in the world is going on in my head? I need to temper my distracting thoughts. Giuseppe suddenly saves me from me.

"Our visitors always want to hear about the crocodile pit. I understand your group is going out for dinner after the tour. I hope I don't ruin your appetite."

Giuseppe's face lights up. It's obvious he loves this part of the tour.

"The crocodile pit originally referred to the pit of millet. It had been used for grain storage during the *Aragonese* reign which we discussed earlier. The more intriguing aspect of the pit is that it has also been used to lock up prisoners for serious crimes, and the crocodiles would, of course, eat the prisoners in the pit. We tell tourists they better behave in Napoli. *Supposedly*, crocodile pits have been abolished, but you don't want to take any chances while visiting. Am I right? Think about that as you go to indulge in the true delight of Napoli…our pizza."

We erupt into laughter, giving Giuseppe the reaction he deeply craves.

~

During the quick ride from the castle to downtown Naples, Maura leans forward and elevates her voice to overcome the rumble of the bus. "If I were home, I would be comfortably tucked under the covers, engrossed in a book."

"Unfortunately, this is about the time I eat back home. Many nights, I sit down for my only actual meal of the day, even later than this. One of many reasons why I'm too old for all of it. Not only am I here to write my book, but I'm also doing some soul-searching. I just don't know if I have it in me anymore...the hours, the pressure, the missed family events...the overall lifestyle is so demanding."

"I think in our own unique ways, there is a lot of 'soul searching' going on around here," Lauren assures Francesca.

The driver parks the bus not far from Piazza del Plebiscito, the historical and pedestrian square anchoring Napoli's city center. The energy level is invigorating. Restaurants, cafes, and shops line the cobblestone streets throughout the heart of Naples.

Gianni leads us into one of the many lovely, quintessential pizzerias. Once seated, I gaze outside the large windows of the quaint pizzeria. A parade of vibrant Italian's walk by our window, drawing attention towards them. They are so demonstrative as they stroll through the streets. It's like watching a cast of Broadway performers dance their way from one via to another. Friends and lovers laugh, hold hands and drape arms over one another, comfortably expressing intimacy. You don't see that back home between friends, especially between men.

Lauren, Francesca, Maura, and I sit next to one another. Penny sits next to me, and Diane, next to Lauren, opposite me. Initiating conversation with someone exceptionally quiet like Penny is uncomfortable for someone like me - nonsense for chatter is better than no chatter.

"Lively crowd outside, isn't it?"

She looks up from the menu and offers me the slightest hint of a smile. "So, Penny. I think I heard you say you're from Des Moines?"

"Born and raised." I'm going to have to work for this but I won't be deterred. I keep the conversation puttering along. "I went to your state fair one year when I was in Des Moines for work. It didn't disappoint." She seems to perk up.

"It never does. My family always enters their livestock in the fair competition." She's a tough nut to crack. I press forward.

"Oh, really. I remember going to the animal pens. Is that what they are called?" I'm obviously a pig out of the mud with my attempt to relate to Penny or her turf. "Do you work on a family farm?" I ask.

"I don't but my parents still have a working farm. I'm the head librarian at the university library. I have my master's in Library

Science."

Library Science ... I didn't see that coming. Admittedly, I placed her somewhere on a dairy farm in middle America. Come to think of it, why am I stumped? Small in stature with a juvenile figure, shoulder-length mousy brown hair and oversized, ill-fitted glasses that she constantly pushes up on the bridge of her nose, Penny actually does give off stereotypical librarian vibes.

With excitement in my voice, I respond. "Library science. I didn't know that existed." Hearing myself say that out loud just sounds ridiculous. Rather than retreat, I continue to vomit words. "Wow...And I want to call myself an author? I didn't even know there was a master's program in Library Science. They will let anyone write a book these days...Am I right?"

I barely glean a half-smirk from her, let alone a smile in response. The exchange makes me think about my girls. They're right. I'm nowhere as funny as I think, and I'm every bit as awkward as they tease me to be.

Despite Penny's desire to bury her head in the menu rather than talk to me, I'm determined to push forward. I make connections with people. That is what I do best. I *will* break Penny...she will like me. I persevere and ask more questions. "Are you writing anything having to do with the Iowa fair animals or libraries?" As perfect timing would have it, Francesca looks up as I ask that bizarre question. Understandably so, she shoots me a well-deserved puzzled look from across the table. I barely know my three new friends, yet somehow, I'm certain we will be laughing about my odd question later.

Penny responds. "No. I'm writing a romance novel, actually." For the second time in five minutes, Penny has befuddled me. I love it when people surprise me, but now I fear the shock is clearly displayed with every line on my face. I stumble through a response.

"Romance. How...ahh...how interesting."

Diane, who is sitting directly across from Penny, saves me myself. "Oh, so we are talking about our books. Stephanie, what genre is your book? I don't remember hearing you mention that before."

I respond to her with conviction. "My novel is a murder mystery - family saga."

Diane looks at me, squints her eyes and asks me in a strangely argumentative tone, considering we just met three days earlier.

"Murder mystery - family saga! That's not a genre." I no longer feel saved by Diane but rather embarrassed by Diane. I suddenly want to return to the farm in the middle of Iowa. My manuscript, in process, is a story that has been sitting dormant in my head for years. I haven't thought about a genre or how to label it. I stutter-respond with much less confidence. "Yeah. Yes. it is?"

Diane doesn't let up. "Where in the world have you seen murder mystery-family saga as a genre?"

Our half of the table is suddenly quiet. I feel all eyes peering at me. "Ahhh, google?"

Diane shakes her head in disbelief, lecturing me for all to hear. "Google? Really? That's not how this works, and if you think you will ever sell even one copy of your book, you need to think again. You have to identify an actual genre. I'm not saying your book isn't good, but if you can't put it in a box…you know, with an identifiable genre and market, readers won't find you."

She very well might be right about my uniquely labeled genre, but her delivery is excessive, especially when cultivating new relationships. Like the middle schooler who subscribes to the adage that any attention is good attention, Diane seems to take the shock value approach to ensure she is heard. I enjoy banter and teasing with one another as much as the next person, but I already feel like I'm treading water on this trip without her badgering me.

Lauren throws out a lifeline. "You will have at least one

book sold, Stephanie. I can't wait to read it. Diane, her story sounds fascinating." She winks at me. I mouth to her, 'Thank you' in return to Lauren. Maura and Francesca follow suit by boasting about my book in progress. I immediately feel their warmth as if Ellen, Janet, and the rest of my crew are sitting at the table with me. I really like these ladies.

~

"Let me introduce you to the most exceptional pizzaiolo in the entire world. And yes. If you did not know it, there is a word for pizza maker. The things you learn on this trip are endless. Signor Franco Liveri is the third-generation owner of this world-class pizzeria. He started learning how to make pizza from his grandfather when he was just eight years old. I asked Franco to share with you what makes his pizza so spectacular."

Gianni waves to Franco. *"Franco, per favore, viene, viene."*

I whisper to Maura, sitting to my right. "Everyone in this country is a tour guide, even the, what did Gianni call him, the *pizzaiolo*."

Maura teases. "And shockingly enough, he is the best in the world."

I turn to her and laugh. We are all amused by Gianni's penchant for embellishment. It's as if Gianni plucked Franco from 'central casting' and plopped him in front of our table. He is a middle-aged, short, portly man with slicked-back salt-and-pepper hair. He completes his look with a white chef's jacket, black and white checkered trousers, and a professionally tied neckerchief that he undoubtedly mastered by the time he was 10 years old. Franco begins speaking in a thick Italian accent. "You only need to know three things about Napoli." Franco holds up his thumb, his index, and his middle fingers.

"Number one. Pizza is beautiful like the people with the blend of colors that represent the Italian flag. Secondo, like the city, pizza can be *caotica*, ahh, ahh, chaotic…even gritty, but it's *deliziosa*. Finally, the most important lesson. If you care for your dough the sauce, and show love to your cheese, your pizza will take care of you with an incredible culinary experience. Are you with me…Neapolitans can be a little rough, but if you treat them right, then you are like family for life in return." He pauses, looking at the nine of us for a reaction.

"Who wants to know how Napoli became *'Gianni, come si dice sinonimo?'* Gianni yells from behind Franco. 'Synonymous.'

Franco continues. "Ah Sí, Sí…Synonymous. Who wants to know why Naples became synonymous with Pizza?"

Cheers erupt in our corner at our table. Servers deliver multiple, perfectly round, thin-crust pizzas topped with delicacies. Each pie is garnished with a variety of options, from melted fresh mozzarella, sliced tomatoes, a mirage of meats, veggies, and fresh basil. Franco shouts *'mangia…mangia.'* Our group digs in while we listen to Franco walk us through the origins of one of Italy's culinary favorites.

Franco holds our attention with his playful delivery and humorous insight by intertwining pizza facts and city folklore. Emphasizing the importance of using fine ingredients, the last few pizzas transfer from the servers to Franco who gracefully releases the piping hot pies to an already full table.

"Gianni will tell you all about the tomatoes tomorrow. Right, Gianni?" He looks back at Giani and smiles. "He won't bring me customers anymore if I ruin his big show tomorrow. I won't say too much about our world-famous tomatoes." He dangles a teaser for us to think about.

Franco turns to Gianni as the banter continues, switching between Italian and English. It's obvious they are enjoying the back and forth like it's performance art. Their affection for one another seems sincere. As soon as Franco resumes his presentation, I peek over his right shoulder and catch Gianni's eyes locked in on me. Out of embarrassment, I quickly look away. It's difficult for me to imagine that he feels the same attraction to me that I feel for him. Surely, someone as handsome, confident, and successful as Gianni must have young, inspiring, beautiful women flocking to him. I don't even know if he's married or not. It's got to be a coincidence that he's looking my way.

Walking back to the bus, Lauren facetiously asks. "Does anyone even remember what day it is?"

Francesca responds. "The days are really running into one another...it's hard to keep them straight... and Stephanie, I shut down when I heard you ask Penny, 'Are you writing a book about fair animals or libraries?" Francesca shakes her head from left to right as she laughs. Maura and Lauren look confused as I try to explain.

"I knew that was coming, but I was…" Francesca interrupts me by elevating her hand up and stating, "I'm gonna stop you right there. You are saved by my exhaustion. I am way too tired to comprehend whatever ridiculousness you had goin' on with Penny, who apparently either works in a library or has fair animals."

Like four old friends, we giggle together as we round the corner, noticing the headlights of our bus. Lauren and Maura quietly mutter to one another. "Library and fairs...what are they talking about? No idea. I am sure we will hear more about that tomorrow."

We reach the parking lot and see our driver pacing outside of the bus. A stream of smoke fills the dark night as he takes a final, long drag and then flicks the cigarette to the ground. Before jumping back into his bus seat, he grinds the cigarette butt into the ground with his heavy foot, extinguishing the lingering flame. Like a teacher leading a school trip, Gianni counts off each of us as we enter the bus. Another exhausting but amazing day comes to an end. It's a full-size bus with plenty of room for the nine of us, Gianni, Ella and Ana, to spread out for comfort. Gianni signals an "all clear" to the driver, then sits down right next to me in the adjoining seat for the 10-minute excursion back to the hotel. Another coincidence, or is this guy messing with me?

Chapter 25
Muse or Inspiration
Day 4 - San Marzano, Sul Sarno

Despite barely sleeping, I feel well-rested when I join my friends for a quick breakfast.

"You look like you are glowing this morning and that outfit. So adorable. I feel so drab." Lauren looks down, assessing her cropped jeans and sneakers. Francesca responds. "We are perfectly fine. Our glowing friend is the one overdressed for frolicking around a tomato farm...to say the least."

Maura says. "Full disclosure. I will feel inclined to take a video of you in those shoes, squishing through the dirt. Fair warning. The compulsion will be out of my control."

"Maybe that bus ride home last night got you all steamed up. Something has motivated you to wear this get-up for an outdoor adventure." Francesca says quietly as she leans into the center of our breakfast table. I pretend to brush off the suggestion, but Francesca has read right through me.

"She's blushing," says Lauren as she turns to Francesca and Maura. Lauren adds. "Would you look at her? We are witnessing an actual real-life crush."

I act indigent at the suggestion that Gianni purposely sat next to me or that I even noticed. What they don't know is that I spent half the night tossing and turning, replaying in my head the layout of the bus. Was my chair the most convenient, or did he go out of his way to sit next to me? Did I imagine him staring at me during our pizza dinner, or did he just happen to be gazing in my direction? I had the same confused feeling when he stared deep into my eyes in Rome while analyzing my writing. I would never confess any of this, so I purposely direct the conversation back to my over-the-top outfit. If they are going to tease me, I prefer it to be about my cold shoulder dressy shirt and chunky earrings selected for an outdoor rendezvous, not emerging feelings for our course instructor.

"You guys are too much. You remind me more and more of my girlfriends back home every day." As I tuck my hair behind my ears, I explain. "Ya know, it's a casualty of growing up Italian in New Jersey in the 80's. We just wouldn't be caught outside, albeit at the beach, the store, or some tomato farm in Italy, without the perfect lipstick, just the right bag and a stylish wedge. You should be pleased to know I decided against the stilettos and don't think I didn't have them on first."

Margaret and Diane, seated just behind us, overheard the three of them poke fun at me.

"We need clarification," states Margaret. "You four are laughing over here like lifelong friends. You never knew each other before this tour began?"

After a brief pause, Francesca, Maura, Laren and I simultaneously burst into laughter without ever acknowledging Margaret's question. Our group of budding authors, board the bus, drive down the coast then divert inland from Naples. Although only an hour from the bustling city, the picturesque, rural setting sneaks up on us. Tranquil compared to Naples, the entire landscape opens to rows and rows of vines, the lifelines to clinging, red tomatoes.

Even at this early hour, the radiant sun pours down on the enormous open fields, breathing life into the expansive gardens. Farm workers pull the ripe tomatoes off the vine and drop them into tightly gripped buckets held stable on their shoulders. They look well-choreographed in their movements. One bucket after another topples with one of the treasured crops of the region. After we exited the bus, Gianni herded us into a circle on a small patch of the tomato field.

"Gather around...viene...viene. Today we welcome my good friend Marco Rossi to tell us about San Marzano tomatoes. If you are not familiar with San Marzano tomatoes, they are the best tomatoes in the entire world, and there is no one more knowledgeable about them than Marco. I'm going to interpret for Marco as he tells us why they are so delicious. After touring the fields, we will make our way to the rustic farmhouse just behind us for today's writing clinic." Gianni points as we simultaneously look behind us at the large structure sitting high on a hill.

"Our friends are kind enough to allow us to use the house for a couple of hours. *Alora.* Imagine your senses literally waking up by touching the flesh of the tomatoes, spending time walking through the fields and finally, eating the local treasures. Marco is letting us pick tomatoes if you would like. I see almost all of you got the memo to dress for outdoor activities, so you will be comfortable maneuvering through the vines." Gianni, ever so slightly, turns his eyes in my direction, revealing a slight grin. My writing colleagues are less conspicuous as they chuckle while shifting their eyes in my direction. I play into the joke.

"Just think of me as an additional muse to inspire your writing." That generates vigorous laughter from the group. Gianni responds.

"Agreed, Stephanie. You are inspirational to all of us. Anyone who has the talent to navigate this rough terrain in heels clearly has talents beyond developing a narrative through the written word." Gianni holds his focus on me as his words linger in the air. Our group quickly transitions from laughter to silence in a nanosecond. His statement doesn't at all feel innocuous to me or, apparently, my eight writing colleagues. This day has become a whole lot more interesting. Thankfully, Marco starts talking as Gianni interprets.

"What makes San Marzano tomatoes so loved throughout the world is their sweetness. We are standing at the bottom of Mount Vesuvius. The fertile, enriched, volcanic soil is one of the reasons the tomatoes are so spectacular. There's a perfect storm between the volcanic soil, the Mediterranean climate and the water levels that combine so beautifully to give us this amazing gift. Our tomatoes are beloved by chefs, too, who go to great lengths to come to our very farm for tomatoes."

Marco kneels and allows soil to dribble through his fingers. My Italian is good enough to recognize that Gianni is taking latitude when interpreting for Marco.

"San Marzano tomatoes are not all made equally. The seeds of San Marzano are grown in many places in the world, but without the fertile soil and climate, the results are not as delicious as the ones grown right here under our feet." Gianni uses his two pointer fingers to firmly point to the ground. Listening to Gianni brag about San Marzano tomatoes reminds me that my father always loved San Marzano tomatoes. They were his 'go-to' canned tomatoes when creating any of his tomato-based sauces.

"When we walk up to the farmhouse a little later, we will have a bucket of washed tomatoes to eat. The flavor will explode to create a party in your mouth. Take your time to walk around, pull some tomatoes from vines, rub the smooth skin, touch the soil, and become one with the land. Words will drain from you like the juices from tomatoes draining through a colander."

~

"Wow, this is as beautiful as a wedding venue," Margaret announces.

Although a modest exterior, the farmhouse interior is fit for hosting an elegant event. Lights stream through each elevated wood beam, then drapes around the pillars anchoring the structure.

Wildflowers with hints of baby's breath fill mason jars, adding a shabby chic yet classy touch to each farmhouse table. Bowls of beautiful, ruby red tomatoes rest arm's length from each chair, evenly aligned side by side. Candles intertwine with greenery and complement the decorum throughout the room. A buffet table parallel to the rear wall is covered with delicious goodies, including sliced tomatoes, fresh mozzarella cheese, a variety of breads, assorted meats and cheeses, scrumptious pastries, and seasonal fruit. Carafes of red, white and sangria put the final touch on the display. Overachievers Ana and Ella arrived early to create a magical experience for us. Gianni directs us to the feast and then invites us to sit at the large extended table in the middle of the room.

We eat with such zest it's as if we hadn't just eaten a full breakfast just a few hours earlier. Gianni wastes no time and begins his presentation as we relish our final bites.

"Why did we come here today? We want you to feel and taste the texture, breathe in the air from the open space, and touch the soil. I saw everyone getting their hands dirty when we were out in the field. Let's pick up a tomato and take a bite."

We are apparently not moving quickly enough to pick up the tomatoes.

"*Prendi...Prendi,* Grab one and bite it...like it's a peach. Enjoy the sizzle of the seeds in your mouth and feel the juice trickle down your arm. Taste the touch of sweetness like any other fruit combined with the savory sensation as if it were a vegetable. As you write over the next two hours, think about those tomatoes outside, clinging for life on vines like our reader will be hanging on your every word." Gianni gives us additional instruction. "Pick up wherever you left off yesterday. Maybe there is a transition needing to be fine tuned or even a romantic encounter to be further developed. Your writing should be enhanced just like a chef boosts her tomato sauce. Add spice, be sensual, be bold or be robust...we are adding zing for the reader." Gianni pauses for effect.

"After the chef adds a little of this or a little of that, she tastes it again and says 'ahh... Just right.' That's what you need to do with your words. Make it just right." Gianni gestures as he continues. "Between the succulent tomatoes, the alluring farmhouse, scrumptious food and of course inspiration watching Stephanie hobble around in her clunky shoes, you have every tool you need to re-read your chapter and say 'Ahh. just right.'"

Laughter erupts. All eyes are on me, and I don't even mind the attention, but Gianni is confusing the hell out of me. I act as if I hardly notice his comment. Two could play this game of cat and mouse. We are playing a game, aren't we? Picking up my laptop, I move to one of the small tables in the rear of the room. Gianni approaches me 20 minutes into our writing session as my writing colleagues curiously look back at us. Can you blame them?

"Stephanie, I hope you know I was only teasing you about your outfit. It's all in good fun. Besides, you look fabulous. In Italy, that's everything."

"Oh, no big deal," I say as if I barely noticed he made any mention of me. "I do like my clothes. Fashion is one of the many things that I love about Italy. Besides, I have a good sense of humor. Hey, if you can't laugh at yourself, who can you laugh at?"

"I figured you could handle it. Not everyone can, ya know, but I pride myself on my ability to read people. You're confident and strong."

"I don't know about all that, Gianni. Your radar might be veering off track. I never really thought that confidence was my strong suit." I look down as I further disclose.

"Believe me, I am working on that, but I'm not sure I am quite there...not yet anyway."

"Let's face it. We are all a work in progress, one way or another. Sometimes, others can see us more clearly than we see ourselves."

I'm rarely speechless, but literally, I got nothin'.' Me? Confident? Strong?

"Based on your submitted writing sample, it sounds like you pushed through adversity over the past year trip. That alone takes strength and confidence."

If only he knew how much I self-talk. I often exhaust myself by self-analyzing the road I have traveled and the road that awaits ahead of me.

"My point is, don't sell yourself short. Let's take a look."

I turn my computer towards Gianni, and he reads my newest additions.

"I thought about what you said earlier. I added spice to my main character, Cassandra. I mean, that was my goal. Her neighbor, Gloria, was murdered, and Cassandra's gut is telling her there is more to Gloria's story than what meets the eye. Cassandra struggles, though."

"Struggles, how?" Gianni inquires.

"She lacks confidence." We both smile at the irony. "Some of the family dysfunction from her past and her current marriage causes her to question herself. I want her to…Cassandra wants to find her own strength…her confidence, but there is this internal battle she confronts often. Like you said, I feel like something isn't 'just right.' I'm not sure if I'm capturing Cassandra's essence. I know her inside of me, but I don't think I'm transferring her voice to the reader. Playing off your metaphors, I think I need more seasoning to captivate the reader."

Gianni remains quiet as he continues to read. He suggests a few structural changes and word choice alternatives. He then provides a deeper analysis.

"As the author, it is your responsibility to breathe life into Cassandra. She's a woman who is attempting to find her own strength. Cassandra is complex. Although she knows how much she has to offer, it feels like she has a proverbial anchor on her ankle dragging her down."

Gianni takes one of his now familiar dramatic pauses.

"Here is what I need from you. I want you, Stephanie, to understand what limits you. What holds you back. I believe you are almost there, but you need a breakthrough. I want you to have that breakthrough." It's as if he is pleading with me. "You don't need to have answers today, but I have homework for you, Stephanie. I want you to do the hard work to release yourself from the anchor around your ankle. When you free yourself, and I mean truly free yourself, you will then free Cassandra."

We sit for another moment in silence as I process his words. He then stands up and walks away. I keep hearing the same word over and over in my head: 'Free.' What does that even mean? Why do I always feel like I'm in a therapy session when he analyzes my work? Two steps forward and three steps back…

Gianni finishes his rounds and then calls us back together. "I had a chance to meet with each of you. I see such spectacular progress in your writing. If you would like me to read a chapter of your book before our next writing session and provide feedback, email it to me anytime tonight. While you are laughing and eating, or who knows, dancing, I will be hard at work proofreading. Okay. As always, I have talked too much. Let's get a volunteer to read a few paragraphs."

Penny slowly raises her hand, much to the shock of the whole group. The only time I ever heard her speak more than one or two words was during our awkward farm-library discussion at the Napoli pizzeria. Even Gianni seems surprised.

"Penny, let's hear what you have for us."

Penny stands up, takes a deep breath and nervously begins.

"No words are exchanged between them once William enters the house and joins Haley in the kitchen. Haley pushes her body up against William's. She extends her long, slender, manicured pointer finger and thumb into the bowl, sitting on the island. She plucks the biggest, juiciest strawberry from the bowl and slowly inserts the strawberry into William's mouth. His tongue welcomes her finger with an intense circular motion as Haley removes her thumb from his mouth. He sucks and twirls her finger with such passion that Haley's eyes roll to the back of her head. William roughly grabs the

back of Haley's head and pushes her mouth into his. Their tongues intertwine with the strawberry as they playfully take turns chewing it until it's gone. William presses Haley against the side of the newly installed, enormous, custom-designed island. His pelvis thrusts against hers as he grabs her firm ass and lifts her on top of the finely sculpted, beveled-edged marble countertop. Haley swipes at the bowl of strawberries, and it crashes to the gunstock hardwood, splattering red shreds of strawberries across the previously spotless new floor. William climbs to the top of the island, straddling Haley. William and Haley tear off their shirts then he presses his entire body on her firm breasts punctuated with erect nipples. After removing their pants, William slides deep inside Haley, her hot, sweaty back leaving streaks on the cold slab of marble. William slips his hands under the small of Haley's back and flips her on top of him. She rides William so hard that she nearly bangs her head against the glass, modern pendant lighting dangling from above. William and Haley reach a climax and release a year's worth of stress with a high-pitched, simultaneous scream. Haley climbs off William, and while standing adjacent to the elegantly curved island, she looks fiercely into his eyes and says, "Now that's how you christen a new house." She then boldly walks away.

Penny remains standing for an additional moment after reading her passage. Her knees buckle then bounce back and forth, right then left, waiting for a verbal cue from someone. Anyone. She pushes her glasses up on the bridge of her nose. Finally, she sits and folds her hands on her lap, more like an innocent schoolgirl rather than a grown woman who just read a passage from her erotic romance novel. An uncomfortable silence lingers. After what feels like an eternity, Gianni interrupts the quiet by lifting a barrel of leftover tomatoes high.

"Tomatoes. Who wants another tomato?"

As if we are running from awkwardness chasing us, we rush to the front of the room, dip our hands into the barrel and grab one of the remaining perfectly ripened tomatoes from the bucket. Dan, bringing up the rear, digs deep into the barrel for one of the few remaining tomatoes and as he pulls out the tomato, he breaks the ice with his Manchester, British accent.

"I'll have what she's havin'." He pauses, then says. "Well, someone hadda say it."

~

"Quiet, mousy librarian Penny sure got our attention, didn't she? I will be her first customer. I could use a little of what she's selling," I tell the ladies.

Maura says. "I will never look at my kitchen island the same way."

"I give her credit. She stood up and owned her story. That is why we are here, right? Besides, Gianni used words like 'sizzle', 'sensual,' and 'juicy,' so what did he think would happen; am I right?"

"Absolutely, Francesca. You can't say she didn't follow his lead."

I share, "Penny's demeanor is obviously why her excerpt had such shock value. She probably felt a charge knowing she stunned the group. I always say everyone has a story. I love it when people surprise me, and Penny did just that for the 2nd time since the beginning of this tour."

Maura adds. "It will be interesting to see if she resumes her previous quiet posture, or was that her coming out party."

"Yeah, really. Where does she go from there? Oh, speaking of a coming out party, I know who is happiest about Penny's debut...Stephanie...did you think we were going to just forget about whatever that was with you and Gianni in the tomato field because we were so caught up in Penny's hot kitchen island sex?"

I shake my head. "I don't know, Francesca, what to say about that or think about that. I'm at a loss for words."

"You aren't squirming your way out of this. To steal a word from Gianni...We will save those juicy details for tonight's dinner." Francesca says.

Chapter 26
Missing

Day 4 - Pompeii

"Imagination...It is the spark that paves the way for all mediums of art to be created. Societies before us have been created and sustained only because men and women allowed themselves to imagine another way forward. Albert Einstein said, 'Logic will get you from A - Z. Imagination will get you anywhere.' You all joined this book tour because you have imagined a story and you desire to tell it through writing. We sit in the center of a 2,000-year-old city that developed because of the incredible imagination of those who dared to dream of the realm of possibilities."

Gianni turns from side to side, arms extended.

"Sadly, in 79 A.D., Mount Vesuvius, perched just above us, erupted, burying the city as well as the people in ash and volcanic glass. It remained immersed until the late 1700s when archeologists dug it out. They were amazed by the sophistication of the city built so many centuries earlier. As the brilliant and energetic Giuliana guides our tour through this enchanted city, open your minds to the ingenuity and the originality you bring to your writings just as it was brought to Pompeii. As our old friend Einstein said, imagination will get you anywhere."

As if Gianni had just wrapped up a Ted Talk, he exits the middle of the city's ancient amphitheater then Giuliana takes center stage. How does she compete with the 'One Man Show?'

Maura whispers. "I'm waiting for a director to step in and say cut, take 3."

I smile in response. Maura never misses an opportunity to highlight Gianni's showmanship. Understated and humble, his flair for the dramatic isn't her style. Not that Maura doesn't like Gianni but rather his personality is the antithesis of hers. I find his expressiveness to be endearing. At his core, I see a kind man who uses his embellished language to entertain us. His elaborate performances are tools used to gain our buy-in and hold our attention. My guess is he knows exactly what he is doing.

During the next hour and a half, Giuliana describes how developed the city was for its era prior to the volcanic eruption. White stones were laid as moonlight reflectors, brilliantly illuminating the sky. A complex gully system buried deep into the cobblestone streets allowed for sewage drainage throughout the city. Finally, everyone's favorite brothels with phallic graffiti engravings depicting a selection of sex service options to world travelers speaking a variety of languages passing through Pompeii.

"Where's Lauren?" Asks Francesca as she looks from left to right. "I had been talking with Dan and Stanley most of the tour. I don't recall when I saw her last."

"Come to think of it, I haven't seen her in a while either." I agree...

Before we dart off in different directions to track Lauren down, we see her from afar, rounding a corner and walking towards our bus. Once she sees us, Lauren breaks into a trot and yells out a series of apologies.

Gianni, pushing his palms downward, repeats, piano, piano. "Slow down. It's okay. We have plenty of time. This is Italy, not America. You don't need to rush," Gianni teases.

He politely guides Francesca, Maura, and me on the bus to join the rest of the group. I peer through the window at Gianni and Lauren, talking warmly with one another. Gianni kindly reaches out for Lauren's hand and tenderly squeezes it. He releases her hand then they board the bus. Lauren sits next to me.

"Are you okay? I'm so sorry. I didn't realize you weren't with the group." Lauren, uncharacteristically sullen, replies.

"Don't apologize. I'm fine. Really. I just felt a little lightheaded, so I found a cool place to sit and drink water. Then, I made the mistake of calling my husband. He worries about me. He just wouldn't stop talking. It was like he was badgering and badgering me. 'How are you? Where are you? Are you alone?' He just went on and on and on."

Lauren shakes her head, looks down then takes another sip of water.

"I guess with so many miles between you two, he is just worried about you. He obviously cares about you." I immediately regret my words as soon as they fall out of my mouth. Even though Lauren paints a picture-perfect marriage, people reveal what they want others to see. Our foursome has talked and laughed in the few days we have spent together but we don't really know one another. Lauren has been nothing but pleasant and cheery; she is obviously irritated by her husband's line of questioning, and it isn't for me to assure her that his behavior is simply out of love. There could be more to their story than meets the eye.

"Sometimes what I need from him is a little more space and a little less caring."

I instinctively reach out and gently squeeze her hand that is resting on her lap. This time, I do what she needs most. I sit quietly and listen.

Chapter 27
Lemon Path
Day 4 - Amalfi Coast

Driving through winding roads defined by the Tyrrhenian Sea, the coastline opens in front of us. Gianni scheduled a visit with one of his dearest friends, Adolfo Percini, owner of a restaurant in the darling town of Minori, centrally located on the Amalfi Coast.

"This is exactly the kind of tour I need right about now," I suggest once our bus stops. Stepping off the bus, a light breeze drifts by me. I catch a glimpse of Lauren laughing with Margaret. She seems to be bouncing back.

Adolfo leads us out back to a quaint patio adorned with lemon trees and stunning views. A delicate whiff of lemons permeates the outdoor space. As the sun descends behind us, we are treated to a variety of lemon-infused delights, including an Italian favorite, limoncello. Adolfo looks to be in his mid-50s. He's well dressed in tailored slacks, a stylish short-sleeved shirt and well-structured, designer loafers. He speaks English with a touch of a British accent.

"Limoncello is made with water, sugar, and zest from the best lemons in the world. Oh, and let's not forget the grappa." *Stai Attento*...these drinks are strong. Before you know it, you will need to be peeled off the pavement like a lemon. I can't resist. A little lemon humor."

Adolfo is looking for his joke to land, but we are too drained to respond. I take a sip and quickly pucker. "Wow. Adolfo, you aren't kidding."

"See. I told you. Drink too much, and you might need lemon - aid…get it…lemonade…Tough crowd."

"We like your lemon jokes, Adolfo, but at this point, we are squeezed."

Dan points at Adolfo. "You like that. Squeezed." Dan repeats as he chuckles.

I turn to Lauren and see her throw the whole drink back and ask for another like she's a freshman pledging a sorority. Back in Rome, she told us she shouldn't drink. How do I say, 'Should you be drinking that?' There's no discrete way to ask nor is it any of my business to do so.

"That is sooo refreshing." Lauren professes.

Maura, Francesca, and I look at one another, but we remain silent. Plates of glorious lemon treats, one after another, arrive at our tables as Adolfo insists we eat.

I say. "Forget chocolate. These desserts are to die for. This Delizia al Limone truly takes the cake, pun intended."

Maura asks, pointing to the disappearing dessert. "What is in that?"

"This is a sponge cake, lemon cream and limoncello syrup. It is delizioso." Margaret adds. "This lemon sorbet is wonderful in this heat."

"You have to try the cafe scurzette, which is a lovely coffee with lemon zest on top," Adolfo promises as one of the servers delivers multiple cups to our tables. Servers present additional cookies, cakes, and candies as our group melts in a sea of Minori's lemon desserts. We slurp the scurzette and relish in the sweets.

"While you are enjoying our lemon treasures, I will share some facts about the lemons in Minori and throughout the Amalfi Coast. We are proud to boast that we might be small, but Minori is a world hub for this bold and beautiful fruit. It's easy to forget it's a fruit, right? They were originally grown to provide vitamin C on long sea voyages to prevent scurvy. The Amalfi Coast has a deep maritime history. Going back to the 9th and 10th centuries, this port was what you would call a gateway between what we know to be the Middle East today, as well as throughout Africa and Italy. Our climate is perfect for these large, gorgeous lemons to flourish. We get that nice, cool sea breeze and it is trapped in the mountain valleys. You can see we have them all around us."

Adolfo pauses to give us a moment to take in the majesty of the surrounding mountains and sea. "As it turns out, this unique phenomenon is perfect for lemon growing."

Adolfo's finesse is enticing. He's no Gianni, but he does an admirable job of enlightening us about the evolution of lemons in Italy. However, our group seems to have reached our limit for processing new information. To his credit, he has the emotional IQ to recognize it's time to allow our group to sit with our own thoughts while enjoying the literal fruits of his labor.

"I know Gianni wants you to gain inspiration for your writing. It looks like you are all drinking and eating a lifetime of inspiration to write any best-selling novel."

We smile at him. I catch a glimpse of Gianni, proudly grinning ear to ear.

"I leave you with this. Lemons, like most people, are complex. They represent freshness, healing, love and even friendship."

Maura, Francesca, Lauren, and I instinctively look at one another and smile.

"However, lemons also signify bitterness and disappointment." I turn to the right and notice Lauren immediately bows her head. I can't help but wonder why his statement seems to deeply resonate with her.

"If you return to our beautiful coast, hike the Sentiero dei Limoni - The Path of Lemons. Start in Maiori and finish the hike right here in Minori. There are lots of ebbs and flows throughout the trek, just like we find in life. With each step, inhale the magnificent lemon aroma, soak up the sun and feel the breeze from the sea. As you walk along the lemon path, contemplate your life's winding road. Think about where you have been and where you are today. It's truly a spiritual journey. Oh, and make sure you come back to see me. You will have all the lemon delights you want, offre la casa – on the house."

Our group appears to be processing his profound words. We continue to pick at the desserts and sip our drinks as Adolfo and Gianni slowly step away from our group. Like Giuseppe in Naples, Gianni and Adolfo seem to have great affection towards one another. Once again, I'm drawn to Gianni consumed with his every movement. It's as if I forget I'm sitting with my tour group until I hear in the background Diane musing about me and my three friends.

"Margaret, when we sit with these four, don't you feel like we are hanging out with the popular girls in school." Margaret smiles big, seemingly for no other purpose than to appease Diane.

She's an easy-going woman with a warm vibe and pleasant disposition, Diane's antics don't appear to annoy Margaret like they agitate the four of us. Completely out of character from the Lauren we have seen over the previous four days, she pushes back at Diane.

"If you mean fucked up when you refer to 'the popular girls,' then yes, we are the super popular group. Right ladies?" Laughing as she leans in, Lauren pours herself another limoncello.

None of us care about her 'impolite' language. Hell, I have always been one to relish in an appropriately placed F-bomb. My concern is that Lauren sounds like she's unraveling. An hour earlier, she was clearly angered by her husband. Now, she appears driven by liquid courage.

Although I've only known Lauren for a short time, my gut is telling me this is about something else. Diane plays off Lauren's response.

"Well, that isn't exactly what I had in mind, but hey, if that's what defines the popular group, then maybe it isn't what it's cracked up to be." If Adolfo, on a scale of one to one hundred for emotional

IQ, is a 100 for his ability to read the room, Diane drops in at about a 2. Rather than recognizing that Lauren isn't in a mind space to engage, Diane chooses to do just that.

"Lauren, I never heard you mention anything about your book. How is your writing coming along?" Diane is like a dog on a bone. She tried to shake this lemon tree once before with Lauren, and it was abundantly clear, for whatever reason, Lauren didn't want to talk about her writing. In a quiet and solemn voice, much to our surprise, Lauren responds.

"Love letters. That is what I am writing. Lovely love letters." Diane doesn't let it go.

"Love letters? Do you mean like a romance novel? I don't understand. I don't get Stephanie's genre, and now I don't understand what you are saying."

Oh, here we go again with my mystery family drama genre. I can't worry about that, though.

Diane is antagonizing Lauren. Making matters worse, Lauren's jovial mood is diminishing while her alcohol blues are seeping in. Playing to Diane's ego, I blurt something out that will surely take her off Lauren's trail.

"Did you all know Diane's book is already 35,000 words?" Francesca and Maura immediately picked up on my lead. Get Diane to talk about Diane. Francesca gives Diane a high five.

"Go, Diane! 35,000 words! That's fabulous."

Maura keeps it going. "Fantastic! You must be halfway done with your novel. What is your book about?" Game over. I heard all the details when we were in Pompeii. Admittedly, it sounds intriguing. If she isn't instigating Lauren, I'm happy to hear it again.

"I'm writing a dystopian fiction, a well-defined genre, I might add." I think we all do an imaginary eye roll, but it takes all types to make a group of nine strangers gel.

"Imagine a worldwide virus that has a 50% chance of death

if infected. Governments all over the world fight to balance preserving their existing population and maintaining personal freedoms while perpetuating human life going forward. Scientists develop a vaccine, but the problem is, the vaccine renders you infertile." I look around and notice everyone locked in on Diane. "Older people quickly get vaccinated and resume their lives, ya know, they don't want to have kids, but many of the young people don't want the vaccine. Our government is tracking down and forcing people to get vaccinated so the virus can be suppressed. People of childbearing age who want to have children someday go into hiding from the government while the military police track them down. The most controversial part of the book is that the government selects young people who they deem as their 'most exceptional' to live unvaccinated in a contained society so they can procreate. They choose the smartest, most athletic, and most creative people. After they live in this contained environment and have a baby, they get the vaccine, and they are pushed back into society, but they have to leave their babies behind for nurses to care for them. There are multiple underground, secret communities and I focus on a few characters. I have a long way to go, but I know a vaccine that doesn't cause infertility will be developed. It will have a happy ending but, in the meanwhile, there's all this chaos."

Francesca responds. Diane, that sounds fascinating. I want to read it. It sounds like it forces the reader to think about moral questions like who decides who is worthy to live in the contained society and have kids and what role the government has in our personal lives."

Maura adds. "Absolutely - personal autonomy versus the government's responsibility to manage what's right for the good of society. When I had bioethics classes in med school, we considered scenarios with all sorts of similar, ethical dilemmas."

I offer... "Can you even imagine a virus traveling throughout the world? It's scary to even think about it but nevertheless, your book will be amazing."

"No, I can't imagine something like that," says Lauren. "That would be a nightmare. Diane, kudos to you. It sounds like it will be a thrilling read," Lauren graciously offers.

Gianni thanks Adolfo for his hospitality and leads us back to the bus for a quick drive to our boutique hotel in Positano. Gianni stands up in front of the bus.

"There aren't enough available rooms in the hotel for me. I have friends who spend the summer on the coast. Don't worry about me. I will certainly be fine."

I don't think anyone is concerned that Gianni Ciabatinni will find a comfortable place to lay his head tonight. No one other than me, is probably even curious as to where that will be.

"Enjoy your evening. Explore the nearby walking area of Positano. If you want to buy gifts for loved ones back home, there are lots of beautiful shops in Positano. Some of you may want to branch out. Extending from Salerno to Sorrento, one coastal town is more beautiful than another: Amalfi, Furore, and Praiano, each glorious yet unique. No matter what you decide to do, you can't go wrong."

Dan asks. "What is the must-eat along the coast?" "Ah, Si, Si, Si...Look over there."

Gianni bends his head and points out towards the sea.

"What do you see? You want to eat seafood while on the Amalfi Coast. My favorite dish in Amalfi is a classic for the region, scialatielli ai frutti di mare. You got your shellfish, shrimp, mussels, whatever the kitchen has fresh that day. They will make it with any pasta. Most restaurants will have a homemade pasta selection. I usually choose whatever pasta is homemade that day, but this is important, only if it is a long pasta like linguini or I love it with bucatini. Long pasta holds the sauce and the fish. Shrimp, clams, mussels, cling to the dangling pasta like your readers will hang onto your every word."

We all hoot and holler, and Gianni flashes one of his big

smiles, as he expands his hands open as if he's inviting the applause.

"I'm startin' to regret askin' for a recommendation." Teases Dan.

"You should know me by now. I will turn anything into a writing session. Kidding aside, you don't want a pastina. Short pasta like ziti doesn't work as well with the dish. The fish just falls off the pasta. Okay. Enough of that. You can check off your list, 'pasta intertwined with writing' from your things to learn on this tour."

Like any performer, Gianni waits for his audience to respond, and he earns the applause.

"If you need me, text or call. I will remind you each night. I barely sleep. Email me your writing if you would like me to read it and give you feedback." With that, we exit the bus and check into our lovely hotel.

Chapter 28
"What happens in Amalfi stays in Amalfi."
Day 4 - Amalfi Coast

Clinging to the coast, the inside-outside restaurant boasts glorious seaside views. We walk in and catch a subtle whiff of garlic and seafood. It reminds me of Friday nights during Lent when I was in high school. None of my friends wanted to get dressed at my house for a night out after my dad cooked a feast of fish and sauces steeped in garlic. Boys at the party wouldn't want to talk, let alone kiss us if we were drenched in the aroma of his culinary creations.

"Another fantastic Gianni recommendation," says Francesca. "I hope the food matches the magnificent view."

Once we are seated by a window, I ask. "Should we order a bottle of wine to share?" Lauren quickly responds. "That's a hard pass for me, especially after today. By all means, don't let me stop you from getting wine." After a brief pause, Lauren continues. "Listen. About today... I am so sorry for my behavior earlier. I do not know what got into me. You all must think I am some sort of closet lush. Really. I swear. I almost never drink at all at home. Especially now." Lauren looks down and pauses again before transitioning. The three of us remain silent, giving her a moment to gather her thoughts. "Oh, and my language, especially with Diane. Was I rude?"

Lauren covers her face and shakes her head. We all trip over one another to tell her no need to worry. I assured Lauren that Diane could handle her response and Diane knew exactly what she was doing. Then I say, "Hey, what happens in Amalfi stays in Amalfi. As far as your language, it certainly didn't offend me. Hang out with me and my Jersey girls for a week, and you will get a taste of next-level potty talk."

Maura quickly insists. "Really. Don't even think about it. As long as you are okay."

"Exactly. Do you want to talk about anything else from today?" Francesca asks.

"No judgment zone here. Sometimes it's easier to talk with people not as intimately involved in your life rather than long-term friends and family back home." Maura says.

"You know," I respond, pointing at Maura, "that is such a good point. I once had a phone sales job, and people would call in and tell me the most personal things about their lives."

I'm babbling. Nervous energy. Based on the look on their faces, I'm driving the conversation off-course. There is a momentary pause before Lauren responds.

"You all are so sweet. I appreciate you making me feel better about my display. Full disclosure, I had a few tough moments today, but I'm feeling better. I called my daughter when I got to my room, and she was such a hoot. She always makes me laugh. I'm fine. Really. In fact, I'm more than fine, sitting here with three amazing women looking out on this fabulous view. No more talking about me."

"Stephanie, you know what that means."

Francesca, Maura, and Lauren stare at me as Francesca continues. "You are up. Spill the beans."

"I'm not getting out of this, am I?"

~

I take a big breath and shake my head. "I don't know if there's anything to tell. It's hard to explain how I'm feeling. It's like Gianni has gotten inside me."

Francesca quickly quips. "Well, it certainly appears like he wants to get inside of you." We all chuckle.

"As you all know, my husband left me a year ago. I fell apart. Thanks to wonderful friends, my amazing daughters, and a good therapist, I've been putting the pieces of my life back together.

After 10 months with my therapist, Sondra, I feel strong. Or at least stronger. Confronting childhood issues with her was one of the best things I have ever done for myself. Oddly, I have Michael to thank for that."

"Hey, gifts are often delivered in the strangest boxes," Says Francesca. Maura and Lauren nod in agreement.

"This might sound ridiculous, but on our 2nd day in Rome, when we were driving over Ponte Sant Angelo on our way to the Vatican, I felt...victorious. Up until this trip, Rome lived in my head as a reminder to me of how chaotic I am…or was. Driving through the city, I felt like a Roman conqueror returning home after winning the war."

"That must have been such an empowering feeling." Suggests Francesca.

"It was. But, after just a couple conversations with Gianni, it's as if he sees right through me. His provocative questions force me to reconsider if I've progressed as much as I thought."

"Okay. What has he said to make you question yourself?" Asks Maura.

"Well, Gianni gave me feedback. You know about my writing. He told me I needed to go deeper and push more. He said I should release the handcuffs from around my wrists."

I throw my hands up in the air.

"He told me to figure out what is holding me back, personally. He said it would help breathe more life into my characters or something like that. What does Gianni see in my writing that speaks to him about me as a person?"

Maura weighs in. "You lost me in handcuffs?' My imagination is going in all sorts of directions, and none of them have anything to do with writing." Maura waves her hands in a circular motion. "As someone who has spent most of her life in therapy, what you are feeling is so normal."

Francesca teases Maura. "Really. You spent most of your life in therapy? Shocking." Francesca slyly smiles at Maura. "I know. I should ask for my money back."

Maura has a wonderful self-deprecating personality and appreciates Francesca's poking at her.

"Notwithstanding my ineptness after years...and years...did I mention...years of therapy, I can tell you this...therapy is a process. Like Adolfo talked of ebbs and flows on the path of lemons, there are similar ups and downs in therapy. Look at it as an Olympic hurdle jumper. She clears the hurdle and is closer to the finish line but then there are additional hurdles to jump over. It doesn't mean she didn't clear that initial huddle and make progress. Sometimes, people have one challenge that is holding them back, and after six months of therapy, they resolve that issue and no longer need therapy. For others, it could be a year, a two-year or a lifetime commitment of jumping over a variety of hurdles. Obviously, I'm more like a marathon runner than a hurdle sprinter. The point is, don't minimize your growth over the past year just because you may or may not have more hurdles to clear. Mental health growth could be a long haul; have patience and give it the time you need."

"Okay, Maura." Francesca pauses. "You crushed it."

"Maybe I have learned a thing or two after all. Of course, it's always easier when you are on the outside looking in rather than working through your own shit."

Francesca rhetorically responds. "Isn't that the truth?"

~

Francesca takes a piece of piping hot bread from the basket, dips it in the oil, herb, and parmesan blend then passes the basket to me.

"It's easy to get caught in the weeds of our own challenges. But Stephanie, I have to believe you already scaled hurdles to use Maura's metaphor? We didn't know you last year, but in the short time we have known you, I don't associate you with chaos. Would Stephanie from last year flourish on a trip like this?"

I nervously laugh as I respond. "Are you kidding? After Michael left, I was completely incapacitated. I wouldn't have been able to pack a bag, let alone get on the plane...forget traveling and writing."

I pause before addressing Francesca's other observation. "It's interesting that you don't associate me with chaos. Michael never missed an opportunity to point out my chaotic traits. I mean, he wasn't wrong."

"Wrong or not, pointing it out didn't help, I assume." Laurn comments as she picks up a piece of bread.

"Yeah, no kidding… Over the past year, I can honestly say I feel more settled. I feel more put together than I ever remember feeling. Yeah. Therapy has been good to me. Then, enter Gianni Ciabatinni, and here I am questioning that evolution."

Francesca asks. "Why does Gianni have such an impact on you? I know he is our instructor and all but are you attracted to him or something else?"

"Well, I do find him to be attractive. Am I the only one?" I ask. My eyes move from one to another, looking for a reaction.

Maura responds. "I can see why someone would find him to be...alluring. He isn't my type. I'm more of the big classes, a pocket protector with a 'kick me' sign taped on his back kind of girl, but I get the appeal. He's just a bit suave for my taste."

"Maura, you crack me up." I lean in. "Okay. Don't laugh at me. It's like he's flirting with me, or maybe I'm flirting with him? Do I even know how to flirt? I know. It's crazy. Why would he even be interested in me?"

Francesca's voice slightly elevated, "And why wouldn't he be interested in you?"

"Oh, I don't know. He's handsome. A famous author. 'Friends' everywhere. I feel so dull compared to him."

Lauren says. "Please. You are also a beautiful author...in training. You are Interesting. We have all had so many great conversations, so I know you are intelligent, you're funny, and most importantly, you're an amazing human being."

I provide Lauren with a smile of gratitude for her kind words.

"Look at us. We are women..." Francesca clears her throat "approaching a certain age yet we are still making moves in life. We are all first-time authors. At some point, each of us woke up and said you know, I think I will write a book today. We are following through with it. That automatically makes us awesome. He probably sees you as a confident, empowered woman who has said I don't care how old I am, but I am putting it out there. I have new adventures to pursue. You are strong, compelling, and, yes, Stephanie, a desirable woman."

"I see life as something to fight for...to the end, no matter how old and no matter how much time is left to live. We are all on this trip for a variety of reasons, but we each are taking a risk to be here. Gianni would be crazy not to find you attractive," says Lauren.

Maura adds. "Forget if he is interested in you...are you interested in him? Think of it in terms of you being the catch, not him."

Francesca responds. "Amen, sister!"

~

"Excuse the moaning. This is divine."

Francesca, Maura, and I join Lauren in savoring the blend of shellfish, flavorful light tomato sauce and hand-crafted pasta. As predicted, Gianni's recommendation is spot on.

As we enjoy the diverse flavors of our tasty pasta dish, Lauren asks. "Hypothetically speaking, if Gianni took things to an elevated level, how would you respond? I'm a hopeless romantic, so it is easy for me to be sucked into a good love story, albeit real or imagined."

I smile. "Confession. I couldn't sleep last night thinking through that very question. Embarrassing, I know."

"It's not embarrassing. It's fun to dream," Suggests Lauren.

"Well, there is a small detail I haven't told you about my first marriage. I mentioned I had been married prior to my soon-to-be ex-husband...words I thought I would never utter... but what I didn't share is that I met my first husband here, in Italy...on the streets of Rome, literally walking through one of those enormous, ancient arches not far from the Colosseum."

Lauren gasps. "That is so romantic. How wonderful that you opened your heart to love after a chance meeting in a foreign city."

Maura suggests. "Well, before we pop the champagne, he is an "ex" so maybe it's better left for a romantic novel than real life."

Francesca says. "This explains your reflective Spartacus moment, crossing the bridge early on in our tour."

Lauren continues. "Why didn't you tell us when we were in Rome? We could have visited the exact place where you met."

"I guess I preferred to leave it in the past. Imagine being in such a mixed-up place in your life that you would meet someone literally on the streets of a foreign city and, within 2 months, marry him."

"Well, that's exactly what I love to do. Imagine the possibilities."

Lauren caught up in the romantic aspect of finding love in a foreign city, smiles big, engrossed in the details of my ill-fated relationship.

I explain, "I would love to paint a picture of something risqué yet beautiful, but it was more like watching a train crash. I barely spoke Italian at the time, and he didn't speak any English. Much of the allure was figuring out how to communicate. If you are thinking this all sounds really nutty, it was."

Lauren has a different take. "I don't know. It depends. Maybe not marrying someone you meet in a foreign city is a missed opportunity. It's all perspective."

"Trust me. It was far from a Hallmark movie ending. I guess I thought telling you all this while we were in Rome might have scared off my new friends."

Francesca assures me. "It would take a whole lot more than that to scare me off. I'm sure we all have skeletal bones rattling in a closet somewhere."

"If only my life was interesting enough to share that I had some foreign, untold paramour," Jokes Maura.

Lauren says. "I wish I had the ability to take risks when I was younger. I'm not saying there's anything wrong with the path I took, but my mother was so controlling. I didn't have the courage to step outside the sandbox and follow my heart. I've spent much of my adult life full of regrets."

Lauren, every now and again, drops small, surprising hand grenades that jolt us. There's a dynamic narrative to be told beyond her perfect husband, 2.5 kids, and a white picket fence.

After slurping a muscle from a shell, Francesca responds. "Stephanie, you were young, and it sounds like you had a lot to process from your upbringing. Your first husband is ancient history, like the arches where you met."

"You are right, Francesca. It's old news. It's just that starting a relationship with my ex, Sami, turned my dream of an amazing Italian cultural experience into a calamity. Fast forward to today, not only am I on this trip to write a novel but this trip is a chance to rewrite the script from my first Italian journey. I'm off to a good start, meeting you three!" I smile and they return a warm response.

"Do you see why my attraction to Gianni is so complicated? It's like Deja vu all over again. Here I am in Italy looking for one experience, and once again, I find myself attracted to some guy. It begs the question – do I ever learn?"

"That is a whole lot to process. I don't advocate for you to pursue Gianni or not but as the senior student of therapy at this table, I challenge you to trust yourself. When you got involved with Sami, it didn't sound like you were in an emotionally healthy place to meet someone. You're a different person now. If you initiate a relationship with Gianni in Italy or with someone else back home, it's because you know yourself and you're entering the relationship for the right reasons and from a healthier place. Just because it was a mistake then doesn't mean it is a mistake now."

Lauren concludes. "Honey, follow your heart and have faith in your head."

Chapter 29
Get Around

Day 5 - Amalfi Coast

The four of us plan for a morning adventure, exploring the glory of the Amalfi Coast seaside. As soon as we walk outside of our hotel, a delicate sea breeze rolls over us. Pointing across the street at a line of shops, I suggest, "How about we pick up espresso, cappuccino, brioche..."

Lauren excitedly interjects. "Oh, I love those cornettos...we have to get some of those too."

Francesca adds. "Perfect. I spoke with Elena, ya know, the hotel manager or owner? Not sure which. Anyways. She said we should hit Arienzo Beach if that works for everyone. Before you commit, remember when we said we need to walk off all this food we've been eating? There are apparently a ton of steps down to the beach...Is everyone up for it?"

After leaving the cafe with our breakfast in hand, we begin the long descent down the stone steps. We take a few breathers along the way. I share an observation.

"I was just thinking about that cafe back there. Some things have not changed since I was previously in Italy."

"Oh yeah. Like what?" Lauren asks.

"For starters, has anyone else noticed that if two cafe employees are talking, they aren't going to let a little thing like a line of customers interfere with their conversation? I remember I found that to be amusing all those years ago, and I still love that their human interaction is more important than waiting on customers. It's such a good reminder that we all need to slow down."

Francesca says. "I guess that's why they say, 'when in Rome.' I appreciate the more relaxed approach to serving customers when I'm here. But, when I'm at a Starbucks in Brooklyn, I'm in a completely different mindset, and that wouldn't fly, not for me and not for my fellow New Yorkers. I'm not saying the Italians don't have the right idea, but city culture is what it is."

I agree with her sentiment. "You're 100% correct. I think there is a lesson about how to live life, though. Speaking of which, I once had a job..."

Maura stops me. "Starting this very moment, I am going to put a euro aside every time you start a conversation with 'I once had a job.'"

As we walk, Maura pulls out a euro from her pocket and puts it into her change purse for effect. "Okay. Go on. Tell us about your job."

Francesca adds. "Maura, you are hysterical and not far off the mark. Stephanie, you have mentioned a lot of jobs."

I stand tall, slide on my animal printed Maui Jim sunglasses as I confess. "What can I say, ladies? I get around."

~

"This is living." Maura declares as she sips her espresso and takes a bite of her brioche streaked with chocolate.

I suggest. "Maybe we should play hooky and spend the entire day out here. It's amazing. Plus, what goes down must go up. We have quite a hike ahead of us going in the other direction.

Francesca counters. "Nice try. And miss watching whatever interaction that will transpire between you and Gianni today? Not a chance." She pauses and sips her cappuccino. "It is beautiful out here, though, isn't it?"

Lauren buries her feet in the white, pebbly sand. "I'm channeling Gianni right now - between the morning sun, the beautiful blue sea and the dramatic mountainside cliffs all around us, what better inspiration could we possibly need not only for writing but for living? I am going to soak this all in."

We all follow Lauren's lead and silently absorb our surroundings for the next few minutes, sitting in orange high-back beach chairs. A warm air wafts through our foursome. Francesca rejuvenates the conversation.

"By the way, I took Diane's advice. After we got back to the hotel from dinner last night, I couldn't sleep so I worked on my book. I sent Gianni a couple chapters to review…shut down my computer at about midnight. Do you know, when I woke up, he had already provided all sorts of feedback? The man wasn't kidding when he said he doesn't sleep. He responded to me at 2:00 am."

In a playful tone, Lauren asks. "I wonder what thoughts were keeping him up until all hours of the night?" Lauren shoots a look directly. It's endearing to see how vested she is in my and Gianni's imagined relationship.

"Haha. Yes, it's me. He's up all night thinking of all of this." I run my hands up and down, emphasizing my body's silhouette.

"Was the feedback helpful?"

"Absolutely. He's so insightful. I know we have fun teasing about the way he embellishes, but he knows his stuff. There's a reason he's so successful, that's for sure. I don't know about the rest of you but spending this time focused on my book makes me realize how much I want to make changes in my life."

Lauren observes. "Okay, Francesca, that is at least the 2nd time I have heard you say that. Maybe you need to reshuffle the deck when you get home."

Francesca smiles. "Maybe I do. I'm really enjoying the writing process so much that it got me thinking, I won't have anywhere near this kind of time to write when I get home. The moment I step off the plane, I jump right back into the rat race. Roman is in college, but I still have my son Devon at home. As the head chef, my job is so demanding. I had to insinuate I would quit if I didn't get these 2 weeks off from work. My husband --- God knows I love him, but oh lord, he can be needy."

Lauren slips in. "Aren't they all?"

Francesca continues. "I think so! I don't know. We are just so busy. His job is also demanding. It's a lot. Between our mortgage and Roman's college tuition, then, Devon isn't far behind so it's not like I can just quit my job."

"Maybe there's a happy medium between quitting and a lifestyle change," Lauren suggests.

"That's what my husband and I need to figure out." Francesca looks down, picks up a handful of rocky sand, and opens her fingers, allowing it to trickle through her fingers. It's obvious she has more to say. We wait for her to continue.

"You know. I own a lot of this. Wanting more. Needing more. I have always felt like I had something to prove. I've had to work harder than the next person. I pushed and pushed to get ahead. Maybe I pushed my husband, too. Is it awful to say I want to bury myself into a hole for the next six months and just write or sleep?"

"It's not at all awful. It's understandable. Maybe this is your 'aha' moment for you..." Suggests Lauren.

"Well, I know it's cliché, but things do happen for a reason. Maybe you're right," says Francesca.

Lauren explains. "You need to decide you don't have anything to prove to anyone. You have to live your life for you. Besides, you're a superstar with nothing to prove."

Francesca chuckles. "Thanks. You're giving me something to think about, Lauren."

Maura says. "Between my family and my patients, I'm right there with ya. Where am I going to find more time? I'm a runner, and that's time consumable but a non-negotiable for my mental health."

"Not to brag, ladies, I'm almost divorced, my children are off at college, and I have a job I love, but as we have already discovered about me, who knows for how long. Well, it sounds like we are all figuring out how to return home better than when we arrived. I know keeping up with therapy will certainly be key for me since I have a history of reverting to unhealthy habits. Well, just ask my husband. He'll tell you all about it."

Lauren says. "Forget what he thinks! Sounds like you're doing great without him."

I share. "I listen to a really interesting podcast. They talk about re-imagining a path forward. We are accustomed to thinking our story is already written, but they say that there is no reason not to rewrite the next chapter of our life story no matter how old we are."

Francesca reacts. "Okay. I like that. 'Re-imagine' a path forward? I guess my husband and I need to put pencil to paper and figure out if we can make life changes. Francesca pauses. "I think I am just tired."

Maura says. "It's settled. We go home, we define our plan and rewrite our next chapter."

Lauren looks down as if she is contemplating whether to say something else. She lifts her head and slightly opens her mouth, but nothing comes out. Lauren holds back. It takes everything inside of me not to tell her to spit it out, but whatever she wants to say, it's obvious that she isn't ready to share...

~

"Francesca, I want to hear more about your book. Do you focus more on your family history or recipes?"

"I blend both throughout the book. I still have such a long way to go but the structure is coming together. Gianni has been helping me organize it."

I push further. "You have mentioned your Italian grandmother a few times. Does she play a significant role in the book?"

"She's very significant. My first chapter is about how my family got started in America, starting with my maternal grandmother. Maura, when you were talking about your grandmother, I thought about my own grandmother. She wasn't formally educated like your family, but my grandmother was also fierce. What a feisty, hardworking woman."

Maura smiles at the comparison. Francesca appears pensive when she continues.

"The other thing that made her uniquely special was her mentality. Back then, she would have been called 'forward thinking.' Her life perspective was ahead of her time, and she demonstrated that in her cooking, how she treated people and how she lived her life."

I add. "The concept of integrating family lore with family recipes sounds amazing."

"Hopefully, the reader will find the stories amusing. I hope it shines through that my grandmother was so cool. Not only was she passionate about cooking, but she had an understanding of how and why foods worked together. Because of her, I developed a true curiosity about herbs, spices and how flavors intertwine with one another." Francesca interlocks her fingers.

"When we cooked together, I asked what would happen if we added this or did some alternate process, and she would say I don't know. Let's give it a try. I came to understand there was a life metaphor...be open-minded, be curious, and be adventurous. When I started culinary school years later, I realized how much she taught me about food and cooking but also about life."

"How old were you when you started cooking?" I ask.

"Oh gosh, I would say I was five or six when we began cooking together. Our conversations would start out with something like…" heat the pan so it gets nice and hot before you throw in the garlic…" then she would transition to a family story or tell me how to stand up for myself.

Sometimes, she would just talk with me about something random like flowers...she loved flowers." After a brief pause, she continues. "Yeah, she really raised me during those early years. My mom...struggled at the time... My father was killed in a car accident when I was about a year old. Needless to say, I didn't exactly fit in well in our Brooklyn neighborhood in the 1960s and 1970s." Francesca pauses. Lauren, Maura and I awkwardly look away from Francesca, not knowing what we should say or even if we should say something.

"Yeah, she was something else. I didn't understand it at the time, but she empowered me and built up my confidence. Two main lessons I learned from her were to work hard and that nothing would be handed to me. In fact, it was understood I had to be even better than the other kids. She got it."

"Wow. She sounds amazing. She taught you amazing life lessons. What else is in the book?"

"I've got classic recipes from both sides of my family, some fusion creations, then there is an underlying theme focused on overcoming...what are we calling them this week...hurdles.

Apparently, it is not only a theme of my book, but it sounds like the official motto of our trip."

Chapter 30
Owes Me One

Day 5 - Amalfi Coast

Additional sun seekers begin to fill the beach. We enjoy a few final minutes while inhaling the subtle sea smell and enjoying the site of the gleaming blue sea water.

Maura asks. "Are classic southern Italian recipes included in your book?"

"Yes! That's what my grandmother taught me. Some recipes were based on what she called 'poor man's food' in Italy. Years later, those foods started popping up on Italian restaurant menus, and suddenly, they are high-end cuisine with inflated prices. I write about that in a humorous way. Well, I think it's funny."

"I know exactly what you mean. When did Polenta with roasted red peppers become high-end cuisine?" I ask. "Yeah, that was just how we ate when I was a kid.

"Right!" Francesca chuckles, smiling big. "Gnocchi is another one. The restaurant I owned several years ago became well known in Brooklyn because of my gnocchi, thanks in part to a food critic."

I blurt out. "Potato or ricotta cheese?"

Francesca quickly assures me. "Potatoes, of course. The only way to make 'um. I used to spruce up the gnocchi with a variety of sauces. Occasionally, I made a pumpkin or a sage version. But for the most part, I followed grandma's old-school recipe. Shortly after the restaurant opened, this critic ate there. He went crazy for my gnocchi with my tomato sauce that had cream, spinach and pine nuts. At the end of the night, he asked to meet the chef. I walked out of the kitchen, he took one look at me, and I could just see the shock in his eyes. I was not unfamiliar with that look when someone realized I was a chef who specialized in Italian food. He didn't expect to see a black woman standing before him. We talked for a while, and he was truly fascinated with my back story. He wrote a fabulous review about my restaurant, and we have remained friends. But what impacted me was his genuine interest in my story; that was when I decided that one day, I would write a book."

~

We trudge back up the 300 steps to join our group for an afternoon writing session. As if we are on a planned cruise excursion, our group is ushered onto our bus and driven through the now familiar winding Amalfi Coast roads. We reach the port and then board 2 dinghies for a short ride through gentle waves to a 75-foot yacht. Gianni, standing barefoot on the bow, the wind blowing through his wavy hair, casually dressed in cuffed, white linen pants, an untucked long shirt, sleeves rolled up his forearm, welcomes us on the yacht. He looks even more handsome than when we left him the night before.

"Now you know why I didn't sleep in the hotel last night. Someone had to try out the yacht to make sure it would be acceptable for you all."

"Poor, poor Gianni takin' one for the team." Muses Dan.

We are in awe as our heads bounce from left to right, taking in every detail of the wealthy man's Mediterranean toy.

Diane suggests. "I know you want us to be inspired, Gianni, but how do you expect us to focus? This is unbelievable."

Margaret throws her arms open. "Look at this place. Now I get how our money for this tour has been spent."

We all laugh at her jab at Gianni made in jest as we walk through glass doors into the front room. We peer out the wall of windows, and then each of us sinks into luxurious leather chairs.

Beautiful artwork hangs on the walls opposite the enormous windows. Gianni directs us to look back to the coast.

"Do you see just over that blue-topped roof back to the right? That is where we were in Minori, and you can almost follow with your eyes down the Path of Lemons. Adolfo challenged you all to hike one day."

Lauren recalls. "Oh yeah, that will forever be my drunken lemon villa."

Francesca smiles and warmly reaches out to grab Lauren's hand. We dart from the bow of the yacht to the stern to take in every inch of the coast, more like eager 4th graders on a class trip than adult author hopefuls in a writing class.

"I'm so glad you're all enthralled by the yacht. A dear friend of mine has allowed us to enjoy it for the rest of the day and early evening. Let's just say this CEO and I have done business in the past and he owes me one." He pokes fun back at Margaret. "So, Margaret, yes, money has been wasted on adventures, but this isn't one of them."

"I wouldn't care if I did pay for this. It would be money well spent." Margaret responds.

Who in the world is this CEO, and why is he indebted to Gianni? If Gianni hasn't yet written a memoir, he needs to. He pushes perfectly polished teak doors open into a conference room where a scrumptious food display has been provided for us.

"Please help yourself before we get started. One more surprise awaits us."

After each of us pile our plate high with a variety of meats and cheeses, bread, fruit salads and gorgeous desserts, Gianni announces.

"Let's give a warm welcome to our latest special guest. We are fortunate to have the talented and amazing author Rebecca Chadsworth with us today. Many of you might be familiar with her work. Rebecca is from Massachusetts and calls Sorrento, right here on the Amalfi Coast, her home three months out of the year. She has had many best-selling crime thrillers. Her dramatic plot twists captivate readers, who hang on every turn until the very last word. Because of her many years as a criminal attorney, she realistically describes crime scenes and legal proceedings. Rebecca is a bit of a local celebrity, too. She includes Amalfi Coast subplots in some of her novels. Everyone gets excited to see their hometown in a book. Who knows, maybe something from this tour might end up in a novel someday. Wouldn't that be intriguing?"

Laura leans in and looks at me then Gianni. She then whispers to me. "My imagination is running wild with the subplot." I smile back at her.

I'm not sure how or when she slipped in, but standing in the back of the room, Rebecca smiles big, listening to Gianni boast about her. Did she spend all night with Gianni, or did she board the boat just before us? I recognize how ridiculous it is that I'm jealous of this woman whom I didn't even know existed until two minutes ago.

"Rebecca, come up here and lead today's session."

Dressed in khaki slacks, a black V-neck t-shirt and white sketcher sneakers, she has a hop in her step as she walks to the head of the conference table as the nine of us sit comfortably on brown, leather swivel seats. Athletic in her strut, Rebecca exudes an enviable level of confidence. She wastes no time on niceties.

"Information plot dumps...they lead to the death of any well-developed storyline."

Like a highly skilled litigator, she begins speaking with her fingers cupped in front of her body, and then she separates them to act out dropping piles.

"When you unleash your plot to the reader, imagine letting go of breadcrumbs along a path rather than dumping an entire loaf of focaccia for a flock of birds. Mastering that timing is an art. Many of us struggle to find the proper balance between giving the reader enough red meat to chew to hold their interest without over-saturating the reader with superfluous information. What I want you to do today is look through your book and find segments of writing where you drone on and on but say nothing to move your story forward."

She uses her finger in a forward-spinning motion to emphasize her point. "Let's get rid of those dumps and transition them into lively conversation exchanges or find ways to disclose pertinent information in smaller chunks throughout your book. In some cases, delete altogether. How many of you attempt to purge your closet, and you can't get rid of your favorite trousers because you are convinced they will fit again or come back in style?"

Several hands go up, including mine.

"Puffy shoulder pads are gone. Leave them in the 80's. Let them go. I remember my courtroom power suits all too well. Gone. All of them, I'm pleased to report." Looking at one another and nodding, we laugh at her relatable reference.

"You might struggle at first, but trust me. Hitting delete is often the best remedy for irrelevant filler paragraphs. Like those pants that are now a little snug, once you purge your paragraphs, you won't even miss them."

Rebecca raises two fingers high above her head. "The second technique you should implement is "show, not tell. We don't want to tell...tell...tell...Let your words describe your character's action and let the reader use their imagination. For example, don't tell us, "Gianni is a nervous guy."

We all laugh at her example, knowing it is the farthest thing from the truth.

"Who wants to take a shot? Give us an example showing us that Gianni is riddled with anxiety instead of telling us he is a nervous fellow."

Silence fills the room. Heads ever so slightly turn towards

me. An adrenaline rush flushes over me, and I take the bait, completely aware that I might regret the decision.

"I'll go."

"Fantastic. What's your name?"

"Steph...Stephanie. My name is Stephanie."

"Okay, Stephanie. Let's hear it."

"Gianni's hand drips with sweat. It's shaking like a buz, no a rattlesnake. He takes a deep breath, then slowly extends it and delicately grabs Lenora's hand for the first time."

"Perfect example. Round of applause."

I receive an exaggerated applause for minimal effort. She smirks and turns her head to look directly at Gianni.

"I imagined you to be smooth with the ladies but what do I know?" Looking back at us rocking in our comfy leather chairs, she continues.

"If I were to read that passage, it would be irrefutable that Gianni is nervous with the ladies, but Stephanie never used the word. What she did sparked my curiosity. I want to know more about the story."

Dan pipes up. "Trust me...we all do." The entire class erupts into laughter. Gianni stands confidently in the corner, arms crossed, grinning ear to ear. Rebecca looks around the room, confused, as she realizes she has walked into a subplot in the making.

"Any good author knows when it is time to move on. I sense that is exactly what I need to do." Lauren whispers directly in my ear. "You are feeling naughty today."

"I read the room and gave the people what they wanted."

I feel a surge of excitement listening to Rebecca. After all, she's literally living my dream life. It's like I'm trying to capture her essence just by standing in the same room with her. Rebecca instructs our group about the power of dialogue, the proper use of an appropriately placed plot twist and how to dangle a carrot at the end of a chapter to keep the reader wanting more. She commands the conference room with her energy, her sophisticated wit and by individualizing the conversation to each of us. Rebecca concludes her mesmerizing presentation and then turns the conversation back to Gianni, who provides us with instructions for our next writing seminar.

"Please, feel free to stay here or find a private space anywhere on the yacht other than the bedrooms. Make yourself comfortable. We are all billionaire yacht owners for the day."

We all cheer, and Dan suggests. "Don't tell me that. Your CEO friend might need to evict me to get me off the boat…excuse me - yacht."

I gather my belongings and find a secluded location on an outside deck far from the conference room to enjoy a well-needed moment of solitude before I begin writing. Sitting on a deck chair overlooking the sea, the air wafts through my hair. A strand tickles my chin. I dig in my bag, find a scrunchie and pull my hair back. While soaking in the afternoon sun and absorbing the views, I'm relaxed by the sound of the sea swishing below me. I contemplate my afternoon writing approach. My last conversation with Gianni was more debilitating than motivating and I need to find clarity if I'm going to make progress. Following through and finishing the book is significant to the changes I'm making in my life. It might take months or even a year but if I don't finish, it would affirm that Michael has been right about me all along.

He never had confidence in my ability to follow through with what I started. I don't want to prove him right. Fuck him that his assessment of me occupies space in my brain. This is supposed to be about following my dream, not proving him wrong. I exhale big, then open my computer and place it on my lap. Just behind me, I hear the pattern of steps approaching me.

"There you are. May I join you?"

"Of course. Welcome to my office." I extend my arms towards the open sea. Gianni grabs a deck chair and then places it towards me.

"You created quite a stir in there."

I laugh in agreement. "Don't you love how I threw a fire stick and then got out of there as quickly as possible? I couldn't resist. I sensed it was what they wanted."

Are we dancing around the fact that it is confirmed there is a mutual attraction between us?

"Ahh, yes. The intuition of a professional storyteller." We sit in silence for a moment before I restart the conversation.

"Wow...Rebecca. She's amazing." I shyly look down as if my 'girl crush' is written all over my face. I look up at Gianni.

"Yes, yes. She's outstanding. Her schedule was so busy yesterday and this morning. We're lucky she squeezed us in today." I suddenly feel relieved to hear she didn't spend last night with him.

These feelings are taking on a life of its own. "I think she's my idol." I quietly admit.

"I thought you would all enjoy her. Why is your idol?"

"Oh, I don't know. She's a successful author living part of the year in Italy. Let's see. I love her confidence. Rebecca is who I aspire to be...when I grow up."

Gianni laughs. "Okay, so if that is your goal, make it happen. I realize you can't just snap your fingers, but think about putting steps in place to get there. Let's start with your book. How are you doing since our last conversation?"

I hesitate before I respond. "Making some headway with the storyline, but I'm struggling with filling in the details. It's not that...I'm by no means...I'm not blaming you, but I think you got in my head the last time we spoke."

"Hmm. How so?"

"I thought I was transparent in my writing. Apparently, I'm holding back. Your critique hit me personally. I spent nearly a year in therapy working on my mental health, and to hear that after all that work, I still have, I don't know, this blind spot...maybe I'm not as self-reflective as I thought. I just don't know where to go from here." I take a breath before finishing my thoughts, feeling embarrassed that I implied he is hindering and not helping my writing.

"Saying this out loud makes me realize I took your feedback personally, and I know that was not your intention."

Gianni gives me the space to finish my thoughts without interruption. "It's probably difficult for someone in your position to understand the battle some people endure when managing their mental health."

"Are you done? It appears that you have a lot going through your head right now. Don't let me stop you if you have more to get out."

"I really just dumped on you, didn't I? I'm so sorry. Wow. That was a lot. And yes, I'm done." "It's okay. Sometimes, you just need to let it all out." Gianni assures me.

"Well, I let it all out, then shoved it on you. My apologies."

"No need to apologize. Writing a book can have a huge emotional component to it. When you stir the pot, everything at the bottom bubbles to the top."

I nod in agreement, thinking about all the residue kicked up over the past year.

"First of all, I want to better understand how I threw you off your game so you can actively write more productively again. Secondly, Stephanie, you have me all wrong. Unfortunately, I am better acquainted with mental health challenges than you could imagine. Haven't you ever heard not to judge a book by its cover?"

Gianni leans in and rests his elbows on his knees. "Forgive

me if this sounds odd to you." Gianni looks as if he is reconsidering his next statement.

"Let me know if I am crossing any boundaries."

All I could think is oh God, please. Cross boundaries. I'm embarrassed by my quiet thoughts and hope that in addition to everything else amazing about him, Gianni doesn't also have the ability to read minds.

"When you submitted your bio and your writing sample at the time of registering for the tour, there was something in your voice that resonated with me."

I do a quick data search of my brain and can't even begin to imagine how Gianni, given all his successes and charitable endeavors, finds any connection to me or my writing. What the hell is he thinking? I wait. He swallows big, then takes a breath.

"I was once married. My wife and I had two beautiful children together." He pauses and smiles before continuing.

"Alessandro, named after my father. Americans have juniors, but we name our sons after paternal grandfathers." I smile warmly back at him, sensing how proud he is of speaking about his children.

"Then there is my amazing, smart and beautiful daughter, Giorgi; she is my heart." Gianni places his right hand on his heart and presses it tightly with his left hand.

"My son, Alessandro, was sensitive, even as a child. In many ways, he was like me."

He lets out a nervous laugh as his voice elevates. "But a far superior version of me. You couldn't find a more kindhearted and loving soul. He became a vegetarian when he was eight years old because he couldn't bear the thought of eating animals."

Gianni emphasizes. "Eight years old!! Ale...we called him Ale...was a poet, a painter, a sculptor." Gianni extends his hands, palm up. "He had these magical hands full of talent. His work was just so profound, especially for a young man."

Gianni is talking about Ale in the past tense. My heart sinks.

"Ale always poured his emotion into his work, and the results were tremendous. When it was time for university, he wanted to study in England, and I encouraged him the move to London. My wife was adamantly against it. She didn't believe he had the emotional maturity to live so far away. There's certainly no shortage of art schools in Italy. He could have lived with us and studied locally. But I thought starting over somewhere else could be a fresh start for him. He never had many friends. I told my wife…my ex-wife, if he was surrounded by other artists, he would socially thrive. I pushed and pushed until she caved. I felt like her apprehension was more about holding on to her son, you know, like typical Italian moms. I won…We…No, I sent him."

"You did what you thought was best for Ale. That's all any of us do. Make decisions that we believe are in our kids' best interest."

Gianni's level of emotion elevates. "That's true, but my job should have been to protect my child despite what he said he wanted."

Pointing to his temple, he continues. "In my head, I was imposing my personality on him. He was sensitive like me, creative like me but not social or strong."

Gianni takes a deep breath. I see the pride wrapped in pain all over his face, just talking about his son. It's his turn to get it all out. We sit in silence until he's ready to continue.

"My ex-wife, Silva, and I flew with him to London and got him settled in his apartment. We stayed a few days to help him move in, probably like your experience taking your girls to university for the first time."

I kindly smile in agreement, even though that was a traumatic weekend that will always represent the beginning of the end of my marriage.

"It was finally time for us to leave. I gave him the biggest hug and kiss. I grabbed his head...I could still feel his hair in my hands."

Gianni extends his two large hands, with his fingers spread wide as if he could still reach out and hold on to the locks of his son's hair.

"I stared into his gorgeous, gray eyes and said figlio, ti amo. Son, I love you. I told him, you got this. I told him how much I believed in him. His eyes were so piercing, yet...pained. It was as if they were saying, 'Don't leave me - take me home with you.' Silva and I turned and walked away. My heart, you know, just dropped like it's difficult to describe the sensation that rushed through my blood. I just knew my wife was right. I have replayed the moment in my head so many times. Why didn't I say no! This is a mistake. Why, at that moment, was I too weak to reverse course and insist he return home with us? A week later, we got a call from a hospital in London. My beautiful, sweet boy was gone. He succumbed to the pressure of distance, the emptiness of loneliness, his struggles with mental health and maybe even shame. His mental health was more fragile than I knew. Silva knew and I didn't listen to her. I wasn't hearing her concerns."

My internal voice says a mother always knows her child. Of course, I would never reveal that thought. It isn't that Gianni is to blame for his son's death, but I could understand why he feels like he bears responsibility. Oh God. I feel sick to myself. To think, I told Gianni he knows nothing about mental health, and his son died, literally because of his battle managing mental well-being.

"All I could think was that it was my fault he was dead."

Gianni's eyes well up with tears. I struggle to control my emotions and fight back tears. I reach out and hold his trembling hands. His pain is palpable. It's as if he just learned of his son's passing yesterday. I can't even imagine how tormented he must feel. Since the first day of the tour, Gianni lights up every room he enters, confidently commanding our attention whenever he speaks. Who knew it's been a façade? How stressful it must be to paint a perpetual happy face for all of us. Today, he reveals himself as a broken man, riddled with guilt. His stature suddenly appears more diminished. The twinkle in his eyes I have grown accustomed to seems dim.

I continue holding his hands.

"Gianni, I am so deeply sorry for the loss of your son. I can't even begin to imagine how devastating that must have been for you, for Silva and your daughter Giorgi. I also owe you a huge apology. I feel so stupid for making the assumption that you know nothing about mental health challenges. How naïve of me to think I could judge you or…or…easily sum up your life experiences based on the charismatic, upbeat personality you have shown to us."

Oh God. Did I say that out loud? I might as well have used words like hot and sexy.

"Please. Don't apologize. I realize how I project myself to others. The pain is something I live with every day, but I have learned to push forward. My son is my very first thought every morning, and before I shut my eyes at night, he is my last thought. I'm aware that I mask that pain publicly and only allow people to see what I want them to see. Maybe it's my way of coping."

I'm just devastated for Gianni listening to his revelation. It's a challenge to process his every word.

"I imagine you're wondering how to connect the dots between my son, his death and your writing." I don't know how to respond, but he's right. I am curious. After what he just shared with me about Ale, I certainly wouldn't ask. There's nothing in my life that brings me more joy and pride than my girls. Although I've had my share of life impediments, I know nothing of the despair that he lives with every day. I struggle to imagine how my writing intersects with his family's tragedy.

"Ale died in 2014, and I plunged into the deepest, darkest place imaginable. I couldn't even look into my wife Silva's eyes after his passing. It was as if she looked at me with such contempt.

She never said she blamed me for his death; she didn't have to. I blamed myself. Neither of us could imagine remaining together and moving on as a couple. I lost the love of my life in addition to my son. The pain of losing him is overwhelming, but the guilt that I contributed to his death is heart-wrenching." Gianni sits back in his chair. Our hands slowly release from one another.

"Silva and I dissolved our marriage. At the time, we owned several apartments in Rome. I moved into one of them and sat there, immobile, day after day, alone and full of despair. I'm fortunate enough to have wonderful friends and family, and I, too, started seeing a great therapist." For the first time since he started talking about Ale, he responds with a warm smile. "Over the past four years, I have been digging out of that dark hole. Initially, I couldn't get out of bed. I then managed short walks, which led to occasional good days. It has been a work in progress, but little by little, I have learned to cope."

He pauses, turns his head to the left staring out into the sea of blue. We sit in silence as he stares. His eyes, normally lighting up every room, look vacant. The sun bears down on his fine lines and wrinkles. I had never before noticed such lines. He looks back at me and continues.

"About a year after Ali's death, an old friend from my days as a political speech writer invited me out for coffee. We began chatting about the arts, the need for additional funding for programs, and how immersing yourself in a creative outlet is often a significant part of either healing or finding hope. At the time, there was a surge of refugees throughout Europe who needed support on every level. A lightbulb went off in my head. I thought, what better way could there be to honor my son than by helping people heal through the arts. After extensive research and fundraising, *Centro de Arte y Sanación de Ale* opened its doors in Rome."

"Ale's Art and Healing Center. How beautiful."

Gianni talked about his charitable work, including an art center, during our orientation in that Roman hotel but I never imagined it emerged from such tragedy.

"Thank you. We offer all sorts of instruction in multiple forms of art or just a safe place for someone to work on their art of choice. Our doors welcome anyone who wants to be creative. Clients pay almost nothing and receive not only a beautiful, comfortable place to gather, but we provide supplies and volunteers who provide instruction. The generosity of people is simply amazing. Our clients tell us they feel safe and respected when they visit the center. Nobody judges them. It is easy for people who are either impoverished or new to a country to feel invisible...disposable...as if no one cares about them. I want them to know they are loved and that their contribution matters. They matter."

"Gives me the chills," I say as I grab my left arm with my right hand.

Gianni continues. "Not only is it therapeutic for our guests, but it has also been life-changing for me. I would say, critical to my healing process."

"There is such a huge personal return on investing in others. You and your volunteers are doing amazing work. Speaking of investing, how is the center funded?"

"My own money, for starters. Fortunately, I had the capital to build out the building and get the lights turned on. You know what I mean?"

He asks rhetorically, then he chuckles before I can even acknowledge him.

"I hit up many of my rich friends and the support from them is truly remarkable. Plus, metaphorically speaking, I'm not afraid to remind some of my old buddies that I know where the bodies are buried, if you get my drift."

"That's one way to get friends to open their wallets. In any case, I'm sure when you turn on the charm, the euros come rolling in." I suggest.

"Well, humbly speaking, I do have the power of persuasion."

"Humbly indeed," I quip.

We enjoy a much-needed moment of levity.

"Honestly, the fundraising never ends. It takes a lot of money to keep the center not only open but thriving. In addition to going out hat in hand, we had our first annual gala, where people got all dressed up and paid way too much money for mediocre food. I have negotiated favorable rental credits with the city of Rome. You know, every bit helps."

"It sounds like the need is endless, and you are doing everything you can to keep the center active.

"It is. It is. Silva and I have also begun rebuilding a relationship with each other. She has moved on with a new man. I like the guy. I'm relieved she isn't alone. She loves volunteering at the center with the small children." He smiles warmly, talking about Silva. What a tragic love story. He cares about her so much but recognizes there is no path forward for them. If it weren't so disheartening, it would be beautiful.

"My daughter is an interior designer. She has created a beautiful layout and lots of comfortable spaces for our visitors, oh, and she is my sidekick in fundraising. Donors are like putty in her hands. Not only is Giorgi beautiful and smart, but she is also so charismatic."

"Really...where does she get that trait?"

Oozing with pride when talking about Giorgi, for a moment, he reveals a spark of the man I had come to know.

"I'm always thinking of additional fundraising opportunities. If this book writing tour ever makes any money, I would gladly donate the profits."

We both let out a hearty laugh.

"Like you said, nothing feels as good as giving to others. I'm a much better man today than I was four years ago. Ale would be so proud of who I am becoming. He has inspired me to be ... more like him. Supporting underserved populations would be right up his alley. It's sad that his death had to be the catalyst. Ya know. I'm going to be honest with you, Stephanie."

My heart skips a beat when he says my name.

"I can see now how self-absorbed I used to be. I was so intoxicated with my own image and my success. Ale loved me. I know he did, but he didn't like that side of me. He was always so wise beyond his years. Oro Zecchino. Pure gold. I have changed since his death. It sometimes horrifies me to think what a pompous ass I could be at times."

"I have a feeling he knows exactly who you have become. Besides, if it makes you feel any better, I can't even comprehend you and pompous ass in the same sentence."

"Thank you. That does. I pray to God you're right, and he is somewhere proud of me."

"You give so much of yourself to the center. Why do you even bother with the book tour, if you don't mind me asking?"

"Yes, yes, of course." He smiles and then continues. "Why would I torture myself with such an undertaking?"

"Exactly. Nine amateur nuisances."

"So before my son..." Gianni clears his throat. "When Ale was alive, writing was my art. It was like breathing to me. I never ran out of ideas. I would stop in a corner grocery store and come out with characters popping in my head."

Gianni extends one hand then his other from his head.

"When Ale died, my imagination died with him. My brain was suddenly a blank slate. I felt like if he couldn't perform his art, why should I have the pleasure of performing mine."

"There is that guilt creeping up again," I tell Gianni.

"Exactly. It's debilitating. When I started getting back on my feet, I began working on opening the art center, yet I still had no vision when it came to writing."

I suddenly recall how uncomfortable Gianni appeared the first day in Rome when Dan asked a perfectly reasonable question about the book he is currently writing. Gianni's awkward response now makes sense to me. The question took him back to that dark place, remembering why he no longer writes.

"One day, Giorgi suggested that I teach a writing class. It's funny how life changes you. I used to think I was troppo importante, troppo significativo to teach a writing class. I was too good for that. You know. Someone like me teach amateurs? No offense, by the way. See what I am saying, though?"

"No offense taken. You had a bit of an ego. I get it. As they say, you believed your own publicity."

Gianni smiles. "To say the least. I'm not proud of that now, but I was arrogant. That's part of who I was back then."

Gianni is a man who has gone through a metamorphosis in response to a trauma. I relate to the process. I have become honest with who I am, and I'm working towards becoming a better version of myself. While his trauma is beyond my comprehension, the process is the same. I'm beginning to see a potential connection? Maybe? It's a stretch but is that the connection between us he is referring to?

"Giorgi reminded me one day how much pride I have in Italy, the beauty, and the culture. Why not combine my love for writing with the love I have for my country? That is the genesis behind Write Italia. She thought it would be a win-win. I could help others write, and maybe I would be inspired to start writing again."

"Is it working?" I ask.

"I guess it's too soon to say. I mean, I haven't begun writing again. I'm still a blank slate. But ya know, I feel fulfilled helping at the art center, and so far, I'm enjoying the writing tour. It's the first tour, so we'll see. My hope is that I will return to writing, but I'm content with what I am currently doing."

"There are nine people sitting on this insane mega-yacht who think it's been a huge success." We sit calmly in silence, gazing outward at the slight rumble of the waves.

"My apologies. I digressed again…connecting dots. Stephanie, when you submitted your bio and your writing sample, you were so transparent. Your writing was raw...exposed. It was real. You mentioned that you took creative writing classes?"

I respond, almost embarrassed about my low-level training relative to his great successes. I tried to remember what I had said about my previous instruction, hoping I didn't make it sound like some extensive writing course.

"Oh gosh. Nothing big." I flip my hand. "I've taken a few writing clinics over the years. Ya know…here and there. I also read a lot." Ugh. I sound like such an amateur. I read books on how to write. Wallah! I'm an author. Can I possibly sound any more ridiculous than I do right now?

"For sure. When people ask me how to become a writer, I tell them to read. You are quite good. Really."

I struggle so much with self-doubt that it's painful to hear his flattery. I don't know if I even believe him. "Then...thank you."

"You have a knack for telling a good story. Some of your structuring needs work. Your tenses sometimes don't align. We want to look at some of the plot dumps Rebecca talked about, but overall, nothing a good editor can't fix. You have an appealing writing style. However, your original registration submission was very honest. Many of your colleagues were very guarded when they submitted their bios. I get it. Who is this guy wanting me to reveal personal information?"

We both laugh.

"You…You were different. I was immediately engrossed in what you wrote. Before you and your group arrived, I thought, "I want to know more about her."

"I don't know what to say. I never really thought of my personal story as being of interest, especially to someone like you, given your life experiences."

"Well, on the contrary, when I read your bio, I found the combination of your writing skills and your vulnerability to be quite intriguing. Since you arrived, what you have written so far is witty, introspective, and well-crafted. However, as you continue to write, you are becoming more guarded than your original submissions. Your story is progressing well, but look back at your original submission when you registered for the writing tour and tell me if you see what I mean.

In the short time I have known you, I sense...I could be wrong… that you are still wrestling with something that holds you back.

Gianni leans forwards. "I connect with your struggle with guilt. You now understand why. I want to see that same rawness, that same honesty from your characters. Let it hurt when you write. You have earned the right to be successful, to win, to not be invisible. I know my situation is more severe, but we both are working on giving ourselves permission to be free of our past and to be happy."

I sit there, silent. It's as if Gianni had been a fly on the wall in my therapy sessions this past year. It seems like I continue to wear my ongoing turmoil on my sleeve, and Gianni picked up on it. I think about what Maura said about therapy; it isn't linear. I have made progress, but I still have work to do...and that is okay.

"That is a lot to take in. I think when I wrote my bio and writing sample, I was deep into my therapy, and I just put it all out there."

"That makes sense. You were open and transparent in your therapy sessions."

"I want to be successful. I don't want to, you know, inhibit my success because of guilt or fear. I thought I had unpacked all this with my therapist. Maybe I am stuffing it back into my suitcase."

"Now that's a good visual. Pull it all out of the suitcase…the pants, your blouses, and shoes…you love your shoes."

We both smile.

"Live with the mess. Life is messy, but it is also full of lessons if we allow ourselves to learn. I hope I'm not too off base. I'm supposed to be your writing coach, not your therapist."

We both laugh but I was literally feeling like I was sitting in a therapy session. "I was about to ask you for a bill. I forgot for a second where I was."

Gianni says, "I know. I know. I sound a little like both. Strictly looking from a writing perspective, be honest with your feelings, find those old habits, those triggers and allow them to hang out with your consciousness. I'm not saying it in an unhealthy way, of course. I don't want to get an angry email from your therapist. I just mean from an awareness perspective. Trust me, it is not easy to hold on to those rough edges. It hurts a little, am I right?"

I nod in agreement. I'm so lost in Gianni's every word I would have agreed to anything, "However, I personally believe it will not only release your writing, but it will be good for you in the long run. Come to think of it. You're right. Maybe I should give you a bill for my therapy services."

"I can't afford any more of your bills."

"Touché. Touché."

This is all so surreal. I am sitting on the deck of a mega yacht in the Tyrrhenian Sea with an accomplished author as we dig deep into our most intimate thoughts. I think to myself, 'How did I get here?' It dawns on me that Gianni and I are tormented souls battling to maintain internal peace, oddly enough, in similar ways. I would have never imagined we had anything in common when I met him the first day of our tour. We sit in silence.

"Well, what can you do? Keep on going, right?"

I smile in acknowledgment. Gianni stands up, grabs the railing and walks away. Moments later, I walk back to the conference room and finish the session with my writing colleagues. After our session wraps up, we enjoy our sunset cocktail, return to port on the dinghies then jump on our tour bus for the drive back to the hotel. I'm not only physically worn out after our walk up and down to the beach earlier in the day, but I am also emotionally exhausted. I return to my room, drop my computer bag in the corner of the room then I plop myself on the end of my bed. I reflect on my earlier conversation with Gianni, take a long, deep breath and pull out my phone.

"Hey, Steph. How are you?"

Chapter 31
Revisit the Past

Day 5 - Amalfi Coast

It's time to initiate a long overdue conversation. Gianni's right. Despite multiple months of therapy, something still weighs heavy on my heart. As a witness to the abuse my brother Anthony endured, I was a bystander who did nothing to interfere. I get it. I do now. I was just a kid. I just need to close that door with my brother.

We've talked with one another about our father throughout our lives, but I never acknowledged to him the guilt I have always felt about how I was treated compared to the abuse he endured. Anthony spent his early 20s processing the abuse inflicted upon him and struggled to overcome his own addictions. To his credit, unlike our father, Anthony entered recovery and took control of his life. He figured his shit out.

Here I am, well beyond the mid-life marker, sitting in a hotel room on the Amalfi Coast, and I can't imagine letting another hour pass without having a conversation I avoided for over 40 years. Gianni struck a nerve, suggesting something still holds me back. I have no illusion that one productive talk with Anthony will be a life-changing event but it's another important step on the trail leading to my mental well-being.

"Is everything okay, Stephanie? I know how exciting it is to talk to me, but I didn't expect to hear from you until you got home."

"I need a moment to gather my thoughts."

"Stephanie, you are scaring me. Is everything okay?"

I assure him. "Yes. I'm fine. I have a question, though. Do you remember when we were kids? I was about 7, so you must have been nine or ten years old, and mom and dad had this huge fight." Anthony chides. "Yeah, sure. Sounds like a Tuesday. Go on."

I laugh. "You're funny. I suppose I should be more specific. Those two fought all the time. Okay. So this particular night, who knows why Dad was yelling."

I took an uncomfortable pause before calling out the obvious.

"Yeah, like he did all the time. Go on." Anthony encourages me.

"You were playing with your racetrack and cars. You loved that racetrack."

"I do remember that racetrack. One of my favorites when I was a kid. What about it?"

"Well, they were screaming and yelling, and Dad's temper escalated. He then...He threw you against the wall, then broke your car track."

Anthony pauses to try and remember. "That sounds familiar, but why are you bringing all of this up now?"

"I remember that night so vividly because after he screamed at Mom, got violent with you, and then broke your racetrack, Dad and I went out for ice cream. You and I had this long gaze before I ran out the door with him. This has stuck with me my entire life. I could never shake that feeling that I betrayed you and mom. I mean not just that night, but I never stuck up for either of you."

Anthony takes a deep breath.

"Damn, Steph. I don't know what to say. You are calling me from Italy, 45 years after the fact, so I can absolve you of the sin of going out for ice cream with our horrible father? Since you are quite literally in the land of Catholicism, do three Hail Marys and two Our Fathers, and then you will be absolved of your sins."

We both laugh. "Come on, Stephanie. I don't want to minimize how you feel but I wish you would have found the time over the past 45 years to talk with me about this. Have you been lugging this painful memory about me on your back all these years because I barely remember it? Dad was often an abusive prick. He yelled, he hit me, he tormented Mom, he broke things...the specific events are a blur to me at this point. Maybe I blocked a lot of it out. Either way, we were all victims of his behavior, and you were not responsible for any of it."

"Yeah, that's what I've been hearing, so why do I feel so guilty?"

"Would you ever put that responsibility on Sienna or Livie? I wouldn't do that to AJ or Nicolette. Dad was a sick, abusive alcoholic who hated himself and took it out on his family. I have long since let go of the trauma. It is time for you to do the same."

"I guess I needed to hear that from you. Intellectually, I know you are right. I have struggled to shake this feeling all these years."

"Come to think of it. There is one thing you can do for me to make everything better." "What?"

"Italian leather...I have a vision of myself in a beautiful, soft leather, brown jacket this winter." "Goodbye, Anthony. It's been good talking to you."

"I guess that's a no? Call me when you get home. We can talk more. But seriously. Let it go. Trust me when I tell you. If you hold on to it, there is only one person it destroys."

While I never believed Anthony had animosity towards me, I'm surprised to hear he barely remembers an event that has been chiseled in my brain. I regret not having this conversation with him sooner.

I retrieve my bag from the corner of the room and pull out my computer. I jump back on the bed and prop the pillows behind my back.

"Plot dumps. Rebecca said we all have them..."

Chapter 32
Safe Zone

Day 5 - Amalfi Coast

"With every destination, I have a new favorite place. The Amalfi Coast is just spectacular." Francesca says as she picks up her wine and takes a sip. Sitting on the small, stone hotel patio at one of the three wrought iron tables overlooking the moonlit sea, we celebrate our final night on the seaside coast region.

Rather than another dinner out, the four of us opted for comfy clothes, a charcuterie spread, Pellegrino water, wine, and desserts. "Amalfi is amazing, but tomorrow, Tuscany - I know that will be the best part of the trip." Lauren exuberantly promises, reminding us once again that she has high expectations for the Tuscan villa and Florence city tour.

Scooping up fresh mozzarella and tomato with a crusty edge of bread, Maura asks. "Stephanie, you disappeared on the yacht today. Did you get a lot of writing done?"

I won't share the details of my private conversation with Gianni. His story isn't my tale to tell. Gianni's loss and enduring grief have been on my mind since our conversation earlier in the day. I attempt to redirect the conversation so as not to blurt out something he told me in confidence.

"I got lost in my plot dumps and ended up having one of my best days of writing since we got here. Wasn't Rebecca fabulous?" That's not a complete lie. I must have felt liberated after my conversation with Anthony. Once I started typing, the words tumbled across my laptop screen.

Before I knew it, I knocked out two chapters. I want to talk more with Anthony when I get home, but I feel so much better after just one open and honest conversation with him.

"Good for you! Yeah, Rebecca's a cool lady. Oh, and your little display about Gianni being nervous with the ladies got everyone talking. You were up to no good," says Francesca.

"Lauren, what did you say?"

We both yell 'naughty' simultaneously. The four of us laugh.

"Maybe it was Rebecca's energy level. She really got me going, too. I dug into family dynamics from my childhood," Maura says.

"Maura, your family history is always so interesting. What did you come up with?"

"Few things. Growing up as an Italian Jew, I never felt like I fit into any one group. Most American Jews are Ashkenazi – ya know, Polish and Eastern European. I grew up with lots of Italians, but they were traditional Italian Catholics. When I was a kid, all this stuff mattered, ya know? We didn't share the same religion or celebrate the same holidays. Then there were my parents and grandparents. They didn't trust Catholic Italians because a lot of them supported Mussolini. My grandmother always told me not to tell anyone I was Jewish. I had an identity crisis, not knowing where I fit in. I questioned where I belonged and who I should or shouldn't trust. It was all so isolating." Maura shakes her head as if she is once again that lonely child. "I know my family was responding to their experiences, but it was tough growing up with that negativity. On top of all that, I was naturally awkward." She pauses and then makes a self-deprecating joke. "I obviously grew out of that."

Francesca bends her head, looks at Maura, and says, "Obviously."

An attractive middle-aged couple holding hands pass behind me. I scoot my chair in for them to get by. My gaze follows them to their table. The man pulls the chair out for who I assume to be his wife. She looks over her shoulder and smiles at him as he pushes her chair in. They look like they are in love. Are they empty nesters on a romantic getaway, or are they new lovers enjoying a 2nd act?

"Did you ever talk with your parents about how you felt?" Asks Francesca.

I'm jolted back to our conversation after briefly losing myself in a couple who represent what I won't get to enjoy as I age.

"Tell my parents? God no. One of the many struggles of being raised by a holocaust survivor - my mom, especially, didn't have much empathy for my brother and me when we weren't happy or didn't feel well. We were reminded regularly how my family left everything behind and risked their lives to escape fascism. We needed to be appreciative of how easy we had it."

"What a burden for children to carry. Who did you turn to when you needed comfort?" asks Lauren.

"No one. We kept everything bottled up inside. When my brother was, oh, I'd say, 12 years old, he had appendicitis but waited until he was doubled over, reeling in pain before he told my parents. We laugh about it now, but it was no joke. He was so conditioned not to complain that he was curled up in a ball on the floor. When his doctor performed an emergency appendectomy, his appendix was close to bursting."

"Oh, that's pretty intense…" says Francesca. "Yeah. Tell me about it. I hate to complain, but…"

I interrupt. "Go ahead. This is a safe zone for registering complaints."

Maura laughs and continues, "Alright, I will enjoy complaining and sharing that it did affect me. God, it's no wonder I have always been riddled with anxiety. Part of that stems from burying my feelings my whole life. Obviously, I've talked with my therapist for years about all of this, but even to this day, I'm programmed to plow forward and just deal with pain or a bad day. You can only push down all that junk so much before it bubbles to the top. In my case, it manifests in all of my quirks. I spent my childhood and into adulthood pushing ahead. I put my head down, did my work, and hoped no one noticed me."

Maura pours the bubbly water for herself and for Lauren. They each quickly gulp the water, place their glasses back down, and Maura refills them.

"You know, Maura, I totally get what you're saying about not knowing where you fit in. As a black girl in the 70's and 80's in a mostly white neighborhood, I dealt with a lot of racism from a young age. Did I fit in with the black kids, with the white kids, neither? Like you, I responded by working hard. I was probably more outgoing than you and not exactly someone people wouldn't notice, so all that was maybe a little easier for me."

I turn my head to my right and catch a glimpse of Mr. and Mrs. Perfect enjoying their wine, talking and laughing with each other.

Maura ponders. "I don't know which was harder, your situation or mine. I could just melt into the background without drawing attention to myself. You couldn't do that."

"Either way, everyone wants to fit in, and it sounds like we both looked for a soft-landing spot," says Francesca. "My grandmother pushed me to be strong. She wasn't even black, yet somehow, she understood that I would have to work harder for the same opportunities, and when I did succeed, my success might be questioned. I outworked others to prove my worth, and that drive stuck with me my whole career, to a fault, I might add."

Lauren reminds Francesca. "And now you know you have nothing to prove. When you go home, you're going to make life changes. There's nothing more important than inner peace and happiness."

~

"So, was your mom out of the picture throughout the early part of your childhood?"

That's one way to get to the point. Francesca speaks highly about her Italian grandmother but hasn't mentioned her parents. I'm curious, too, but I hadn't planned on such a direct approach as Lauren has taken. Francesca doesn't miss a beat.

Francesca asks in jest. "Promise you will still buy the book if I give you all of my life, juicy details."

She then tells us about her that her parents met in college. Her father moved from Ghana to New York to study engineering. Francesca explains that they were so different from one another, and she could never understand how they got together. Growing up, she was told he walked around with a huge pile of books under his arm, opting for the library rather than parties. Her mom was more likely to be found tripping on shrooms at a festival than at a library, studying. I think about how different Michael and I were. They say opposites attract, but I'm not so sure they make strong, sustainable couples.

Francesca further explains. "To my mother's credit, she was active in the civil rights movement. "If you meet her one day, she will tell you all about it. Trust me."

I reach in for a slice of prosciutto, a thick chunk of parmesan cheese and a slice of bread. It has a chain reaction. Maura and Lauren spoon some olives and cheese onto their plates as Francesca continues. "But their relationship somehow worked, according to my mother and grandmother, despite the challenges they faced as a bi-racial couple. My parents were well accepted in my mother's free love, party crowd but outside of that, their relationship was mostly taboo."

"Could you imagine - that must have been so hard in the 60's," I suggest rhetorically.

"They didn't care. My parents were in love. Then I came along. My mom never said I was unplanned, but what 20-year-old college student tries to have a baby."

"I'm pretty sure we were all unplanned back then," Lauren

says as she chuckles.

"Isn't that the truth? My grandmother said once I was born, my mom settled down. One night, my father was driving late at night in a storm and got in a car accident. My mom was devastated and drifted back into the party scene. She was active again in the civil rights movement, which I admire, but she also had me at home. My mom dropped out of college, and she was in and out of my and my grandmother's lives."

Francesca pauses. Sips her wine, looking like she's in deep thought. We wait.

"It took time, but my mother finally got her shit together. She went back to school and became a teacher. She came a long way from her party days, but I'm not gonna lie. I was angry at her for years. She dropped the ball as a parent during those early years, which explains the close relationship I had with my grandmother. Eventually, our relationship healed. My mother and I became very close, and we are best buddies now. We hadn't talked about her past for many years, but when I decided to write the book, I told her I would be brutally honest when disclosing family stories. To her credit, she told me it's my story to tell. She also said if I tell the world how gorgeous she used to be she supports whatever I write. Did I mention my mom is vain?"

We all laugh. Lauren says. "Sounds like your mom is a real character."

"Oh yeah, to say the least, but she wasn't lying. My mom was so beautiful. Still is but when she was young, she was gorgeous."

"And she wants everyone to know," I comment.

"You know it wasn't that I missed love or wanted for anything growing up, but I wish I would have had my father in my life."

Lauren responds. "Of course. God knows I needed my father, especially because he was a buffer to my crazy mother."

Maura asks. "Do you know anything about your family in Ghana?"

"I actually have an aunt, my dad's sister, who lives in Maryland. We're pretty close to her, but we met the whole family about three years ago. My husband and the boys visited Ghana, and ya know, they were a lot like my Italian family - really warm, and it was all about food and family. They teased one another relentlessly, like my Italian family. It was really cool. I would like to get back there, but..." Lauren interjects. "Let me guess - you haven't had the time."

"I sound like a boring old broken record with the same song on loop, don't I?" "That's okay. I'm here. Changes are coming, right?"

"Lauren, I have a feeling you're gonna make sure of it."

After a brief silence, Maura asks. "How was the food in Ghana?"

"We loved the food. One of their main dishes is jollof rice which is with meat or fish and a tomato sauce. Everyone fights over who's jollof is the best, like Italians fight about whose pasta sauce is the best. One of my fusion recipes in the book is a jollof rice - Italian sauce combination. It's delicious if I do say so myself."

"Sounds delicious...oh, excuse me. I need to get this." Lauren picks up her phone from the table.

"Hi, Robert. I'm fi...I'm, I'm. I... I know. Let me...I'm. ROBERT. I'm fine. I am with my friends. We are at the hotel finishing dinner. I will call you later."

She abruptly hangs up as Francesca, Maura, and I uncomfortably look around, not wanting to embarrass her.

"I apologize, ladies. My husband...he worries. A lot. I know he means well. It can be suffocating, though."

Maura responds. "No need to explain. It can be difficult for families back home, right ladies? We are on this amazing adventure, and they are home not knowing where we are, how we are."

Lauren smiles. "Thank you. I know you are trying to make me feel better. It is...complicated." She exhales and then continues. "I feel so good here, in Italy...traveling from city to city, the sites, the writing clinics and especially with you three. It's like I just want time to stand still. My husband calling me is a reminder." She pauses and then abruptly ends the conversation. "Well, we had such a lovely night. Sorry to change the mood yet again."

Maura, in a comical voice, squeezes her fists tight and shouts. *"HUSBANDS."*

One by one, we stand up and gather the leftovers and the trash from the table. Before walking inside, I allow myself one last glance at the loving couple enjoying a romantic night. I can't decide if I'm pining over what could have been or imagining what could be.

After giving each other a hug, we retreat to our individual rooms. My heart goes out to Lauren. She seems to have her hands full with that husband of hers, or maybe something else is going on that she hasn't yet shared. My sense is that she wants to confide in us, but she hasn't found the right moment. I hope she knows we are all here for her when she's ready to talk.

Chapter 33
Coveted Antiquities
Day 6 - Chianti, Tuscan

"Good morning, ladies. How did everyone sleep?" Lauren's floral summer dress swishes with every step as she saunters through the lobby.

After her emotional breakdown the previous evening, the spunky Lauren we have grown to adore is back. The four of us grab the remaining lobby chairs while we wait for a van to drive us to the train station; next up our Tuscan experience. I sip my bold, double espresso and slip a final bite of a cookie in my mouth. I think about how the scrumptious lemon sweets will be missed.

"I can't wait to see the Statue of David, the wineries...Oh, I hope we get to Volterra. One other thing…" Within a split second, Lauren transitions from sounding like a gleeful child to a stringent parent. Maura, Francesca, and I instinctively lean in to listen to her. "When we are in Florence, I want to go out dancing one night to a fancy nightclub, drink fancy cocktails and feel the music, just for a night. Who's in?"

Francesca quickly gives her a high five.

"I am totally down for that. I can honestly say I did not see that coming, but sure…I can let loose on a dance floor."

"I don't promise that my dance moves won't embarrass you as much as they embarrass my girls, but yeah. Let's do it. I can't wait to pull out my stilettos. I also packed a few perfect nightclub dresses that are probably a little tight right about now." I stare at the remaining crumbs of my now-deceased lemon cookie. I then make a promise, as if it really matters to anyone. "Don't worry though. I will squeeze myself into one of them."

All eyes turn to Maura as she nervously twists her tightly

curled hair through her fingers. It's as if she's attempting to be invisible, like she told us was often her goal growing up.

"Not exactly my wheelhouse, to say the least. I don't have anything with me to wear. Who am I kidding? I don't have anything in my closet back home, for that matter, that would even remotely resemble nightclub attire. Well, unless buttoned-up blouses, oversized cardigans and long, patterned, pleated skirts are all the rage nowadays at European nightclubs."

Once we stop laughing, I try to put Maura's concerns to rest.

"Oh, don't you worry about that? I have options tucked away in this bad boy."

I tap my enormous animal print suitcase like it is a temple holding the most coveted antiquities thought to have been lost in Pompeii after Mt. Vesuvius' volcanic explosion.

"Let's just say I've got us both covered. Hell, I have us all covered." It's amazing what magic can happen if you release your wishes to the universe. When I first met Maura, I imagined how I would love to give her a makeover. Opportunity has come knocking on the Tuscan villa doors.

After yesterday's conversation, I know I need to tread lightly with Maura. Her oversized clothing is a shield, protecting her emotionally after a childhood that conditioned her to fade into the background. I have the tools to create magic if she will let me in.

"Looks like I am fresh out of excuses. I won't be the party pooper. Count me in. Does anyone even say that anymore? Party pooper?"

Francesca teases. "YOU DO, Maura. And that is one of the things we love about you."

"Buon giorno, buon giorno, buon giorno a tutti."

Gianni enters the lobby, greeting everyone like he's a politician strolling through a parade. The nine of us and our bags engulf the entire small hotel lobby. Our group claims every black, modern leather seat leaving no room for any other guests. Gianni pushes himself to the middle of our scrum and delivers his morning address like he is Churchill preparing us for our next military advance. Once again, in overdrive, he projects the very image of confidence and strength. I would imagine that the others see him as I had viewed Gianni prior to our intimate conversation on the yacht the previous day. He discloses no evidence of the broken man riddled with sadness, guilt, and fear that I discovered while soaking in the Tyrrhenian Sea. Since learning about his tragic family story, I suddenly noticed lurking behind his mysterious eyes, torment reflected in every wrinkle on his face. Distracted by his good looks and charismatic personality, I didn't see a spec of his pain and anguish just 24 hours ago.

"Okay, authors. Who's ready for two amazing days in a Tuscan villa followed by two days touring Florence?"

We all hoot and holler.

"D'accordo. Andiamo." We grab our bags and follow Gianni to the bus for the short ride to the train station. New adventures in the notorious Tuscan region await us.

~

"Amazing! Exactly what I imagined."

Staring at the villa from just outside of the bus, I hear Lauren quietly announce to no one in particular. We are all exhilarated as we swarm every corner of the expansive, traditional Tuscan home. Wood beams extend from one ceiling bulkhead to another throughout the first level. Cotta floors create a rustic yet elegant charm. Solid Mahogany cabinets topped with thick, earth-toned tile countertops line an enormous kitchen that leads to the backyard patio. Rolling green hills flow for as far as the eyes could see. Standing on the exterior stone, I gaze in awe to the right at the pearl of Tuscany, rows and rows of vines dripping with plump grapes that blanket the rich soil.

"I wonder what the other villa looks like?" Dan and Stanley are spending the two nights in a nearby villa with Gianni, Ana and Ella to accommodate the size of our group.

"This outside space is glorious. Will anyone else be up for a late-night dip?" I ask. "It's as if you are reading my mind," agrees Maura.

We meander through every room of the house and then retreat to our respective bedrooms for a quick reprieve until Chef Belazzio arrives.

~

"Buena sera."

Signor Beppe Belazzio shuffles through the house, pulling a dolly topped with multiple crates that are stuffed with perfectly ripened vegetables, garden-picked herbs and freshly cut meats. Our Tuscan villa experience includes a cooking lesson from a local, renowned chef. It's of no surprise that Beppe and Gianni 'go way back.' Gianna told us that the expert chef would demonstrate to us how to create a masterful, traditional Florentina dinner. He and his assistant methodically flow through the gourmet kitchen as they pull out pots and pans, wash herbs and chop vegetables. Our mouths water as the fragrance of fresh basil, garlic and rosemary drift throughout the entire villa. We eagerly wait to be summoned to join them for our cooking lesson. Several of us take turns peering through the massive, arched entryway that separates the dining room from the kitchen to steal a glimpse of their magic in action. It reminds me of a time when I caught my girls who must have been six or seven years old, hiding behind a couch, spying on a dinner party Michael and I threw for a few neighbors. I smile to myself, recalling their innocence. Michael, me, and our guests listened to the heartwarming giggles of little girls as they huddled together, thinking we didn't know they were there.

"Allora." Let's get started. Gianni calls us to the kitchen as we organically form a circle around the expansive island. Gianni initiates the conversation.

"Prepare to be amazed. Your taste buds will be somersaulting in your mouth. You might be inspired to write a trilogy after this meal." Laughter erupts as Gianni, in true form, pumps up expectations.

"Beppe is an extremely sought-after premier chef in all of Tuscany. Amongst other dishes, he is known for one of the most well-known specialties from the region, Bistecca alla Fiorentina. Let me turn it over to you, Beppe."

Speaking in a thick, Italian accent, Beppe begins. "A fine bottle of wine starts with exceptional grapes. Just the right soil and climate are vital to grow the perfect grapes to create a luscious bottle of wine."

In dramatic form, Beppe picks up the huge slab of meat and holds it up high to present it like a priest presents a newly Christened baby. Watching his kitchen theater, I can't help but wonder if Gianni and Beppe are long-lost siblings.

"Look at this." Beppe points to the features of the meat. "Look at the marbleization. See the coloring and the T-bone? Start out with good grapes to make exceptional wine. By comparison, the best Bistecca alla Fiorentina begins with the finest of meats. You are in the right region of Italy for that."

Beppe explains the process of aging the meat, proper seasoning and ensuring it is at room temperature prior to cooking. As he speaks, he rubs the Bistecca with fresh garlic, thyme, rosemary, and sea salt.

"We will grill this over an open flame in just a moment, but for now, I'm gonna put the meat aside. Let's work on our primo piatto, another Florentine classic, tagliatelle funghi porcini e tartufo."

Beppe uses premier Tuscan ingredients like truffle and porcini mushrooms to create a smooth and creamy sauce then covers the long, flat pasta. We intently watch him sauté greens, toss salad, and whip up a Tuscan dessert favorite, Schiacciata Alla Fiorentina.

"We will bake the Schiacciata while we are eating, then after cena, ahh, ahh, dinner, we will enjoy it with a nice cappuccino. The light cake has a touch of orange flavor."

Even with my slight buzz, I make the executive decision not to eat the cake. I don't need another love affair with a local dolce. Lemon treats sucked me in while on the Amalfi Coast, and I'm determined not to be drawn in by a new local citric favorite.

Devine wine is flowing, cured meats, devoured, flavorful olives and tasty pecorino, Tuscany's most popular cheese, top slices of Tuscan bread. We dip the classic, crusty Florentine bread in seasoned olive oil. Maybe it's the wine, the ambiance created by the classic Tuscan decor, the savory flavors from our charcuterie or perhaps the bond that has evolved amongst our group, but a feeling of warmth and pure serenity rushes over me. You would think we were in the third month of a study abroad program rather than the second week of a book-writing tour. Of course, Lauren, Maura, Francesca, and I have developed an especially close relationship, but something undeniably special has emerged within our group. Our backgrounds and personalities are as diverse as the regions of Italy, but tonight, we have come together like Italy unites as a country. I look around the kitchen and realize that I am exactly where I'm supposed to be. I take another sip and, internally, toast my good friend Ellen for knowing what was best for me, even if I couldn't see it myself.

Beppe continues. "I hope you all left room for the meal."

I put my hand over my stomach and reply. "I hope so, too. It all smells so amazing."

After wrapping up a few final touches, topping the food with a garnish of parsley and other herbs, Beppe announces,

"Mangiamo."

Wine glasses in hand, we move from the kitchen to the outdoors to indulge in our traditional, Tuscan feast. We sit at the expansive live wood farmhouse table, illuminated above by a strand of white lights attached to a pergola ladened with greenery. The courses begin to roll out.

Diane asks. "Beppe, I don't mean to be rude."

Oh dear. There goes our peaceful night. Audible gasps are heard. Based on our experience with Diane, there is no telling what she might say.

"The bread is a bit bland...tasteless even. It's just not good. Why is that?"

Beppi responds. "Ahh. Si' Si' good question." Beppe is so proud of Florentine cuisine and culture. I would think her question could be perceived as rude but given his inviting response, we exhale in relief. Beppe picks up one of the many loaves on the table and forcefully taps it with a knife as if it were a solid piece of wood, demonstrating its firmness.

"Florentina bread is dense and crusty because it is made without salt. There are many theories as to why Tuscan bread was originally baked without salt. I think it's because salt was heavily taxed during the Middle Ages, so Tuscans just made bread without it, and the tradition continued. Maybe we have damaged taste buds in this region, but we think it is the best bread in Italy."

Once our exquisite dinner ends, Beppe and his assistant pack their crates, load up the dolly and leave. Gianni, Ana, and Ella retire to their nearby villa, but Stanley and Dan stay a little longer to enjoy the festive mood. The nine of us relax as we drink, laugh and talk. Tuscany is already living up to our expectations.

"What a night! Here I am, havin' the time of my life, and the wife is home, juggling the kids and her job...ya know...I feel guilty."

Dan pokes at Stan. "Well, Stan, if ya' stop your moanin' and write a best-selling novel, make millions, your wife will be thankin' you for making her struggle for two weeks without ya.' Easy fix."

"You Brits and your sense of humor - Honey, I know I put you out, but don't you worry. We're gonna be rich as soon as I finish my novel, find an agent, get picked up by a publisher and sell it in numbers that rival Harry Potter, so hang in there."

We all laugh at the suggestion that writing a bestseller and making millions of dollars is an actual game plan and an easy one at that. Deep in our private thoughts, who amongst us hasn't dreamed that our novel, in the process, will be a treasure with a dedicated following. However, statistics don't lie. It's not that realistic for a first-time author with a limited social media presence to write a breakout best-selling novel. One thing is clear; we are enjoying one hell of an experience, with or without a big payday.

Francesca responds. "Stanly, I sorta feel your pain. Why do you think I always have a drink in my hand? I feel bad that my husband has to handle everything on his own, but if I'm being completely honest, drinking helps me forget about what is falling through the cracks. What's my house gonna look like when I get home? This might come as a surprise to you all, but I'm a tiny, tiny bit of a control freak." Francesca squeezes her fingers together.

Maura teases. "Oh, no, no…we haven't noticed." Francesca smiles at her.

"I like to call it decisive, and every friend group needs someone to take the lead." Francesca lifts her glass to Lauren. "See, Maura, I'm decisive, not controlling."

Maura bows her head to signal her concession.

"The sad thing is, as much as I worry my husband is struggling on his own, I'm equally concerned that he and the boys are enjoying the break from me. Hell, they might even be holding it together and enjoying the break."

Francesca finishes off a final sip and pours another.

Margaret offers. "Maybe it's both. If you are…ahhh… decisive, your husband and boys might initially enjoy the break from you. At some point, their world begins to unravel. They realize how much they need you." Francesca ponders before concluding. "Interesting Margaret."

Francesca nods her head. "Yeah. I can live with that. I'm still gonna drink, though."

Penny looks at Stan, then Francesca. "Maybe you should both embrace the uncomfortable feeling you have while you're here," Penny speaks so infrequently that when she does talk, it grabs our attention.

"Hmm. What do you mean by that, Penny?" Asks Francesca.

"Yeah, I am curious. I would love to find a reason to lean into my guilt." Stan says.

"Then do it. Lean in. The more you feel, the better you write. Think about Gianni wanting our senses activated to inspire our writing. I think that has really worked for me."

Dan says what we were all thinking. "Penny, we heard ya reading. It certainly is working for ya, isn't it?"

Who could forget her sexy expose after picking Marzano tomatoes? Penny seems completely unphased by Dan's comment. Maybe it is the farmer in her, but I have come to realize Penny is not to be underestimated. She might seem meek, but she's no wilting flower. Penny plows forward.

"Whether it's guilt, excitement, sadness, I think if you own your feelings instead of pushing them away, those feelings will enrich your writing."

"Penny is right. Think about some of the most highly acclaimed authors – Tennessee Williams, Emily Dickinson, F. Scott Fitzgerald, Ernest Hemingway, and even Mark Twain. They all dealt with either depression, mental health issues or alcoholism. They did okay for themselves. Well, from a writing perspective, anyway.

Penny, you're onto something." Lauren agrees.

Diane chuckles, shakes her head then sips her wine. "You don't agree, Diane?" Lauren asks.

Diane offers a snarky response.

"Oh, no, I wholeheartedly agree. I'm laughing to myself, out loud…or maybe out loud to myself…either way, what do you know, Lauren, about struggle?"

Diane's last part of that statement is abrasive. She stares directly into Lauren's eyes as if she is provoking her to respond. The festive mood immediately evaporates like a post-Christmas letdown. I attempt to mask the awkwardness since cold water has been poured over our jubilant evening.

"I don't think…"

Lauren, utterly and uncharacteristically, speaks right over me as she maintains a firm gaze into Diane's eyes. "What is it that you think you know about my life to suggest that I don't understand what it's like to struggle?"

Diane is clearly out of line to suggest she is either in a position to or has the right to assess Lauren's life. Although she should apologize and back down, *that* would be uncharacteristic for her. Instead, she fires back at Lauren. "I don't claim that I know everything about you, but I see how you dress, how you look, your ring probably cost more than my car. I heard you mention a beach house or some sort of vacation home, or, or maybe it was a boat. I don't even remember, but It was something big like that. You have a loving husband who calls ten times a day, plus two perfect children. You don't exactly strike me as someone who has an intimate relationship with the word struggle."

Another awkward silence seeps in, but this time, Francesca attempts to intervene in defense of Lauren. "You know Di…"

Lauren again flagrantly interrupts, and this time, it is Francesca who takes a back seat.

"Well, Diane, you are right about one thing. You don't know anything about me. I don't need to be lectured about my lack of understanding when it comes to managing life's struggles. Trust me, I think I know a thing or two about pushing through tough times."

Diane has yet another opportunity to bow out of the conversation, but instead, she doubles down. "Look, Lauren, I'm just calling it like I see it. Yeah, sure, everyone has perceived struggles. I don't know. Your favorite shampoo might be out of stock, and choosing another one might cause you a great deal of anxiety. Maybe you need to plan a dinner party and have your luxury car serviced on the same day. These could be your big life struggles. I am just spitballing over here, but you get my point, right?"

Diane's comments are utterly disrespectful and wholly condescending. This time, rather than attempting to lead a response, we all turn our heads toward Lauren. She has made it clear that she will battle Diane's unfounded accusations. Lauren stands up, points her finger at Diane and fires back. "How dare you. I don't know what you see or what you think you see."

As she raises her voice, it cracks. "You have no right minimizing me like that by suggesting that an out-of-stock hair product or a dinner party is somehow my biggest life concern."

Diane interrupts by saying, "I was obviously being facetious, but..."

"Facetious? Do you think that my life is a joke? I'm a punchline to you? How dare you draw conclusions about me with your insulting, demeaning comments. Just because I have nice things doesn't mean life isn't hard for me. Life..." Lauren pauses. Her whole body is shaking.

Francesca reaches up and grabs her hand. She then continues.

"Life. Is. Hard. Life is really…. really…. hard for me. I. I. I. I'm dying. Is that a sufficient struggle for you? You're right. I am blessed with a loving husband, fantastic kids, and, yes, plenty of money. But at this point, that money doesn't mean anything to me. I'm pissed off that I will be leaving them behind. I am so fucking angry."

Lauren's lip quivers as she pauses. Diane remains seated, jaw dropped and seemingly stunned. We are all stunned. Lauren releases Diane her frustration, her fear, and her sorrow that she has masked with a huge smile and loving persona since our first day together. Diane deserves every word of it. Lauren, now hysterical, continues to scream at Diane.

"None of that, Diane…not the fancy clothes, not my diamond ring, not even my amazing fucking husband or my perfect fucking children protects me from metastatic cancer. Tell me, Diane, does my terminal illness qualify me to comprehend the word struggle? Do you think I'm in the position to infuse struggle into my writing?" Lauren is now screaming even louder.

"In your humble opinion, Diane, is it enough?"

Everyone remains completely still except for Diane. She stands up and looks around as if she is searching for an ally. Not even Margert rushes to her side. Diane's color appears to drain from her face. Turning towards Lauren, she ever so slightly opens her mouth, but nothing comes out. Diane then abruptly turns and swiftly walks away. Like a bully, she collapsed almost instantly when Lauren stood up to her. Lauren is relentless, though. She continues to yell at her even though Diane is now out of sight.

"Do I get life struggles? Tell me, Diane, do I understand what it means to struggle?" Lauren is inconsolable as she continues to repeat herself over and over again, despite the fact that we can't see Diane, who presumably is locked in her bedroom by this point.

Crying and simultaneously repeating, she says. "Do I understand what it means to struggle, Diane? Diane, where are you? Let's talk about what you think you know about my life. Tell me, Diane. What do you know about struggle? You know nothing, Diane. You don't know anything."

Francesca, Maura and I surround Lauren and hug her. Holding on to her tight, the four of us literally fall to the ground. Slowly and quietly, Margaret, Penny, Stan, and Dan leave the patio while the four of us sit on the cold, stone patio holding Lauren, holding one another, and crying profusely. No words are spoken. Each of us is left to our own thoughts to process our shock and grief. I feel such sadness knowing that my kind and loving friend, skilled at spreading joy and inspiring others, is dying.

I ponder how to wrap my head around this awful reality. In moments of stress, you think of the strangest things. As we sit on the patio, intertwined, the oddest image creeps into my brain. It's like I'm watching a puzzle come together. Each puzzle piece represents something I've observed about Lauren or something I've heard her say. It now makes so much sense. Her overly concerned husband, her beautiful clothes that appear to hang off her body, not feeling well in Pompeii, not drinking because of medication and the multiple prophetic statements she has made about living life in the moment and getting the most out of every moment. I suspected all along that Lauren had a deeper story to tell. The fully assembled puzzle I'm envisioning isn't what I wanted to piece together.

~

"I think I scared her."

Sitting by the fire pit, we rehash Diane and Lauren's fight. Francesca stands up, pokes the fire then sits back down.

"Oh, she's scared, alright. She bolted out of here like she was on the run. I think Diane is traumatized at this point." Lauren fake slaps Francesca as she laughs. "Oh, Stop. I already feel terrible."

"Why should you feel bad? You lost it on her, and she had it coming to her. Diane was completely out of line, and it wasn't the first time. Remember how she kept pushing you about your writing when we were at that pizza place in Naples and again when we had that lemon feast? You were rattled both times. Not this time. You firmly stood up to her."

I add. "Based on the short time we have known Diane, I have a feeling she is used to getting yelled at. Her personality invites it." We manage to find humor despite the sense of gloom hovering over us. "I'm just sayin'." I swing my hands wide open, horizontally, for effect.

"Look, Lauren," Maura warmly says as she leans in. "If you want to share with us anything about your illness, we are here for you. If you choose not to, that's completely your choice. Whatever you want, we support you."

"I'm so sorry I didn't tell you about my illness earlier. On several occasions, I wanted to, but I've been having so much fun I didn't want to change the dynamics between us."

We assure her she has no reason to apologize to us.

"Maybe it's been a welcome break from talking about it…your illness. This trip has allowed you to escape the battle for a couple of weeks."

"You're so right, Maura. And let me tell ya. It is a daily battle, and I've loved the break. Since we got here, we've been talking and laughing whenever we are together. It's been so long since I have had that freedom. It's like I have been able to pretend I'm not sick. I know that sounds crazy, but I have had days where I hardly think about my cancer other than when I'm popping my pills. Back home, my cancer defines me. My husband, Bob."

Lauren pauses. "You guys have heard all our fights first-hand."

I confirm. "Admittedly, I jumped to conclusions. I thought your husband might be the jealous type or maybe controlling. I judged him without knowing the facts. I feel bad about that."

"You didn't know. The man worries that's for sure," Lauren utters in a sarcastic tone. "I know he just wants to take care of me. I get it. That's what he is supposed to do, but sometimes I feel smothered. It's as if he is satisfying *his* need to know I'm alive and well. What about what I want from him? If he really listened to what I wanted, he would give me space. I know it sounds like I'm calling him selfish and maybe I am. It's such a confusing dynamic."

The three of us remain silent and let her get out what she has bottled up inside of her.

"Look. Bob is the sweetest man in the universe. Here I am making him sound like this terrible husband, and all he wants is for me to be healthy so I can live as long as possible."

Maura comforts Lauren. "I can tell you this all sounds so normal. You aren't wrong and I would guess Bob isn't selfish. When you get home, maybe the two of you should meet with a counselor. Sometimes, it's a matter of talking through a plan that works for both of you."

"I will consider it, thank you. We have always had a happy marriage. I certainly don't want us to spend our remaining time together bickering. How awful that would be for him, ya know...when the time comes." Lauren's voice cracks. I instinctively reach out and grab her hand.

Lauren is working through her raw emotions in real-time. Her pain is palpable, she simultaneously wants to live her life to the fullest while balancing Bob's need to protect her.

"My friends back home have treated me differently since my diagnosis. It's like everyone walks on eggshells around me. I see pity in their eyes. I don't want to be pitied." Lauren's voice elevates. "They treat me like...like...like I have cancer."

We all pause for a moment to allow the gravity of her statement to set in. Francesca injects much-needed levity into the conversation.

"Don't you worry. We are not going to be any nicer to you now that we know about your illness. Right ladies?" Maura and I nod in agreement.

"Absolutely not. Nothing between us will change. You will still be teased mercilessly where appropriate. You won't get any royal treatment from us."

Maura and I concur. "Absolutely. No special treatment around here."

Lauren laughs. "You guys are hysterical, but that's exactly what I need. I want things to be normal. Back home, it's like every conversation revolves around how I look and how I feel. Did I take my medicine? I want us to talk and laugh like we have been doing since we met."

Maura says. "Well, if you want normal, you might want to find a different friend group, but if you want to talk and laugh a lot, you've come to the right place."

The four of us, sitting in Adirondack chairs surrounding the fire pit, remain silent. We soak in the heat from the fire as if it's a warm blanket providing us with much-needed comfort.

"Lauren, there is one thing ..."

Lauren smiles as if she was waiting for one of us to ask.

"Given everything you are going through, what made you decide to join this particular tour?"

"Well, something like that." I gently admit in a shy, quiet tone.

"Now *that*, ladies, is a long and complicated story."

Lauren is wise enough to know that it is a curious choice for a woman who potentially has limited time to live. We head off to bed, knowing there is so much more to our dear friend Lauren than we could have ever imagined.

Chapter 34
Perspective

Day 7 - Chianti, Tuscany

"The bus is outside. Stanley and Dan are already on it."

Standing in the middle of our villa living room, Gianni attempts to herd us from the house to the bus. We are in a variety of stages of preparation for the wine tour, from finishing up with breakfast dishes to packing a bag for the day.

He looks at his watch and flashes his right hand, extending his long fingers to signal. "How about I give you all five? We have a little time before our tour, but the quicker we go, the more wine we can drink."

His shameless attempt to appeal to our senses by dangling low-hanging grapes goes in vain. Even the promise of aged wine can't revive the bleak mood in the house. Gianni turns and walks back to the bus. Based on his demeanor, it sounds like Stanley and Dan told Gianni about the previous evening's blow-up between Lauren and Diane.

Negative energy penetrates the shared space like smoke lingering in a speakeasy. Awkward small talk is initiated, but nothing catches fire. Lauren and I are the last ones to leave the house. As luck would have it, Diane is holding the door for us when we leave. I mumble a weak thank you as I pass by Diane to join the others on the bus. I overhear Diane quietly, asking Lauren if she could sit next to her during the bus trip to the vineyard.

Diane and Lauren follow each other to the last seat like the cool kids sitting in the back, far away from everyone else. Who wouldn't want to be a fly on the seat cushion for that conversation? Just as Gianni has done every other day, he stands up and announces the itinerary for the day.

"Today is our Castello di Verrazzano wine tour. Enjoy the peaceful scenery during our 30-minute drive through Tuscany's spectacular wine country."

Gianni attempts to rally us but even he isn't himself. "Between the climate, the rich soil, and the improved farming equipment over the years, the finest grapes flourished, resulting in the production of some of the finest wines of the world. We will enjoy a wonderful private tour and then a wine tasting. Word of caution. Don't overindulge. You will need to have your wits about you for our afternoon writing clinic back at the villa. Between last night's dinner and the wine today, your imagination should run off your proverbial page when you start writing." He carefully selects words to hype the wine tour, as we have seen from him, but his delivery is lackluster in comparison to his usual energy level.

He gets one thing right. My imagination is bubbling over, not about agriculture and a favorable climate but about the conversation taking place eight rows behind me.

"If you remember yesterday, which feels like a week ago at this point..." Gianni looks down momentarily, massages the back of his neck, and pauses. He's off his game. This is the first time since the start of the trip that the demanding schedule seems to have caught up with him. Maybe talking about his son stirred emotions, or last night's drama is perhaps more than he bargained for when organizing this tour. Whatever the impetus, his mojo is drained.

He continues. "We talked about movement. Think about the act of picking grapes, wine flowing, walking through vineyards...how would you describe these actions? During our writing seminar later today, we will discuss how movement enhances the depth of your writing."

I'm only half listening to him. Like Gianni, my energy level is also depleted. I feel my positive aura slipping away. My heart is aching just thinking about my dear friend. I didn't even know Lauren existed a week ago, yet I am despondent over her illness. Looking out the window, I soak in the view of winding roads, the running landscapes, and the succulent grapes that are all flying by me outside the window. I know when I exit the bus, I need to be cheery ready to appreciate the flavors of the day. I need to put on a happy face for my friend.

"What a glorious ride," says Maura.

"Absolutely stunning. The bus ride was serene. I was comfortably lost in my thoughts," says Francesca.

Standing with Francesca and Maura, I put on my game face while Lauren finishes her conversation with Diane.

"Don't look now, but Lauren and Diane are still deep in conversation."

Maura abruptly turns her head precisely in the direction of Diane and Lauren.

I tease Maura. "It's as if I said conspicuously and quickly turn your head and stare directly at them."

Maua apologizes as she simultaneously laughs. "Sorry. I always fail the 'don't look now' test."

"Oh God. Lauren just gently touched Diane's hand," observes Francesca.

Stealthy, I steal another glance at the two of them, hoping they don't notice the intrusion.

"Leave it to Lauren. She is the one who is sick, yet she's comforting Diane. Would it be rude if I scream over to Lauren and tell her not to be sucked in?" Francesca rhetorically asks.

Maura says. "Okay. Act normal. They seem to be wrapping up their conversation."

"I'm afraid the three of us wouldn't know what acting normal was if we fell over it."

Francesca laughs as she strategizes. "She's walking over now, so pretend we are talking about the beautiful view. Just look at the natural beauty. It, it, it…"

"Beautiful. just beautiful." Maura leans in for the save. "Can you ladies do me a favor?"

"Sure thing, Lauren, anything." Maura immediately responds.

"When I decide to check off *robbing a bank* from my bucket list, remind me not to ask you three to join me."

"Were we that obvious?" I ask.

Lauren dramatically rolls her eyes, throws up her hands abruptly, turns her head, and marches forward without saying a word. Maura, Francesca, and I smile at one another and dutifully follow behind Lauren then join the rest of the group for a two-hour vineyard tour. After the tour through the grounds, the caverns, and the castle, we have a scheduled lunch at the winery restaurant.

"What an amazing tour. I had no idea there was Chianti wine and Chianti Classico wine." I admit that fact as if it was a significant life discovery.

"To think, I have managed to drink Chianti all of these years without knowing the differences in Chianti grapes."

Lauren agrees and then says. "Chianti Classico requires 80% Sangiovese grapes, and Chianti has 70% Sangiovese grapes. Did I get that right?"

Maura confirms. "That was my understanding. Roberto said that the Sangiovese grapes are found all over central Italy, especially throughout Tuscany."

"I need to remember this stuff," I tell them. "The next time I'm with the ladies back home, I can casually drop my newly found knowledge like I'm a cultured wine connoisseur."

I flip my hair, then sip my wine, pinky finger extended. They laugh robustly. Looking through the beautiful wall of windows at the picturesque view of the Verrazzano castle, I wonder if our laughter is sincere or if we are forcing ourselves to rekindle the spirit we created between us four on the first day of the trip. Our hearts are heavy since learning about Lauren's illness. I know it's important to set those feelings aside and respect Lauren's wishes to proceed forward with the same level of delight we have enjoyed since the day we met.

The underground cellars, the lush grounds, and the stately castle create the quintessential Tuscan experience we had been talking about all week. Lauren is all smiles. Following my lead, she projects her own version of a cultured connoisseur queen. I respect her commitment to enjoying the moment rather than focusing on what lies ahead.

Margaret, Diane, and Penny slowly approach. Lauren quickly reacts.

"Oh, let me move my bag. Come. Sit. Sit. There is plenty of room."

Maura, Francesca, and I follow Lauren's lead and welcome them to the large, round table. Dan and Stanley join moments later. Just like that, the nine of us are once again breaking bread like we did the previous evening before the epic throw down. I'm sure Lauren will share with us details about her conversation with Diane later but for now, their fight and reconciliation is wine under the bridge.

"It's crazy to think that the castle is over 1,000 years old," Margaret says.

Francesca concurs. "I know. We get excited back home when a building is over 100 years old, let alone 1,000 years old. Despite multiple trips to Europe, I'm still amazed when I think how ancient everything is in Europe."

Dan doesn't hesitate to lean into the conversation. He sits up tall and crosses his leg over his knee like an Oxford sophisticate.

"You Americans are such amateurs. It's cute how you are easily impressed with cobblestone streets, fancy architecture, and old castles. We are so accustomed to our aged culture and architecture back home."

"Oh, here we go. Let's all bow, ladies. The Royal Prince Dan has entered the conversation."

We all laugh with Stan. Given his Manchester, working-class roots, Dan is far from an elitist, but occasionally, in good fun, he unleashes his inner 'faux aristocrat.' A warm rapport and delightful banter have developed between Dan and Stanley. They are both gentile souls comfortable revealing their sensitive side. They differ so much from the men in my old neighborhood who never miss the opportunity to pump their chests and outdo one another. It's my turn to poke fun at Dan and rattle his cage.

"You know, Dan, when I visited China several years ago, I remember this British couple on our tour who were amazed by how old everything was in China. Of course, Asian culture is significantly older than Europe. I guess it is a matter of perspective, wouldn't you say?" Dan pretends to tip his imaginary cap towards me.

"Touché, Stephanie. You got me there."

Diane perks up. "You are right. Stephanie. It's a little something I have learned this week. Perspective is everything." She glances at Lauren, who quietly nods back at Diane.

Chapter 35
Grateful Dead

Day 7 - Chianti, Tuscany

After a week of touring, we know the drill. We have eased into a routine like students adapt to a new school year. Upon our return to the villa, Gianni rolls out a writing activity.

"To demonstrate the importance of how movement adds depth and texture to your story, each of you will pick a card from the basket and use movement to describe the prompt."

Gianni lifts the basket over his head and then lowers it to the table. "Who wants to pull the first card?"

Margaret steps up. "I throw down a pretty good game of charades. I'll give it a go."

She pulls a card and reads it to herself. "Ok, I have a bit of experience with this." She uses an exaggerated movement to sling back a sip of her wine.

"Margaret slurps her red wine," says Gianni. He pauses and then announces.

"Snooze fest, right? Right? Who wants to provide a more captivating observation of Margaret's Oscar-winning performance?"

Stanley stands up. "What the hell. I'll take a stab at it. How difficult could it be?"

Stanley takes a huge breath. A bead of sweat rolls down his face. After mustering the courage, he begins to speak. "Margaret's del...deli..." Stan clears his throat. "Margaret's delicate hand gently lifts the ahh stemless wine glass to her soft, red lips. She extends her tongue to the top of the glass, lick...she then licks the glass rim then tilts her head back. The red...no, the, the robust red, cherry red? wine swishes in her mouth like a seductive ahhh...I got nothin' else." Stanley's face suddenly turns as red as the wine. Poor guy is embarrassed.

"Margaret, did I make you uncomfortable? I'm so sorry. I don't even know what I am saying. I write sci-fi."

We all laugh. Stanley is exceptionally kind and respectful; there isn't anything threatening about him. The cringe-worthy moment somehow is heartwarming as opposed to intimidating; it's far from the lustful scene he attempted to describe but he gave Gianni what he asked for.

"Uncomfortable? Hell no. Please. I want to hear more. This is the most excitement I've had since the '89 Grateful Dead, East Rutherford show, and that was epic, from what I could remember." Margaret is an affable person with a huge heart. I adore how considerate she is about Stanley's feelings.

"Fabulous, Stanley. You captured the essence of movement in describing the simple task of drinking wine. It was a fantastic contrast to my boring description. You might need some practice mastering the art of seduction, but maybe your next book. For now, stick to scientific imagery."

The living room comes alive. The atmosphere, re-invigorated, replaces the dreary mood from the morning. We each take a turn describing movement in a variety of scenarios. We learn, we laugh, and we tease with one another. I secretly steal glimpses of Lauren and it warms my heart to see her so happy. After Gianni wraps up the activity, I pack up my computer and find a secluded spot by the pool to finish the afternoon writing on my own. Opening my computer, I revisit where I left off.

"How's it going, Stephanie?"

"You know. It's going." I respond to him in a way that suggests I am struggling.

"I don't know why I said it like that. It's actually going really well. I feel like I have found my groove since yesterday..."

"Own your successes, Stephanie. It's okay to admit to me and to yourself that you are making forward progress."

I smile and look down. I know he's right. I need to be my own biggest cheerleader, yet I'm more at home playing the role of leading self-critic. "It's amazing how much I have learned. Writing meaningful dialogue feels more natural, too. You and the guest speakers DO know what you are talking about, don't you?"

"I suppose we know a thing or two," Gianni proudly responds. "I read the chapters that you emailed me."

My head is awkwardly cranked back. I use my hand to shield my eyes from the glare of the glowing sun. He notices my uncomfortable positioning and pulls up a chair to sit next to me.

"Agreed. You are progressing. Your main character, Cassandra, is getting stronger. Needless to say, there is a correlation. Cassandra is also becoming more complex. More mysterious. Her character is pulling me in. I want to know more."

Gianni stares deeply into my eyes. I can't handle the intensity. I look down to break the connection.

"From what I gather, comparing your initial bio submitted with your tour registration and what I am reading about Cassandra, there's some overlap between your personal story and Cassandra. What made you decide to disclose so much about yourself through your main character?"

I respond without giving a second thought. "They say write what you know. Oh, and what's the other rule? Sometimes truth is crazier than fiction."

Gianni laughs. "True. True."

"I mean, Cassandra is not me, but a lot of the reflection we hear from Cassandra about her childhood is, unfortunately, pulled from my own life experiences. Strangely, it is cathartic to talk about me through her."

"It sounds like your family went through a lot with your

father. I can understand why there is something therapeutic about giving a voice, in essence, to yourself through a character."

Gianni allows for an appropriate moment to pass before he segues to his next sentence.

"Cassandra is turning out to be an interesting character. One part suburban homemaker and one part sleuth." He smiles affectionately with his description.

"Growing up, I loved Nancy Drew, the Boxcar then Agatha Christie as I got older. It was such a rush to piece together small details to solve the crime. I'm still a huge fan of crime novels, and I listen to crime podcasts. It's a little morbid, I know, but honestly, I can't get enough of it. One of my friends back in my old neighborhood is an FBI agent. I emailed him, and he agreed to meet with me when I get home. Cassandra puts pieces together from her gut, but I have some forensic questions for him. You know. I want the crime scene science to be realistic."

I feel myself babbling, nonsensically, from one topic to the next. Gianni has that effect on me. A funky, nervous sweat begins to brew under my arms. I squeeze them tight to my body, fearing an odor will expel.

"Meeting with your FBI friend is a good idea. You never want your reader to be distracted by inaccuracies. Keep in mind though…as far as research goes, your novel is bedded deep in character development. Don't overthink the research. Touch on the science and move on."

"Ahhh. I will remember that, thank you." I respond.

"What is it about Cassandra solving a crime that intrigues you?" Gianni asks.

"Cassandra, on the outside, is a nondescript, average woman living a typical suburban life, yet quietly, she has a secret ability. You know, like it's her superpower. The murdered woman, Gloria, is also a seemingly 'regular' woman, but we will learn more about her backstory. Cassandra and Gloria are anything but average, to say the least."

"Do you see that as a metaphor for your life?" asks Gianni.

"I guess I see it as a metaphor for people in general. We all have something special about us. It doesn't matter what it is or how old we are when we discover it, but buried in all of us is a unique trait or a well-developed story waiting to be revealed."

Gianni nods in agreement. "Unfortunately, many people go through life not recognizing what they have to offer is unique. They don't realize they have a story to tell." Gianni reveals a big smile and asks. "What's your superpower?"

"I don't know. Maybe it's that I make connections with people? I'm a good listener? Oh, hopefully, I'm a good storyteller. Can I have dual powers?" laughing as I ask, as if there are literal rules for identifying superpowers.

Gianni laughs. "Indeed, you can, and you do. Was that hard to admit about yourself?"

"Well, you read my bio. I'm gaining confidence, but like Cassandra, I'm a work in progress."

"Something else I noticed about Cassandra. You write that she was married in Italy early on in her life. Creative liberty or pulled from a true event?"

"True event. I left that out of my bio, didn't I," I ask rhetorically. "I spent a year in Italy after college. I met a guy. Married him, and it was all a disaster. That is the very abbreviated version. I only touch on that debacle in my novel, but I could have written an entire book about the whole ordeal."

"I'm sorry to hear that in the land of romance, your love story ended in disaster," says Gianni.

He pauses then expresses. "However, it is also intriguing to discover that your past includes an Italian love story."

Intrigued? Again, I'm confused. I never know if Gianni is

flirting with me or prompting my writing creativity. There's only one way to gain clarity. Much to my own surprise, I walk out on a limb, take a risk, and search for answers.

"Intriguing? Gianni Ciabatinni, if I didn't know better, I might think you were flirting with me."

Oh God. Did I really just say that? Maybe he didn't mean that at all, and I completely misread his statement. How do I walk that back? My face must be as red as Stanley's was an hour earlier. It feels like I am dangling out on that tree limb all alone, waiting for a lifeline. After what feels like a century, Gianni looks deep into my eyes and responds.

"Would that be so surprising?"

~

"What a day! I'm simultaneously exhilarated and exhausted."

"Stephanie, I get the exhausted part. Not sure I'm feeling all that exhilarated. That was a tough writing seminar for me."

Francesca puts Maura at ease. "We all have those days. I made some progress today, but some days I sit in front of the computer and truly understand the meaning of writer's block."

"Yep, for sure. Hurling my computer into the pool was very seriously under consideration earlier today. I wrote, reviewed, and then deleted it. I couldn't get a rhythm going, so I packed it in, went to my room, and talked with my sons, so it was not a complete loss."

Francesca adds. "Catching up with the family hopefully brought you positive energy. By the way, I was wondering where all my girls were hiding out. Maura, you talked with your boys. Lauren excused herself after the charades activity and went back to her room. Stephanie, where were you?"

"Oh no. Is Lauren okay?" I don't purposely ignore Francesca's question. In theory, nothing is suspicious about sitting by the pool and talking with Gianni. After all, he is our writing instructor. I know if I tell them where I am, I will somehow manage to make it all weird, and Francesca always seems to know when I'm hiding something. My real concern is sincerely with Lauren.

Gianni quietly walks into the kitchen and leans against the island, just a few steps from where I'm standing. I feel a jolt rumble through my body, standing near him.

"Is Lauren still in her room?" he asks.

"Yes. Maybe we should check on her?" I suggest.

"We have had a couple of long days, plus, it was hot today. I'm sure she is fine, but…" Maura quickly jumps in. "How about I check in on her."

I respond to Maura. "I don't want to put that pressure on you, but I was kind of thinking that you would be the best person to…"

"Best person to what?" Lauren suddenly emerges from behind me, looking more refreshed than any of us. We all greet Lauren enthusiastically as we awkwardly look at one another.

"Are we volunteering the best person for something?" Lauren pushes.

"Well, we are talking about bringing dinner in since we are on our own tonight. We thought maybe Gianni would have an idea for some options. He is the best person to recommend a takeout restaurant."

Maura and Francesca make an unconvincing attempt to nod in agreement. "Well, that sounds like a whole bunch of bullshit."

Francesca responds. "Well, bullshit or not, Gianni. What do you suggest we do for dinner?"

~

"Oh my God. I…am…stuffed." Maura emphatically states. Maura allows for a thoughtful minute before continuing.

"We've said that very statement more times than I care to remember since starting the tour," I respond. "What do we have, four or five more days? Not that I'm rushing the rest of the tour, but when I get home, I'm immediately getting back on track with eating right and yoga classes. Having said that, that's next week, but right now, do we have more of that delicious apple torte?"

I push the plates around and then find the remaining sliver of the torte. I quickly shove it into my mouth as if the torte has the ability to resist my force.

Sitting under the patio white lights, the four of us are enjoying food from a local Maura, Francesca, Lauren, and I brought dinner into the villa, from a local trattoria. Given the cooler-than-usual temperatures, it's the perfect way to end our Tuscan villa visit.

"This was such a good call. I'm sure downtown Chianti is adorable, but I just wasn't up for all that tonight. Penny, Diane, and Margaret will tell us about it."

"Ladies, I must say, I am impressed. We got through dinner and not one question about my conversation with Diane."

"Amazing, isn't it but you aren't going to get by the whole night without telling us," I suggest as I pile the remaining food on top of one another to ensure I'm done picking at the remnants.

"Okay, here's the short version. What a bizarre turn of events in the past 24 hours."

"Just a day later, and you two seem like besties." Jokes Francesca.

"I wouldn't go that far. She isn't…"

Lauren's head turns in every direction, looking around the property for a Diane sighting.

She's not…exactly my type. Look. She's fine, but we wouldn't actively pursue one another as friends back home, not like us. I knew from day one that we four would get in all sorts of trouble together if we lived near one another. I left my conversation with Diane feeling sorry for her more than anything."

Maura, Francesca, and I look at one another.

"I know. I know. I see it in your faces. I am the one dying. How is it that I feel sorry for her? We haven't talked much about my illness and how I am doing emotionally. I'm sure we will get into that at some point. One thing I will share is that I have a sense of peace."

Lauren sits up and points her finger to emphasize. "…and don't think I mean acceptance. I am fighting like hell to live. I have the best medical care available and lots of love and support, so there isn't anything I want more than to beat this."

Maura, Francesca, and I remain silent. Lauren pauses. She has more to say. I have so many questions, but the floor is hers. Lauren lowers her voice. "Have you ever really listened to someone who is…. close to their end of life."

Maura says. "In my practice, I have known children, 8, 9, 10 years old, who are more perceptive and reflective than adults. It's sad anytime a child is terminally ill, yet it's amazing to see how some children approach the end of life with such grace. Sometimes, they comfort their parents. I take it that you are seeing life through a clearer lens than ever before."

"God bless those babies. I can't even imagine. Yes, Maura, I have become hyper-focused on what is important in life. I know in my heart who loves me and who I am as a person. I've gotten to know myself in a more real way than ever before. Even if I do die, I'm at peace with myself and my loved ones. In full transparency, I do have an old wound to tend to, which is a whole other story, but overall, I have gotten to know myself more intimately than ever before."

Open wound? Is that why Lauren is here at this point in her life? I have more questions than answers.

"I know this is so deep into my feelings. I'm sorry. I didn't mean to go in this direction. Here we are, enjoying such a beautiful night."

I respond. "Don't be ridiculous. No need to apologize. It's beautiful. I mean it, it, it's heavy, but it's beautiful. You're so inspiring."

"Thank you, Stephanie. The thing is, talking with Diane reminds me of what makes me thankful rather than focusing not on this disgusting, horrific disease. Diane is a lonely, sad person with hardly anyone in her life. Ya know. She finds ways to compensate for her personal struggles with outbursts and by instigating others."

"I don't wish that on anyone, nor do I want to sound insensitive, but she doesn't make it easy for people to want to get close to her. She isn't the most..." This time I lean in and whisper in fear they might walk in at any moment. "...likable person. I know that sounds insensitive, considering what you are telling us, but her energy is so negative. She doesn't draw people in."

Maura says. "She's probably so insecure that she doesn't love herself. She probably can't imagine someone caring about her."

Lauren points at Maura. "That's exactly right. It's like she uses her bombastic personality to cover up all that self-loathing. That's why my heart goes out to her. She had it rough growing up. Even as a kid, Diane struggled to make friends. Her mom passed away when she was 12 years old. It sounds like her dad was fine enough, but he was gruff and cold towards her. She needed her mom, or a more loving father or anyone in her corner."

Lauren looks around again, expecting Diane to walk through the door. "To make matters worse, she said she was bullied as a kid, mostly because she wasn't attractive." Lauren throws her hands up in the air to clarify. "Her words, not mine. She felt lost and alone throughout her life."

"Okay. Now, it makes sense. She has always masked her own insecurities by poking at people with her snap judgments. It's not right, but I guess it better explains her behavior," says Maura.

"She told me she assumed that I was the pretty, popular girl with money who grew up and married the perfect husband and yada, yada. She put me in this nice little box and tied it up with a perfect bow."

There is a moment of silence before we look at one another and laugh.

"I know what you are thinking. Sure, maybe I did, you know, have friends, and maybe people thought I was pretty. Money was never much of an issue or not at all an issue. Okay. Some of her superficial assumptions weren't completely off base, but that doesn't give her the right to jump all over me."

Maura, Francesca, and I quickly assure Lauren she didn't deserve any of what Diane said to her. "She saw an opening and took a shot," I add.

"By the way, some assumptions were correct but my childhood was far from rosy like she seems to think. That's beside the point, I know. I might have been popular and whatnot, but I was never *that mean girl* in school. It really irks me that she assumed that I would have been mean to people as a kid. I have been nothing but pleasant with her and everyone else since this tour began."

"You're kind to everyone." Francesca agrees.

Maura says. "I empathize with some of Diane's struggles. I was always that weird girl in class. I didn't dress well. I wasn't super attractive. I was odd. I mean, I still am all those things, but unlike Diane, I have a sense of who I am. My parents weren't exactly warm and fuzzy, but they were both always there for me."

Francesca responds. "Okay, Maura, I accept you calling yourself and your family weird, but I reject that you aren't attractive. You're gorgeous."

Maura smiles at Francesca.

"You know it's funny. Diane and I had similar social struggles, but we coped differently. All I wanted was to be invisible. I'm not saying that was a good thing, but my goal was to go under the radar and not ruffle feathers. That probably wasn't Diane's style then, and it isn't her approach now," says Maura.

"I guess negative attention is better than no attention at all," I suggest.

"That's pretty much what she said. She couldn't get attention for her looks, her clothes, her grades, or her athleticism. Again, these are her words, not mine. Her way of attracting attention was to be the class clown or to hurl insults. She used the word obnoxious to describe herself."

"Well, that is some first-rate self-awareness. I will give her that."

"You are not kidding, Francesca. Diane said she got a 2nd job and emptied her savings to pay for this trip. She said she was jealous that I don't have the same financial stresses she has. She also told me some other more personal stuff that I won't get into, but Diane has a lot of issues."

"Yeah, it sounds like Diane is a hot mess. Look, we can all understand that life has been stormy for her, but that doesn't give her a free pass to insult people. If she doesn't want to alienate everyone she meets, she might want to find another way to deal with her issues. For her sake, hopefully, she will learn from this whole experience."

"Maybe I'm naïve, but I think this was a wake-up call for her. Diane said that she has always been so consumed with her own issues that she never stopped to think that other people also have struggles. She said she was going to work on being more empathetic. Now, do you see why I was so understanding when we talked?"

"It makes more sense, but you're exceptionally kind."

We sit in silence and enjoy the quiet of the night. It's been a long day but it's as if we are all too exhausted or maybe too comfortable to retire to our rooms.

"What do you say we call it a night? I'm excited to meet up with my old friend David tomorrow." Jokes Lauren.

"Ahhh, as in Statue of…You really loved Florence, didn't you?"

"I did, Stephanie. It was a magical time in my life. Robert has always wanted to take me to Italy. He never could understand why I wouldn't want to visit Florence with him. I guess I wanted to leave my memories of my time there untarnished. It also never felt right for me to return here with my husband."

"I don't know what I am more excited about, seeing Florence or hearing about this magical time in your life." Says Francesca.

"I'm going to hit the sack, but I leave you with this teaser." Lauren stands, turning her head to speak to each of us. "Always be willing to take a chance on love. You never know where it might lead you. If it feels right, and there aren't any crazy red flags, of course, be willing to see where the road goes. That is a cookie crumb for you three to nibble. Juicy details will follow. Oh, and Stephanie, if you feel like this is directed at you, it's because it is. Don't think I didn't see you and Gianni deep into each other's eyes today at the pool. It was as if you were sitting next to a hot tub, not a pool, with all that steam rising."

Maura and Francesca simultaneously look at me, jaw dropped. Lauren adds. "I thought I was watching a scene from Penny's novel." Our laughter escalates.

Maura looks at me. "And you said nothing to us. I feel so deceived." Francesca responds directly to Maura.

"We can't trust this one, can we?"

Teasing, I respond. "You know me. I'm hiding a passionate love story waiting to be written…by Penny."

The delightful evening ends with laughter and warm hugs. We head off to our respective rooms, putting an end to another insightful day. I lay awake thinking about Lauren and the respect I have for her. Despite her illness, she is so full of love and remains committed to following her spiritual journey. Fearless, whether confronting Diane or facing what she calls unfinished business in Florence, Lauren is squeezing every ounce of life out of each day. I drift off to sleep, thinking about my awe-inspiring friend. My life has been enriched by this tour in ways I never could have imagined when Ellen convinced me to take a 2nd look at the website 10 months ago.

Chapter 36
An Old Friend

Day 8 - Florence

We depart from the two villas, leaving behind the serenity of rural Tuscany. Less than two hours later, our bus reaches Florence's cultural center.

"We will be surrounded by beauty today and tomorrow. Fortunately, I was able to get my…" Dan interrupts Gianni from the second row. "Let me guess, a fabulous, dear old friend."

Even Gianni joins in the laughter.

"I've become predictable or so you think. You're right, Dan, about one thing. Someone fabulous will be joining us. But not a dear old friend but rather my niece. Margherita is studying Art History with an emphasis on Renaissance art in a PhD program in Florence."

Gianni, speaking in Italian, directs the driver to an exact location to park the bus. We descend into a parking lot adjacent to the Piazza Di Marca, where Gianni, already several strides ahead of us, embraces who I assume to be his niece. As we briskly walk towards Gianni, the whistling of multiple languages reverberates throughout the piazza. Tourists from all points of the world unite to devour the city's world-renowned art as summer rolls closer to an end.

Breathing heavily after what felt like a jog to meet up with Gianni, he introduces us to his niece.

"Margherita, please meet nine authors who are looking for inspiration from Michelangelo, Botticelli, Donatello, and any of the other greats the city offers. We met these famous artists in Rome, but we will reacquaint ourselves with them from a whole new perspective."

"Benvenuti a Firenze." Family traits run deep. Speaking

English perfectly with a slight accent, we immediately latch on to her every word.

"Like my uncle said, there is plenty of inspiration and lots of beauty to motivate you in Florence. It's actually the birthplace of the Renaissance movement. We will start with the Galleria dell 'Accademia and then the Duomo, which are two main attractions in Florence."

Margherita leads us to the rear end of the piazza center. Walking backwards to face us as we follow, she continues. "Not only are our statues and artwork amazing, but Florence also offers so much more to our visitors. It's a smaller city than Rome, but it's charming, comfortable, and even romantic."

For some unknown reason, I instinctively look in Gianni's direction when Margherita says 'romantic' as if that word connects the two of us. 'God, did anyone notice?' My eyes slowly transition to the group, looking for signs that someone noticed.

"We have lots of lovely, small cobblestone streets, cafes, and vendors in Florence. Shopping in Florence is fantastic. It's no Milan, of course, with their posh high fashion." Margherita offers a slight eye roll. "But I like to think Florence is more inviting. You don't need to be runway ready to feel like there is a style for you in Florence."

Margherita smiles when gushing about Florence, revealing her perfectly aligned white teeth. Her bold, red lipstick, showcasing her confidence, and glistens against her blondish brown hair, pulled tight back off her face. She wears her tight, cropped summer jeans and silky blouse well. After following her skillful backward march for a 10-minute walk, we reach the Accademia Gallery.

"Before we enter, let me suggest other tourist spots while you are here, if my uncle allows you any time for fun."

"You know me, cara mia. We are all business and no time for fun."

"Ok I am in charge in Florence, so I give you all free passes."

We smile as we enjoy their loving banter.

"Make sure to walk over Ponte Vecchio, which is the Old Bridge. Something interesting about the Ponte Vecchio is that it is an old, medieval stone bridge with lots of shops built into it, which was a common practice back in medieval times too. The bridge extends over the Arno River. The Boboli Gardens are tranquil…a fabulous place to visit. Do you like people watching?"

We all shake our heads in acknowledgement.

"I know it's a favorite Italian pastime. The Basilica of Santa Croce is a lovely church. Michelangelo and Galileo are buried there but the excitement is outside of the church on the piazza. You will see musicians, people of all ages dancing, kids playing. It's always entertaining."

"I don't know. That sounds like too much entertainment for your uncle's liking." Muses Stanley. The rest of us laugh and look to Gianni for his reaction. He extends his long arms.

"What do you Americans say? I'm a buzz kill."

We follow Margherita into the dell 'Accademia for our tour. Gianni watches his niece intensely, bursting with pride, as she guides us through the Renaissance art collection. I envision him calling his younger sister later in the day to boast about Margherita. As we turn a corner, a large crowd fills the marble hallway. The enormous Statue of David, cut from a slab of Carrara marble, as Margherita explains, is on full display before us.

It is truly an awe-inspiring work of art to be admired. I didn't have the same appreciation for its glory when I was in Florence as a young woman, but at this age, it takes my breath away. Margherita tells us he often makes grown men cry the first time they see David. Our group walks up to the black, rod iron barrier that surrounds the statue on all four sides like a team of bodyguards surrounding a movie star. While his size is enormous, David's life-like features make him mesmerizing. Every defined line of his realistic body pulls your eyes up and down his outstanding physique in a way that a man undresses a woman with his eyes. Michelangelo was a true genius. Standing before the 17' wonder, his presence does make me feel like I want to be a better writer. I can't sculpt my way out of a stone quarry but the degree of perfection in creating David leaves an indelible impact on me.

Margherita discusses the extraction process from Fantiscritti quarry used to create David and how the statue was moved from its original outside location to inside the gallery. When I look to my right, I notice Lauren standing alone on the far side of the statue from where our group is standing. She seems to be having a moment. The Statue of David is a marvel to all of us, but it has significant meaning to her for reasons she has not yet disclosed. Lauren lingers even longer when we exit the exhibit. She seems to be soaking in every grain of him as if he is an old boyfriend meeting up after years apart. Finally, she releases herself from David; it's as if she and her old lover know it's time to say goodbye one last time. Lauren slowly strolls towards us all while turning her head back every couple of steps to get a final glimpse of his beauty.

"You okay girl?" I ask. I wrap my arm around Lauren's shoulder, and she easily drops her head into mine.

"Yeah. I'm good. My old friend and I had a lot of catching up to do. He is gorgeous though, isn't he?"

"He's handsome, but not my type." I quip.

The three of us match Lauren's slow pace as we exit the gallery to join the rest of our writing group. Standing together, we wait for our next direction from Margherita.

"After the Duomo, I have a meeting at a Synagogue. I assume we are still planning on dinner tonight?" Says Maura.

"Dinner, absolutely." Lauren looks at Francesca and me for affirmation. "I know we haven't talked about it yet today but don't think I forgot about dancing. Is everyone still up for it?" Lauren smiles as she asks.

I'm pretty sure Maura hoped that it was just a fleeting and

forgotten discussion, but she knows dancing is all part of Lauren's trip down memory lane. There is no way any of us would disappoint her.

"Oh yeah. We are all in." Proclaims Francesca.

"And we can't wait." Adds Maura.

We all give Maura a suspicious look.

"What? I can't wait."

As we spend the rest of the day taking in the sites, it's clear Margherita didn't oversell the stunning city. After enjoying the vibrant atmosphere outside of the Basilica of Santa Croce, I was drawn inside the cathedral to light a candle for Lauren. That's the funny thing about religion - it pulls you close in moments of despair. I know it's naive, but I convince myself that somehow our collective energy and prayer in Florence, the city that is so meaningful to Lauren for God knows why, could somehow save her.

Chapter 37
Road Not Taken

Day 8 – Florence

"I love this neighborhood. It's so hip, don't you think? Well, as much as someone who sleeps in flannel pajamas and is in bed by 9 with a book knows what hip is."

Francesca responds directly to Maura.

"Not that I'm the aficionado on hip either, but I did read that San Frediano was voted one of the coolest neighborhoods in the world. I can see why."

Located on the other side of the Arno River from Punto Vecchio, San Frediano is impressive with its cool shops, swanky bars, and trendy eateries. After a full day of sightseeing, we decided on an early dinner. Time is of the essence! Before hitting the nightclub, we need to get all gussied up for dancing the night away.

Margherita recommended one of her favorites, a trattoria called *Azzurro*, meaning blue in Italian. It's early by Italian standards. We easily find a table at the restaurant located not far from our hotel. True to its name, the walls are painted in a two-tone blue, the floor, a mismatch of blue tiles, and the chairs are a blue crushed velvet. Modern, chrome touches flow throughout the welcoming eatery. The diverse menu is a blend of old world classics and contemporary selections.

A young, attractive woman with multiple piercings and several vibrant tattoos imprinted on her youthful skin greets us.

"Buona Sera."

We figured out early on that Lauren and I speak enough Italian to get us in or out of trouble. Francesca and Maura, both fluent, do the talking for the four of us.

"Let's see. Margherita said we have to try the oysters. They sound wonderful, baked with *parmigiano, aglio, pane e prezzemolo.* Maybe we should share a few dishes."

I suggest. "Ok. The oysters for sure, oh, the black truffle risotto? That sounds amazing." Lauren agrees. "Sounds delicious. How about the chicken with a spinach puree, prosciutto, and mozzarella in a wine sauce?"

Maura teases. "Sounds amazing, but I hope that doesn't revisit us while we are getting down on the dance floor."

Francesca, Lauren, and I smile sweetly at one another. Maura's jargon might be outdated, but she's certainly feigning excitement for Lauren. Francesca selects a perfect Vernaccia for the table, a white wine from the Tuscan area.

"Maura, how was your synagogue visit?" Asks Lauren.

"Amazing. The architecture was just stunning, both the interior and exterior. It's one of the largest synagogues in Europe."

"That's wonderful. Who was your meeting with?" asks Francesca.

"This absolutely lovely, elderly woman whose family has been part of the congregation for over 100 years. She's going to request permission from local families for me to include their personal stories in my book. Hopefully they will agree."

"We are going to read about you one day. You will be one of few premier experts writing about Italian Jews during the holocaust."

"I don't know about that, but sadly, my competition is dwindling with every passing year. Everyone I speak with is so eager for me to keep their stories alive."

Maura asks. "How was the rest of the day?"

"New bag." Proudly, I varnish a huge smile as I pull my bag from the back of the chair and hold it up, framing it with my two hands.

"Very cute. Oh, and thank God. I was just thinking you needed more bags because you don't have enough." Maura teases.

"Well, you know. You can never have too many."

"True, true. You never know when one will desperately need a red bag with…oh, wow, what are those gold studs?"

"Cute, isn't it?" I rhetorically ask.

Maura smiles and tilts her head. She doesn't even pretend to like the bag best suited for the set of housewives of New Jersey.

Lauren adds. "Shopping was a lot of fun, but the Santa Croce Cathedral didn't disappoint either. Margherita was so right. We experienced first rate people watching."

Francesca jumps in. "And when we say 'people watching,' we are talking in part about Margaret and Dan."

"Why doesn't that surprise me?" Responds Maura.

"Our whole writing crew ended up at Santa Croce at the same time. That might have been the highlight of the afternoon. It was hysterical."

The three of us laugh, Maura smiling as she looks at each of us, trying to understand what happened.

"Dan and Margaret were dancing on the piazza with each other and pushed themselves in the middle of a large crowd."

I move my hands in a circular motion to describe them. "A huge circle formed around them. While they were in the middle of the circle, everyone was dancing and cheering and clapping for them. Apparently, their lunch included plenty of vino."

"Accordion players and guitar players were all rockin' it. There were all sorts of nuttiness happening in the best way possible." Francesca explains.

"Sounds hysterical. Hopefully someone got it on video."

The server returns with four glasses and a bottle of white

wine. She pours a small amount for Francesca to taste. All four glasses are poured as the conversation continues.

"It was a fun day. Gianni and his niece are so cute together, aren't they?" Just mentioning his name makes me blush. I nervously take a sip of my wine.

"Lauren. Was seeing the Statue of David everything you expected it to be?"

"It was everything and more. But not for the reasons I thought it would be."

"How so?" I ask as I lift my elbows and rest them on the table.

"Before this trip, I *thought* or should I say feared, I would visit the Statue of David and feel a sense of loss or even regret."

Lauren pushes her hair behind her ears and pauses as if she is choosing her words carefully. Francesca suggests. "Sounds like this trip has been more of a plot twist."

Lauren smiles. "Yes. The trip has changed my perspective, sort of like a plot twist."

"My husband..." Lauren gathers her thoughts.

"Bob. You know I adore him. He is worried about me because of...my situation...and driving me nuts this whole trip. But I love him more than anything. My kids. Claire and Christopher. They are my everything. I couldn't love them any more than I do. But I have spent so much of my life wondering about what 'coulda' or 'shoulda' been. Florence, especially the Statue of David, represents doubt that has tugged at my heart throughout my marriage. Visiting David today...It's like I sold my family short all these years. I know now, life brought me right where I needed to go."

Francesca says. "Don't beat yourself up. Who doesn't look back on decisions made when they were younger and have a flicker of regret. It doesn't change the love we have for your family."

"Exactly. I agree 100%. I can't count how many times I have thought about Glen, my college boyfriend, especially since Michael left me. Songs are written about the one who got away. It's normal to wonder. I'm not saying I regret not staying with him, but I have allowed myself to imagine what my life would have been like with him."

Maura adds. "It's human nature to think about roads not taken…and there are poems written about that."

"Robert Frost would agree. Is it safe to assume this has something to do with another man?" Asks Francesca.

"Don't tell me you also married a random man when you were in Italy before?" I suggest.

"Noooo! That didn't happen. You alone have that honor, Stephanie. But, yes, there was another man when I studied abroad."

"Glad it wasn't as complicated as a marriage. Tell us all about him."

"We didn't have a marriage to untangle, Stephanie, but…" Lauren exhales.

"But things with us did get quite complicated."

~

"I met Bob at a frat party during the spring semester of my second year at Vanderbilt. I was drawn to his kind eyes. You hear people use this description…kind eyes…. What does that even mean? If you were to meet Bob, it would be obvious. Maybe it's the shape of his eyes or the way he looks at you when you talk to him." Lauren looks off in the distance as if she is imagining Bob's face.

"During college, he was the type of guy that everyone wanted to be around. He still is."

This is hard for Lauren. She pauses again and we wait. I take the last sip of my wine. Francesca notices me looking at the bottle and pours me the remaining few sips from the bottle.

"We started dating, casually at first, but things progressed rather quickly. Claire recently asked Bob and me if it was love at first sight or if we knew immediately that we would get married. You know, those questions that your kids naturally are curious about."

"What did you and Bob tell Claire?" I ask.

"Bob immediately said that the minute he laid eyes on me, he knew I was the one. He told Claire how he was attracted to my beauty at first, but he loved me for my intelligence, my kindness and he loved how I looked out for the underdog. He then said that I was even more beautiful than the day I walked into that frat house all those years ago." Lauren nervously chuckles then looks down in embarrassment.

"Looks like Bob got it right about you, day one," Francesca says. "What did you tell Claire about your first impression?"

"I was perspiring while Bob was talking about me. I always found him to be handsome, kind…an overall great catch, on paper. But I didn't have that same *"he's the one"* feeling about Bob that he had for me. Of course, I told Claire and Bob that I too immediately knew, blah. I stretched the truth, but it was the right thing to do in that situation. Bob didn't make my heart stop…you know, I didn't have butterflies in your stomach when he walked in a room like you read about in, dare I say, a saucy novel by Penny."

"We have gotten a lot of mileage out of her reading, haven't we," I suggest.

"Like I said before, props to Penny. She nailed the element of surprise. I digress. Go on Lauren," declares Francesca.

"This is why I love you ladies," Lauren says as she smiles big. "We just jump from here to there…it's like we are on the same page. Anyways, back to Bob."

We all laugh in a way women laugh together when they have an undeniable bond.

"It was always so comfortable and safe with him. You know? He takes care of me. Always has. I love him. I adore him."

"But…" Francesca asks.

"But…You guys already know I'm a hopeless romantic. Early on in our relationship, I expected my heart to pound out my chest or some signal that says this is it! He has never made me feel weak in the knees. God. It feels so good to say this out loud."

"Let it out. It's okay," I empathize. "Your relationship…My impression is that you and Bob get along well, no?"

"Oh yeah. That has never been an issue. Not surprisingly, Bob turned out to be a wonderful husband. We've always gotten along well. Since becoming ill, I couldn't have asked for a better partner and support system to be by my side. Sometimes overly supportive as you have all observed, but nevertheless, he's been amazing. I have always loved him, just not in the way I imagined I would have loved my husband."

"Honestly, strong marriages look different from one relationship to another."

"Yes, Maura agreed. There's no such thing as one size fits all when you are talkin' marriages."

"If you weren't crazy in love when you first started to date, why did you stay with him?" I ask.

"Well, my mother was a real game changer."

"Oh no. Not the mother."

"Yes! The mother. Bob and I dated all spring semester, and then over the summer, he visited me at our beach house."

Lauren looks uncomfortable mentioning the family beach house. We could probably thank Diane for that.

"I may not have been sure if Bob was the one for me, but my mother certainly did."

"You must have been serious since you invited him to meet your family, right?" Maura confirms.

"I mean, he was my boyfriend, sure, it was serious-ish. I guess, but in no way was I thinking about a future together. My fatal error was telling my mother about him. She badgered me until I invited him to our beach home. That woman was like a dog on a bone when she got something in her mind."

The server returns with the oysters and crusty, Florentine bread. Rich with flavor, we enjoy the bread dipped in the thick sauce while mesmerized by Lauren's story.

"mmm. Delicious." Says Lauren as she chews. "We were so young. I was only 20 years old, and Bob was just a year older than me. Once my mother met him she determined that the suit fit, if you will. My mom honestly believed I was in college to get my 'M.R.S.' degree and I found my mister. I'd like to think that wasn't my goal, or at least my only goal."

"What did you want to do after college," asks Maura.

"What did I want, or my mother want because those were two very different things. I wanted to be in the art world. Maybe as a curator or a dealer. That was my dream."

"That explains why you are so knowledgeable when we visit the museums."

"Yeah Stephanie. Lauren is like a walking art Wikipedia," Francesca adds.

"You guys are too kind. I have always loved art, art history. I am not a bad artist either but enough of that," Lauren shyly states. "My mom told me that a career in the art world was never going to happen. She never believed in me. She thought it wasn't appropriate for a woman to be in a career like that. Among other things, she was the original anti-feminist. I was given 'permission' to be an art teacher for a couple of years, then I would stop working to have a family.”

Lauren puts her fork down on her plate. She takes a moment and then she declares.

“And that is exactly what I did. She had an agenda and I fell in line. I did. I succumbed to her demands.” Lauren appears aggravated as she loses herself in unpleasant memories of her mother.

“Don’t get me wrong, I loved being home with my kids. I know it was a privilege but what kind of mother shoots down her daughter’s dreams? I certainly would never suggest to my daughter that she needs to go to college to find a husband and give up her career goals. That would never happen anyway; another story for another time.”

Lauren is full of surprises. I can’t help but wonder what that comment means but clearly it isn’t the time to ask.

“Okay. You were dating Bob…you liked him well enough, but you weren’t thinking about marriage at that point in your life. Why did you listen to your mom if you weren’t sure about him?” asks Francesca.

“Well, if you knew my mom you’d understand. My father, my brother and I were scared of her. She was a bully, really. Ya know my younger sister, Kelly, was the brave one of the family. She stood up to my mom for the rest of us.” Lauren chuckles, seemingly reflecting on her sister’s resistance to their mother.

“Bit controlling, was she?” I suggest.

“Yeah. You can say that again. But it went beyond that. She was also mean and miserable. My dad was such a good, sweet man and my mother was absolutely brutal with him too.”

“Would you say you married your father?” Asks Maura.

Lauren gives that thought before responding. “Bob is kind like my father, yes, but…and I mean no disrespect to my father. My husband has a backbone. He wouldn't allow a wife to treat him or his children the way my mother treated our family. I know my dad was a victim too of her wrath, but he didn't protect any of us."

"Other than Kelly, none of you pushed back at her?"

"Oh, every now and again, I would do something passive aggressive to feel in control. One time, she insisted I wear this dress, which she bought me because it was the 'perfect dress' for some dumb party. It was hideous. I was 20 years old, and I wasn't allowed to even decide what damn dress to wear. Right before we walked out of the house, I purposely got it stuck on a door hook, so the dress ripped right along my breast. Of course, I had to change, and she was furious. We all paid for that, but I remember thinking it was worth it. My dad looked at me and smiled. He understood that sometimes you had to push back in small ways to feel in control."

"Yeah. That makes sense. You had to do what you could to fight back. What specifically did your mom like about Bob?" Asks Francesca.

"My mom thought he was so handsome. He was polite, but most of all, he had the right pedigree for her. He was and is a banker and he comes from a long line of bankers. Based on my mother's logic, his family met or even surpassed our family's stature, so he was a keeper. My mom made up her mind that I would marry him. Fortunately for her, Bob was thrilled to have an ally in that arena. He certainly didn't care for my mother otherwise, but he appreciated her endorsement."

"Do you think your mom's actions came from a good place? Did she think you would be happy with him?" Maura asks.

"Oh, hell no. She didn't care about us."

Lauren sounds uncharacteristically angry.

"My mother thought about her image with her friends or how our family was perceived at the country club. What we wore, where we went to school, where we vacationed, who our friends were. It was never about our happiness but her reputation. She could care less if I wanted to be married to Bob. She only cared that she could brag that her daughter was marrying someone she deemed to be…elite. Everything was about her."

The three of us sit quietly as Lauren vents about her mother. She needs to get it out and we are a non-judgmental sounding board for her. Francesca uses a slice of bread to soak up the remaining sauce from the oysters. As she is still chewing, the server brings us our risotto and the chicken dish. Passing the culinary creations from one to another, we comment on the aroma of the unique blends and the generous amount of grated truffle used on the risotto.

Lauren explains that she returned to Vanderbilt for her 3rd year, his last year of college, and continued dating. They got along and rarely even bickered but something was missing for her. When she thought about breaking up with him, she called her mother.

"Knowing your mother, why do you think you would have told her about breaking up with him?"

"Oh, I don't know. Maybe it was conditioning, living under her control. I never consulted her like my daughter comes to me for support or advice. It always felt like I was asking permission from her."

"Permission not granted?" I ask.

"Are you kidding? She told me I wouldn't find anyone better and even accused me of thinking I was prettier than I was. She said with every passing year, Bob would get better looking and my looks would diminish."

"Wow. She was horrible." I blurt out, momentarily forgetting this was Lauren's mom.

Lauren doesn't even blink.

"Horrible. Right? And that isn't the half of it. I can go on for hours. I guess part of me feared my mother was right. After years of being minimized, you start believing it. I guess I thought I should ignore my feelings and feel lucky I got this guy who was sooo much better than me…according to my mother. I thought I didn't deserve to be any happier than I was, so I stayed with Bob."

Thinking back to Diane's assumptions about Lauren, admittedly, I'm also guilty of coming to certain conclusions about her. Listening to Lauren reflect on her past, I'm shocked. Like Diane, my perception of her was way off. Rather than an idyllic life, she has had more than her share of struggles.

"Well, your mom was so wrong about you. Sounds like Bob was a catch and he recognized that you were too."

"Aww. You are so sweet. He really helped to rebuild my self-esteem. Bob has always put me on a pedestal."

Lauren tells us that she decided to study abroad in Florence 2nd semester of junior year and her mother fully supported the decision.

"I'm surprised that your mom agreed to allow you to study abroad," says Maura.

"It fit right into her narrative. That would give her something to brag about with her friends. She also thought it would make me more interesting when I accompanied Bob to cocktail parties. It was all about laying the groundwork for our marriage. Trust me, even my study abroad reverted to her. At least she did see a personal benefit or I wouldn't have been allowed to go at all."

Lauren isn't holding back. She paints an honest, albeit difficult to hear, picture of the woman who raised her.

Lauren resumes after a short pause. "Like Gianni talked about yesterday, conflict is key. If I were writing a novel based on my life, which I'm not by the way, conflict would enter the picture when I studied abroad in Florence." Lauren takes a deep breath, sips her wine then tells about her time studying abroad. "I lived with two other young ladies, Sarah and Liz. They didn't go to Vanderbilt, so I didn't know them before meeting them in Florence. There were a few small apartment buildings with a courtyard just on the edge of Florence. We weren't quite downtown but not really far from this neighborhood, actually. It was basically a glorified dorm full of students from a bunch of different colleges. Not long after we moved in, I noticed a group of guys in the courtyard playing hacky sack. I don't know if kids even play that anymore?"

I recall. "Oh yeah. I remember that. Everyone played back then."

Lauren resumes. The three of us listen intently to Lauren. Animated in her expression, she takes us on a trip, recalling a joyful time from her past.

"One of the boys caught my eye in a big way. Oh God was he cute."

Lauren appears to drift to another time in her life. "He had this messy dark, brown hair with lots of curls. His big, green eyes sucked me in. Part of the attraction was that he was so different in every way from…from what I had grown accustomed to. Bob was always so clean cut with his perfectly quaffed hair. He looked like a banker even as a college student. This boy, Andrew. Everyone called him Andy, was so hot. We talked, we flirted. He…"

Francesca finishes Lauren's sentence. "Made you go weak in the knees."

"Yes. Exactly…I felt something radiate throughout my body. I was flooded with emotions. Meeting Andy made me quickly realize exactly what was missing from my feelings for Bob. I knew it was wrong, but I started dating him. I'm so embarrassed to admit that. It feels so good to talk about it."

The server returns to the table to check in with us. We continue to slowly eat our shared dishes, more consumed with Lauren's story than the exquisite flavors.

"You were young, not married and not even engaged. You have the advantage of time and experience now but what were you 20, 21?"

"Yeah. I turned 21 while studying abroad but I was old

enough to know it was wrong. All these years later and it still feels cathartic to talk about it. I'm glad you guys don't judge me."

"Judge?" Maura responds. "You just picked up a boyfriend in Italy. Our friend over here ran off and got married in Italy behind her boyfriend's back."

The four of us laugh. Strangely, it warms my heart to hear my new friends tease me about my past transgression. Our laughter trickles out and Francesca gets the conversation back on track.

"Okay. Did you tell your study-abroad friends that you had a boyfriend back home?"

"Don't ask me why but I never told my new friends about Bob. Sarah and Liz each said they didn't have a boyfriend. For some reason, I told them I didn't have a boyfriend either. I swear it was never my intention to go to Florence and claim to be single. I just said no. It's like I wanted to be someone else for a few months. Eventually, I told Andy as things progressed with us but no one else knew about Bob. You can't get away with that these days with social media but then, I easily recreated myself, even if it was for a few months."

The server approaches our table. I slide the remnants of the risotto onto my plate as we hand her our empty dishes.

"When you meet people, you have the right to disclose whatever part of your life you want to share. Who knows. Maybe I'm an international spy."

"International spy? You don't exactly blend. Between the shoes, the bags, the hair…we would all be dead by now." Maura loves poking fun at my style, and I love every bit of it.

"What were your study abroad girlfriends like?" Asks Maura.

"Those girls were a hoot. We had a blast together. Andy, me, and the friends we made partied, traveled, danced…a lot. It was a four-month party."

"Dancing. I think I'm beginning to understand. Are we recreating the magic from your experience studying abroad when we go dancing later tonight?" Teases Maura.

"Absolutely and I can't imagine better dance partners in crime to recreate that time in my life." Smiles Lauren. "I felt so free as when I studied abroad, like I have felt with you three over these past couple of weeks."

The server returns to our table and Maura orders four double espressos. "We are going to need it to get through the night. Well, I need it."

While we wait for our punch of caffeine, I suggest. "It sounds like you and Andy developed a pretty serious relationship."

"Very serious. Things heated up with Andy and me quickly. I felt closer to him in four months than I did to Bob, at that time."

We drink our espresso then walk back to the hotel. Once again, Lauren leaves us wanting to hear more about her path not taken.

Chapter 38
Back to the Future

"Maura, I'll be waiting for you in my room for us to get ready. I already pulled out a few things for you to try on."

"Do you travel with the assumption that you will meet the poster child for what not to wear? Looks like you found her, right here."

"I have my deficits - Makeovers and packing like a rock star…that's where I shine."

It's as if we are twentysomethings heading back to our flats to get ready for a night out on the town. I wonder what's running through Lauren's head. Like a scene from Back to the Future, she must feel like she has one foot planted in the present and the other, reaching far back to an earlier era completely removed from her current reality, even if it's only for one night. A few minutes after returning to my hotel room, I hear a light tap on the door I slightly propped open with a security bar.

"Doors open!"

As Maura walks in, I greet her as if I hadn't just seen her 15 minutes ago. Shortly after meeting Maura, I imagined giving her a make-over and here we are! This is going to be fun, however, I need to be mindful of her insecurities. Maura's eyes slowly roam the room. Four dresses hang on the bathroom door like it's the outside of a fitting room.

"I feel like I just walked into a high-end department store."

Maura then looks to the left at the solid, wood desk pushed up against the wall, opposite the double bed. It's covered from one end to another with hot rollers, a flat iron, a variety of hairbrushes, hair serum, and enough makeup for a movie set.

"Or maybe a salon. Just how many bags did you pack for this

trip? I have been squeezing every drop out of the hotel bottles of soap and shampoo this whole trip." Says Maura as her eyes wonder from one corner of the room to the next.

"I like to have my home tools and supplies when I travel. Besides, you want to stay away from hotel shampoos. They usually are cheap, high in sulfates so they will strip your hair of moisture."

"Oh, I didn't know that. I'll keep that in mind the next time I travel. I will be sure to lug my cheap shampoo from home instead of using the cheap hotel shampoo."

I smile at Maura.

"I know the room looks a little messy, but I prefer to call it organized chaos."

Maura probably isn't even thinking about my room. She's more consumed with what in the world I'm about to do to her. I walk to the bathroom door and separate one hanging dress from another.

"Take a look at these dresses. All of them would look great on you but since you are taller and thinner than me, I think these black, tight, form-fitting dresses would work best."

It looks like Maura is going to break out in hives with words like tight and form fitting. She's been wearing nothing but flowy dresses and skirts, loose jeans, and baggy shirts this whole trip. "Keep an open mind and I promise you won't regret it."

"I'm going to go with the flow tonight, for Lauren and I promise you I *will* regret whatever I decide to wear as soon as I walk out that door, so it doesn't matter what I put on. Somehow, I'm okay with that."

I ask Maura to sit in the leather back chair that's tucked under the desk. I pour her a glass of wine into one of the glasses I borrowed from the hotel bar.

"Enjoy your wine and relax." I suggest.

"Isn't this wine supposed to be for one of your friends back home?"

"I have plenty. Besides, I only have room to stuff a couple bottles in my luggage." Maura looks from left to right. "I would imagine so."

Over the next 30 minutes, I bring out all the stops. Every hot roller is needed for her curly, thick, dark brown hair. After the rollers came out, I shape her face with more defined smaller curls using the flat iron and then straighten her long bangs. I add hair products for a final touch.

"You can stand up and look. What do you think?"

"Holy shit. That's my hair? Did you put a wig on me without me noticing? I look like I just stepped out of 'As the World Turns.'"

"I know right. Isn't it fabulous? Soap opera hair is the Holy Grail of hair perfection. Sit, Sit. Time for makeup."

Maura looks progressively more panicked.

"Can you pass me my wine glass?"

"You seem a little nervous."

"I repeat. I'm going with the flow. Wine is helping me with that commitment."

"As we age, blended lighter tones are best on our eyes to make your eyes look bigger. You see how that looks?"

Maura instinctively nods and then takes a big gulp of her wine.

"Door's open," I shout in response to the faint knock.

Francesca, confidently enters the room, dressed in a red, V-neck tight fitting wrap dress that accentuates her curves. Large dangling earrings pull the outfit together. Her gray, modern styled, close-cut hair reveals her high cheekbones. Lauren dazzles in a cobalt blue jumpsuit and silver strappy heels. Her gorgeous blue eyes pop between the outfit and her heavier than usual make-up. She looks like a picture of health; It's so hard to comprehend that a killer is quietly invading her body.

"Wow. Maura. Look at you!" screams Lauren.

"Wait until you send your husband pictures." Lauren says.

"Pictures? Not a good idea. There would be a rescue squad at our door in 10 minutes. Marty would take one look at my hair and all this makeup and assume I am being held against my will." Maura twists and turns her head, taking a closer look at herself. "I can hear him now. Help! My wife has been kidnapped and forced into some 80's TV remake. The poor man would be distraught."

"Maura. You are too much."

Maura stands up, picks up the heels Francesca brought her, grabs the dresses from the back of the door and enters the bathroom…We wait…

"I'm coming out," announces Maura.

Francesca and I are standing at the foot of the bed and Lauren is sitting on the chair that had previously been converted to a makeshift salon chair for Maura.

Maura steps out of the bathroom and stands in front of us like we are assessing her bat mitzvah outfit. She pulls and tucks at the dress like an awkward teenager who doesn't recognize her own beauty.

"You look amazing. Dear God. Those legs. I knew you had an amazing body, but I didn't know you had all that going on under your long skirts." I wave my hands in a circular motion in the direction of Maura's body.

Francesca says. "I love how the thin straps show off your toned arms. All of that running and working out shows."

"Thanks ladies. You all look amazing too. This is out of the box for me but who knows, maybe it is time to add a little spice to my boring wardrobe. Hiding under baggy clothes is part of how I have always gone under the radar. Ya know. It's a security thing."

Maura stands in front of the mirror attached to the back of the bathroom door, turning, front to back, taking in her new look.

"It's so weird to see me like this."

"Well you look great and you can keep the dress. I will never look at it the same again. I can assure you, I don't look like that." I say as I point to Maura in the mirror.

"Oh stop." insists Maura. "Seriously ladies. You three look great too. What do you all do to stay in shape?"

"Yoga, this past year, ya know…since I started working at the studio. I have always been an on again off again exerciser. I hope I stick to it this time," I respond.

"Yeah, I go to the gym when I can but with my crazy hours, I don't work out nearly enough."

We all look at Lauren. Did we enter awkward territory? Since learning about her illness, I have been cognizant of the fact that Francesca, Maura, and I will pick up our lives back home where we left off. Family, jobs, errands, social events, and yes, working out, will keep us busy like before. Lauren, presumably, will return to managing her cancer, new drugs, good and bad days. I know she didn't want us to treat her any differently but God! Our conversation suddenly feels frivolous given the magnitude of what awaits Lauren upon her return home.

"I'm a big walker." Lauren smiles. "My neighborhood gals and I go early in the morning before starting our day. We get our heart rate up, ya know talk. It's good for the body and soul. Lately, of course, the walks have been more hit or miss but when I can, I still join them."

"Well, you do what you can." Why did I say that? It's like I minimized her. Sometimes silence is the best response. I gotta work on that. I don't know how to walk that back, so it's dangling out there, awkwardly." I quickly transition the conversation.

"You girls pour yourselves some wine and keep talking. Margherita said the clubs don't get going until late, so we have about an hour before we need to leave. I'm gonna slip into my dress."

~

"Lauren, you have a huge smile on your face. What are you thinking?" Francesca asks.

"This feels so right. I'm literally transported in time. The four of us sitting here, all decked out, reminds me of my study abroad friends in our flats. Before going out dancing, we would share clothes, put on make-up, drink, laugh… Much tauter skin back but everything else is the same."

"Tell us more about Andy, other than the fact that he was hot." I ask.

"Let's see. He and I loved going to museums and traveling together. We loved being alone but we also loved socializing with the friends we made. It was four months of bliss." Lauren's whole face lights up as if she has been transported back in time.

"Andy was also an Art History major. We had that in common. Bob has always humored me by doing all that artsy stuff with me, but he doesn't really care for it like Andy did."

It's incredible to watch how wistful Lauren looks talking about Andrew.

"Who knows? Maybe our relationship was always destined to be nothing more than a short term fairytale with the two of us fluttering around Europe for the semester. Life is more than parties, museums, dancing, and travel. Would the relationship have sustained itself in the real world when you add real life responsibilities? I will never know the answer to that question and that's what has always haunted me."

I ask. "Did you guys think about maintaining your relationship after you got back home after studying abroad?"

"Oh yeah. We worked out our whole lives together. After the semester was over, the plan was for me to fly out to see Bob and break up with him. Of course I was gonna wait until after graduation, so I didn't ruin it for him. None of that happened and in fact, I never even told Bob about Andrew. And I mean Never. Years later, he asked if I had met someone in Florence. I was so distant from him while I was abroad. He knew something was off. I never fessed up."

"Am I correct to assume someone prevented you from staying with Andrew?" Francesca astutely asks.

"Exactly. Someone decided for me."

Lauren sits quietly, shaking her head. She takes a sip of her wine.

It's obvious that after all these years later, the mere thought of her mother interfering with her relationship still infuriates her. I guide her back to what seems to bring her pleasure.

"Ok. I have to ask. What is so special about the Statue of David?" Lauren begins to laugh as she covers her mouth.

"It's so embarrassing. Promise you guys aren't going to laugh." Maura explains. "Absolutely not. You know we can't do that."

"Ok fair. Andrew and I were both good artists and we loved the Statue of David. Each time we visited the statue, which was often, we then returned to our flats and sketched one another, naked, striking David's pose but we would add a twist to the drawing by including something in the drawing that we were wearing that day. If I had a hat on that day, Andrew would add a hat to the drawing. Maybe I would add socks or a scarf to my drawing if Andrew wore socks or a scarf. I know it sounds so corny, but we really connected when we would sketch one another like that." Lauren becomes quiet, seemingly deeply immersed in her thoughts.

"It sounds beautiful. Sensual," Francesca quietly suggests. "Yeah. Lovers doing loving things together," says Maura.

"I can understand why you felt so connected to one another. You were close on multiple levels. It must have been difficult saying goodbye to one another at the end of the semester."

"I have such a vivid memory of that day. Andy and I went to the airport together, he walked me to my gate. We hugged and cried, then I boarded my plane. We weren't as sad as you would think though because it was only supposed to be a temporary separation. When I got home, I told Kelly all about Andrew. Since she was so feisty and took pleasure in standing up to my mother, I looked to her as an ally."

Lauren has a sparkle in her eye talking about her younger sister.

"I would have thought Bob would be waiting for you at your parent's home," Francesca says. "I got lucky. Since it was his senior year, he was busy with all those pre graduation events and parties. He was waiting for me to join him at Vanderbilt for his graduation."

We wait. Lauren needs time, space, a few deep breaths and more wine.

"When I got the nerve, I sat my mom down in my bedroom with Kelly by my side. I told my mother that I met a guy and that I was ending my relationship with Bob. I said we have so much in common and that we were so happy together. What else could a mother want for their child but for her to be happy?" We nod in agreement. "She. had. a. meltdown! When I said we wanted to be museum curators or maybe art history professors one day, she wouldn't hear of it. She said something like what kind of man thinks he could support his family as a curator or as a professor? As if there is anything wrong with either of those professions."

"Based on what you have told us about your mother, I'm nervous just thinking about this conversation," says Maura.

"Oh, I was terrified. She was that awful, Maura. It's as if I reverted to a child when I was around her. She emasculated my father and she infantilized my brother and me. She was just so controlling. Kelly said something like, do you hear Lauren? She met a man. She and Andrew are in love. Your daughter is happy with him. Why can't you be happy for her."

I am hanging on to her every word like I'm watching a drama unfold before me. I ask Lauren. "How did your mom respond to her?"

"First, she wanted to know details about Andrew so she could assess his status. She wasn't impressed with his career path but maybe his family could redeem him. If they surpassed Bob's family, based on her criteria, she would have dumped Bob. She was literally that transactional. As much as she supposedly adored Bob, if Andrew's family came over on the Mayflower or his last name was Carnegie or Mellon, we might be having a different conversation."

Lauren makes us all laugh. We each sip our wine, giving her a chance to gather her thoughts. "I take it he didn't pass the founding fathers' club test?" Francesca says.

"No. Not even close. My mother was such a snob. Andrew came from a very middle-class family. They sounded like wonderful, genuine, loving people yet my mother thought his family wasn't good enough for us. Andrew went to a state school in Indiana. God forbid, a state college boy. How could she possibly tell the ladies that? She commanded me to call him and tell him it was over, then I needed to get on a plane to join my boyfriend for his graduation, immediately." Lauren gets quiet. We model her silence. It was obvious she needed a moment.

"Kelly kept repeating for me to tell her. Tell her. Lauren, tell her everything."

Lauren's eyes well up. We plowed too far down this path. Sitting in my hotel room, enjoying a pre-game drink, we are supposed to be reliving a wonderful moment in time from Lauran's past, not reviving an awful memory.

"I knew that once I came clean, things would get even uglier. I felt like I had no choice though." I recall earlier how she referred to her relationship with Andrew as complicated. At this very moment, it's become crystal clear just how complex their relationship was.

"Lauren, how far along were you?" asks Francesca.

"By the time I got home, I must have been only about seven weeks pregnant. We were so careful. I was on the pill when I was at Vanderbilt and when I went abroad, I had about a 2- month supply of pills with me. They ran out. I swear, I only had them with me because the pill helped regulate my periods. I didn't go to Italy with the intention…"

"Look, it was your choice to be on the pill, no matter what the reason," Maura assures Lauren. "How did you tell your mom?"

"Kelly pushed and pushed, "tell her" so I finally blurted out, I'm pregnant."

"My mom lost it. She called me a whore. She even slapped me across the face. Could you imagine hitting your pregnant daughter?"

Lauren stands up and turns around to look at the mirror hanging over the desk. "Look at me. I'm a mess."

"Don't you worry about that. You are in the right place. Stephanie will have you all fixed up in no time. There isn't a color on your face that she can't match," Teases Maura.

I hand Lauren a make-up face wipe. She gathers herself and continues.

"My mom would not let up. She said I would get an abortion and break up with this boy. She accused him of taking advantage of me. Kelly stood up for me but there was no reasoning with her. My mother wanted what she wanted. I can't even explain why I would allow her to bully me into such a life changing decision, but I did. I have lived with that guilt my whole adult life. Rather than celebrate the birth of a baby and our relationship, I gave in to her demands. She made an appointment with my private doctor. 'Girls like me didn't go to clinics.' She literally said that."

"I am so sorry that she pushed you into such a huge decision," Says Francesca.

"Do you know the worst part? She was such a hypocrite. My mother pretended to be so religious and against abortion. Push came to shove, her reputation was far more important than her beliefs. People would talk about how I cheated on my boyfriend and got knocked-up while studying abroad. Scandalous!"

Lauren pauses again then reveals.

"I love my husband and children but how can't I wonder about the family I lost? I have such guilt for many reasons. Not only did I abandon Andy, I lied to Bob. Now that I am closer to the end of life than not, I'm conflicted about the fact that I had an abortion. The crazy thing is, I'm full-heartedly pro-choice yet, it weighs on me. Ya know. You start questioning things like do I have to answer for my lies to these men and what if I'm wrong about abortion. Will my death be a time of reckoning?"

Lauren is spiraling, deep into her internal thoughts. So much pain has been bottled up inside of her for literal decades. She must feel such a sense of relief to get this off her chest even if it does derail the night Lauren has talked about for the past three days.

Maura says. "You are carrying so much on your shoulder."

Maura leans in and hugs Lauren as Francesca and I rub her back and hold her hand.

"None of us have the answers as to what happens in the afterlife but the God I know sees you for the loving and beautiful person that you are."

"Thank you." Lauren says as she blows her nose.

"Boy, this night really took a turn, but It feels so good to talk about everything. I can't tell you how fortunate I feel to have met each of you. You're stuck with me. I literally divulged my deepest, dark secrets."

"Well, you couldn't get rid of us if you tried," says Francesca. "Like Maura said. This is heavy stuff. Maybe think about continuing the dialogue back home with a therapist, a pastor or priest and you can always call us."

"I have thought about that, and I think I will talk with someone. I'm clearly still looking for closure. I'm a mess, aren't I? Let's do the math. Bob and I need to see a marriage counselor. I need to talk to a therapist or a minister. I have my work cut out for me, don't I?"

"You haven't lost your sense of humor," I tell Lauren as we laugh. "You're not alone. Each of us are returning home with more to work on than our books."

"Okay. I gotta ask. Do you know what happened to Andrew?"

We seemed to be moving forward so it's probably time to let the story go but curiosity got the best of me.

"I called Andrew and told him I had a miscarriage. I didn't have the heart to tell him I aborted our baby. There was no reason for us to both live with all that. I told him I decided to stay with Bob. We both cried. We talked every so often for a short while. He tried to convince me I was making a mistake. The calls eventually stopped. I looked him up on Facebook a few years ago and he seemed happy. He appears to have a lovely wife, children and you know what, he is an Art History professor. That made me smile. One of us got there."

"Looks like you both ended up where you belong." I reassure her.

"We did, didn't we." Lauren continues to pat her eyes with the crumpled make-up wipe. Instinctively, I pull another from the container and hand it to her. "Aww thanks… My mom has been dead for years and I still don't forgive her. I am not in any way justifying her actions, she was wrong. But, I did have a moment of clarity standing in front of the Statue of David. I thought about how lucky I am to have Bob and my children. Who knows where 'the road less traveled' would have taken me but I know the road I took was wonderful."

Lauren looks pensive. She then says. "I know one thing; I am a happier person than my mother ever was. We didn't have a great relationship before that but afterwards, our relationship never repaired. She died a miserable woman."

We sit still, in silence, allowing the negative energy to dissipate. "Tonight was supposed to be a night of celebration. Look at me!"

"It's Italy! The night's young!"

"You ladies are amazing. What do you say I get my face cleaned up and we go dance our hearts out?"

"You sit right here. Sit back and let me do my magic."

Lauren smiles and closes her eyes as I dab a brush into what seems like a similar shade of copper eye shadow. After touching up her hair and makeup, we leave my hotel room then take the elevator to the lobby. As we walk towards the front door, we see Gianni walking towards us.

"Look at you ladies. I might need to hire a bodyguard for the night. I will be sitting in that chair all night waiting for your safe return." Gianni points to an orange, plush chair in the center of the modern hotel lobby. As we exit the hotel, Gianni turns and yells to us.

"No excuses will be accepted if you are late for our morning writing clinic."

"Don't you worry about us. We will be up early, ready to write, waiting for the rest of you," Taunts Francesca.

We walk outside of the hotel, jump into a taxi and head off to our dance club adventure.

Chapter 39
Let It All Go

Day 8 - Florence

While crossing over the Ponte Santa Trinita, returning to the center city not far from where we had been earlier in the day, our short encounter with Gianni in the hotel lobby lingers with me. I fight to shake that feeling I get every time I see him. He's deep in my head, and I know it's obvious to everyone.

Adjacent to the Piazza Della Repubblica, music thumps from a free-standing building. With much trepidation, we walk past a well-dressed, handsome young man who doesn't look like the burly bouncers I remember from my clubbing days in Philly and the Jersey Shore. Looking around the nightclub, we are obviously out of our element.

I ask rhetorically. "How many levels does this place have?"

"It's not that crowded. I guess 11:00 is still early," Maura clumsily looks at her watch, coming to terms with the fact that we are locked in for a long night. Aimlessly, we walk through each level. Classic 70's and 80's disco on one floor leads to a 90's techno vibe on another. More current music blasts from the top floor.

"And we thought Santa Croche was good for people watching," I yell but fail to overpower the force of the pounding music.

The young and the beautiful of Florence slowly fill the club, dressed in a vast range of attire from barely clothed to trendy, and theatrically flamboyant. They strut from one level to the next like their singular goal is to be seen. We're drawn to them, enjoying their styles, their movements, and their attitudes.

Fancy cocktails flow from the multiple bars anchoring every corner of each floor. Music thumps through us from head to toe.

Multi-colored lights bounce from one wall to another. The DJ rocks the front stage, igniting the atmosphere with his gyrating moves and rhythmic beats. Francesca leads us to a bar, nestled in one of the far corners of the 2nd level, far away from the DJ.

"How about we do some shots? If I drink wine, I will fall asleep right there." Maura points to one of the many contemporary white couches that complement the club's hip vibe.

"Have you tried Frangelico shots?" I ask.

"You mean those Italian Biscuit shots?" asks Francesca. "You drink it with lime dipped in sugar and an Italian cookie. Could you imagine if we ordered that shot? Here? In this place? We might as well hang a sign around us that says old ladies in the house - young man, don't forget my cookie on the side," muses Francesca. "Tequila will do," I concede.

We toast and down our Tequila then we wait. We look around, we fiddle with our clutch bags. I pull out my lipstick, a small pocket mirror and apply a fresh coat.

"Maybe this was a bad idea. I'm sorry I pushed you all into this. What made me think we could revive my past."

"Are you kidding? We don't give up that easily. We need a minute to adjust. That's all," says Francesca.

Francesca orders another round of shots…then another. I feel my body loosening up. I begin to move my arms, albeit from the comfort of a stool pushed up against the bar. Francesca and Lauren also start to sway. Looking at Maura, stiff as a stale baguette, I can't help but wonder if there is enough Tequila in the bar, or all of Florence for that matter, that will get her going. I stand up but hold on to the stool with one hand like it is a life preserve; I'm not ready to let it go. Suddenly, Lauren shoots up from her stool and grabs us.

"That's it. It's time. If we are going to do this, it's now or never ladies."

We push our way through what suddenly has become a packed dance floor. After securing our piece of real estate, we begin to move our body, awkwardly at first. Slowly, we shake our legs, we swing our hips, and wave our arms. Our heads bounce to the beat. Little by little, we absorb the music through every part of our bodies. Our movements become larger and larger. We smile, we punch our arms above, and kick our legs below. I look to my right and see Maura shaking her bootie like nothing in the world matters other than letting go on this dance floor. Her beautiful, long legs extend from the black fitted dress in a way I'm sure she could have never imagined 24 hours ago. We move our hips from left to right. None of us care how we look or who is looking at us.

We just dance. We dance and dance. We dance to release Maura's anxiety, her unease, and her awkwardness. With every move, we flush it right out of her. We dance for Francesca to know she is enough. She has always been more than enough. It's as if, with every thrust of our body, Francesca regains control of how she lives her life. We dance to cleanse me of all my self-doubt and insecurities. Swishing and swinging makes me care less about needing to prove anything to Michael. But mostly, we dance our hearts out to destroy Lauren's cancer. We move our hips and sway our heads. We punch our fists above to knock out cancer so Lauren could live not only next week or next month but for years to come. It's as if the more we unleash our bodies, the more each cancer cell will be obliterated. The four of us leave it all out there on the dance floor like we are letting go of baggage and letting go of anguish. We release our pain and soak up our power.

Our energy is like a magnet, pulling those around us, 30 years our junior, into our orbit. We hold hands, we touch, we smile, we sweat, we cling to one another as we jump, thrust, and spin. After hours of dancing, our bodies are drained, but our hearts are full. We came to the club to accompany a friend through time travel, to revisit a previous era when her life was care-free and joyful. We leave feeling nourished, as if there isn't anything we can't do, including 'will' Lauren back to health. Feeling simultaneously exhausted yet rejuvenated, we jump into a taxi for our 10-minute ride back to the hotel.

"I don't remember the last time I had so much fun. It was as if all my inhibitions washed away on the dance floor," Maura says.

"I can't thank you all enough for humoring me. I'm so glad you enjoyed it. I was afraid I was pulling you three to that club by your earlobes and you didn't really want to go."

"Oh, don't get me wrong, I was dreading this all day. You were most definitely dragging me by my earlobes, my whole ears and everything else you could hold onto," teases Maura.

"Well, I don't regret 'forcing' you to go."

I add. "Oh my God, all those young people dancing with us and…"

"…so close to us, weren't they?" Lauren says, laughing as she finishes my sentence. "Oh my God yes. We caused quite the stir on that dance floor."

"Four Signore Robinsons hit Florence."

Lauren says. "At least I'm consistent. Whenever I'm in Florence, I get myself into trouble. This time, I can't wait to tell Bob all about it."

We laugh. We chat and relive the highlights from our night as our taxi pulls into the hotel. Heels in hand like college co-eds strutting the walk of shame, we walk into the hotel and find Gianni sitting in one of the plush hotel chairs, dozing in and out. Feeling the scrutiny of us peering down on him, he opens his eyes, seemingly out of sorts. He wasn't kidding. He really did wait for us.

"I was resting my eyes for a minute," he quietly mutters. "What? You all know I have trouble sleeping."

Chapter 40
Blessing and a Curse

Day 8 - Florence

I take a seat next to Gianni, and almost immediately, Francesca, Maura and Lauren announce they are heading upstairs. He and I watch my dancing queens cohorts lumber towards the lobby elevator.

"Did you have a good night?" I ask Gianni.

"Yes. Wonderful. I took my niece and her boyfriend out to eat."

"Margherita is amazing. She's smart, she's funny, and beautiful. I could see how proud you are of her by the way you look at her."

I immediately regret alluding to the fact that I was secretly staring at him.

"Yes, yes. She's terrific. It's always good to see her. Then later in the night, I met an old friend for a drink."

"Of course you did. The most popular guy in Italy."

I wonder if this was a male or female friend, but of course, that's not a question I would ask.

"What can I say? It's my blessing and my curse."

"How about you? Did you have fun?"

"It was a blast. I hadn't danced like that in years. It felt like we walked back in time with Lauren to her days as a student studying here. There was something special about tonight. It was much more than just dancing."

I pause, looking for the right words to describe our evening. Gianni takes a shot at helping me unravel my thoughts.

"Dancing is a great way of letting go. There are so many endorphins released between the music, the movement, sweat pouring down everybody's crevices, bodies in close contact with one another...touching. It's like getting lost in another universe."

Here we go again. Are we talking about dancing or something else? I open my mouth ever so slightly, but before I can release anything from it, he saves me.

"How's Lauren doing? Does she seem okay, you know, physically?"

"She was great tonight. It's hard."

I look down, feeling myself getting choked up.

"She seems fine, and I know she isn't."

"As cliche as it sounds, take one day at a time and hope for the best," responds Gianni.

"I'm hoping and praying with all my heart."

I pick up my shoes and stand up; Gianni follows my lead and together we meander to the elevator. "At this rate, I can hopefully squeeze in four hours of sleep."

"Well, Francesca set high expectations for the four of you. Aren't you all beating me downstairs tomorrow?"

"We might. You are in no better shape than us, Signor."

"Well, I at least had some cat naps on that chair. It's surprisingly more comfortable than it looks. Fortunately, or unfortunately, I wasn't exhausting myself by moving and grooving all evening. To be honest, I probably should have been."

Gianni gently taps his stomach. We are all our own biggest critics.

I push the button, and the elevator door opens. Gianni instinctively reaches out his arm to hold the door open for me to enter first.

"What floor?" he asks.

"Oh, 4, thank you."

"You are one below me."

Standing side by side, inches from one another, as the doors slowly close in front of us, I suddenly feel flush. Making our way to our respective bedrooms, alone, in the middle of the night feels intimate. There's something about an elevator that is inherently risqué'; dangerous; sexy. My heart is pounding out of my chest. I look to my left as Gianni looks at me to his right. Our eyes instantly lock. Somewhere between the 1st and 2nd floor during our ascension, he reaches out his right arm, puts it around my right hip and slowly turns me inward towards him. Shoes still dangling in my right hand, I reach up high and put my hands around his firm shoulders. Gianni and I tilt our heads, lean in and kiss. After just a few seconds, he pulls away.

"Stephanie, I am so sorry. This is very inappropriate. Please forgive me."

Still facing one another, he begins to release his hand from my waist. Gianni lowers his chin, seemingly embarrassed. I reach in with my left hand, lift his chin and continue what he started. Gianni pulls me in by my waist even tighter. His lips press hard against mine. I feel his tongue in my mouth. I'm lost in our embrace until I hear a ding in the background. We release from our embrace. The elevator stops and the doors open. I walk off the elevator and turn towards the elevator. We each stand face to face on either side of the opened doors. No words are exchanged as we hold our gaze. The metal doors close, slowly diminishing our view of one another. I remain standing in front of the doors for an additional moment, even after they are completely shut. I flip my shoes over my shoulder, smile then walk down the hall. I enter my hotel bedroom, knowing I will spend the remainder of the night reliving in my head...that kiss.

Chapter 41
Day After

Day 9 – Florence

"Hey…I'm here on time like I promised Gianni. I said nothing about functioning at even a low level," says Francesca, gripping her temples.

"I don't know, Francesca. You made all sorts of unrealistic promises on our behalf, but lucky for us, Gianni isn't even here yet. Does anyone else still hear the music pounding in their head?" Asks Maura.

"Stephanie, are you with us?"

"Oh, yes. Yes. I agree. What an amazing night."

"You didn't hear a word we said, did you?" Francesca looks me up and down, assessing my slightly more put together outfit than one would expect after a night of drinking and dancing.

I take another sip of my double espresso and mumble a lie. "Oh, I'm… you know. Just tired."

More like exhilarated. I got back to my room and replayed every moment leading up to and including that kiss.

Margaret asks. "We aren't gonna read about four philandering American women of a certain age causing havoc in Florence, are we?"

"Oh you might. Florence's young and hip nightlife crowd will be talking about us for a long time."

"Impressive stuff. Showing up for the AARP contingency. I love it," teases Margaret.

"Hey, Where's Lauren?" asks Diane, seemingly concerned.

"Oh she's fine. She just needs more sleep after last night,

that's all."

"I'm not surprised Gianni's late. Even he seemed exhausted when we got back to the hotel," says Francesca.

Using a napkin to clean crumbs off the table, I do everything possible to avoid eye contact with Francesca.

"You okay? You seem a little…I don't know… off," Francesca quietly asks. Before I have a chance to respond, an ebullient Gianni walks in. I guess he got his second wind at 4:00 am.

"There he is, ready to!" Francesca announces, saving me from having to answer her.

Rather than acknowledging his presence, I pick up my handbag sitting by my feet and pretend to be looking for something. Score! I find a battered piece of gum, pull it from the bottom of the bag and lift it up as if that was my actual mission. Francesca takes a sip of her American pour coffee and gives me a particular look that suggests she thinks I'm up to something.

"Buongiorno a tutti. Buongiorno. Buongiorno." Gianni repeats, as he buzzes through the hotel restaurant until reaching our group's table.

"How are we feeling about a brisk morning walk to wake us up?"

~

After a 10-minute walk under an especially glorious morning sun, we reach the Boboli Gardens. It's immediately obvious why Margherita finds peace in visiting the historical open-air museum. Ancient structures, statues, and grottos dot the perfectly manicured landscape. We stroll through the grounds as a warmup to awaken our creative engines.

"Walk around in silence and absorb the environment. Take

it all in. Try to clear your brain to make room for your writing," instructs Gianni.

Clear my brain. Is he kidding! He couldn't possibly think I have the power to resist re-playing what I have privately dubbed, the passionate elevator kiss. Well, if nothing else, I certainly feel inspired. My senses are tingling from head to toe. It felt so good to be touched by Gianni, to be held by him and to be kissed by him. I loved feeling so wanted by him.

During a brief tour of Boboli, we are told that the gardens were designed by the famous Medici family. The layout became a model for future European garden designs. Gianni declared the morning a 'free' writing session. Rather than lead a writing session, he tells us to tighten up our chapters, revisit areas needing more work or work forward. I assume he's too tired to lead a writing session. Perhaps he, too, is distracted by something spectacular that happened between us and can't possibly think about providing formal instruction. I'd like to think it's the latter.

Gianni roams the gardens to help anyone who wants it. Sitting on the grass in front of the steps, with my legs crossed, I rest my computer on a raised, stone slab in front of me. I return to where I left off in my manuscript. I know who killed Cassandra's neighbor, Gloria, and why she was killed. I'm working on further developing the characters and I need to drop additional, thoughtful clues to lead the reader through the murder plot, like Gianni suggested. I feel the presence of someone approaching. I look up. Gianni is flashing one of his warm smiles at me.

"May I?"

"Of course. Step into my office!" I muse. I scoot down to allow room for Gianni. Facing me, he rests one elbow on the stone slab. Business as usual, I repeat to myself. Don't make this weird. There's an obvious elephant in the garden, and it's my mission to normalize our early morning elevator interlude.

I jump right in. "If you remember where I left off, Cassandra had her suspicions about the dead woman's husband, but he has an alibi. We also know by now that Gloria was having an affair, but her lover was out of town at the time of the murder, so we think. Then there's Gloria's undercover work with the government. Was she some double agent who got in over her head? I want the reader to find doubt in the alibis so they can't be eliminated as suspects. Thoughts on cookie crumbs to create that doubt?"

"Ahh yes. I like this direction. Think of the characters' small timeline inconsistencies. Maybe Cassandra casually talks with a neighbor at a cocktail party, which reveals holes in the husband's alibi. He might have lied about his alibi, but that doesn't mean he's the killer. He could be covering up another secret. Identify character traits that might be unique to each of them."

"I like that. Throw them off the trail maybe. Oh…Maybe I could…"

"Look, Stephanie. Sorry to interrupt. I really like the progress you are making on your manuscript. I want to circle back and pick up on this conversation. About last night, or should I say this morning, I apologize. I stepped over a professional line. As the instructor…I…"

"Gianni, it's okay. It's more than okay. If I were being completely honest, I made it abundantly clear that it was invited. And I enjoyed it, I might add."

"Well that's mutual. It's just that since….our elevator intimacy."

I thought to myself, elevator intimacy That sounds so sexy.

Gianni continues.

"What concerns me is that you told me about your previous relationship with the man you met in Italy. I know that you are going through a divorce. I don't want you to think I preyed on your vulnerabilities. I wanted to kiss you because you are easy to talk to. You are kind. You intrigue me."

Gianni suddenly looks shy as he looks down. There's that surprisingly vulnerable side of him again.

"And beautiful. I mean. I think you are beautiful."

I turn Marzano tomato red. It's overwhelming hearing Gianni, my 9-day crush, compliment me. I nervously clear my throat.

"Wow. What kind words. Thank you. Trust me. You don't need to apologize. I never felt like you were exploiting your knowledge about me to your benefit. We are consenting adults who enjoyed a wonderful kiss."

The flirty, confident Gianni returns.

"Oh. So, you enjoyed it, huh?"

"Guilty as charged," I respond.

"Something else we have in common."

"Yes, I could tell."

"You could?" Gianni continues. "Next time I won't be so obvious."

"Well, if you are granted a next time," I tease.

"No no no…of course. I don't mean to assume. Only if you want…"

I smile, listening to him trip over his words.

"Oh, I get it. You're joking."

"My weak attempt at flirting. Obviously, I'm a little rusty," I admit.

"You and me both. Don't look now but we have eyes on us."

He stands up and takes one step away then turns his head back to me and asks.

"By the way. Who did it? Who murdered Gloria?"

"Come on now. You know I can't tell you that. Once I finish writing, you will find out."

Gianni smiles and moves on to assist Dan.

Chapter 42
Love Letters
Day 9 - Florence

After walking back to the hotel, we find Lauren sitting alone on the same chair where we had found Gianni after our night of dancing. Lauren appears deep into her writing.

Lauren smiles big. "How were the Boboli Gardens?"

I say. "They're beautiful. It got hot out there. I wanted to grab a taxi back here, but these guys wouldn't let me."

"How are you feeling? You look well rested, and all put together, unlike the three of us," remarks Maura.

Dripping with sweat, hair flattened against our head - after the mile walk back to the hotel under the piercing sun, we don't resemble the dancing beauties from the night before.

Lauren says. "I feel good. Those extra couple hours of sleep were just what I needed. I had a productive writing session this morning. Tuscany really got my juices flowing. It's been an eventful few days."

Francesca grabs a bottle of water, four glasses and a lemon from the bar. I immediately gulp most of it then I dip a cocktail napkin in the remaining few sips. I press the damp napkin on my forehead, face, and neck in an attempt at cooling myself down.

Francesca, Maura, and I join Lauren on adjoining chairs. Our bodies are tired, arms hanging limp.

"Lauren, do you want to get back to your writing? We barged in and interrupted you."

"Oh, I am good. I really did make some good progress today in the short time I have been down here."

Maura, Francesca, and I look at one another, hoping

someone asks. Since joining the tour, Lauren has provided very few details about her novel or whatever it is she is writing. She senses our curiosity and is astute enough to know we won't ask.

"Love letters. That's what I'm writing. I know I haven't said much…or anything, really about what I have been writing. If…I die, I want to leave something special for my family. I came on this trip to write Bob, Claire, and Christopher each a beautiful love letter."

"Oh my God. That is lovely." That makes sense now. I remember in Naples when Diane was pushing Lauren about her writing, she quietly said love letters. We sit quietly and allow Lauren the time and space to gather her thoughts.

"After my cancer returned, I put together a bucket list. Bob was in such denial, and I needed to take control of my own destiny. I knew statistics were not necessarily in my favor, so there were things I needed to do. One of them was to return to Italy, for all the reasons we have already talked about. Bob couldn't wrap his head around why I would want to vacation without him. I get it."

"He didn't know anything about Andrew and the closure you were looking for. It probably made no sense to him."

"Exactly, Francesca. Can you blame him? I needed to take this journey alone. In fact, originally, I was going to travel entirely on my own, but now you know how he is. Bob begged me to at least join a tour. I guess he thought if I got sick, someone would be with me. It worked out. I met you guys." Lauren smiles at us and we smile back at her.

"I looked at different art tours but nothing spoke to me. One was a renascence tour that I thought was intriguing."

"That sounds like it would have been in your wheelhouse," says Maura.

"Yeah, it did sound interesting to me but then, I got some ad for this tour. A light bulb went off. I could write letters to my family and leave for them, you know, if need be. I emailed the trip organizer."

"AKA Gianni Ciabattini, I presume."

For some reason, we all laugh when I say his name.

"You got it. The one and only. I told him my whole story and asked if he could help me with letters rather than a novel. He was so kind. He emailed me back and said it would be his honor to help me write each of them the most beautiful letters for them to hold forever. Isn't that sweet?" I love hearing that Lauren has the same impression of Gianni on a personal level that I have of him.

"We wrote back and forth before the trip. He asked me to tell him a little about my family, our dynamics; you know, he was trying to get to know me and them. He assured me that he wanted the letters to sound like me, not someone else. He read my mind. That was so important to me, ya know. He was very empathetic. I know he's a big showman, but he's a big softy inside."

"Why is everyone looking at me?"

"I think you know the answer to that," says Francesca.

Lauren is right about Gianni. She reinforces that he's the gentle soul I have also come to know. We sit a few minutes longer, relaxing in the warmth of our friendship.

"How about we get ourselves together before our train ride to Verona? Looks like you ladies could use a shower," Lauren says, looking us up and down. She packs up her laptop and leads the way to the elevators.

Standing in the same elevator where Gianni and I stood together at 4:00 am, it's difficult for me to maintain composure. The doors close. As if it's completely out of my control, I unleash the biggest grin. Francesca can't ignore something so obvious.

"Stephanie…There is something up with you. I don't know what it is but we will get it out of you eventually."

Chapter 43
City of Love
Day 9 - Verona

After a 90-minute ride on the 'bullet,' we arrive in Verona, Venice's smaller sister city, for an overnight visit to the most romantic city in Italy, according to Gianni.

"Any author traveling through Italy must visit Verona," he insisted when leaving Florence.

Gianni seems exuberant even by his standards. He talks about Verona to anyone sitting within ear shot of him as the train coasts into the Verona station. It seems as if something or someone special has surely impacted his impression of Verona.

After settling into our downtown hotel, I sneak out on my own for a quick solo tour of the city. I'm not the kind of person who usually needs alone time, but after these past couple of days, decompressing on my own is required for my mental well-being. I need to settle the noise rattling in my head before reconnecting with the ladies.

Verona's city center immediately draws me in with its charm, its winding cobblestone streets, cozy shops, and trendy cafes. The medieval city, divided by the Adige River, has the warmth of a small Italian village yet offers the culture and characteristics of a vibrant metropolis. I walk through the Piazza delle Erbe and take in the sites, the smells, and the sounds. City guides approach me, peddling their tours of palatial palaces and ancient gardens. Verona isn't on our itinerary for the palaces, cathedrals, or piazzas. There is only one thing that brought us to Verona; we're here to explore how far someone is willing to go for love.

I find a bakery then grab a small table to enjoy a cappuccino with a torta di Verona, a dessert originally made for a Russian girl traveling on the North Seas. The treat is topped with a heart of chopped almonds. I guess everything is based on love stories around here. My thoughts immediately transition to my tryst with Gianni. It still thrills me to reflect on our kiss and his hands around my waist, pulling me close to him. I can't stop thinking about the way we looked deep into each other's eyes, standing on opposite sides of the elevator threshold. I crave a second act.

After my well-needed time on my own, I return to the hotel, drop my shopping bags in my room then rush back to the lobby to meet the ladies.

"How was your walk?"

"Wait until you see the city center. It's adorable but I gotta tell you, I'm running on fumes. I thought I would have slept on the train but that didn't happen."

"I feel your pain. I am happy to grab a quick dinner and hit the sack. No crazy clubbing tonight." Francesca turns her head to look at Maura.

"Sorry Donna Summers."

"Last week you could barely get me out after dark and now I've earned the disco queen title."

We continue strolling through the bustling city center. A slight scent of the sea floats through the piazza.

"You're so right, Stephanie. This town is adorable," Lauren says as she looks around Piazza delle Erbe.

I point to my left. "I had a cappuccino and some sort of delicious Russian-Veronian torte right over there. Remind me after dinner that I already ate dessert. I somehow manage to forget these things when I am staring at a dessert menu."

The concierge recommended a small bistro on the other side of the piazza, right on the Adige River. We walk through the piazza to the lovely river path, lined with restaurants adorned with greenery and flowers.

"This is perfect. I love the water view. I'm thinking seafood might be the way to go. Captain Obvious, I know."

"An appetizer and two dishes should be enough for us to share, don't you think?" asks Francesca.

"Absolutely. Starting tonight, I am beginning the process of weaning myself off three course meals three times a day. It was fun while it lasted."

Maura's comment is another reminder to me that we're nearing the end of our trip and an uncertain future for Lauren. There is also the realization that leaving Italy means saying goodbye to Gianni, most likely for good. We order typical Northern Italian dishes to share; mussels in white wine sauce, a pasta dish with a light summer seafood sauce, and white fish filet over creamy risotto with peas. We pair our meal with lots of water, rather than the usual bottle of red and white. The four of us talk, we laugh, and we even sit comfortably in silence, enjoying the ambiance, like old friends.

"Wait until you see what I bought for Gianni."

I immediately notice the shocked look on everyone's face.

"Oh, from everyone. A group gift from the nine of us."

"Oh, yes," says Maura. "I thought…Good idea."

"What did we get for Gianni?"

"Picture frame. I thought we could have it engraved, then take a group picture and frame it. What do ya think?"

"He'll love it." Francesca says as she plucks a mussel from its shell then neatly twirls a forkful of bigoli.

"We can give it to him on our last night."

I must have an overly expressive look on my face relative to how one should react to a group gift for a tour instructor. I look down to avoid eye contact. I sense their eyes peering down on me. I suddenly regret not drinking wine; I could have blamed my flushed face on the alcohol.

"Ok Stephanie. What's going on?" asks Francesca.

I don't deny anything.

"Oh. So, something really is going on, isn't it?" concludes Maura.

"Well. I mean. Nothing is going on, per say but…"

I lift my head and minimize my smile in an attempt to not look so creepy.

"Last night."

Before I could even finish my sentence, Francesca jumps in.

"I knew it. It has been written all over your face all day."

"Oh wow. You could be the detective in my novel. I haven't even 'confessed' and you have already solved the mystery."

"I'm calling it like I see it."

"Ok Nancy Drew. You got me. Last night, when you all went to bed, Gianni and I sat in the lobby and talked a while longer. We then got on the elevator together."

I pause before asking. "Does everyone agree that there is something sensual about an elevator?"

I notice the shocked look on their face as they wait for me to drop the bombshell.

"I suppose one can argue that when two people are alone on an elevator…you were alone, right?" teases Francesca.

I laugh. "Yes, of course, we were alone. We weren't offering a performance for other hotel guests."

Maura teases. "Thank God for little things."

"We were standing there together, looking at the doors. Something just happened. We looked at each other and then we started kissing."

"You kissed. That's so romantic, isn't it," Lauren asks

rhetorically.

"I don't want to be negative, but do you think he crossed a professional line? He runs the program. Maybe I'm thinking of it as a teacher and student relationship, and I shouldn't?"

"I get what you are thinking. Gianni immediately felt the same way and pulled away. Then I…leaned back in towards him. We had a long, passionate kiss."

Maura says. "Wow. If those elevator doors could talk. You have had time to process what happened. How do you feel today about it?"

"I honestly feel great about it. Kissing him…"

I pause before finding the right words.

"It makes me happy just thinking about it. He certainly didn't coax me or take advantage of the situation. I enjoyed it as much as he did. Gianni and I have gotten…close? Maybe close is too strong a word but we have shared some special moments with deep, open conversations. I have no illusions that this will progress past this trip or anything like that, but I feel a connection with him. We both wanted to kiss one another at that moment, and it felt right."

"You are undeniably happy. It's obvious how you feel just by looking at you," Francesca says. Lauren says. "If I have learned nothing else over the past few years it's do what makes you happy. Life is shorter than you think. Sometimes that might mean taking risks. Don't go through life overthinking your decisions. And Francesca's right. You're absolutely glowing."

"Thank you."

We sit quietly for a few minutes, processing the conversation.

"Does this mean you will be receiving special attention from Gianni? I don't want to have to register a complaint. I paid handsomely for this program too."

"I don't know Maura. After all, I did 'put out' on the elevator. Aren't I entitled to extra attention?"

Our young friendship continues to blossom. It feels good to tell them how I'm feeling about Gianni. It's been liberating to talk with one another about our inner thoughts. Laughing together has been nourishing to our souls. I will return home with a partially written novel and so much more than words typed on a laptop. We end another delightful meal and return to the hotel for a much needed night of rest.

Chapter 44
Day 10 - Verona

Just off one of the many narrow Veronian streets, the hotel's private stone patio blends with city streets. While drinking our morning coffee and eating a variety of breakfast pastries, Gianni, standing before us, delivers a soliloquy about love.

"What force in nature is stronger in life than the power of love? Murders have been committed over it. Wars started over love. We sing along to lyrics written about a new love…or the one that got away. Is there anything purer in life than a mother or father's love?"

Gianni swallows hard and pauses for a moment.

"As authors, no matter our genre, the essence of love can't be ignored. Center to many love stories throughout history is a narrative that creates intrigue, sorrow, or happiness. Shakespeare's Romeo and Giulietta reminds us all how deep and unrelenting love can unfortunately end in tragedy. We will walk over to Casa di Giulietta in just a few minutes and stand in the courtyard. Put yourself in Romeo's place and imagine how he would have felt when he called up to Giulietta as she stood on the balcony above."

He spins his pointer fingers in a circular motion.

"Then switch roles in your head and become Giulietta, standing on the balcony, listening to her lover proclaim his unyielding dedication to her. We have all heard it a million times…'Romeo, Romeo!'" Gianni takes an artistic pause and assesses the group's interest.

"We have another writing clinic scheduled this afternoon before we catch a train to our last destination, Milan. During the Casa di Giulietta tour, your challenge is to think about opportunities to intensify emotion, love, or passion in your writing. Whether your story is a romance novel, includes a romantic subplot or if there is just a splash of love, you will pull in your reader while pouring your heart into your storyline."

All of us are undeniably engrossed in his oration about love. Or maybe not. Maybe no one is immersed in his message in the way I am. The irony of listening to Gianni pontificate about love after I told the ladies about our kiss is not lost on me. Certainly not lost on my friends either.

As a group, we walk together to the Casa di Giulietta. I take Gianni's instructions to heart as I imagine myself on the balcony. Despite attempts to push his image from my head, I can't help but imagine Gianni, serenading me. I walk away, smiling, feeling a scene of embarrassment with myself. Well, no one can say I didn't follow his instructions.

After the tour, we have time before our writing clinic. Lauren isn't feeling well. Her energy level has diminished since our big night out dancing into the morning. Maura assures Francesca and me that she's keeping an eye on her. We find a quiet spot by a fountain rather than join the others on a tour of the Scavi Scaligeri Underground Museum.

"Stephanie, Don't tell Gianni, but the whole thing is sort of cheezie with a line of people waiting to touch Giulietta's boob."

"Apparently, the "me too" movement hasn't made its way to the Casa di Giulietta. Like you said, Maura, everyone surrounding the statue waiting to cop a feel of her breast for good luck is a little weird for me. Who came up with that anyway?" says Francesca.

"Who knows how that started but yeah, it's an odd tourist tradition…" I pause then say, "I love how Maura tells me not to tell Gianni. One long and passionate kiss in an elevator and I am now his inside operative."

"Absolutely. We need to watch what we say in front of you now."

"You're right, Maura. We don't know if your allegiance is to us or him," says Lauren.

"You guys are going to get a lot of mileage out of that kiss, aren't you? I get it. I would do the same if the tables were turned."

"Kidding aside or should I say kissing aside, Verona is lovely, but next time, I'll pass on the Romeo and Giulietta museum."

Lauren, ever the romantic, disagrees. "I understand why Gianni would include this in the tour. Love is a crucial part of each of our stories in one way or another."

"I don't need to wait in line to touch Giulietta's boob again either, but I think I would explore this region more. I also like what Gianni said about infusing more passion in our writing and I'm talking about my novel, so don't let your imaginations run wild."

They don't look convinced. I don't even believe my own fairytale, how can I expect them to believe me?

Chapter 45
Stand Down
Day 10 - Milan

I enter my Milanese hotel room and immediately walk to the window to check out my view like I have done with every hotel. I lift the latch, pull the large casement window inward and stick my head outside. Center to Milan, the Duomo, consumes the skyline. Gianni promised us a fabulous hotel for our last city. He is a man of his word. I feel invigorated after taking a nap on the train from Verona. Ella and Ana organized a rooftop sunset cocktail hour to kick off our last city tour. I change my clothes and quickly reapply make-up. Primping feels intentional. My crush will be up on that rooftop, and I want to look good.

"This is crazy," I utter out loud to myself as I brush blush on my cheeks then line my lips.

The following day will be our last full day of exploration in Italy. Gianni has a jam-packed schedule with planned tours, a group dinner, then the grand finale, tickets to the world-famous Milanese opera. Gianni insists that no trip to Italy would be complete without experiencing the opera.

I leave my room, walk briskly down the hall, and take the stairs up two floors to the rooftop. The expansive concrete balcony, edged with stone column guardrails, illuminates beautifully as the glowing August sun begins its final descent for the day.

"It's absolutely beautiful." Diane proclaims as she pops a piece of cantaloupe wrapped in prosciutto in her mouth.

Penny, Margaret, Dan, and Stanley all nod in agreement. I join the conversation.

"The colors are bursting in the sky," I announce as I pick up a white sangria stuffed with a variety of chopped fruit.

We talk about our writing. We discuss details about the upcoming Milan tour, and we lament that the trip is coming to an end.

"Where's your posse?" asks Dan.

"I don't know…oh, there's Francesca."

Francesca looks out of breath. She also appears to be uncharacteristically frazzled. As she approaches us, Francesca cordially greets the group.

"Stephanie, can I talk with you?" We step away from the group.

"What's going on?" It then hits me. "Lauren." My shoulders drop, and my mood deflates.

"Maura wants her to see a doctor."

"Oh no. What's going on with her?"

"Maura said Lauren seems lethargic, her coloring is off, and she might even be a little disoriented. Maura said she would feel more comfortable if she were to get checked out at the hospital."

"She's trying so hard to push through to the end of the trip. Lauren hasn't looked herself since our big night out, has she?"

"She is a little off, right? What concerns me is that she didn't protest going to a hospital."

"Yeah, that is telling."

"Maura and Gianni left already. They didn't even check into the hotel. I threw their stuff in my room and came running straight up here. I'm going to the hospital now and assumed you would want to go."

"Of course. I'm so sorry. I had no idea all that happened." I feel a tinge of guilt. I was in such a hurry to check into my room so I could freshen up my make-up. I feel so frivolous. My friend is ill, and I'm consumed with primping like I am going to see my new squeeze at a high school dance.

"How would you have known? It all happened so fast."

I take a long sip of the refreshing fruit-laden wine then we dash from the glowing sunset down to the lobby to catch a taxi. Francesca gives the driver the address.

"Gianni assured Lauren, Maura, and me that the Italian health system is excellent. They are at a private hospital, which is apparently better than the public facilities."

We enter the modern-looking facility and receive instructions to Lauren's room from an older woman sitting at the desk. As we approach her room, we could hear Lauren from the hallway.

"Robert, I'm fine. No. I don't want you to come here. I am getting checked out. This hospital is lovely. Everyone is taking excellent care of me."

Lauren's voice elevates. "NO. Robert. Listen to me. You aren't hearing me. I said I am finishing this tour without you here."

Gianni and Maura are talking with the doctor. Francesca and I slide into the room and attempt to blend into the background. The faint odor of disinfectant permeates the small, private room.

"Nice room." I awkwardly comment to Francesca.

Lauren, dressed in a hospital robe, is sitting in the bed at an incline. Wires extend, connecting her to beeping machinery.

"Robert, the doctor wants to talk with me. I'm hanging up. What? No Robert."

Francesca and I approach the neatly made bed, crisp white sheets tucked tightly under the mattress.

"Robert here, talk with my friends." Lauren holds the phone away from her body and I instinctively grab it from her.

"Robert, hi. I'm Stephanie."

I make myself cringe hearing my own elevated and overly cheery voice, given the situation.

"Oh my gosh. We have heard so many wonderful things about you."

I look back at Lauren, and she rolls her eyes. The phone rests on my shoulder, pressed against my ear. I extend my hands as if to say what am I supposed to say.

"Let me tell you. This hospital looks amazing. Blows away the one near my house."

I let out a nervous laugh. I'm exaggerating, but I just want to comfort an anxious husband.

"Maura and Gianni are talking with the doctor. You know Maura is a doctor and speaks Italian fluently, right? How amazing is that? Oh, and most everyone speaks English, but the point is..."

I think to myself. Stephanie, what is the point?

"The point is they are communicating really well together."

I'm babbling on and on and saying nothing. Robert can't even get a word in. Maybe that is my intention. The last thing I want to do is field questions from this man when we both know there aren't any good answers to give. I let my guard down. I pause to take a breath, and he seizes the opportunity to pepper me with questions.

"How does Lauren look? How does she sound? Is the doctor going to run tests? Is there an Oncologist on staff? Does the doctor know about her current medications?"

He runs through a litany of questions one asks when they are protective of the person they love. I reflect on Romeo and Giulietta. Robert is combatting a potentially tragic scenario the best way he can because of his deep and steadfast love for Lauren. It would be beautiful if it weren't, well, so heartbreaking.

I assure him that Lauren came to the hospital only for precautionary measures. I tell him that Maura told the doctors about her medication. Robert is understandably frightened. This must be utterly confusing to him. He doesn't even understand why Lauren wanted to take this trip to Italy at this moment in her life. It's clear that he loves her deeply. Authentically. Even enviably.

Robert wants to jump on a plane and accompany her back home. As difficult as it is, I need to take control of the conversation and advocate for Lauren.

"You know, Robert, I think what I am hearing from Lauren is that she needs to finish out this trip on her own. On…On her own terms."

After spending the first 10 minutes of the conversation drowning in a word soup, we suddenly are marinating in silence. I look at Lauren and she is giving me the thumbs up. Francesca looks stunned. I have known Lauren for less than two weeks, yet I am telling her husband, a man who has loved her more than anything for 25 years, to stand down. While I empathize with his pain, Lauren knows exactly what she wants. As my voice quivers, I promise Robert from deep in my soul that we would look out for her with love and care.

Doctors and nurses scurry about taking vitals, administering tests, and talking with Lauren. A young, handsome doctor walks into the room. His brown, curly hair is pulled back in a ponytail. Peeking out from under his white coat are modern-fit slacks, a shirt with cufflinks and a stylish tie. Even the doctors in Italy look like they just walked out of a photo shoot. Lauren recognizes that he isn't sure if he should speak freely.

"Go ahead, we are an open book around here." Lauren winks at Gianni.

"Signora Clarkson, you have an infezione del tratto urinario, ahhh, urinary tract infection. We can take care of that with a regimentto of…of… antibiotico."

We look at Lauren and wait for her to respond.

"Ok, well, that's good news, right? Certainly not the worst

diagnosis I have ever received.”

She turns her head and looks at Maura, then Lauren looks back at Dr. Rizzero.

“Why don’t you two look like it’s good news?”

“It’s good. It’s fine.” Dr. Rizzero responds. “But given that you have cancer, we always need to be extra cautious. I would like for you to get plenty of rest. Take antibiotics. Drink lots of water. When do you return home?”

“Ahh. Oh geez. The days are running into one another. The day after tomorrow. Right?”

Maura responds quickly. “I have completely lost track of time too. Today is Tuesday. Yes. We fly back home Thursday.”

“Ok. You go back home Thursday. Follow up with your doctor when you get home. Maybe Friday, you can see your doctor?”

“I will call Robert. No. I will text him. I’m not up for another inquisition. I’ll let him know I have a UTI and ask him to make a follow-up appointment. He will be thrilled to have something to do for me.”

We all laugh but I could identify with that sentiment. There’s nothing more frustrating than feeling helpless. We give Lauren privacy so she could change.

Out in the hall, Maura shares explains. “Look, I’m going to recommend that Lauren skip the tour tomorrow. I will stay back with her so I can sort of keep an eye on her. You know she is going to push back, but I’m going to strongly recommend it.”

“Tomorrow is a busy day. It will be a lot for her between the heat and going in and out of tours. Should we all stay behind to keep you both company?”

Maura says, “Honestly, I think it would be best for just me to hang back with her. It will be calmer…quieter that way. You know I am a big bore. The two of you raise the excitement level."

We all chuckle.

"Do you think she will be okay?"

I ask Maura like I'm a child looking for reassurance. I made a promise to Robert that we would look out for Lauren. It weighs on me.

"Well, when someone has cancer, you want to monitor them if there's an infection or any kind of illness for that matter. Her immune system is compromised. Even something that we battle regularly and don't give it much thought, like a UTI, can be more precarious for her. The good news is we caught the infection, she's on antibiotics, and she has time to rest."

We all smile big when Lauren walks out of the hospital room. The five of us walk back to the hospital lobby, call a taxi, and return to the hotel.

Chapter 46
Overstep

Day 10 - Milan

Once back in my hotel room, just as I was about to change into a nightshirt, I heard my text ding. Meet me on the rooftop in 5? After a quick mirror check, I walk out my door, down the hall, then up the two flights of stairs like I did earlier in the night. I reach the rooftop door, push it open and see Gianni leaning against the stone columns, elbows resting on top of the flat slab. I walk up to him, and as he turns towards me, his silver hair glistens in the summer moonlight. Gianni smiles warmly at me. We immediately hug one another. It's a hug of comfort not of intimacy.

"Tough night."

"It was, wasn't it," I agree.

Gianni is holding a bottle of wine in one hand and two glasses by the stems. We walk to one of the outdoor couches and make ourselves comfortable next to one another.

"We missed the sunset cocktail so I thought we could have a moonlight drink."

Gianni pours me a glass of wine.

"Thank you. It's exactly what I need."

"It sounded like Robert was upset," says Gianni.

"I felt so torn when I was speaking with him. His wife has cancer, and she calls from a hospital in a foreign country. It's all just awful for him. I mean, obviously it's awful for Lauren, but I can't imagine how he must have felt getting that call. He doesn't even understand why she took this trip in the first place. That's a whole other..."

I stop in my tracks. I don't know if Lauren shared with

Gianni anything about Andrew.

"Exactly. It must have been difficult for him to grasp. He clearly doesn't have, you know, all the details. Like you said," Gianni says, also choosing his words carefully.

"Lauren doesn't have control over much of anything in her life. She wants to finish this trip on her terms. That is something she can control."

"You did a great job explaining that to Robert."

"Did I? I felt like I was overstepping my boundaries. God. I have known her less than two weeks and I told him, in so many words, that he needs to back off. Awkward, right?"

"I could understand why it felt like that, but sometimes in life we overstep. Robert was thinking from his perspective, and I don't mean that to say he is selfish. Quite the opposite. He loves her so much, so he was advocating for what he thought was best for Lauren. You let him know she was receiving great care and Lauren is driving her bus or train or taxi or whatever analogy you want to use based on what we are driving from day to day." We both smile.

"Speaking of driving, on our way back to the hotel from the hospital, I thought about our visit to Verona and what you said about love. We would do anything for love. It was like Robert was out of his mind. I could feel his pain. It was so sad and yet so beautiful."

Gianni suggests. "It's the dichotomy of love. It can be a scary thing, or it could be exquisite."

"Exquisite," I repeat. "What a lovely word to describe love."

"You like that? It's been said that I am pretty good with words."

"Oh yeah, it's been said, huh? A critic or two may have mentioned that."

After a brief pause, Gianni continues. "When I talk about what it means to love, I should have included not only what people do for love but also the extreme measures people will take to avoid love. That can also be a painful journey."

"Is it worth it? In the end? Is the risk of pain worth the potential for deep love?" I ask.

Gianni smiles and nods his head.

"It depends on who you ask. For me, the risk of loss is always worth the potential for what you might gain. But we Italians are hopeless romantics."

Our bodies edge up next to one another. I lean my head on his shoulder. The warmth of his body next to mine is comforting. I'm attracted to Gianni's good looks, his charisma, and his humanity.

I could sit there in silence, feeling his body touch mine until the night's vibrant moon completely descends and the sun begins to rise. I don't even care to question how or why I got here at this point of the trip. I prefer to just enjoy the moment.

"I guess we should head back in."

"I guess. If you insist," I respond.

We allow ourselves to enjoy an additional few minutes, then simultaneously stand up and begin the return trip to our rooms.

"This is me," I tell Gianni, standing in the stairwell.

Gianni extends his arms and gently pulls me close to him. We give each other a long and warm hug. Before departing, Gianni leans sweetly and softly kisses me on my lips then on my cheek. We gradually pull away from one another. I walk through the stairwell doors back down the hall to my room. Crawling into bed, once again, Gianni Ciabatinni is the last thought before I drift off into a deep sleep.

Chapter 47
Mayor to Italy, friend to the world
Day 11 - Milan

"Man. Milan is awesome. Mark my words. I'm returning to Milan with my wife."

Stanley says as he slurps down the last bite of his anchovy pizza. Before the San Siro Stadium tour, we grab a quick bite at a typical pizzeria not far from the heart of the city center.

"Ya think your wife is gonna appreciate watching your head dart in every direction every time a beautiful woman walks by, now do ya?" Dan says as he directs his pointer fingers, one after another, in multiple directions.

Dan is right about the Milanese women. We have seen beautiful women everywhere in Italy, but everyone in Milan is especially stunning. The city of high fashion lives up to its reputation.

"Dan, I'm gonna call you every day when I get home just so you can abuse me. We haven't even left yet, and I already miss it."

We all laugh. Stanley and Dan's taunting of one another has entertained us the entire trip. They complement one another perfectly.

Milan isn't meant for a one-day tour, but we are getting a good feel for its majesty in the short time allotted for the city. The duomo, including a rooftop panoramic tour, was magnificent. We walked through the main piazza, meandered through the open atrium shops, and took the *Da Vinci Last Supper* tour.

"Dan, you must be excited about touring the soccer stadium. You've been talking about it nonstop since day two."

"Come on, Margaret. We're in Italy. The futbol stadium tour is gonna be great. But please, no posting pictures of me on

Facebook. My mates back in Manchester won't let me live it down. They'll call me a traitor for tourin' another stadium."

"I don't believe it. They could only wish to take a premium tour like the one we are taking. The stadium is state of the art."

"Stan, you're right. But that's beside the point. All you have ta do is give these fuckers a smidge of an opening, and you are done. Pardon my Italian, ladies. Anyways, if they see photos like that, they will be on me for life. Mates will find any opportunity and ride ya mercilessly."

"Ahhh. I get it. What you are saying is your mates are all like you."

"Exactly. Ya think I'm the only pain in the arse in Manchester? The whole lot of them back home are like me."

After lunch, we drive to the shared stadium for both AC Milan and Inter Milan in the San Siro district. Gianni takes his usual post in the front of the bus.

"Here we go. It's a spectacular stadium. And remember. Lots of pictures of Dan and post them everywhere; Instagram, Facebook, My Space. Don't forget to tag him."

"My Space." Many of us repeat as we laugh.

"See. Looks like Gianni would fit in with the boys back home. He's a natural ballbreaker. Apologies again, ladies, for the slip of the tongue."

Dan loves to flaunt his humble Manchester, England roots when he isn't using his faux royal, proper English accent. Regardless of which persona he's projecting at any given time, we have all been seduced by his sense of humor and his splendid readings. It takes a skilled writer to balance a gruesome murder with satire. From what we have heard so far, he manages to do just that.

After the extensive stadium tour, we returned to the bus.

"I can't wait to give my kids the jerseys." Stan pulls the

jerseys out of the plastic bag, opened each of them to take another look. "They might even be excited to see me when they see these."

"Who you kiddin' mate? Your kids can't wait to see you."

"I know nothing about futbol, but I was blown away by the stadium."

Margaret shares as she cools herself down with a cold water bottle.

"The locker rooms alone were phenomenal. I could live in them."

Dan leans over and I overhear him not so quietly whisper to Margaret.

"Now, is that when the locker rooms are empty or full of the young, half-naked, sweaty lads?"

Without even missing a beat, Margaret responds.

"Do you need to ask?"

They erupt into laughter like two old perverts who have known each other for years. Margaret and Dan connected almost immediately because of their common worldviews, mutual music interests and similar past experiences experimenting with illicit drugs. While sharing whiskey nightcaps, you could hear them exchanging stories about their rambunctious hippie years tripping on shrooms or debating the literary significance of the classics.

Upon our return, it's a relief to see Maura and Lauren sitting in the lobby, enjoying cappuccinos and cookies. Lauren looks significantly better than she did 24 hours earlier.

"How was your day?" Lauren enthusiastically asks as she pats the couch, inviting Francesca and me to join them.

"It was a lot of fun. I don't know what I enjoyed more, the tours or listening to Dan all day."

"Oh, he was in rare form today, wasn't he? I think he was

extra hyped up because of the soccer stadium tour," Francesca says.

"You guys look great, by the way."

Lauren looks comfortable yet fashionable in khaki, lightweight summer slacks and a black V-neck t-shirt. She applied a full face of makeup, and it looks like she even put a few loose curls in her silver-gray hair. Her meds seem to have kicked in.

"I'm a little tired, but I feel much better with my concierge doc by my side all day."

"I was of no help, but we had a good time, didn't we?" Maura affirms as she turns her head and smiles at Lauren.

"I took a walk down to the main Piazza and saw the Duomo, then I picked up a panini and brought it back to the hotel for Lauren and me to share."

"It was so good, too, with pancetta and cheese. Also, in case you were wondering, I called Robert. You all are off the hook. I'm keeping him in the loop, so I won't be throwing the phone at any of you to try and figure out what to tell the man."

"Thank God. I feel horrible about telling your husband to back down, we got this…in so many words."

"He was impressed by how committed Gianni and all of you are to my well-being."

"Sounds like you had a good day," I comment.

"Yeah, it was nice. We even went up to the rooftop for a while before it got too hot up there. What a view."

I smile, reflecting on my alone time on the rooftop with Gianni. I can't keep him off my mind no matter how hard I try. Drifting off in my own world, I hardly notice when Francesca stands up, suggests we get ready for dinner and she starts packing for our trip home.

~

Since it's our last night together, Gianni arranged a group dinner at a classic Milanese restaurant near the Piazza Paolo Ferrari. He herds us into our bus for a quick drive to the restaurant. The nine of us, Gianni, Ellen and Ana, are seated at a large table in the back of the modern space, accented with sophisticated touches.

"Do you have the gift?" Lauren leans over and whispers to me.

"Yep. Got it right here," I respond as I tap the bag resting on my lap. We are good to go."

"Tonight is our last night of the inaugural Write Italia tour. I thought we should enjoy a family-style dinner. After all, by this point, we are like family."

Dan quips. "Yeah, and like any family, we have had plenty of drama."

No doubt referring to the now infamous battle between Lauren and Diane. Our whole group, including Gianni, simultaneously boos Dan.

"See, just like family, none of ya can take a joke. Everyone is so sensitive."

We can't help but laugh this time.

"I hope you don't mind, I ordered for us. I chose traditional Milanese standards for dinner. Hope everyone enjoys it. Buon Appetito."

We dig into Gianni's selections; the Costoletta alla Milanese, a breaded veal cutlet fried in butter, pass around the Risotto alla Milanese and sink our teeth into the ossobuco.

Reminiscing about my father, I share. "My dad used to make ossobuco. He prepared it so well that I have never eaten it in a restaurant."

For a fleeting moment, I think about my father in the kitchen, cooking, singing, and telling stories like he was playing to an audience. It often saddens me to recall how sensational he was in so many ways, yet his toxicity is what I often remember most.

"What is it?" Asks Diane.

"You braise veal shank with vegetables in a saucy rue. It's best served over a creamed polenta, in my opinion. It's a fabulous dish."

Additional meats, vegetables and risotto dishes continue to flow, as does the conversation. Compared to our first day when we nervously met one another, like Gianni said, we have truly congealed. Throughout dinner, we recall funny moments from the trip, poke fun with inside jokes, and spew our favorite "Gianni-isms." We talk about how we will spend our fortunes when we become famous novelists and promise to promote one another's books.

"Let's bring out the desserts. Cafe, cappuccino, who wants what?"

Gianni asks as if he has become the server. Along with the coffees and after-dinner drinks, the server brings us each panettone, a popular dessert in Milan.

Gianni stands up, taps his wine glass with a butter knife to get our attention and delivers farewell words.

"I am not one for long, drawn-out speeches."

As we all laugh, Dan pipes up.

"And you're gonna say that with a straight face, are ya."

Gianni grins. He knows he dangled low-hanging fruit for someone to pick.

"We don't have a lot of time before we walk over to the Teatro alla Scala to enjoy a wonderful Milanese tradition, the Opera. I do want to share a few words. This tour has meant more to me than you know. My talented marketers got all of you to click on some links to register, somehow, I don't know how, but I am glad you all did. Hopefully, you learned a thing or two about writing. Such amazing progress was made over the past two weeks…each one of you." Gianni pauses.

"More importantly, hopefully, you learned a thing or two about each other and about yourselves. I know I personally have grown as a person on this trip, getting to know each of you." Gianni rests his hand on her heart.

"Bravo. Bravo." We yell in chorus.

Gianni continues, "Ella and Ana…are these ladies amazing or what? We would be lost somewhere in Tuscany if not for these ladies."

We hoot, holler and clap in agreement. Many of the other patrons look over to see what's going on at the table in the back of the restaurant.

"Gianni, this has been amazing. I have been writing my book for years, and I now know it's going to get done sooner than later. I now know that with certainty. I had to put up with this guy for two weeks…" Stanley points to Dan to his right. "But other than that, it's been a fantastic life experience."

"You're gonna miss me as soon as you get on the plane. Did you all know Stan is going to visit me next summer."

"You all know what I am going to say…" says Stan.

Margaret takes the bait. "You have to ask the wife. Come to think of it, do we even know her name? It's just been the wife."

"Rachel. Her name is Rachel. And yes, if she says yes, I am going to Manchester."

"You think I'm hard on ya. My guys are going to sniff out your weaknesses and taunt you relentlessly."

"Who could resist an invitation like that? I will be calling you guys to come save me."

"I'd like to say something." Diane stands up. "I came here to work on my book but to your point, Gianni, I'm leaving here learning so much more about myself and about life."

Diane looks at Lauren, who warmly nods back at her. Diane then continues.

"I want to thank you, Gianni, Ella, Ana and all of you."

"One last thing."

Diane pauses. She almost looks like she is going to cry. "I haven't always had close friends in my life. I feel like I connected with all of you. It means a lot to me."

"Right back at cha, Diane." Yells Dan as we clap for her.

"Ella, Ana and Gianni, we have a little something for each of you to show our gratitude for everything you have done for us."

I present each of them with a small gift bag. Ella and Ana pull out bracelets from their bags then Gianni opens his gift. He took one look at our tour group photo we took in Verona and reads it out loud.

Mayor of Italy, Friend to the World

"That's beautiful. I love it. I am going to hang it up as soon as I get home."

"When you are sitting at the opera, take in the surroundings and the sounds. Now, let's walk to the opera house and watch how love intersects with tragedy."

Chapter 48
Perfect Ending

Day 12 - Final Day in Italy

After squeezing the last few items into my bags, I roll them down the hallway and, for the last time, meet my friends for breakfast.

"What are you smiling about?" I ask Francesca.

"I'm thinking about our first breakfast together almost two weeks ago."

"So much has happened since then yet it feels like just yesterday, we were sitting in that Roman hotel, getting to one another."

"And here we are, two weeks later, I feel so comfortable I could say anything to you guys."

"Well, you know all my deep dark secrets. I've got nothing else, I'm happy to say," remarks Lauren.

"Me too," I respond.

Francesca looks to her left then to her right to make sure no one could hear us.

"Do we, Stephanie? Do we know all your secrets from this trip?"

"Now that you mention it, I might have a couple more up my sleeve."

We stand up, laughing, and join the rest of the group in the hotel conference room for our last writing session.

"*Buon giorno.* Before I send everyone to the airport to catch flights home, it's only fitting that we talk about how we want to end our novels. It's never too early to think about how you want to leave your reader. Do you want to wrap up all your plot lines and put a bow around each subplot? Will you leave the ending open so the reader writes their own ending, or maybe leave room for a sequel? If you would prefer to talk about the plight of the tragic heroine Violetta from last night's opera, *La Traviata*, that's okay too. Creativity will always contribute to writing, even if you harvest that inspiration for another day."

As usual, I slip away to a quiet spot and open my laptop. Scrolling through pages and pages of text, it's gratifying looking at the thousands of words that have come together like an orchestrated performance, dancing from one page to another. Gianni approaches me. My stomach drops.

"How are you, Stephanie?"

I love how he says my name. He elongates the first syllable, making my name sound sensual. Maybe it's just who is saying it, not how it is pronounced.

"Doing well."

Gianni pulls out the chair adjacent to mine and sits down.

"To be honest, I am just scrolling through my book with delight. I can't believe how much I have written."

"I'm so appreciative of the instruction and how all my, you know, senses have been stimulated."

I smile and twirl the bottom tip of my hair that falls just below my shoulder. Dear God, who am I? I can't wait to tell Ellen and Janice. "You said what?" I can hear Ellen now.

Thankfully, he warmly smiles back, or I would have been mortified.

"I'm glad I could be of service to you."

"Have you thought about the ending of the book?"

"Oh, I have lots more research and writing but yeah, I have a good feel for where the story is going. My main character,

Cassandra, and Gloria, may she rest in peace, will be neatly wrapped like a Christmas present. If only I could see my own future as clearly as my characters." I release a nervous laugh.

Gianni chuckles. "I could relate. It's funny to hear me say that out loud. The old me always had a plan and had everything precisely planned out. Who knows? Maybe not knowing makes life exciting. Just enjoy the ride and see where it goes."

"You're right. I spent this past year working on my personal growth, motivated by this tour. I know I need to maintain forward progress."

"Maybe go home. Marinate in your successes then think about new goals and how to reach them."

"Sounds like a plan. I hope you decide to keep going with *Write Italia*. It suits you well."

We sit, staring a little longer than we probably should. Gianni double-taps the table and stands up.

"I should wrap things up." We stare intensely, lost in one another's eyes. It feels like we are the only two in the room.

We maintain a long gaze. "Stephanie, you know, I gained so much personally by knowing you. You take care, Stephanie."

I open my mouth, and before I can get anything out, I hear a faint voice from behind me. I look up, and Diane is standing over us, looking back and forth between the two of us.

"Um. When will the bus be here?"

Gianni looks at his watch. "*Allora.* Look at the time."

Just like that, he moves to the front of the room to address us all.

"The bus will be here in a few minutes to drive you to the airport. Again, thank you all. It has been a pleasure."

We all gave Gianni a robust applause.

"Make sure you yelp or like or share or whatever the heck it is that you do on social media."

"Don't forget My Space in honor of Dan," teases Stanley as he looks at Dan.

"I trained him well. Look at Stan landing a punch on me."

Chapter 49
This Isn't Good-Bye
Day 12 - Milan Airport

Gianni guides us through the lobby then outside the hotel like a homeowner walking his guests out the door after a dinner party. Hugs are exchanged with him. Some of my colleagues began boarding the bus. Gianni and I lean into one another and exchange an anemic hug not representative of what has developed between us.

Gianni walks over to Lauren. They seem to be engaged in a sweet conversation. Their special bond began well before we ever stepped foot in Italy. It warms my heart watching them.

I look back and forth between the bus and Gianni. As the driver continues loading the luggage in the cargo space of the bus, Gianni delivers one last wave and walks back into the hotel. I feel conflicted. It's not like I expected anything to materialize between Gianni and me beyond the tour, yet we had more to say to one another before Diane interrupted our conversation in the conference room. Lauren, always astute, walks up to me, leans in, and quietly says, "Ya know, when I think about my life, I have some regrets. One regret I will never have is having loved too much. Go give him a proper goodbye. I will cover for you."

I silently mouth to her. "Thank you."

I run back into the hotel and find Gianni in the conference room where we had just been ten minutes earlier.

"Gianni."

He turns around. "Stephanie. Is everything okay?"

"Yes. Everything is fine. Thinking about our earlier conversation, you're right! The knows where we are going in life. I need to embrace the unknown. My future chapters are still undefined, but I know one thing, I don't want this to be the last time

I ever see you."

We stand in silence for a moment. Gianni slowly steps towards me. He reaches out and pulls me in, close to his body.

"I am so glad you came back. I wasn't sure…I didn't know what…"

No words are required. He leans in and kisses me deeply. After the long, lustful kiss, we remain standing in each other's arms.

"Wow. Now that's how you say goodbye. Now. I have a plane to catch." He smiles. "Yes, you do. It's settled, then. This isn't goodbye."

"I hope not."

He affectionately smiles back at me. We release from each other's arms, and I run back outside and quickly jump on what is now a full bus waiting for me.

"Sorry. When you gotta go, you gotta go."

Lauren and I each smile at one another.

~

Once we reach the airport, like campers at the end of summer, we all hug one another and make promises about future reunions. Francesca, Maura, Lauren, and I have a few remaining minutes together before we walk to our respective gates.

"Well ladies. I guess this is see ya later."

"I can live with see ya later. I can't accept goodbye," Maura says.

"When we get home, I will give you ladies a week or two to get settled back home then. I am going to throw out some dates. I would love for you to visit me," Lauren says.

"I'm in."

"Me too."

"I wouldn't miss it."

With heavy hearts, we walk towards our respective gates. I turn back and watch Lauren walk away before she disappears into the crowd of travelers.

Part III

Chapter 50
Right Direction.

Dulles Airport, Virginia

"Hi! ladies."

I enthusiastically greet Janet and Ellen on a cooler-than-usual early summer night.

"Thanks for picking me up."

Janet seamlessly lifts my larger bag of the two into the boot of her BMW SUV.

"What in the world did you bring for two weeks?"

I smile as if to say have you ever met me before. I hoist my smaller bag with all my might and shimmy it into a small space next to the large bag, then jump in the back seat.

"We have lots of catching up to do," says Janet.

Janet begins rattling off a laundry list of work items as if we are in the yoga studio.

"I added another early morning Wednesday class. Wait until you see the juice bar reviews. They are fabulous. Oh, we need to talk about…"

"Janet. Really? Put a sock in it. She just spent ten hours traveling, for God's sake."

Ellen to the rescue. Once again, she's looking out for me.

"Thanks, Ellen. You will get your gift. Janet, at this point, I'm not so sure."

"You got us gifts? Okay. I will play nice. There will be plenty of time to talk shop. How about a glass of wine at my house so we could hear about your trip?" says Janet.

Once we reach my old neighborhood, I sit quietly in the back of the SUV. I stare out the window, lost in a gaze on the way to Janet's home, nestled on a court amongst the other most ostentatious homes in a neighborhood of grand homes. Janet and Ellen probably think it's difficult for me to travel back in time by returning to the place I always assumed would be my forever home. I guess I just always assumed Olivia and Sienna, along with my not-yet-identified sons-in-law and future grandchildren, would join Michael and me for birthday brunches, holiday dinners, and backyard BBQs. However, rather than feeling disappointed as we turn down the very streets where I watched my girls play kickball, the drive reinforces that I no longer feel connected to the perfectly manicured shrubs, wrap-around porches, and kids' play sets. I had the privilege of raising my daughters in this wonderful community. But I now feel removed from the cookie exchanges, play dates, and neighborhood gatherings. I no longer identify with that woman who lived on Meadows Way, burdened with insecurities because of a messy kitchen or unfolded piles of laundry. As we turn from one winding street to another, I remind myself I no longer strive to be that wife, desperately trying to please a husband who would never have accepted me for who I am. I was devastated when we sold our beautiful red brick colonial, but today, I can't imagine living in any of these beautiful homes like the one I once cherished. While there are still plenty of unknowns about my life going forward, the drive through my old neighborhood is a reminder that I'm going in the right direction. Gianni was right. I don't need to have all the answers. Just enjoy the ride to wherever it leads me.

Once we reach Janet's house, Randy is also pulling into the driveway.

"Randy. How are you?" I give him a warm hug.

"Good to see you, Stephanie. I hope you enjoyed your trip."

Randy leans in and whispers, pretending Janet and Ellen can't hear him, but we both know they can.

"I'm glad you're back. Janet was going crazy without you."

Randy over-exaggerates the impact of my absence, mostly because he's kind. I flash him a reassuring smile.

"I will be right in," I tell them.

After digging in my suitcase, I walk into Janet's living room, double-fisted, and hand Ellen a bottle from the vineyard in Chianti, then hand Janet a Pinot Noir that I picked up in Milan. I strive to impress them with my newly acquired vineyard knowledge as if I'm now a sommelier.

"I got you each something else, but they are buried deep in the caverns of my bag."

They pepper me with a battery of questions. Did I finish writing my book? Where did we go, and what were the other travelers like? I take Ellen and Janet on a journey through the cities we visited, the sites we saw, and the expert guest authors who assisted us.

"I forgot just how amazing the food is in Italy. We ate one sensational meal after another. I think I put on a few pounds, but nothing a few yoga classes can't fix."

"Since you are bringing that up, that reminds me, next week…"

Ellen immediately intercedes. "Zip it. Did you forget already? Give Stephanie a chance to get re-acclimated."

Janet takes two fingers and slides them across her lips as if she is zipping her mouth shut. "The true highlight of the trip was meeting the most amazing three ladies."

I share with them Maura, Lauren, and Francesca's back stories, the books they are writing, and the relationship that developed between us in less than two weeks.

"I know it sounds crazy. We immediately clicked, and somehow, over the course of the trip, we developed an amazing connection."

I tell them about Lauren and how we learned, in dramatic fashion, that she has cancer.

"I am so sorry. She sounds like an incredible woman. That Diane sure sounds like a real pill, though," Janet remarks.

"Lauren is an incredible woman. She's sort of like a sage, too. Because she views life with her own mortality in mind, she pushes aside life's bullshit drills down to what really matters. Her advice is spot on. She's a fighter."

"There are so many new treatments available now, both traditional and alternative approaches. I hope she has the best care available." After a pause, Janet says, "You really did develop a close relationship with these ladies, didn't you?"

"We did. I hope you both meet them one day. You will love them."

"It sounds like a fantastic life experience. When I think about where you were a year ago and where you are today, I can't help but feel proud."

"Thanks to both of you for helping me get here."

"Well, even if we are a little jealous of your new friends, I'm glad the trip was a success. I'm also glad you're back. Plus, we were worried you would run off with a man in Italy…again. Weren't we, Ellen?"

Ellen nods in agreement.

"Well, I didn't run off and get married or anything like that, but there is a man…"

Chapter 51
The Other Side

6 months later

It's an uncharacteristically warm and sunny February day in Connecticut - So fitting given the radiant woman Lauren was. The church and graveside services were lovely. Claire and Christopher delivered beautiful eulogies in honor of their mother. They captured the essence of the woman I grew to know and adore. Francesca, Maura, and I drove together to the celebration of life luncheon at their stunning colonial home set on an expansive lot in a country club community.

"There were a ton of people at the services. I'm not surprised, of course. Lauren was such a giving person," Maura says.

"Oh, I just loved the red, green and white flower arrangement from our writing group. It was so perfect to make it the colors of the Italian flag."

"I can't believe it's been two months since we were last here."

Francesca reflects on the visit she, Maura, and I made to Lauren's home in early December, just as we promised when we left one another at the Milan airport. Although Lauren had declined significantly between August and our December visit, she was still her bright, funny, and affectionate self. Robert was hospitable and every bit the pleasure I had expected him to be. When I initially met him, the first thing I thought was that he does have kind eyes, just like Lauren described. His love for Lauren was pure and seemingly infinite. I relished the opportunity to observe firsthand their beautiful relationship in action.

As Lauren's family and friends unite in the stunning eat-in, gourmet kitchen, the three of us stand alone in the warmly decorated family room, next to a large, heavy console table. Lauren decorated it perfectly. It's not overly cluttered but rather splattered with just the right number of coordinated pictures and decorative, accent pieces.

Maura looks down, smiles, and picks up a picture hidden behind a small bouquet of flowers that had been sent to the family.

Quietly, she stares at the photo, seemingly reminiscent of our friend. She turns the wood frame towards us.

"I don't remember seeing this photo of us at Trevi Fountain when we were here in December, do either of you?"

I reach out to take the picture from Maura, but rather than passing it to me, she quickly jerks it back towards her.

"Wait, What's this?"

Maura scrapes a piece of masking tape attached to the back of the frame to reveal a coin. She holds up the euro that Lauren presumably, taped to the back of the frame. We didn't understand that day, in front of Trevi Fountain, why Lauren gave us each a euro and requested we promise to return to Rome together in the future to toss it in the fountain. Her intention is clear to us now. She hoped with the entirety of her huge heart that she would be around for a future visit.

"It's as if she is talking to us from the other side," Francesca suggests.

"I don't know when or how, but we owe Lauren a trip, don't we."

"I can only imagine what she wished for when she threw her coin in the fountain that day."

As Maura returns to the table the picture of us smiling big as we toss the four coins behind us into the fountain, Claire approaches us. She has her mother's same inviting smile. Tall and slender, Claire is beautiful in a 'girl next door' kind of way.

"Hi. I'm Claire. I am so happy to meet you."

Claire warmly hugs each of us as she apologizes for not making it over to us sooner.

"Of course. You have all your family and friends here." Francesca assures Claire. As if she is speaking on the behalf of the three of us, she expresses condolences to Claire. "We are so sorry about the loss of your mother. What an exceptional woman...She really was amazing. I don't need to tell you." Maura and I smile as we nod our heads in agreement and then we each offer our own warm sentiments about Lauren.

"You and your brother each described Laur...your mom exactly as we knew her. Just beautiful," I comment.

"Thank you. She was the best mom. I don't know what I am going to do without her." Claire looks down and tears up. I affectionately put my arm on hers.

"I saw you looking at the picture of the four of you. My mother talked about her trip to Italy until...well until she no longer could. She would just go on and on about how she loved you three. It was as if you were lifelong friends. She talked about how you connected on such a deep level and how you laughed and laughed together in a way she hadn't done with girlfriends in years. Oh, there was a crazy night of dancing at a nightclub?"

We immediately start laughing and looking at Maura.

"Did she tell you I am the most awkward human on the face of the earth, and somehow, I completely let all my anxiety go on the dance floor that night? I have your mom to thank for that, and I mean that in the best way possible."

"She described something like that."

"Maura now takes dance classes," Francesca shares.

"You have no idea how huge of a leap that is for me."

"That's awesome. What kind of dance?" Claire asks.

"Hip hop. I'm with a few other older ladies in the class. Our dance studio has its recital in June. I'm going to be on stage performing in front of actual human people."

Maura shakes her head as she covers her face.

"I don't know what I got myself into, but I honestly wouldn't be putting myself out there if not for your mom. It feels good to step out of my comfort zone. Scary, but good."

"It makes me feel so good to hear that. Honestly, I'm not surprised. My mom empowered others. That is…was who she was."

"We all became better versions of ourselves because of your mom."

Francesca adds. "Stephanie's right. I made real-life changes in the months since returning home from the trip. Your mom helped me realize I needed to give myself the gift of time and I'm happier for it."

Claire looks so proud of her mother. She then cases the room to ensure no one hears her.

"When she got back from Italy, my mom told me about Andy. She said she never told anyone about him other than Aunt Kelly, her mother and you three. She wanted me to know because she didn't want anyone to do to me what her mom did to her. My grandmother was horrible. I never liked her."

"Yeah, your mom mentioned she was a difficult woman," offers Francesca.

"It was important to my mom that I live my authentic life. It sounds like she did a lot of reflecting and soul-searching on the trip. Rather than wait for me to come out to her, she told me she knew I was gay and encouraged me to be open with others. She understood…you know… time wasn't on her side. You would think being gay wouldn't be such a game-changer these days, but around here, it's like an apocalyptic event. Not with everyone, but you know, some people are so close-minded. She told me, 'Let one person say something about my sexuality, and they would have to deal with her.' My mom was 100 lbs. soaking wet. You know. As time went on, she was fierce."

"No messin' with momma bear," says Maura.

"When we visited her here two months ago, she told us how proud she was of you for coming out to everyone. She loves Michelle, too. Looks like your dad likes her, too."

We all turn and see Robert and Michelle engaged in conversation.

"If my mother told him he needed to play nice, he would honor her wishes. My father was always the best dad but believe me, this is hard for him. He always imagined me in a big princess dress, him walking me down the aisle with a male banker or lawyer waiting for me at the altar. He is trying. I will give him that. Oh, and Michelle is studying to be a lawyer; at least I fulfilled part of what he imagined for me."

We laugh with Claire. She then turns to walk away then she remembers something else.

"Oh, by the way, my mother left my brother, my father and me each a letter. She called them her love letters."

Claire smiles like she's recalling the conversation with Lauren.

"She asked us not to open them until she passed away. I read mine last night, and I found it to be so comforting. I cried. I laughed. It felt like she was talking directly to me. You know. Like we were in the same room or something. I never knew my mom was such a fantastic writer. I guess she was full of surprises."

Claire gives us each a hug, then turns to walk away.

Part IV

Chapter 52
April- Return to Trevi
2 Months Later

I pull out my lightweight, navy-blue jacket from my small built-in closet, slip it on then throw my brown leather satchel over my shoulder.

"*Piccolina*? There you are."

Piccolina does a full-body shake. Her tail thrusts from left to right when I tell her we are going bye-bye.

"Oh no. Your bow fell off. Let mamma put it back on."

I pick her up, put her on the small, light wood coffee table sitting in front of the small, brown leather sofa. I pluck a few pieces of her hair from the top of her head and intertwine them with a pink bow.

"*Che carina,*" I tell her in a loving tone.

After clipping the leash to her rhinestone-studded pink harness, I walk down the three floors holding her in my arms. Once I reach the pavement of Rome's hip, eclectic Monti district, I put Piccolina down. It's a perfect sunny day for a walk.

"*Buon giorno Stefani. Ciao Piccolina.*"

"*Buon giorno Alfi. Come va?*"

When you are on a first-name basis with the corner grocer, you're truly one with the neighborhood. At least, that's how I feel every time Alfi and I engage in small talk. I stroll through the Piazza Della Madonna, then turn right onto one of the many quaint, cobblestone streets. Lined with wine bars and trendy restaurants, the budget-friendly-ish neighborhood is a perfect fit for me. I stop at a cafe and grab an American pour coffee and cornetto. Less than a mile from my apartment, I round the corner, and the world-famous landmark emerges in front of me.

Like I do most every week since moving to Rome two months earlier, I wait for the crowd to disburse, then squeeze in to sit on the cement slab barrier that separates the piazza from the flowing fountain. My tiny, middle-aged rescue Yorkie sits by my ankles. Soaking in the energy from the crowd, I enjoy my coffee and cornetto. Tourists from all over the world are laughing, tossing coins behind them, and snapping selfies.

Rather than feeling sad, on the contrary, I feel at peace whenever I visit Trevi Fountain. Wonderful memories of my beautiful friend gush over me. Before I leave, I pull out my change purse, remove a euro, and toss my coin behind me into the turquoise blue water in memory of Lauren. Before zipping up the change purse, I see a specific coin tagged with a piece of tape, air-marked for a future date.

"Let's go, Piccolina."

She and I take a quick, 5-minute walk to the Barberini terminal and board a bus for a 15-minute ride to a more suburban Roman section of the city. Once exiting the bus, I walk just a few blocks to my destination in the Tuscolana neighborhood. Even though I'm only about five miles from the heart of Rome, Tuscolana is worlds apart from the bustling city center. It's a charming area but lacks the same energy as the Coliseum, the Spanish Steps, or Trevi Fountain. I look up and confirm I'm at the right place. 'Centro de Arte y Sanación de Ale,' I mumble to myself. I open the door and immediately hear a familiar voice.

"Stephanie. Benvenuta." Gianni gives me a big hug.

"Piccolina. Come stai?"

Piccolina has loved Gianni from the first time she met him. He squats to her level and then pulls a small treat from his pocket. He knows how to butter her up.

"Gianni, you are irresistible to the ladies, albeit human or canine."

He picks her up, snuggles her under his chin, and receives lots of kisses in return. He then hands her to me as we continue to walk through the art center. I look around in amazement at the multitude of colors, geometric shapes, and the open floor plan for gatherings. The space is buzzing with energy; people of all ages from a variety of countries gather in groups or work independently.

"Gianni, this is fabulous. It's so vibrant. I love the layout, the colors, and the atmosphere is so inviting."

"Thank you. I couldn't be happier with how this place has progressed. My daughter, as you know, did most of the design. Georgie is a genius."

He oozes with pride as we tour every corner of the center. Painters, skechers, and sculptors create works of art ranging in all levels of expertise. Computer designs pop from screens, canvases, covered with montages of colors, attract my attention. Instructors support all the students in a variety of art genres.

"Are the instructors all volunteers?"

"Yes. Yes. Every one of these wonderful instructors is a volunteer."

As we walk through the center, all eyes turn to Gianni. Appreciative artists shake his hand and thank him profusely. It's like he is a living legend walking through the halls.

"Please, have a seat."

Gianni pulls my seat out in a secluded section of the center. I've seen Gianni several times since moving to Rome two months earlier, but it's my first visit to the center.

"You look well. How are things going?"

"Things are coming along, ya know, since those first few days when I thought I must have lost my mind for picking up and moving to Italy. I joined that yoga class we talked about last time. I met a couple nice ladies. You know me. I need my girlfriends."

"I'm so happy you are finding your way here. You are adjusting quickly to your new life."

"Yeah. It's coming together. Oh, I started an outline for a new book. The storyline came to me a few months ago. Last week, when we had all that rain, I just started typing, and we will see where it goes."

"Writing can be addicting. Once you get into that rhythm, you can't stop."

"Totally. I can see that. It's the best kind of addiction."

Gianni chuckles. "Yes, yes, indeed it…well it can be." He leaves his statement at that.

Gianni leans back into his tan armchair and folds his arms in front of him.

"Stephanie, I remember that day on the yacht when you told me you always dreamed about moving back to Italy for a redo. Do you remember that?"

"Absolutely. I think that's the day we began opening up to one another. I have thought many times over the past 25 years about returning to Italy for a second shot at the whole Italian experience. Over the years, I guess I imagined it would have been with Michael, but that wasn't in the cards. Maybe I was always meant to fly solo for the redo. Who knows. In any case, here I am, and I couldn't be happier." I pause for a moment recalling something Michael said to me.

"You know, when Michael told me he was leaving me, he said I would be happier without him. He got that right. I'll give him that."

I flip my hands out to my side, palms up.

Gianni says. "I guess he was onto something, and here you are, taking in the whole Italian experience. You're working. Going out with the ladies. Taking yoga classes. You're writing now. I'm happy to say, you even spare a little time for me."

We both chuckle. He's right, though. When I lived in Italy before, I was locked into a dysfunctional relationship, living a one-dimensional, unfulfilled life. This time, I'm entrenched in a diverse lifestyle, complete with activities, cultural outings, new friends, and, yes, carving out some time for a man I'm crazy about. He's important to me, but Gianni's not the entirety of my Italian experience.

"Kidding aside, you should be so proud of yourself. I know I'm proud of you."

Gianni leans back into the round table. He squeezes my hands that are now resting on top of the table. I'm beaming with pride hearing him compliment me. Our conversation pauses momentarily.

"How are your Italian language classes?"

"Give me another couple of weeks, and we will only speak Italian with one another."

"I will hold you to it. Any other updates with Maura and Francesca since we spoke last?"

"Maura was asked to speak at some Italian cultural event about the plight of Italian Jews during the holocaust. We teased her during the writing tour that she would become a subject expert and here she is presenting at some forum. What else? I told you Francesca self-published her memoir cookbook on Amazon, and it's also in some local bookstores in Brooklyn. She even did a book signing at a few restaurants. This restaurant critic she befriended years ago wrote a good review about the book so that has given it traction locally."

"That's fantastic," says Gianni, smiling big, undoubtedly thinking about his impact on their success.

"We confirmed dates for September. Francesca and Maura are visiting. The three of us have some unfinished business we need to tend to."

I quietly think about the tagged coin in waiting, sitting in my change purse.

He taps my satchel that is sitting on the chair between the two of us. "I assume your manuscript is in here?"

I pick up the satchel from the chair and plop it on top of the table. After opening the bag, I pull out the manuscript.

"Here it is in all its glory. I will also email you a copy."

"Did you make all of the changes I suggested?"

I smile and tilt my head to the right.

"Not all."

"That's okay. It's, in fact, more than okay. A confident author follows her instincts."

"It was good to finally find out who murdered Gloria," Gianni says.

"Yep. Lizzette didn't appreciate that Gloria was sleeping with her husband," I respond.

"Very clever. Cassandra began to put the pieces together after finding blue nail polish chips in Gloria's house that matches a dress she recalled Lizzette wearing," Gianni says.

"You don't think Cassandra was bringing a casserole to Gloria's husband after her death to be nice, do you? She was snooping for evidence. That was the beginning of the end for Lizzette."

"The book is good, Stephanie. It's a solid mystery strong character development, and a thorough back story. I like the dark humor that pulls in the reader. Congratulations. You did an amazing job. I spoke to my old NY publisher, and she said she would take a look. We will see what she says."

"I can't thank you enough for doing this. Regardless of what happens, I finished the book. It's a win for me, and I owe you for that, too.”

“You put the time in and did a marvelous job. All I did was help guide you.”

“How is your writing coming along?” I ask.

“Better than expected. I’m beginning to feel that energy again. Unlike in the past, I’m maintaining a healthy balance between writing and managing other life commitments. This art center is important to me. Relationships.” He pauses for a moment, then looks into my eyes. “I want my relationships to remain a priority at this point in my life. Writing needs to be what I do, not who I am.”

“That does sound like a healthy approach. Ale would approve.” I give him a warm smile.

“My daughter helped me with this progression and Stephanie, you have also been critical to me resuming my writing.”

Looking at my dog, I respond. “Piccolina. Look at us old dogs learning new tricks. We are getting better with age, aren’t we?”

Gianni releases a robust laugh. “Indeed we are.”

After his laughter retreats, I continue.

“I heard from my girls yesterday. Their university approved the American University of Rome summer credits. After spending some time back home with their dad and friends, they’re moving in with me for the rest of the summer. It will be tight for the three of us for a few months in my tiny place, but we’ll make it work.”

“That’s wonderful. I can’t wait to meet them. I can always make some room for you at my place while they are here.” Gianni says in a flirty manner.

“Aren’t you kind?”

I respond with an equally flirtatious tone. I pull out my phone from the satchel side pocket to check the time.

“We will have to revisit this conversation another day. I need to get back to my apartment. Janet and I have our weekly budget Zoom meeting later today. I still need to pull some numbers together and prepare to pitch her on a new marketing campaign."

Gianni and I get up, and he walks me outside. Standing on the quiet walkway, we simultaneously lean in and hug one another. We slowly release from our warm embrace, and I turn to walk back to the bus. Just as I take my first step, Gianni calls out to me.

"Stephanie."

I stop and turn back towards Gianni.

"Are we still on for Saturday night?" he asks.

"Of course. I wouldn't miss it for anything."

Gianni flashes a huge, inviting smile and I warmly look back at him. After our gaze breaks, I look down at my furry friend sitting patiently by my side.

As I head back to my apartment with Piccolina, I don't know exactly what lies ahead of me. If I were to write my memoir, my story could go in many different directions. My next life chapters are still in the works. While I don't know all of the twists and turns on the road ahead, I am certain, however, that the path I'm walking along at this moment in time is exactly where I need to be.

The End

About The Author

Marijo Nicoletti is a first-time author who has written many life-style articles for women over 50. Marijo loves everything about Italy – the culture, the language, the food and of course the people. She currently lives in Maryland with her husband and her two dogs but dreams of living part-time in Italy one day.

www.ingramcontent.com/pod-product-compliance
Lightning Source LLC
Chambersburg PA
CBHW071919150726
47999CB00001B/36